Black Notice

ALSO BY JOY ELLIS

JOY ELLIS

BLACK NOTICE

JOFFE BOOKS

Joffe Books, London
www.joffebooks.com

First published in Great Britain in 2025

Cover art by Nick Castle

ISBN: 978-1-80573-174-0

This one is for my lovely friends, Rose and Rachel.
Thank you both for your continued support from way back,
even before Day One, until now. It's been quite a journey
and I'm glad we've shared it together.

Love, as always,

Joy xxx

CHAPTER ONE

It was six in the morning and still dark. Bob Ruston was about to feed the dog his breakfast when the front doorbell rang. He frowned. Who the hell . . . ? 'I've got it!' he called up the stairs to his wife and unlocked the front door.

The sight that met him made him take a step back, and for a moment, Bob just stared.

The man on his doorstep had blood running down his cheek from what appeared to be a head wound, and there was a look of terror on his face.

It took Bob a moment to register that there was also a handcuff dangling from one lacerated wrist.

'Please! Let me in!'

Bob snapped out of his stupor. 'Sorry, mate, but no way!'

Bob was a retired police officer, and everything he'd ever learned about scammers flooded back into his mind. Allowed inside, if the supposed victim didn't suddenly produce a knife and proceed to rob you, he could simply take a professional look around and decide if you were worth a return visit to relieve you of your treasured possessions. The man did not move.

Bob hesitated. 'Okay, what's happened to you?'

'They're going to kill me! Please, for the love of God, let me in!' He held up the bloodstained hand, sending the cuff swinging in front of Bob's face, and glanced anxiously back towards the road.

Bob made up his mind. 'I can't let you in, but hide around the side of the porch. No one can see you there because our hedge hides the road from view. But you must tell me what's happened to you.' Had he somehow escaped police custody? They looked like police issue cuffs to him, but he'd been too long out of the force to be certain.

'They'll find me, and then they'll kill me!'

'Who?'

'I don't know who they are! They grabbed me off the street and bundled me into a car. They drove for ages, then shut me in a stinking old barn.' The man looked close to tears. 'They beat me up, kicked me in the head, hit me with a pistol, handcuffed me to a tractor and left me there.'

Something terrible had obviously happened, but Bob didn't buy the story that this was some random act of violence. The man must have done something to get treated like this.

The man began babbling. 'I got free . . . ran along the side of the main road, but no one would stop to help me. I gave up after a bit, turned into this road. Yours was the first house that had a light on . . . Please hide me!'

'I'm not letting you inside my house, so you can forget about that. I have a wife and a disabled son, and I'll not have them upset. But I will ring the police for you. You need proper help, from the authorities. Come on, lad, give me your name, and I'll call them.'

He started to pull his phone from his pocket, but the man cried out, 'No! Whoever took me said I was dead meat if I tried to contact the police.' With a groan, he sank to the ground and sat, his back against the porch wall, hugging his knees to his chest.

'Darling? What is it? Who is at the door?'

At the sound of his wife's voice, Bob bit his lip. He didn't want Daisy coming downstairs in her dressing gown and seeing a man, covered in blood, cringing in the porch. 'It's okay, Daisy, nothing to worry about, I'll be in in a minute.'

He turned back to the man. He reckoned he must be in his twenties — cheap clothes with dried mud on them, scruffy jeans and a black T-shirt under a black nylon puffa jacket. No shoes, just muddy wet socks.

His tone softened. 'Come on, lad. You clearly need help, and medical attention. I can get someone out here in no time. We're only ten minutes from the police station.'

'No, no, no,' the man whispered. 'They'll kill me, I tell you! They had a gun, one of them hit me with it.'

'Where were you when these people abducted you?'

'On my way to my gran's house.'

'But where? Was it nearby?'

The man shook his head vehemently. 'No, she lives in Huntingdon.'

Huntingdon! That was fifty or sixty miles away. Then his old police head kicked in. Whatever had happened, it seemed the people that took Charlie-boy here wanted him out of the county. 'Listen to me. I can see you're in trouble, but no one will find you here. Just let me call the police. Stay put, I need a minute to check on my wife. Okay? Keep your head down and I'll be right back. I'll do my best to help you, I promise.'

He hurried indoors and raced up the stairs.

'Whatever is going on, darling?' asked an anxious Daisy, pulling her fleecy dressing gown tighter around her.

'Do something for me, will you? Watch out of the bedroom window and tell me if you see anyone coming into the drive. I'm ringing the police. And, Daisy, no questions, right? I'll fill you in later.'

Bob dialled 999, asked for the police and waited. Finally, he found himself talking to someone who was obviously a civilian. He was still answering a series of totally irrelevant questions when he heard his wife hiss, 'Bob! Come here!'

3

He ran to the window, arriving just in time to see the young man at the gate. He looked cautiously up and down the road, and then scuttled off out of sight. With a 'Damn!' Bob turned back to the phone. 'He's on his toes! Can you get a car here fast, something is terribly wrong. Apart from believing he's been kidnapped and held against his will, he needs medical attention.' His call was diverted again, and a voice told him that someone would be with him as soon as a vehicle was available. Bob hung up and sighed. There was a time he would have legged it after the man, and very likely caught up with him, but his arthritis had put an end to that kind of caper years ago.

'Who was that man? And was that blood on him?' asked Daisy, still staring out of the window.

'I have no idea who he was,' replied Bob. 'And, yes, that was blood. He'd been beaten up.'

'The poor man! Why didn't you bring him in? Oh, Bob, that was unkind of you. I could have made him a hot drink, and you should have called an ambulance.'

'Much as I love you, darling Daisy, you can be very naive sometimes. Apart from it being a possible con, imagine if someone nasty *was* after him, and saw him come in here? These days I'm not up to tackling a bunch of heavies.' He threw her an exasperated grin. 'There's a helluva lot more behind this than we know, believe me.'

'Bob, come here.' Daisy's voice was low, apprehensive. 'Look!'

Bob stared out of the window and caught his breath. A big car, a four-wheel drive with blacked-out windows, now sat outside his house. He cursed the hedge, which obscured most of the car, so there was no way he could identify it, or get a look at the number plate. He was about to go downstairs and into the drive to get a proper look when another car, this time an expensive-looking silver saloon, arrived. To Bob's surprise, it drew level with the 4x4, thereby blocking their narrow road. They eased slowly forward, clear of the hedge, allowing Bob a slightly better view of them. He saw the windows of both vehicles go down, and the driver of the 4x4 lean out towards the other car as if he were speaking to the other driver. Then the silver car moved away down the road.

'Damn, damn it!' His neighbour's fence had obscured the plates, and the vehicle was gone before he could even see the make or model. The 4x4 followed a few minutes later, crawling slowly along like a jungle predator patiently stalking its prey. Then it too accelerated away and out of sight. Bob was left feeling angry and inadequate.

A police car arrived ten minutes later. While one officer came in and spoke to him, his crewmate wandered up the road, checking gardens for any sight of the injured man.

Too little too late, thought Bob, while giving an account of what had happened. Thankfully, the constable, who had introduced himself as PC Simon Laker, seemed to take him seriously. He radioed in for another car to check the supposed route their man had taken to get to Bob's front door.

'Right. I'll just go and see how my mate's getting on,' said Simon. 'Tell me, Mr Ruston are you a former copper?'

Bob smiled. 'Thirty years with Surrey Constabulary, for my sins.'

'I could tell.' Simon gave him a grin. 'So, Bob, what's your take on this guy?'

'He was shit scared, no question about it, but since he legged it, I guess he's even more scared of the police — or maybe what they threatened to do to him if he contacted you.' He shrugged. 'I think he's either involved, or got caught up in, something heavy. He mentioned a gun, and they'd taken his shoes too. This wasn't some guy getting duffed up for messing around with the boss's wife.'

Simon stood up. 'Thanks, Bob. I'll call it in. Let's hope we find him before they do.'

'So do I. I really did not like the look of those two cars that appeared after he took off,' said Bob. 'They looked bloody intimidating. Let me know how it pans out, won't you?'

Simon nodded. 'Will do, and thanks again. We'll be needing a proper statement, as you know, so I'll be in touch.'

After he'd gone, Bob went to find his wife and found her still looking out of the bedroom window.

'There's two police cars out here now,' she informed him, clearly enjoying her new position as lookout. 'And look, Bob! A police van!'

Bob looked. So, they *were* taking his report seriously. Had they located the young man? Bob didn't think so. His was a rural village road, with houses along one side, and fields and copses on the other. The houses were a mishmash of properties, ranging from large dwellings with considerable gardens, to one or two tiny bungalows that backed on to a small paddock with stables. There were sheds, garages, outside offices, Wendy houses, and even an old wartime pillbox. After that was the church, the village hall, and the graveyard. On the edge of the village were two small commercial businesses, one that repaired farm machinery, and the other a one-man car workshop. No way could a couple of PCs have searched that lot and found matey-boy, unless they'd been extremely lucky indeed.

'Have you noticed how quiet it is?' he commented to Daisy.

'Oh yes.' Her eyes widened. 'Like last week, when there was that accident on the main road — they closed it while they got the damaged vehicle off the carriageway.'

'Exactly. I think they've closed it again. It's where that lad said he walked from — a deserted barn about fifteen minutes on foot from here.' He nodded to himself. 'Carter's Farm! There's two old barns there that are awaiting demolition if I remember rightly, about half a mile away from the farm itself. Old man Carter leaves that crappy old wreck of a tractor of his in one of them. Drags it out once a year for the tractor rally. I bet that's where that fellow was held.'

'Yes, of course!' Daisy said excitedly. 'And the one adjoining it has no door, so it'd be easy to get in, and no one can see inside from the main road. You're right, Bob.' She looked at him hopefully. 'I'll just get dressed, then we can walk to the end of the road and see what's going on.'

'I don't think we need to, sweetheart. The road runs right along the bottom of our garden, and there's no sound of any traffic. They've definitely closed the road.' He smiled at her. 'I think our part in it is over now, and I wouldn't start watching the local papers for any info either.'

Daisy looked disappointed. 'Why?'

'Because if he was abducted in Huntingdon, it'll be the Cambridgeshire Constabulary dealing with it. As soon as our guys get all they can on it, they'll bundle it off to them. It's not down to the Fenland Constabulary at all.'

'Oh dear. Well, I hope that nice constable who spoke to you gives you an update. After all, it's us who alerted them, and it's only right we know what happens.'

He laughed. 'It doesn't always work like that, angel. Not these days. It's all changed since I was on the beat.' He saw how downcast she looked and relented. 'I'll do my best to find out, never fear. I'll try putting on a "good old boys" act — you know, fellow officers and all that? Anyway, right now we have a starving dog, and our son will be demanding his breakfast. I'm afraid it's back to the real world, Daisy, we'll have to leave the bloodstained kidnap victims to the police.'

* * *

DI Rowan Jackman noted a thoughtful look on his sergeant's face as she entered the CID room. 'Should I be worried by that rather pensive expression, Marie?'

DS Marie Evans raised an eyebrow. 'I've no idea, boss. I'm trying to work it out myself.' She peeled off her leather jacket and hung it over the back of her office chair. 'The thing is, I saw a face I thought I recognised on the way into the station, but she was gone before it properly registered. It's only just come to me now.'

'Friend or foe?'

'At one time I would have said foe, but she looked different, which is why I didn't recognise her straightaway. Remember the Millard case?'

Jackman nodded. 'I'm hardly likely to forget that one.'

'Well, Johnny Millard's wife is in town. It was Anna Millard I saw, but not as we knew her.' Marie smiled. 'Unless I'm very wrong, of course, but that auburn hair is a bit of a giveaway.'

Jackman could visualise her clearly. She had been in court every single day of her husband's trial and had been his staunchest ally throughout. She made a striking figure — a lone woman, and elegant, with long, wavy hair the colour of burnished copper, always in black. He recalled admiring her poise and dignity, even when her husband was sentenced to ten years imprisonment.

'So, in what way is she changed, Marie?' Jackman asked.

'For a start, she was dressed casually. And she seemed, well, *ordinary*.' Marie rolled her eyes. 'I mean, that woman always looked like she'd stepped right off the front cover of *Vogue*. There were days in that courtroom when I felt positively like a bag lady.'

Jackman laughed. 'No one could ever describe you as that!'

'Thank you, Jackman, but let's face it, the only magazine cover I'll ever grace is *Motorcycle News*. Even then, no one will be looking at me, they'll all be ogling my beautiful Triumph Tiger. Anna Millard was in a different class. That woman oozed sophistication. But now? Phew!'

Jackman thought about it. 'Her husband has been banged up for seven years by now, and she adored him. Maybe she hasn't coped and she's let herself go.'

Marie looked doubtful. 'I dunno, Jackman. She's strong. She's never given up fighting his cause. There was something in one of the papers only a few weeks ago about her. I don't buy the not coping bit.'

He was about to answer when Tim Jacobs, Jackman's office manager, approached. 'Sorry to interrupt, sir, but there's a call from downstairs. There's a woman in the foyer who's asked to speak to DS Marie Evans personally. Her name is Anna Millard.'

'Really?' Jackman exclaimed. 'Speak of angels! Or maybe that should be the devil. Now, this I need to see. I'll come with you, Marie.'

He thanked Tim and asked him to ring down and say they'd be there in a few minutes.

'She's the last person I'd expect to see in the nick, unless she were in the custody suite, or in handcuffs,' said Marie. 'She never even tried to conceal her anger at the police for her husband going down, did she? What do you think this is about, Jackman? And why ask for me by name?'

He grinned at her. 'Well, let's go find out.'

In the interview room, any thoughts Marie might have harboured of a woman worn down by the incarceration of her husband vanished completely. Anna Millard might be dressed differently — she wore jeans, a black T-shirt and an old denim jacket — but she sat bolt upright on the hard chair, and the look on her face was the same. No, Jackman corrected himself, that was not quite true. The determination was still there, but there was something else, a kind of desperation tinted with anguish.

He'd told Marie to take the lead, as Anna had asked for her by name, so Marie introduced him, and then asked how she could help.

'I know who you are,' said Anna to Jackman, and turned her attention to Marie. 'I'll keep this brief. I don't expect you will either believe me or take me seriously. You will most likely think it's another calculated ruse to get the press on my side. I don't care. I just need you to listen to me.'

Jackman, watching, noted the woman's body language. It took only seconds to decide they'd be fools not to hear her out.

'I won't bore you with details that you already know. But I will say one thing. I fight for my husband because, although he's something of a villain, he was innocent of the crime he went down for. What you don't know is that he was set up, in a very clever and calculated manner.' She paused, looking straight at Marie. 'Because I believe he'd stumbled on something that certain people didn't want anyone to know about.'

'Can you expand on that?' asked Marie.

'I wish I could,' said Anna bitterly. 'Johnny is either too scared to talk about it, or he isn't fully aware of what he uncovered. Even I don't know the answer to that one.'

Not unkindly, Marie said, 'But how can we help you, Anna? Do you have some fresh evidence, or . . . ?'

'Five days ago, Johnny was released on parole. The day before yesterday, he went missing.' Anna swallowed. 'I want you to help me find my husband.'

Questions raced through Jackman's mind, questions he knew that Marie would be asking herself. Surely, they should have received notice of Johnny Millard's early release on licence, so why had they missed it? He'd be checking on that as soon as they were out of this room. Had Johnny done a runner and gone into hiding? Was his wife even right about him knowing something that was dangerous to him? And if that was the case . . .

'I'm here,' continued Anna, 'because I was watching you, DS Evans. At the trial. I saw your face. There was a look on it that said you weren't happy about some of the evidence. You knew something was wrong, didn't you?' She drew in a breath, but continued without waiting for Marie to respond. 'I'm not blaming you, don't be anxious on that score, but I saw a seed of doubt in you. I am asking you to look back. Look back, and remember.' She took a sheet of paper from her pocket and passed it to Marie. 'My contact details. Not my home, or my usual numbers, these are private, newly set up, and only you have them.' She stood up. 'I'm not stupid, DS Evans. I suspect that when you do find my Johnny, he will be dead, but right now I cannot allow myself to dwell on that. I must give him every chance. Please, help me.'

'Anna,' Marie began slowly, 'say for one moment that I believe you. You do know that I'll have to dig deep into Johnny's background, meaning that everything, and I mean everything, including the worst of his actions, is going to come to light? And you'll have to tell the truth. No bypassing something because it's shady. I'd have to know every single thing that Johnny has ever done, right back to when he was in short trousers.'

Anna looked at her steadily. 'I vowed I'd sell my soul to the Devil to get my Johnny back, and I hold to that promise. I'll do it, DS Evans, if you will help me.'

Marie glanced at Jackman. 'Wait here a few minutes, Anna. I need a word with my boss.'

'He's sitting right next to you,' Anna said. 'Why not have your word here and now?'

'My station. My rules.' There was no arguing with Marie in a situation like this. Wanting to either laugh or cheer, Jackman remained impassive.

'There are other cases to consider before I commit time to you and your husband,' continued Marie. 'So, five minutes, okay?'

Anna raised her hands in surrender.

Outside, Marie leaned back against the corridor wall and exhaled loudly. 'Lord! She's an astute one, all right. I always thought there was something iffy about certain aspects of the Millard trial, and she picked up on it! Hats off to her for her powers of observation.'

'And you want to take this further?' Jackman himself wasn't sure if it was right to take this up, but he had no doubt in his mind that Marie wouldn't be able to let it go.

'If he turns up in the river with a knife in his back after I'd ignored his wife, I'll never be able to live with myself. Plus, I hate to say this, but I think she's right. He's a villain, all right, but I'm willing to bet he's just served seven years for something he didn't do.'

'Then it's a bit of luck we have nothing too pressing on at the moment, isn't it?' Jackman did a few quick calculations in his head. 'Robbie, Max and Charlie can take over the money laundering business, leaving Gary to help you. After you've finished with Anna, we'll get everyone together, put them in the picture and delegate jobs. I've got a pile of reports to sort, and Ruth has a load of new admin stuff to run past me, so I'm leaving it up to you to decide if we have a legit case or not. Okay?'

'Perfect, Jackman. Let's tell her.'

Back inside the interview room, Jackman said, 'Mrs Millard, I'm going to leave you two to talk. I hope your fears for your husband's safety turn out to be unfounded.'

As he left, he heard Marie say, 'Okay, Anna. Talk to me. I'm listening.'

CHAPTER TWO

Marie escorted Anna Millard to the foyer. Just as they reached the main doors of the station, Anna stopped. She caught hold of Marie's arm and said, 'I trust you,' regarding her with an intense gaze, which turned into a rueful smile. 'And that's a first, believe me.'

Marie returned the smile. 'I can't say I find myself fighting on the side of a criminal too often either. Life's full of surprises, isn't it?'

Making her way back upstairs to the CID room, Marie shook her head, amazed at the fact that an unlikely bond had just been forged.

As soon as she appeared, Jackman beckoned her into his office. She sat down and let out a long breath, finally able to relax. In a station full of activity and chaos, Jackman had made this humdrum room into a lovely, peaceful refuge. He had brought in his own furniture — the desk made of oak, the old captain's chair upon which he sat. Instead of the usual photos commemorating life in the force, there was a single black and white picture, representing a different kind of glory, that of his first love — his horse, aptly named Glory.

Jackman sat back and regarded her. 'So, my friend, what is your opinion? As if I didn't know.' As he spoke, he idly spun the globe that always sat on his desk. Each of the countries was inlaid with semi-precious stones which glistened as the world turned.

Marie was glad to see him like this, more like the old Jackman — focussed and seemingly untroubled by unwanted thoughts. He'd been through hell in the last year after losing his partner, but recently Marie had noticed a distinct change in him that she recognised as a kind of acceptance. You can never alter the past, but you don't have to let it ruin the future. Okay, maybe he was a little harder now, but he was, and always had been, a damned good policeman, and he was back on track.

'It's my belief that Johnny Millard *was* a scapegoat, and that his disappearance is a cause for concern. I think we should follow it up, Jackman.'

'As I have no wish to incur the wrath of Marie, that's good enough for me.' He grinned at her. 'But this one's your baby, and a right unholy alliance it is too.'

'Don't worry, I intend to have my eyes wide open every step of the way.' She frowned. 'I've got a bad feeling that this could be the tip of an iceberg, but I've no idea what sea it's floating in, or how deep it goes.'

He raised his eyebrows. 'Marie Evans — sorry, Enderby — waxing lyrical?'

She laughed. 'Evans is fine. As we agreed, I'll always be Marie Evans while I'm at work. I only use my married name when I'm off duty.'

'Exactly what my friend and counterpart at Greenborough told me. It's hard to think of DI Nikki Galena as anyone but that — until she gets home and takes the warrant card from her pocket.'

'Well, you don't spend a lifetime in the force as one person, then overnight expect to be thought of as someone else,'

Marie said. 'My Ralph understands that completely. Now, back to Johnny Millard.'

'Keep me updated, Marie, every step of the way, and as soon as I've caught up with the admin and Ruth's requests, I'll be back with you. So, shall we take this to the others, then you can fill us all in on what Anna had to say.'

She stood up. 'Absolutely. I think we need to hit the ground running on this.'

When the team had gathered, Marie stood by their white-board and gave them a brief outline of what had been said by Anna Millard. Before she could begin in earnest, she was inter-rupted by a surprised little grunt coming from DC Robbie Melton. 'Hey!' he said. 'I know Johnny Millard. Well, I've met him a few times. Harry, a friend of mine from way back, went to school with him, they were good mates, still are as far as I know. They lived in the same village, and I think Johnny's family still does.'

Marie turned to Jackman. 'Can I ask to have Robbie with me on this? If he knows people connected to Johnny, he could be invaluable.'

Jackman agreed at once. It still left three detectives work-ing on the money laundering, which was ample.

'Johnny Millard,' Marie began. 'Known to us as a profes-sional enabler. That is, he provides a valuable service that facil-itates different types of crime. He's a man with extraordinary IT skills, capable of manipulating things like security cameras, and he's thought to be a first-class hacker. He's clever, and prior to being found guilty seven years ago, had never been convicted of even a minor misdemeanour. He was always on the periphery of investigations, and there was never enough evidence to even get him to court, let alone bang him up.' She looked at Robbie. 'Is that what your friend says, that he has brains, not brawn?'

'That's right,' Robbie said. 'He was popular too, nothing like the typical picture of a computer nerd as a rather pathetic "Billy No-mates". Technology came naturally to him, and he treated it as a game. My mate said he was a right trickster, even as a teenager, but never heavy with it. I only met him a few times, but I found him likable, and always willing to share his passion for tech.'

Marie nodded. 'Well, that backs up the wife's story. She told me that he'd been led into using his skills for criminal activities, and he hadn't always been that way. Initially, it had been small stuff. He'd seen it as a bit of fun, a chance to pit his wits against the big guys, and get one over on the Establishment. He then discovered how easy it was to manipulate the transfer of money, and get through security. After he'd been doing this for a while, a very astute villain decided that Johnny might just be his Golden Goose.' She shrugged. 'He took Johnny on, and paid him very well. According to Anna, none of the crimes he was involved in were violent. They enjoyed the lifestyle that the money permitted, and if no one got hurt — why not?'

'So, what went wrong?' asked DC Gary Pritchard. 'How come he was convicted for the Cardinal Cross investigation?'

'I only have Anna's take on this,' said Marie, 'but she is convinced that he either discovered something, or was about to discover it, and someone decided to shut him up before he blabbed. So they dumped him in the shit, while all traces of their involvement disappeared. Every bit of information that Johnny gave the court, things like addresses and names, were checked out thoroughly, and found to be false. Buildings were empty, people he named didn't exist. Whoever set him up covered their tracks perfectly, and the whole burden of guilt fell squarely on Johnny.'

Robbie Melton raised a hand. 'What exactly did he go down for?'

'Cybercrime, on a big scale.'

'Must have been if he got a ten-year stretch. It's usually seven, isn't it?' added DC Max Cohen.

'They threw the lot at him — hacking, fraud and identity theft, including a ransomware attack; the Court found that

16

he highjacked Cardinal Cross company files and held them to ransom.'

'And what's his wife's opinion?' Robbie said. 'He was obviously up to his neck in it somehow.'

'She swears he only accessed information and accounts for the man who pulled the strings. According to her, he was doing exactly what he'd been doing for years — opening doors for his boss.'

'And who is this bossman?' asked Gary. 'Bit of a stupid question, I suppose.'

Marie smiled at him. 'Yeah, that too turned out to be a dead end. I've been told that the Serious Cybercrime Unit are still trying to unravel the complexities of how money changed hands, and where the hell it went. Anna thinks Johnny was part of something far bigger than he realised, possibly even international.'

'So, if he got hold of something he shouldn't, why not just make him disappear?' Robbie asked. 'Surely, if they're that big and powerful, topping him would be the quickest and easiest way to shut him up permanently?'

'Anna said the same thing, Rob. She's shit scared, both for Johnny and for herself. She must have been really desperate to walk in here and ask for help. We are her final hope, and she's terrified that someone might have done exactly what you just said. But seven years down the line? Okay, he's out early, so maybe they weren't expecting him to come out on parole, but why now?'

Marie wasn't surprised when no one answered. 'Anyway, there's no point wasting energy in trying to work that out. Robbie and I will move on this one straight away.'

'And everyone else, plough ahead with the money laundering,' added Jackman. 'If, as Marie suspects, this is going to turn out to be a big one, we can do with tying up everything else as fast as possible. We are close to nailing the organisation responsible for the illegal transactions in the town outlets, so let's pull out all the stops.'

Max started to get to his feet. 'We've got the guy who appears to be the big cheese under close surveillance, and I've just heard that we've isolated one angry ex-gang member who has an axe to grind with his old boss. He's prepared to leak a few names, dates, and times to us as long as we keep his name out of it.' He looked at his watch. 'If it's okay with you, Charlie and I will head off right now and have a chat with him.'

'Then go,' said Jackman. 'We'll meet up again at four, and see where we are. Marie? Robbie? Quick word in my office.'

Marie and Robbie followed him out of the CID room.

Back at his desk, Jackman said, 'You mentioned that Anna was concerned for her own safety as well as Johnny's, so keep your wits about you all the time you are around that woman. If Johnny has been taken, there's a good chance they'll go after her too, and she probably upped the stakes by coming here. Watch your backs, guys.'

'We will,' Marie assured him. 'And I'm also holding onto the thought that today's visit could be some sort of scam in itself. I've no idea why, or to what end, and although I do think Anna is being upfront with me, well, I'm a copper, and I've never trusted a villain, or a villain's wife, before.'

'That's sensible. Just take care. Both of you.'

'We always do.' Marie winked at him as they went out of the door. 'Honestly, Jackman, however likable Johnny Millard might be, and however much his wife seems on the level, it's still a case of trust no one.'

Back outside, she and Robbie made for the coffee machine. 'One drink, then we go have a long talk to Anna, okay?'

Robbie nodded. 'I've never met her, but because of my passing acquaintance with her husband, hopefully she won't be too antagonistic towards me.'

'If we are to help her, I can't possibly do it alone, she'll understand that.' She fed money into the machine and pressed the button for a tea. 'And she's not at home, Rob, she's too scared to stay there on her own. That's how certain she is that Johnny's been taken.'

'So, where is she?' Robbie asked.

'A friend of hers is away for a couple of weeks, and has left Anna the keys to her house. She's also got a burner phone, and only I have the number.'

'Hell! She really is convinced she's in danger, isn't she?' Robbie took his turn at the machine.

'She believes he's already dead, but says she has to do everything possible to find him in case she's wrong.'

They took their tea back to her workstation and sat down.

'Tell me, Rob,' Marie began. 'Does it surprise you that Johnny turned to crime? You said your friend knew him well, and you met him several times, so what was your impression of him, apart from being a "nice bloke"?'

Robbie sipped his tea thoughtfully. 'I could have seen him going into the corporate world, being head-hunted by the big companies, all wanting his expertise. I could also have seen him as a hacker, because of what my friend told me about Johnny liking to get one over on the system. But as to serious organised crime, I'd have to say no.'

'And your general impression of him?'

'Extremely bright. Good natured. Fun guy on the surface, though I think he was pretty deep. Not easily led, so what you told me about him getting into crime surprised me.' He looked up from his tea. 'It's my opinion that if he really had set up the crime he went down for, it wouldn't have gone wrong. It would have gone as smooth as silk, and he and Anna would have had money enough to live the good life forever.'

Marie considered that. 'Okay, but if he was so bloody clever, how come he was set up in the first place? The Cybercrime Unit found all manner of incriminating stuff on his computers, so where was his state-of-the-art security? Surely anything sensitive would have been encrypted, and he'd have used pathways that it'd take GCHQ to follow?'

'Maybe because he's not the only bloody clever bastard out there. Someone as smart, if not smarter, than Johnny turned the tables on him and beat him at his own game.' Robbie shrugged. 'Which tells me that whatever he had uncovered, or was about to uncover, was damn important.'

Frowning, Marie stared into her tea. 'That's what Anna believes, but what if it was all about something completely different? It won't be easy, Rob, but we need to keep an open mind on this one. It seems so obvious, i.e. he's pissed off some serious players, but what if his disappearance has nothing to do with that? Has he even been taken in the first place? Maybe he's squirrelled away a hoard of money from his previous jobs, and he's ditched Anna and buggered off to the Costa del Crime?'

'Okay, so if we're going on that tack, what if Anna herself is behind this? Maybe she knows exactly where he is, or if he is dead, then it's she who killed him? Stranger things have happened.'

Marie was certain that wasn't the case. She had seen the anguish on Anna's face in that interview room, but having said herself that they should keep an open mind, she had to agree. 'Is your friend Harry still around, Rob?'

'Sure. We've been out of touch for a while, but I know he still lives in the area because I caught sight of his car a week or so ago. Want me to contact him?'

'Maybe. Let's go talk to Anna, start to build up a concise picture of Johnny Millard, and then if we think your Harry could help, I'll get you to have a quiet word, okay?'

'Sure, Sarge.' Robbie smiled rather ruefully. 'It'd be good to touch base with him again. It's too easy to let old friendships slip in this job.'

'Isn't that the truth!' said Marie. 'Far too easy.' She emptied her beaker and threw it in the waste bin. 'Ready?'

Lobbing his beaker after hers, Robbie stood up. 'Ready.'

They drove to the address Anna had given her. It was a good place for someone to lay low. For a start, it was one of those peculiar areas in the Fens that was hard to find if you didn't know it was there. There was no village, per se, just a few straggling houses and scattered farms on lanes that seemingly went nowhere. It was less than six miles from Saltern, yet it could have been in the back of beyond. If she hadn't known Dowdyke End from her childhood — a friend of her father's had lived there — she might never have found it. Sat nav didn't have a clue, and she was quietly amused to see Robbie's puzzled expression as she drove confidently along narrow, potholed lanes that zig-zagged with no apparent end in sight.

'Good choice of hideaway, wouldn't you say?' she asked him.

'Just don't ever ask me to drive here alone, Sarge!' he exclaimed. 'I've lost my bearings completely, and I thought I knew this area better than most.'

'Unless you know someone here, you'd have no reason to, Rob. It leads nowhere apart from to a few farms, then meanders back to the main road again. It gives new meaning to the term "backwater", doesn't it?'

Marie slowed right down and checked a faded and weather-worn nameplate attached to an old five-bar gate between high laurel hedges. Here it was — Ambleside House. Robbie got out and opened the gate for her.

She was glad he was with her on this one. He had very good powers of observation and could read people's body language far better than many detectives.

As he climbed back in, she said, 'I'll be *very* interested to hear what you think of her.'

CHAPTER THREE

For the past hour, Jackman and Superintendent Ruth Crooke had been going through the latest directives from HQ, and Jackman was growing increasingly bored. He tried not to let it show, as he knew Ruth hated the bureaucracy as much as he did. Nonetheless, it was part of her job description, what she had signed up for, and she was damn good at it.

'You have that glazed look on your face, Rowan, the one that says you'd rather be anywhere else than here. Am I right?' Ruth regarded him severely; her thin lips were tight, but he caught the hint of a smile in her eyes. 'Is there something bothering you, other than a deep desire to escape this office?'

He told her about the missing man, Johnny Millard, and the unexpected visitation of his wife, Anna.

'Well, that's a turn-up for the books!' said Ruth, raising an eyebrow. 'I'd have thought she'd rather have rolled naked in a bed of nettles than set foot in this place.' She paused, frowning, as if in recollection. 'She was that aloof and rather enigmatic woman who was always present at the trial, wasn't she? Never missed a day in court, as I recall.'

'That's her. Though she's far from enigmatic right now, she's desperate to find her husband, who she believes has been kidnapped and possibly killed. Marie is absolutely certain that she's on the level.'

'I see. Well, our Marie does have good instincts.'

'She does,' Jackman said. 'And fortunately for her, Max and the others are close to bringing the money laundering investigation to a conclusion, so I can afford to let her and Robbie run with it.'

'And you want to join in, I suppose?'

'Only when we are through here and when Max and the rest of the team are ready to snap cuffs on wrists. Marie and Robbie can handle the preliminaries and let us know one way or the other whether we need to take our missing man seriously.' He chuckled. 'Mind you, if he's playing silly buggers, he'll go back inside and serve what remains of the full sentence, but as he's no plank, I can't see that.'

'No, I can't either. Breaking the terms of your licence has serious consequences, as anyone on parole is aware. It means completing the full sentence, plus another two years. That's a lot to risk.' She leaned back in her chair. 'We've almost finished here, and at least I've saved you from another little item that reared its ugly head earlier today.' She gave a dry laugh. 'Listen to this — frankly, you couldn't make it up! Apparently, uniform responded to a call to the home of a retired copper formerly with the Surrey Constabulary. He opened his door early this morning to a man with blood running down his face. He was holding up one of his arms, which had a handcuff dangling from it! He begged to be allowed in, saying someone wanted to kill him.'

Jackman's eyes widened. 'And he'd knocked on the door of a retired policeman? I bet he was given short shrift! Was it a hoax? Someone sending in a scout to case the guy's home?'

Ruth shook her head. 'He was told to wait outside while the ex-copper called the police, but he legged it. Turns out it was for real — two suspicious-looking cars turned up a few minutes later, cruising slowly down the road, and the guy is nowhere to be found.'

'Weird!' breathed Jackman.

'His story was that he'd been kidnapped in Huntingdon, driven over fifty miles, then held in a deserted barn before he managed to escape. While they were searching for him, uniform discovered fresh blood in an old barn off the main road.'

'Phew, that looks like someone trying to dump their crime over the border, doesn't it?'

'Especially if the plan was to kill him and leave him in the old barn,' added Ruth. 'It would have been our problem then. As it is, since the crime supposedly took place in Huntingdon, we've thrown it back to them. I've asked DI Jenny Deane to get all the evidence reports together to pass over to them. I gave it to her as I thought you had enough to cope with regarding the money laundering, and considering what you've just told me, I'm glad I did.' She stared at him, her eyes widening. 'Unless . . .'

'Unless it was Johnny Millard?'

'I wonder . . .' she breathed. 'Although I was under the impression that Johnny was considerably older than this guy, but even so . . .'

Jackman half raised himself from his seat. 'We'd better get an ID photo of Millard across to this retired copper, Ruth. Although if it was Millard, surely, he'd have been taken *out* of the county to kill him. The logistics don't make sense, do they? And what's all that about Huntingdon?'

'Speak to Jenny Deane, Rowan. Get her to send her witness that photo pronto, then you'll know one way or the other.'

'Oh, I will,' said Jackman. 'Marie said that this Johnny Millard problem could be the tip of an iceberg, and the more I think about it, the more I'm inclined to agree.'

Ruth looked down at the folders, memos, and files on her desk. 'Forget this garbage, Rowan. I'll sort it. If there's anything you really need to know about, I'll tell you. Right now, see Jenny, then go help your team to finalise the problem in the town, so you can join Marie. Go, detective, and do what you do best.'

With a grateful smile, Jackman leaped to his feet. 'I will, and we'll update you as soon as we know more. Thanks, Ruth. I owe you one.'

'You *always* owe me one, Rowan. Now bugger off and leave me to these fascinating — no, *riveting*, new accountability and oversight arrangements. Or would you prefer to stay . . . ?'

Jackman was already at the door. 'As you say, Ruth, I'll leave you to do what you do best.'

* * *

On a concrete floor, bound tightly with what felt like nylon cord, sticky packing tape across his mouth, sat a man convinced these were his last hours on earth. Long past panic, the terrors had subsided, leaving him in a state of acceptance, of unreality. This really wasn't fair, he thought. He was still young, and had envisioned an exciting life ahead. No, it wasn't fair. Pain, confronting a violent death, had never featured in his plans for the future.

It was dark, although he could just make out the vague shapes of objects. He knew he was in a garage from the smell of fuel, and paint, and that cloying, slightly chemical mustiness of weedkiller, engine oil, and other old items stored untouched for years.

He was a little disappointed with himself at having given up all hope so quickly. Then again, maybe this was the best way to deal with the inevitable. Did condemned men and women who faced the hangman's noose, the electric chair, or whatever other fate had been arranged for them, feel like this? It wasn't an attempt to maintain dignity, that was for sure. There was nothing dignified in his present state. It was more a kind of exhausted resignation, and a realisation that it was pointless to waste your final breaths in fighting the inescapable.

He didn't think about those he cared about. He didn't dare. He had fast realised that he had to close his mind to them;

25

their fear, their anguish and their grief, would be unbearable. He had to make this ignominious ending entirely about him.

Let his captors come. Let it end. He was ready.

He heard footsteps, the sound of a key sliding into a metal lock, and utter dread and panic took hold of him.

No! Please, no!

* * *

There were still traces of the old Anna. Even if she was looking less than immaculate in casual clothes and no make-up, she still retained a certain bearing, that of a person determined to face whatever was to come without flinching.

'I've not located everything here yet,' she gazed around the country-style kitchen, 'but I have found the kettle, and the coffee and tea. I'm making a cup anyway, so can I get you one?'

They both declined, saying they'd just had tea.

'Well, well, police officers refusing a brew? Or do detectives work to a different set of rules to coppers?' She turned back to the kettle.

When Marie saw the expensive leaf tea she was spooning into a pot, she changed her mind. 'I think I'd like one after all, if you don't mind.'

Anna gave a small laugh. 'I thought that might be the case.' She glanced at Robbie. 'You look like a coffee drinker, young man. You're not really a detective, are you? I must be well out of touch, I didn't know they were recruiting teenagers these days.'

Robbie took the comment in good part. Yes, he said, he was a coffee drinker, and he was actually well into his thirties.

Anna regarded him with a hint of amusement. 'Yes, I can see that now, but you do not look like police. I expect that comes in handy.' She led the way through to a lounge with French windows that looked out onto a pretty, if somewhat overgrown garden.

'Your friend has a lovely home, Anna,' Marie said, 'and it's the perfect location for keeping a low profile.'

Anna sipped her tea. 'I wondered if you'd find it. And it's the first place Johnny would come to — if he were able. He was changed when he came home, Marie, and very frightened, so we made a few contingency plans. This was one of them.'

Although she decided not to say so, this worried Marie. It didn't seem to have dawned on Anna that it placed her in danger, because if he was put under pressure Johnny, no matter how much he loved her, might be forced to tell his captors where his wife was hiding. So, she said, 'I know you're convinced that they've kidnapped Johnny intending to kill him, but what I can't see is why they would have waited so long. It's an unpleasant fact, but we all know that prison is one of the easiest places in which to have someone killed. So why wait seven whole years? Any ideas on that?'

Anna looked thoroughly miserable. 'If I knew why he'd been framed in the first place, I might be able to hazard a guess. I always believed that they only wanted him out of the way, so he wouldn't be able to interfere in whatever they were planning. Killing him wasn't on the cards, he was simply taken out of the picture for a while. We never met the man he worked for, but I always got the feeling that Johnny was appreciated for his skills and paid accordingly. It's as if what happened to Johnny was the work of someone else. But,' she said bitterly, 'I guess if you work with faceless people, you can never know what they are really like.'

'Or how dangerous they can be,' added Robbie soberly, and then he smiled at her. 'I met your husband several years ago, Mrs Millard. I liked him, and was amazed at how clever he was. I imagined him with a senior position in some massive corporation, and I was really sad when I heard about not only the direction he had taken, but what then happened to him.'

'Robbie reckons that if Johnny had been running that operation he was jailed for, he would never have been caught,' added Marie.

'Your detective is right, Marie.' Anna seemed to regard Robbie with slightly more warmth. 'The so-called "mistakes" that led to his arrest were sloppy and stupid, and my husband is neither of those things. Yes, he would have carried it off seamlessly, and we three would not be sitting in my friend's home wondering where the hell he is, and whether he's dead or alive.'

The catch in her throat as Anna spoke those words made Marie realise that she was close to breaking point. 'Why don't we take a look at Johnny's life, right from the beginning, and see if we can pinpoint something that might help us find him. We already have people checking the CCTV in the area around your home. Hopefully, this will give us the date and approximate time of when he actually disappeared. We know he didn't use his own car, but there might be a sighting, or the presence of another vehicle in the vicinity that isn't usually there.' She glanced quickly at Anna, who was looking downcast. 'I know this must be hard for you, and I promise we'll do all we can.'

'It's more than I had hoped for,' said Anna. 'And much to my surprise, I'm actually glad I approached you. Now, what can I tell you about Johnny?'

After half an hour or so of questions and answers, Robbie said, 'Did Johnny tell you he'd received any threats while he was inside? Did anyone attempt to hurt him?'

Anna shook her head. 'No, in fact, he got on well with many of the other prisoners, and even the staff. He told me he made a point of keeping his head down. He was in HMP Marshfield, which as I'm sure you know, is a Category C prison. They aim at rehabilitation, and have workshops and training facilities. When there was no trouble in his first year, he was put to assisting some of the other inmates — helping those with literacy problems and so on. He worked damned hard to get his parole, I can tell you.'

'And there was nothing in particular that worried or upset him?'

'You mean, apart from having ten years of your life stolen from you for something you never did? Oh, he was angry. Of course he was. He wanted out, to get back at whoever put him there, but on the whole, he made the best of it. For seven whole years he survived, taking it one day at a time. I respected him for that.'

Seeing Anna's eyes bright with unshed tears, Marie decided they'd got as much as they could from her for now. They would be back, but in the meantime Anna had given them plenty to work on.

Just as she was about to tell her so, Anna said, 'I think what hurt him most was the loss of his photos. Thousands of images and video he'd shot, going back years — all gone. Places he'd been to, our life together. His family — the brother who'd moved to the States, and his parents; old friends, homes we'd made together, our old dog. His whole life was in those pictures.' She shook her head sadly. 'Some things you can never replace, they only exist as memories, and old photos help you bring them alive again. Not only was it devastating for Johnny, but it's also a tragedy for me. I needed those photos to hold onto, in case I never see him again.' She gave a little self-deprecating laugh. 'Sounds pathetic, doesn't it? After everything that's happened, here I am, fretting over a bunch of old photos.'

Marie thought about her own photos, and what the loss of them would mean to her. Never to look at her mum and her dad, her beloved spaniel, herself at her passing out parade. And Bill, her late husband. What if she could never see his dear face again? 'I don't think it's pathetic at all,' she said. 'But it reminds me of something I kept thinking all the way through his trial. How was it that someone as skilled and experienced as Johnny could have been hacked in that way? I assumed he must have got complacent or become careless for some reason, but whenever I looked at Johnny, I couldn't help feeling that that wasn't the case, and he really was innocent.'

'I could tell from the way you reacted,' said Anna. 'It's why I contacted you. Johnny told me that whoever hacked into his computer was way cleverer than anyone he'd ever come across before. I have an idea he knew who it might have been, but he never told me.' Anna looked from Marie to Rob. 'One thing you might not be aware of — it happened after the trial — was that Johnny had a visit in prison from the cyber-crime investigation team. They wanted to know about the failsafe he'd set up, which eradicated everything from his computer system while it was in their possession under lock and key. They had just finished retrieving information that was needed for evidence in the trial when it closed down, destroying all the files and programs not only on the computer, but also on the Cloud. It turns out Johnny hadn't set anything up, but someone else had. He told the officers that if he had created such a program, he'd have made sure it took effect *before* he went to trial, not when he was already banged up in a sodding prison cell. And surely, they should know themselves that it is impossible to eradicate all trace of someone from the web, dark or not, which they had to admit was so. Not that it did him any good, it just remained an unanswered question. Soon after that visit, Johnny realised that he'd lost everything, including his precious photo gallery. He became more angry than at any other time in his ordeal.'

Robbie frowned. 'But what about the Cloud? How come his information was removed from there? And he could have used block chain.'

Anna shrugged. 'It's beyond me, Detective. I never got the hang of technology. I'm afraid I can't help.'

I wonder? Marie had a sudden picture of Orac, their enigmatic IT expert, in her underground lair in the bowels of the police station. Maybe it was time to have a word with her. It was what she was good at, and Orac always relished a challenge.

Standing up, Marie said, 'I think that's enough for today, Anna. We'll give you a break and get back to base. And, please, I know this house is hard to find, but do be very careful. I'm not comfortable with the fact that you are alone, no matter how well hidden. Keep in touch with us.' She asked Robbie to give Anna his card with his personal number on it. 'If you cannot reach me, ring Rob, okay?'

Anna took the card. 'I will, and I'm glad you met and liked my husband, DC Melton. He did some illegal things, but he's not a bad man. I'm glad you are helping Marie to find him.'

He smiled at her. 'It's Robbie, and as the sarge here said, we'll do all we can.'

As they followed the winding fen lanes back to the station, Marie asked Robbie what he'd made of Anna Millard.

'She is genuinely concerned for her husband.' He screwed up his face. 'But I can't help thinking there are things going on that she's not telling us about.'

'I think that's par for the course, Rob. After all, they are criminals. She's not going to cough to everything he's been up to, is she?'

'Probably not,' he agreed. 'But I meant it was something more personal than that. I got the feeling there was something she wasn't telling us about Johnny himself.'

They drove on in silence for a while, until Marie said, 'What I still don't understand is how come, if Johnny is as brilliant as everyone seems to think, he was hacked so cleverly.'

Robbie shook his head. 'That's what I thought, too, Sarge, but then I got to thinking. Computer science is so advanced nowadays, it's perfectly possible. Look at viruses. Orac once told me about a German computer science student called Jaschan who released a worm that caused worldwide disruption. The British Coastguard had to disable its electronic mapping system, and Delta Airlines were forced to cancel multiple international flights. And he was small fry compared to hackers who bring down huge conglomerates and cost countries billions. If a fifteen-year-old kid can gain unauthorised access to NASA's computer system, and another find his way into the US defence department from his North

London flat and leave a message saying, *"Your security system is crap,"* I guess anything is possible.'

Marie gave a little snort. 'When you put it like that, Johnny Millard's information system was probably like an open door with a welcome mat outside, and a sign pointing "this way".' She looked askance at him. 'And since when have you been having conversations with Orac, Robbie Melton? It's hard enough to get her to even utter a word sometimes.'

Robbie laughed. 'Try getting her on her chosen field. She'll talk all right. Well, lecture is probably a better word for it. That said, I swear she's starting to soften.'

Having worked on some very emotionally challenging cases together, Marie was probably the nearest thing Orac had to a friend. It was a relief to learn that the 'cyborg in the basement' might be taking steps towards becoming human.

'If you say so, though I can't quite see that myself. Softening or not, we are going to need her expertise on this case, so I suggest we make her our first port of call when we get back.'

'Sure, but can we please make one little detour — via the vending machine. I'll need that coffee I refused back at Anna's place if we are to confront Orac.'

CHAPTER FOUR

When Jackman told DI Jenny Deane about the missing Johnny Millard, she at once emailed a photograph of him to Bob Ruston, the retired police officer who had opened his door to a terrified stranger. The reply came back in minutes: it was not their missing cyber-criminal. Jackman informed Marie, and sent his office manager, Tim Jacobs, to Ruth Crooke's office to let her know that they had two separate cases of missing men.

He then went back to the money laundering affair, and found Max, Charlie and Gary all practically dusting the ceiling in their excitement.

'It's on for tomorrow afternoon, boss!' Max said, his eyes sparkling. 'Our man came through! We've got a time and a rendezvous point, and if all goes well, we could be netting the big fish, Lars Westerham.'

'That's great news! Where's the location?' asked Jackman.

'East Street, just behind the town centre,' said Charlie. 'It's a small grocery-cum-off-licence, one of those with adverts plastered all over the windows so you can't see inside.'

'We've been watching it for weeks,' Max went on. 'It's a legitimate business, but our intel tells us that the gang has earmarked it for a prospective hit. It has a good turnover, and takes a fair few cash sales, so it's ideal for the launderers to blend in funds from illegal operations.'

'But if the money is moved around electronically, how are you going to prove anything?' asked Jackman.

Max grinned. 'Ah, but you see we aren't expecting to grab him holding a big bag of readies with SWAG written on it. This is an opening gambit. After his minions were less than successful, Lars Westerham has begun to sound out prospective "business associates" in person. If he's happy with an outlet, he lays out his terms, and that's when we'll have him.'

Gary took up the thread. 'Our informant, whom we are referring to as "Sid", blames Westerham for the death of his brother, and he's very angry about it. Sid isn't in the kind of league to get Westerham taken out by a rival gang, so he's using us to get back at him by taking him off the streets and into prison. Sid has a friend who helps out in that store, and this bloke got hold of a spare backdoor key, and had one cut—'

'And gave it to Sid—'

'Who gave it to me,' said Max, with a smug grin. 'I happened to call in earlier, and placed a handy little voice-activated recording device in the back office. We've commandeered an upstairs room in one of the buildings opposite. It has a clear view of the front door of the shop, and once Westerham and his heavies are inside, uniform will be waiting, front and back of the premises, and they'll take him the minute he sets foot outside. The whole thing will be on CCTV, too, as I've arranged for the pub a few doors away to train their camera on the shop door.'

'And then we'll have a recording of his proposed transaction,' breathed Jackman. 'Nice one, Max.'

'Orac will prove it's him. She has voice recognition technology that's as good at identifying a speaker as a fingerprint. Job done!'

Jackman beamed at them. 'This could be the final piece in the jigsaw. You, along with Orac's team of cyber detectives, have accumulated so much evidence over the months that we have a definite case for the Crown Prosecution Service, but this is hard evidence, and indisputable.'

Jackman knew that Westerham was far from being the only money launderer in the area, but he was, as Max put it, 'the big fish'. Take him out of the pond, and the minnows should be easier to control. He was glad they were only a small market town, and not a big city. Money laundering — so called because in the past, criminals used laundrettes to mask the proceeds of crime — was costing the UK £100 billion every year. Furthermore, criminals were constantly inventing new ways to dodge the money laundering legislation. They would never stop them — criminal organisations go to great lengths to hide the source and the destination of funds derived from their operations — but taking people like Lars Westerham out of the equation gave them all a huge sense of achievement.

'Wrap this one up, Max, and the drinks are on me.'

'Cheers, boss! We'll hold you to that. As OIC, will you be with us when we hit the place?' Max asked.

'Wouldn't miss it for the world. Westerham has been a thorn in our side for far too long. Seeing him in handcuffs will make my heart sing, believe me.'

'And as I want that free drink, I will make sure it happens, boss.' Max saluted smartly. 'We've got this!'

Jackman knew that a dozen things could go wrong between now and tomorrow, but Max's enthusiasm was infectious, and he found himself believing that it would all proceed as planned. 'Okay, keep me updated on times, and I'll look forward to seeing our Mr Westerham being bundled into the back of a police wagon.'

* * *

Lucas lay stretched out on his bed, staring at the ceiling. He didn't want to be here. The Fens were boring beyond belief, and he missed his lively city. *Any* city would be better than this flat landscape full of bloody cabbages, he thought morosely, but especially his beloved London with all its noise and bustle. The silence here felt threatening. All that space allowed his fertile mind to wander to places he'd rather not go. He closed his eyes. Just this one job, carried out to perfection, would secure him a hefty payout, and he could return to the clamour and the frenetic life he so loved. Just three days, four at the most, and he'd be heading back to the Smoke with plenty of money to enjoy himself with. Lucas was a professional. He didn't come cheap, but he was worth the money he earned. He was an expert in what had become a niche market, and his services came at a price.

Lucas yawned. Doing nothing always made him tired, he wanted to be out there working, but he knew better than to start playing games with his schedule. The job had to be carried out to the letter, so he had no choice but to chill for a while, and relax. He'd made sure to exercise, to eat well, and now he had nothing to do but wait. He told himself to breathe. *Relax. You're nearly there now. Soon, you'll be completing stage one of this lucrative little caper, and you know how it goes — as soon as you're out of the starting block, you'll be enjoying yourself, and the time will fly.*

He closed his eyes. In his head, he heard the roar of traffic, the blaring of horns, he heard music pouring out of shop doorways, from sound systems in tuk-tuks. A visitor from the provinces, on a first trip to the metropolis might find it a confusing welter of noise, but to him it meant life, with all its buzz and verve. He missed it terribly.

Only two hours to go, and he would be locking the door to his temporary accommodation and driving the three miles to where it would all kick off. If his intelligence was correct, and it always was, he would see a car with two occupants pulling away from the tree-lined driveway, which was the signal for his work to begin. He gave a little shiver of anticipation. Okay, it wasn't the territory he was used to, but if he was careful, that should play into his hands. And he always was careful. Lucas didn't take unnecessary risks, it made him the pro he was, and a very sought-after one too.

Eyes still closed, he pictured his new client and went over their initial interview. He hadn't been expecting to meet the man himself. That kind of man didn't usually show his face, or even use his own name, let alone fly a prospective business associate hundreds of miles to his home.

And what a home it was. The stuff of dreams. If he could just accrue enough money — he already had some sitting in a tax haven on some godforsaken little island — he might purchase one for himself, though not so grand, of course. This job was the acid test, the key to a regular supply of specialised jobs. And while he carried out his assignments, he would be keeping his eye open for opportunities to feather his own nest, not just that of billionaire Crispin Payne.

* * *

As Orac had been busy, Marie and Robbie had returned to the CID room to check out some of what Anna had told them. Marie watched Robbie's fingers fly across his keyboard as he searched for information relating to Johnny Millard. He had come a very long way since he and his old crewmate, Stella North, had been on the beat. Stella had been shot trying to protect innocent bystanders in a bungled post office raid, and had been retired out of the force. Robbie had taken it hard, and had gone off the rails for a while. He had a heartless gold-digger for a superintendent who refused to acknowledge that he had been seriously affected by what had happened to his partner and did everything she could to get rid of him. Stella had rung Marie to ask for her help, and the rest, as they say, was history. Robbie had proved to be a very good detective, and an asset to the team. Marie smiled, recalling

Anna's comment about his age. His youthful appearance, along with an ability to blend in wherever he found himself was invaluable.

Marie looked back to her own screen and sighed. At the time, it seemed that Anna had told them a lot, but none of it had turned out to be useful. Maybe Robbie would come up with more than she had found.

He looked up for a moment, and she saw that he was as disappointed as she was.

'I reckon it's time I gave my friend a call, Sarge, what do you think? I have a feeling he might know more about Johnny than anyone. Plus, there's a chance, a very slim one, that if Johnny is on the run, Harry might have heard from him.'

'Okay, Robbo, ring him now, and see if he's available for a friendly chat with an old mate.'

'Not coming with me?' Robbie asked.

She shook her head. 'Not this time. He'll probably be more willing to talk when he's not in the presence of a stranger, especially when that stranger is a cop. Anyway, whatever he says, it's got to be more informative than these computer searches. I'm getting nowhere fast!'

Robbie made the call. 'Bit of luck — well, for me anyhow. Harry's off work with a broken wrist, and says he'll be happy to see me.'

'When?'

'Right now,' said Robbie, getting to his feet.

'Nice one. Off you go, and good luck.'

Marie turned back to her own screen and bit her lip. She needed to try a different approach. Uniform were already scouring the area for Bob Ruston's missing man, so she had asked their sergeant to get them to keep their eyes open for anything that might indicate another fugitive, either in hiding or being held captive. There was still some hope that CCTV in Johnny's home area had picked up some unusual activity at the time he disappeared, but even that was unlikely to show up anything useful.

Marie pushed her chair back and stood up. It was time to try Orac again. When they had called in to see her earlier, she had been busy interviewing a prospective candidate for her team. Marie had wondered how the unsuspecting interviewee would react when faced with Orla Cracken's silver Mohican haircut and unnerving mirror contact lenses. Now, that would be an interview worth videoing!

Still smiling, Marie took the stairs down to Orac's basement lair. Hopefully she'd be free now, and Marie could enlist her help.

Orac was in her usual place in front of a bank of computer screens. She looked up and smiled when she saw Marie. 'Sorry I missed you. Philip said you wanted to see me.'

Marie pulled up a chair next to her. 'How did the interview go?'

'Better than expected,' she said with a metallic flash in Marie's direction.

'Good. What did they make of your, er, kingdom?' What Marie really wanted to know was what they made of Orac herself, but of course, she couldn't ask that.

'She was obviously very impressed,' Orac said, and then gave one of her rare laughs. 'Actually, I was the one who was impressed. She was in a different league to some of the others I've interviewed, one of whom kept staring at me like the proverbial rabbit in the headlights.'

Marie chuckled. 'I'd like to have seen that. You certainly sound very pleased with your choice.'

'Oh, she's a rare find, and its pure chance that she heard about the vacancy. She's from London, but her father lives down this way. He's disabled, and she wants to be closer to him.' Orac lowered her voice. 'She was with the Metropolitan Cybercrime Unit for three years, and was afraid she'd end up in a boring job with some big corporation if she moved here. A friend of hers knows my senior technician, Leon Barras, and he mentioned that there was a vacant position here, and I'm bloody glad he did.'

39

'Well, that sounds very good, and it kind of ties in with what I wanted to see you about, especially if your new recruit worked for the MCCU.' She went on to tell Orac about Johnny Millard and his sudden disappearance while out on parole.

Orac nodded slowly. 'I remember the trial. Wasn't it David Serlin and Philip Adisa who worked on it, along with the National Crime Agency's NCCU? Though I didn't hear what happened to him, because just as he was about to be sentenced, I was called in to assist with that massive scandal — you know, the one involving a peer of the realm and the editor of a major newspaper.'

Marie had forgotten that. Pity. She had rather hoped Orac would be able to give her some first-hand info on Millard's case.

'No worries, though. I'll have a word with Phil and David, they can gen me up on it.' She sat back in her ergonomic chair and regarded Marie quizzically. 'Well, if Millard's served his sentence and the case is closed, what do you want me to do for you?'

'I'm wondering if you might be able to get access to Johnny Millard's data. His computer was hacked and somebody wiped it clean. It should still be in the Met's secure evidence store.'

'Phew! That's a big ask.' Orac gave a dry laugh. 'But . . . I do have a fair bit of clout. It might just have some bearing on a new case as well, so I'll give it a shot.'

Marie beamed at her. 'Thank you, Orac. I really appreciate that.'

'Don't hang by your eyelashes, though. If the NCCU couldn't find any evidence of foul play, I'm not sure exactly what more I'll be able to do. It's a real bummer that your man has gone AWOL, because I could do with some inside info about how he worked. I do remember that Philip had heard of this guy Millard before the trial, and had been impressed by his brilliance. He said at the time that he couldn't see Millard making the kind of mistakes that got him convicted, and when his system was hacked, he swore it couldn't possibly be Millard's doing.'

'Apparently, the other investigators said the same thing.'

'So, we have a mystery on our hands.' Orac would never have gone so far as to rub her hands, but she did exude a sort of controlled enthusiasm. 'You know, I rather like the thought of this one, Marie. It could be the perfect first case for Coral McIvor, our new recruit.'

Relieved to have Orac onside, Marie said, 'Fantastic! When does this Coral start work?'

'The day after tomorrow. She already has her accommodation sorted, so she's ready to roll,' Orac said. 'Get me everything you have on him, and precisely what you want me to look for, while I summon my amazing powers of persuasion, and try to get your man's data released from imprisonment in the evidence store.'

'I'll get onto it straightaway, and once again, thank you, Orac.'

'My pleasure. I'm glad you called by. I'm going to enjoy this one.'

Marie emerged from the depths of Orac's underworld with the distinct impression that Robbie had been right. Orac had indeed mellowed — she had actually laughed at one point. She wondered what Jackman would make of it. His terror of Orac was the source of much humour in the station. It was what had given rise to Marie's friendship with her, because he always used his sergeant as a go-between. It was one of those things that cast a little light on what might otherwise be a dark and sometimes hopeless world.

* * *

Robbie arrived at his old friend Harry's house at around half past three. At thirty-five, and despite having plenty of money of his own, Harry had chosen to live in his childhood home, with his parents.

41

Arriving at Barnham Lodge, Robbie thought he could understand why. Gazing up at the windows of the old rambling house, Robbie calculated that it had to have at least six bedrooms. He knew from his past acquaintance with Harry that he had a remarkably close relationship with both his mother and his father, so unless — and as time went on this seemed increasingly unlikely — he fell hopelessly in love, Barnham Lodge was where he would stay.

Let in by Harry's mother, Robbie found Harry in the lounge. He lifted a plaster-encased arm in greeting. 'Good to see you, mate! Sorry I can't give you a hug.'

'How'd you do that anyway?' Robbie asked.

Harry grinned. 'Character building.'

'What?'

'I was teaching a group of itinerant youngsters from the community youth centre how to play rugby. I volunteer there, and I reckoned rugby would be a great game for team-building and all that.' He looked ruefully at the arm. 'It seemed to have been successful, because they rallied round immediately, fetched help and called an ambulance without showing the least sign of panic. I was really proud of them. Anyway, never mind about all that . . . want a coffee?'

'Love one.'

Lorna, Harry's mum, was in the throes of making plum jam, and the kitchen was a glorious mess. Harry rolled his eyes. 'It's the annual plum fest, and just after she'd let you in, mother just discovered she'd run out of jam sugar. She's probably stripping the shelves in Tesco as we speak.'

Harry waved away Robbie's offer to make the coffee. He was getting pretty good at operating one-handed, he said, although he wouldn't mind help with carrying the mugs.

Rob's friendship with Harry was one of those where no matter how long it was since you'd last seen each other, you immediately fell back into the old rapport. Rob told himself not to leave it so long before their next meeting.

'How's the lovely Ella?' asked Harry.

Robbie smiled. 'Still lovely.'

'When are you going to tie the knot then, eh? With looks like hers, you'd better not leave it too long, or someone will pinch her from you.'

Harry led the way into a sunny garden room. 'We're happy as we are, mate. Neither of us feels the need to make a big show of our commitment to each other with a costly wedding. My own parents were hardly a shining example of married bliss, and, well, if it ain't broke, why fix it?'

'I only ever saw your parents on a couple of occasions, but they struck me as being, er, not particularly happy with parenthood?' Harry said, with an enquiring look at Robbie.

Robbie snorted. 'You can say that again. I was a bloody inconvenience, and nothing but a disappointment to them. I spent my school holidays being dragged around the Med watching them getting rat-arsed with their rich friends. When I complained, they said I was an ungrateful little sod who didn't know how lucky he was. The rest of the time I was palmed off on some relative or other, while they played at being socialites. If it wasn't for my auntie Hazel in Cornwall, I think I'd probably have run away and ended up on the streets.'

Harry smiled. 'Instead, you ended up as a copper.'

'Best thing I ever did, Harry. From being an unwanted nuisance who was always in the way, I became a person with something to contribute. And apart from one brief catastrophe, when I nearly blew it, I've never looked back. Of course, I did receive an allowance when I left home, which I can't deny was useful, even if they only did it to get me out of the house and from under their feet.'

'Total opposite to the way my life's turned out. All credit to you, my friend. You've done well. A detective no less! Bit more exciting than being an electrician, like me.' Harry regarded Robbie over the rim of his mug. 'And talking of your job, this isn't just a social call, is it?'

Relieved to be able to divert the conversation away from his parents, who still had the power to upset him, Robbie said,

'No, but I'm still glad of the opportunity to link up with you again. It's about Johnny Millard.'

The smile left Harry's face. 'Johnny! Bloody shame that. He was royally stitched up there.'

'You sound very certain of that.'

'I am. Totally. I visited him several times in HMP Marshfield, and it really upset me. I've never seen a man so changed. He was still bitter, but he kept it all under control because he desperately wanted to get out on licence.'

'Is that what he told you? That he'd been set up?'

'He swore he had, and I believed him. Still do. Come on, Robbie, you remember him? Okay, I don't condone the things he did, but it didn't totally surprise me. He always enjoyed pushing the boundaries — and he was so sodding clever.' Harry exhaled. 'Which is what I still, to this day, cannot fathom. How did this person manage to hack him so successfully? It certainly wasn't some local geek in a basement, was it?'

'It doesn't look that way, mate. The only thing I can think of is that he became involved with some large criminal organisation.'

'But why?' asked Harry. 'He was smart, and he readily admitted to having enabled some shady characters to gain access to information they shouldn't, but he wasn't big-time, Robbo. Whoever closed him down was a master, but why did they think it was necessary to do so?'

Robbie shrugged. 'If only we knew. Tell me, Harry, when did you last see him?'

Harry thought for a while. 'I guess it must have been about two months ago. He was in good form, as upbeat as I'd ever seen him since being inside. He was certain that his parole was going to go through. That was the last time I saw him, and I've not heard from him since he got out. I haven't tried to get hold of him, thinking I'd give him a chance to relax and spend time with Anna.'

'And now he's disappeared. Anna is distraught. So much so that she's asked *us* for our help,' Robbie said.

Harry stared at him. 'Disappeared! As in what? Run away? He can't have broken his parole, surely!'

'Frankly, we suspect that he's been abducted, and we have no idea why. Any thoughts, Harry?'

Harry looked pole-axed. 'Jesus! Abducted . . .'

Robbie was certain that this was no act. Harry Barnham had no idea what was going on, or where his old friend was now. 'Listen, Harry. Do something for me, would you? If you hear from Johnny, or find out anything about where he might be, ring me, okay? Immediately. We are afraid for his life . . . and Anna, well, Anna believes he's already dead.'

'Poor woman,' whispered Harry. 'She adores Johnny, you know? Maybe I should ring her. What do you think? Or call round and tell her I'm here if she needs anything.'

'You won't be able to, mate, and it's no use trying her phone. She's taken herself off, and is now in what they like to call an "undisclosed location".'

Harry went quiet. 'In that case . . . you really are concerned, aren't you?'

'Very.'

'Then of course I'll ring you if he contacts me, but from what you've just said, that ain't likely to happen, is it?'

'Who knows, Harry? There might well be a lot going on that we don't know about. There's even a chance that Johnny has gone to ground for some reason known only to him.'

Harry very carefully set his empty mug down. 'He did tell me that he was going to get his own back. He swore that when he got out, he'd turn the tables on whoever stole all those years of his life from him. He said he'd do whatever it took — whatever that means.' He winced. 'He'd changed, Robbo, really changed. He wasn't the Johnny I used to know. I can understand how bitter he must have felt at having to do time for something he didn't do, but bottom line, Johnny was a criminal himself, and if you choose that sort of life that's a risk you have to take. He must have known that what he was doing carried a custodial sentence, and he was far from naïve.

Perhaps he got too confident of his own abilities. But from what I saw of him in prison, he'd gone far beyond being pissed off about someone taking him out of the game. It's not an exaggeration to say that he was consumed with a boiling rage that was taking all his strength to suppress.'

'Anna told us he was changed, too, but according to her, he was scared to death, not thirsting for revenge,' Robbie said.

Harry shook his head. 'Then I have no idea what the fuck is going on.'

'You're not alone there, Harry-boy. But you will keep in touch, won't you?' He glanced at his phone. 'Time I got back to the nick. Thanks for the coffee, and you take care of that wrist. I'll give you a call — maybe we could have a couple of beers one evening? Assuming you can lift a pint glass with your left hand?'

'I'd lift it with my feet if it meant a couple of jars with an old mate!' Harry grinned. 'And seeing as how I'm not exactly going out much at present, bring it on.'

CHAPTER FIVE

Every couple of months, Bryson Smith made a point of spending at least a week in the Fens with his parents. They had been good to him, supporting him in his ambition to become an artist. Although they couldn't really afford to send him to art school, they had somehow managed to scrape the funds together, and with the aid of a grant, he had graduated from Loughborough University with a degree in Fine Art. Now he was not only an artist in his own right, but also held an important position at one of London's largest auction houses. Bryson specialised in British and Irish Modern Art, and was known to be an expert on the war artists, and the work of Mervyn Peake in particular.

Today, he had abandoned his tailored suit in favour of overalls and an old pair of boots. His parents, who were not getting any younger, saved up odd jobs that they were no longer able to tackle for him to do when he came home, and he enjoyed getting his hands dirty. The nice, detached bungalow he had bought for them was easy to maintain, but some of the tougher garden jobs were beginning to build up.

Today, Bryson was loading conifer hedge cuttings into a barrow and wondering if it had been a mistake to buy this place. The bungalow came with a garden an acre and a half in size, which had initially been a delight for his green-fingered parents. Now, however, it had become something of a burden. His father, Teddy, had flatly refused Bryson's offer to employ a gardener for them, even one day a week. Bryson guessed his dad didn't want to admit the fact of his encroaching old age. Bryson hoped he'd see sense before the winter set in. Right now, in the last weeks of August following a wet and dreary summer, the weeds were rampant. There was only so much he could do in a week, but at least it was dry today, so Bryson could deal with some of the larger jobs, like the hedge, and then plead with his parents to allow him to get them a helping hand.

'Bry!'

Bryson looked up to see his dad walking towards him, accompanied by a skinny young man with longish dark hair, wearing boots and khaki trousers. He flashed a friendly smile in Bryson's direction.

'This is Colin, old Gabriel Reynolds's grandson.'

It took Bryson a few moments to recall one of his parents' neighbours from their previous home.

'Gabe asked me if I might be able to give Colin a few hours' work. The company he worked for have gone to the wall, and the lad hasn't found a new job yet. I thought you might like a bit of help, son.'

Praise be! thought Bryson and stuck out his hand in welcome. Clearly, in his father's book, helping someone out with a bit of work wasn't the same as employing someone. Whatever, this was good news. 'I certainly can! Hello, Colin.'

Colin's handshake was surprisingly firm. 'I'm happy to tackle anything,' he said. 'Just tell me what to do, and I'll do it.'

'Perfect,' said Bryson. 'In which case, I'll leave this for now, and we can have a go at the jungle.'

'Oh, that'll be good,' said his father enthusiastically. 'That area down the bottom has beaten me. I'll leave you to it and go and see if your mother has got the kettle on. If you're going to sort that wilderness out, you'll be needing a brew.'

After Teddy had gone, Bryson explained about the so-called jungle. 'It's a fenced-off area that the previous owner wanted to keep as a wildlife garden. It's even got a little bird hide. There's some straggly crab apple trees, buddleias to attract butterflies, and more nettles and brambles than you've ever seen. It's a two-man job if ever I saw one. Are you up for something like that?'

'No sweat, Mr Smith. Let's give it a go.'

'Ditch the "Mister", Colin. Bry will do nicely. How are you for time today? It's mid-afternoon, and it's a bit of a job.'

'I've got all day, I'm game to work till dusk.'

'Then let's go down to the garage and sort us out some tools.'

Ten minutes later, armed with a strimmer, a long-handled pruner, a small chainsaw and a selection of other implements, they entered the enclosure.

'The plan is to clear the weeds, nettles and brambles, prune the shrubs, make sure the trees aren't diseased, then strim the path and the edges, and finally get the mower in. Oh, and check the condition of that old wooden bird hide. If it's rotten, as I suspect it might be, we'll take it down and I'll have to fathom out a way to get rid of the old timber.'

'I've got a small van, Mr Smi— er, Bry. If we can saw it into manageable lengths, I'll take it to the local tip,' Colin said.

Delighted, Bryson beamed at him. 'Well, I'm mighty glad you turned up today. How are you fixed for the rest of the week? I'll happily pay you whatever the going rate is.'

Colin grinned broadly. 'Free as a bird, Bry. And to be honest, my old employer paid me so little that I was considering setting up on my own anyway. This'll be a good start, and I'll be able to find out what I'm capable of.'

'And if you get on okay, I could be your first paying customer,' said Bryson, considerably relieved. 'Even if we finish this place by the end of the week, it'll need maintaining. If it all goes well, you could have your first regular contract, lad.'

For the next hour they worked in silence, cutting back the overgrown shrubbery and pulling up nettles. Colin then attacked the massive thicket of brambles that had taken over a corner of the area.

Bryson smiled at the lad's enthusiasm, and also at the colourful expletives directed at some of the more tenacious and spiteful thorny stems. Bryson didn't want to eradicate them completely, as he knew they provided shelter and food for wildlife, especially bees, but a harsh cut back, and a root out of any seedlings, would do no harm at all. His mother had expressed a wish to keep it as a wildlife garden; she enjoyed watching the birds, along with the occasional visit of a little vixen. He had put off tackling it alone, but with Colin's help, they might make of it somewhere his mum would enjoy.

While Colin hacked and swore his way into the brambles, Bryson fired up the strimmer and cut a route through to the old bird hide. As soon as the path was clear, he took a good look at the little wooden structure. He had expected it to be rotten, but it was perfectly intact, needing only the ivy stripped off the far wall, a good rub down and a couple of coats of timber preservative. He opened the door and checked inside. The window hatch needed oiling, and cobwebs threatened to engulf it, but basically it was good for a few more years. It could be a first project for his new helpmate, saving him the trouble of doing it himself. His preferred kind of painting was done on canvas, not planks of weathered wood.

'Bry! Got a moment?' called out Colin.

He walked back along his newly trimmed pathway and found Colin surrounded by a huge heap of cuttings.

'Do we have a shredder? Only this is getting a bit out of control.'

'No, I'm afraid not, but we could certainly use one.' He thought for a moment. 'Tell you what, pile it all up by the gate, and I'll go and ask Dad to source one online. With luck we'll get a next-day delivery, and we can be shot of it.'

'Make sure he orders a chipper that takes green leaves. My granddad got one that clogged up if you put anything a bit young in it,' said Colin. 'We don't want him wasting his money like Grandpops did. They aren't cheap.'

Bryson grinned at him. 'Oh, it won't cost him a penny, and I'll make sure he gets a good 'un.'

Having tasked his dad with finding a one-day-delivery shredder, Bryson hastened back to the wild garden where he found Colin staring at the bramble patch.

'What's wrong, Colin?'

'There's something underneath this lot, Bry. Something solid. And big.'

Bryson felt around. Colin was right, there was something there, although he had no idea what it could be. He pulled aside a thorny stem and saw concrete. 'I suppose it could be an old World War Two air raid shelter,' he suggested. 'Although the Anderson shelters were made from corrugated iron sheets, not concrete.'

'Bit before my time,' Colin said.

'And mine, I'll have you know!' laughed Bryson. 'But I happen to know quite a bit about the two world wars.'

'Hey, there's a kind of narrow opening here,' Colin said, tugging away at the brambles.

Immediately, Bryson realised what it was. 'It's a pillbox from the Second World War.'

Colin looked mystified. 'Pillbox?'

'A small, fortified structure, usually made of concrete, and built for use by the armed forces in case the enemy invaded. They reckon around 28,000 of them were constructed along the coast of England. After the evacuation of the allied troops from Dunkirk, they believed that our shores were highly vulnerable to the chance of attack.'

'Wow, you do know your stuff, don't you,' exclaimed Colin.

'I have to, it's part of my job. Well, kind of . . . I'll tell you about it sometime. Suppose we clear the whole front section?

It'll make a rather nice feature, don't you think? A bit of history, right here in the garden. Dad'll be dead chuffed with this.'

'Yeah, cool!'

They spent the next half an hour cutting the brambles and the ivy down to ground level, pulling up clumps of sedge grass and removing overhanging branches from the adjacent trees. As they worked, Bryson told Colin a bit about the different kinds of pillboxes that could still be found in the area. Colin was enthralled. Bryson got the impression that all the lad knew about the war came from films and computer games.

Sweating from their exertion, they stood back and admired it. They could now see its hexagonal shape, although only a small amount of it was clear of brambles, but the two embrasures — the openings that enabled the occupants to use rifles or light machine guns on the enemy — were now visible.

'Where's the door, then?' asked Colin.

'At the back, I should think,' said Bryson, 'and as this bit of the garden backs onto a field, that would probably be about right. There's a bit of a copse behind here, and it runs right along the field edge, so I guess that's as overgrown as this side is. It might even be partly on the farmer's land. Maybe I should get my dad to have a word with him. They have a pint together some weekends down at the local.'

'I'd love to take a look inside,' said Colin.

Bryson laughed. 'Most likely it's full of rubbish and very smelly, but it makes a great garden folly. I'm glad you found it, my friend.'

Colin looked pleased with himself. 'Unreal! Can't wait to tell my mates.' He looked at Bryson. 'Would you mind if I took a few pictures with my phone?'

'Go ahead, I'm going to do the same.'

They both took several shots, and Colin leaned forward to take a photograph of the interior through the narrow opening.

Bryson checked his photos. They'd come out well. The heavy cloud gave them a rather eerie quality that he really liked.

Colin was staring at his phone.

'Is it full of rubbish, like I suspected?' Bryson asked.

'I don't know what I'm looking at,' whispered Colin, and handed Bryson his phone.

Bryson stared at the image. If this was what he thought it was, he needed to see it for himself. 'Colin, clear the rubbish away from the base of the pillbox, would you? I'm going to get a step ladder.' He thrust the phone back at the confused young man and hurried off.

By the time he returned, Colin had cleared enough space for Bryson to crawl inside. He really didn't want to do this, but he knew he had no choice. Maybe it was a trick of the light, nothing but a heap of age-old debris. Maybe they'd be laughing about this in a few minutes. Maybe.

He rested the steps against the stone embrasure, and looked inside. For a moment he had a flashback to some paintings he'd seen by a war artist who had documented the horrors of the concentration camps. He saw tangled limbs that were little more than bones. A skeletal hand reached up to him as if in supplication. Bryson gasped and drew back.

'Mr Smith! Bry! What is it? What did you see?'

'Death. There's someone dead in there. We need the police. Now!'

* * *

Marie rang her husband, Ralph, to say she'd be late home. 'We've got a weird one just come in. Jackman and I are going to assess the situation. It might be a hoax, or, well, I don't need to tell you what else it could be.'

Ralph said that in that case he'd call in at the supermarket on his way home and grab a couple of ready meals, and just in case, he'd stick a bottle of wine in the fridge as well. She might need it.

Marie hung up, feeling profoundly grateful that she'd found a husband as understanding as DS Ralph Enderby.

She and Jackman hastened to the crime scene — if that's what it was. The initial call had been scanty on detail, but it wasn't far to Fendyke Village, and the long evenings at this time of year meant they'd have plenty of daylight left to see just what had occurred.

Two police cars were parked outside the bungalow. Standing beside one of them was the familiar figure of PC Simon Laker. Simon was a good, solid copper, who had become a trusted contact over the years. Marie often sought his opinion on the crimes they had to deal with.

'What have we got, Simon?' she asked, jumping out of the car. 'A time waster? Or something else.'

'Definitely something else, Sarge.' His expression showed none of his normal good humour. 'I must say it's a first for me, and probably you too. Come on, I'll take you to see for yourselves. And prepare for the unexpected.'

Jackman checked his phone and then came over to join them.

'Simon says it's not a hoax, Jackman.'

He raised an eyebrow. 'Okaaay . . . So, what have we got?'

'It was rung in by a Mr Bryson Smith, the son of the couple who live here — Edward and Elizabeth Smith. He, and another man, Colin Reynolds, were clearing an overgrown part of the garden when they came across an old wartime pillbox. Smith looked inside and saw what he believed to be human remains. When we arrived, we took a look, and I can confirm that it was a corpse.' He shuddered. 'Fair gave me the heebie-jeebies, it did.'

'Poor you,' said Marie. 'What a shit way to end your shift.'

'You can say that again. I'll be dreaming about that pillbox for the next few months. Nearly fell off the ladder, I did.' Simon attempted a smile.

'Any idea if it's one body, or could there be more?' asked Jackman, as they approached a rickety gate to a rather unkempt section of the garden.

'Hard to say exactly what's what, sir, but I'd guess at least two,' said Simon. 'We need to clear the whole thing of brambles so we can get inside for a proper look. My crewmate has already contacted the farmer who owns the land behind this property, and he's given us permission to access it. We'll drive a couple of vehicles along the perimeter so we can get some cutting equipment in there.'

'Good,' said Jackman, looking at a partially revealed concrete structure peeking from a mass of overgrowth just ahead. 'This it?'

There was a sinister look to the old structure that caused Marie to be flooded with foreboding. What on earth had happened here?

Bryson's ladder was still leaning against the small rectangular opening that Marie supposed the soldiers must have used to fire at the enemy.

'Right, then, better take a look,' said Jackman, approaching the ladder.

The way he spoke told her he had as little desire to enter as she did, but at least he'd be going in first.

'Give me your torch, Simon.'

Marie saw him stiffen, though he held the torch beam steady. A few seconds later, he stepped slowly back down.

'You were right, Simon. It's definitely no hoax. This a serious crime scene. As you said, we have to gain access to it, but before any chainsaws spring into action, this whole place must be sealed off and forensics brought in. We cannot afford to lose any evidence through contamination. Can you contact your sergeant and update him of the situation, please? We need more officers out here, pronto. I'll get hold of forensics.'

While Simon radioed his sergeant, Jackman turned to Marie. 'You'll have to see it, I'm afraid. But I warn you, it's not pretty.'

'Death rarely is, Jackman.' She took the torch from him and climbed the steps.

Simon had called it a hellhole, and it was. Trying to remain professional, she attempted to work out how many poor mortals comprised this tangle of contorted and twisted limbs. It was impossible. All she saw was a sickening scene that belonged on a film set or in a Gothic horror novel, not in someone's back garden in a sleepy Fenland village.

'Marie? I think you've seen enough for now.'

Marie swallowed and turned to climb down. She certainly had seen enough.

Back on the ground, she stared up into the sky. The sun was going down, and it was starting to feel chilly, but that was nothing compared to the chill that crept through her on seeing that ghastly heap of remains. She felt a pressure on her arm. It was Jackman, giving her a reassuring smile.

'I know, Marie. But those people in there need us to find out who they were and what happened to them, so they may finally rest in peace. It's up to us now, and Professor Rory Wilkinson, of course.'

She looked at him. 'It was just—'

'Believe me, that was my reaction too.' Jackman gave her a weak smile. 'I wish I was as witty as our revered Home Office pathologist. We could do with hearing what he'll come out with when he sees why we've called him.'

Marie returned his smile. 'Me too. It'll save my sanity.'

CHAPTER SIX

Spotting the old-style Volvo making its way towards the lane leading out of the village, Lucas counted the occupants. The timing was more or less spot on — a sign that things should go smoothly. He waited five minutes, and then sent the pre-arranged text. On receiving the go-ahead, he drove smartly through the open gates of Hartwood House and parked outside the front entrance. And what an entrance it was. The double doors were constructed of thick stained glass behind a framework of intricate, geometric design. The doorhandles were made of genuine forged wrought iron. Lucas made a mental note and, pausing for a moment, tapped in a few numbers on the small device in his hand. He waited. The word *APPROVED* appeared on the screen, he pocketed the device and walked around to the back of the house.

He left the vehicle where it was. No one was going to remark on a company van, especially when it bore the name of a pest exterminator specialising in wasp and hornet nest removal.

The curved, metal-framed Crittall bay window at the rear of the building was a beauty, as was the first-floor veranda. He hadn't seen many old buildings that were as lovingly maintained as Hartwood House, and it gave Lucas much hope for what he might find inside.

At the back door he took the small device from his pocket and pointed it at the lock. This was always a tense moment. It opened, and to his relief, there was no ensuing alarm. As he went inside, he noticed that the screen of a wall-mounted home security monitor was blank, just as it should be. Now, to work. He preferred to start at the top and work down, and his watch showed that he had more than enough time to be thorough. Even so, he worked fast. There was always the chance that the occupant might come home unexpectedly.

This was the best part of the job for Lucas. The moment of anticipation. You never knew what you might find, and a single step into the front hall told him he had been right to be optimistic. The decor was pure Art Deco — the fan-shaped wall sconces alone were worth a mint. The entire house was a shrine to the 1920s and 1930s, and as far as he could tell, everything in it was authentic.

This was way beyond all his expectations. He had anticipated finding some beautiful collectible pieces here, but the sheer number of them took his breath away.

He spent the next fifteen minutes taking photos and videos for identification purposes. One upstairs room in particular, furnished like a lounge, had him gaping in awestruck admiration. Unlike the other rooms this one was Art Nouveau, an earlier style than Art Deco, characterised by long, sinuous flowing lines. The room appeared to be a kind of showpiece, and contained what Lucas guessed would be the most precious, and valuable, items in the house.

He checked his watch. He should go. He was well within his allotted time, but he had done what he set out to do, and was beginning to feel slightly uneasy.

Lucas exited the same way he had gone in. Outside, he tapped some numbers on his device, and the doors locked. Back in the van, he drove out through the gates before feeding some final instructions into the iPad. After a short, slightly anxious wait, a message appeared on the screen: *ALL SYSTEMS ACTIVATED.*

He drove away, head spinning, eager to get back to his room and take a look at the images. This visit to Hartwood House had shown him that he was perfectly capable of undertaking a little private work on the side. His client would still benefit from his expertise, while Lucas cherry-picked the very best items for himself. His sight of that glorious Art Nouveau room had shown him the way forward to a new and profitable life.

* * *

Rory peered into the pillbox and uttered a small startled, 'Oh!'

Jackman raised an eyebrow at Marie. 'Is that all he has to say?'

'Most disappointing,' she said.

Rory climbed down the ladder and regarded them with a frown. 'You've been taking bets again, haven't you? Ever since that Romeo and Juliet case, you've been trying to second-guess me.' He folded his arms. 'In which case, I shall up my game!'

'We expect nothing less, Rory,' said Jackman. Glancing over Rory's shoulder at the concrete structure behind him, he said, 'You're going to need a way in, aren't you? It appears that the entrance is probably at the back, in that field. The farmer has given us permission to go onto his land, but we need the help of you and your SOCOs to direct our lads when they go in with the chainsaw. We've cordoned it off, and so far, it hasn't been contaminated.'

'I fear there's going to be no easy way to preserve it, dear heart,' said Rory, looking pensive. 'All I can do is take a look, but the chances of finding anything pertaining to what happened are, frankly, pretty remote.' He stood, hands on hips, gazing at the pillbox. 'Those bodies have been there for a considerable length of time, and given the weather in recent years, any evidence, unless it's something really solid, such as a piece of jewellery, will have been well and truly obliterated by now. Our best hope is of finding something inside this monstrosity.'

'Okay, let's take a look at the back.' Jackman looked about for one of the uniformed officers, and spotted Simon Laker. 'Take us round to where you believe we can get access, would you, Simon?'

'This way, sir. There's a small pedestrian gate that leads directly into the field. We can use that, and then bring the vehicles in from the road and along the perimeter.'

As they hurried across the garden, Jackman saw two men standing by the entrance to the field.

'That's the son of the owner of this property, sir — Bryson Smith. He's here on a visit and was clearing up the garden for his parents,' explained Simon. 'The other man is a local lad who was helping him. I think his name is Colin Reynolds. They came across the pillbox, took one look inside, and rang us. They were pretty shocked, sir, as you can imagine, but they're over it now, and have offered to show you where they believe the entrance is to be found.'

Jackman introduced himself and his companions, and they followed the two men into the field.

'Donald Telford, the farmer, leaves a clear strip of land along the boundary, so that we can get to the trees and bushes and cut them back when we need to. I get a local company in once a year to do the job, but it grows so quickly we could really do with them coming in twice a year.' Bryson Smith rolled his eyes. 'I've told my parents I'm happy to pay for it, but my dad insists it's not necessary. He can be very stubborn when the fancy takes him.'

Jackman asked Bryson where he lived and what he did for a living.

'I live in London, I'm a practising artist, although I also work for one of the big auction houses. I come here as often as I can to help out Mum and Dad, mainly in the garden. To tell you the truth, it's no hardship. I find it quite therapeutic. Our family has always been gardeners, and I enjoy the physical labour, it keeps me rooted, if you know what I mean.' He grimaced. 'Except when you come across something out of Hieronymus Bosch!'

'Hieronymus Bosch,' Jackman said with a smile. 'That's just what I thought when I looked through that opening. Tell me, Mr Smith, how long have your parents been living here?'

'About six years,' Bryson said.

'Do you know who lived here before that?' asked Marie.

Bryson gave a dry laugh. 'Oh yes, good old Barkis. He didn't get his name from Dickens, by the way, but because he was barking mad, and his wife was little better. Their real names were Arthur and Avril Self. The two of them thought they owned the village. They were on every committee and had their fingers in every pie. One thing in their favour, though, was that they were extremely fastidious, and the house was spotless.'

'Not the type to bump off the neighbours and store them in a convenient pillbox, then,' said Rory drily.

'I don't know about that,' said Bryson. 'They were so obsessed with order and cleanliness . . . who knows? Perhaps someone dropped some litter.'

Bryson was reacting to the shock of what he had seen the way they did — by using black humour.

They were now approaching a thicket of trees and bushes that jutted out into the field that the farmer had ploughed around. 'Telford leaves this patch as a wildlife refuge. There used to be an owl box here, but it came down in a storm earlier this year and he hasn't replaced it yet,' said Bryson. 'I'm pretty sure the pillbox is just over there, around twenty-five metres away on the boundary between the two properties. It's pretty overgrown, but not completely inaccessible.'

'Thank you, Mr Smith,' Jackman said. 'We'll leave the next stage to the professor, his SOCOs, and our team of constables.'

Jackman stood back and allowed Rory to take a proper look at the place Bryson had indicated. 'Not too awful, my cherubs. You've presented me with far worse in the past. A saw and a bit of muscle power, and we'll be inside in no time at all.' He looked over the top of his spectacles at Bryson Smith. 'Although I suspect it will not form the subject of your next masterpiece, will it?'

'Indeed, it will not,' muttered Bryson, as he and his silent companion turned to leave. 'I have always detested jigsaw art, but all of a sudden, fluffy kittens and roses seem rather attractive.'

'Any idea of how long this might take, Rory?' Jackman asked. 'It won't be long before you lose the light, and you'll be needing some halogens down here.'

'Most definitely, my lovely friend. It won't take long to get in there; the problem is how to tackle what we find when we do.' Rory frowned, suddenly serious. 'I suspect that there's at least three bodies, Jackman, but judging from that tangle of bones, it could well be more. I have no idea how they came to be that way, but what I do know is that, somehow, I have to disentangle them and put them back together as the Good Lord intended. Our artist friend mentioned jigsaws, but, sadly, that is exactly what we have here.' The corners of his mouth twitched slightly. 'If I were callous enough to be flippant, which of course I'm not, my first impression was of a demonic game of Twister, on which the Grim Reaper suddenly called time.' He fluttered his eyelashes. 'But you know me, I'd never say a thing like that — ah! I do believe our muscles have arrived, armed to the teeth with cutters and power saws by the looks of it, and heaven be praised, the wonderful Ella Jarvis, my forensic photographer extraordinaire! Saved by the bell! Now, run along, my angels, I have real work to do.'

Jackman shook his head. 'And that, I believe, is our cue to organise the lighting, and have the area closed off as a crime scene. But before we go, Professor, please promise me one thing?'

'And that is?'

'Promise me that you'll never change. Without you, my encounters with death would have done my head in long ago. I'd probably have a job as a stable boy, and Marie would be selling motorcycles on the Fenchester Road.'

'Oh, my dream job,' breathed Marie. 'Although I'd most likely blow all my wages on new bikes, so that's out. Looks like I'll be staying.'

'Rest easy, cherubs,' crooned Rory, 'the Rory you know and love will never change — unless, that is, you fail to bring me my lights, oh, and a canopy. It may have escaped your notice, but it's pouring with rain!'

* * *

It was late, but still light, and Bob Ruston was walking his dog along the sea bank. Being hard to find, the area wasn't much frequented, and Bob relished the peace. It was great exercise for Tarka, who had derived his name from the fact that, as his son had pointed out, he could swim like an otter.

More than the exercise, however, the walks were a means of escape. Now Bob was retired and spending almost all his time at home, there were days when his son's disability became just too much to bear. Daisy seemed to cope with it so much better than he did, perhaps because she was a mother, and she saw in Troy the baby she had once nurtured — the feisty, petulant toddler who used to make her laugh, and the exasperating adolescent boy. All Bob saw was a tall, strong young man with a bright future, whom a drunk driver had reduced to a shell confined to a wheelchair with no hope for the future. Hardest to bear was the fact that Troy tried so hard. Every day was a struggle for him, and there were times when frustration got the better of him, and he would hurl a cup or plate at the wall. Those were the times when Daisy really came into her own. She coped, while Bob floundered, and all he wanted to do was throw crockery himself.

He called Tarka to heel, as the energetic dog was venturing a little too close to the marshy area that flanked the Wash.

As he watched the dog race back to him, he realised that for once, he didn't have Troy on his mind but another, unknown young man, with blood on his face and a handcuff dangling from one wrist. Although he knew he'd done the correct thing in leaving the man outside, he couldn't help hearing Daisy telling him he'd been unkind. It bothered him, more than he could explain.

Bob stared out across the expense of watery marshland and watched as twilight began to deepen the shadows. He wished he'd dealt with the situation differently, but what could he have done? He had certainly been right not to allow him into the house, especially when those two sinister cars drew up outside their gate.

He trudged slowly on, oblivious of the light rain that was now falling, wondering what on earth that young man had done to merit being hunted down in that way. Unless it was a case of mistaken identity — and he very much doubted that — matey-boy had done something to seriously piss off whoever was after him. Bob sighed. The rain was getting worse, and Tarka was starting to look like the otter he had been named for. He'd better turn back.

Once he was in the car, he remembered PC Laker, the constable who had taken his statement. He seemed a nice fellow. Promising to keep Bob updated on any developments, he had told Bob that so far, there had been no sightings of the man, and no one of his description had been reported missing. Well aware that he would be pretty low on the list of the officer's priorities, Bob decided he'd let a few more days go by, and then give him a call.

As he drove away from the sea bank in the gathering dark, Bob realised he'd come to feel a certain responsibility for that lad. Whatever he might have done, he was still someone's son, and Bob had let him down, no matter that he'd done it to protect his own family. That did not sit well with Bob Ruston. Not well at all.

* * *

Lucas could never get used to the nights on the Fens, finding the quiet unnerving. Tonight, however, absorbed in his images of the contents of Hartwood House, he hardly noticed it. With a glass of spicy organic ginger and lemon soda — Lucas never drank alcohol — at his side, he had settled himself down to take a proper look at the objects, one by one.

The couple who owned the house were obviously not just collectors, or dealers, for that matter. They were fanatics, that was the only word for the wealth of treasure they had amassed.

He wondered who else might know of it. No one but he could possibly have got in and out again without being detected. The house had state-of-the-art security, but there wasn't a system in the world that Lucas couldn't bypass, not since he had found that genius hacker. He had never met this person, a brilliant software engineer who went by the name of Chaos — which apparently referred to a dwarf planet or rogue asteroid. It was thanks to Chaos having disabled the security system that Lucas had been able to enter Hartwood House and compile his inventory. Chaos's genius lay in his ability to do that without leaving any indication that the security system had ever been tampered with. Time had literally stood still. Or, rather, the clock had speeded up, and only reverted to its normal pace when the system was reactivated. Thus, there was no point when the system actually stopped. For thirty minutes, Lucas had worked in a time warp, as if he had never been there at all.

Deciding he ought to eat something, Lucas went into the kitchen and prepared himself a bowl of salad. Not only did he never drink, he also ate only the healthiest of diets, keeping himself in tip-top physical condition, much as an Olympic athlete might.

He returned to the laptop, went back to the beginning and ran through the entire sequence again, studying each item carefully. It was beginning to dawn on him that what he had here amounted to the find of the century. His client had told him only that the owners were rumoured to be two eccentric brothers living in seclusion in the Fens, but he had never been able to verify the truth of this story. Whoever the owners of Hartwood House might be, one thing was certain; they had kept the extent of the collection, and the rarity of some of the items, a close secret.

Among his many talents, Lucas was an expert in the Art Nouveau and Art Deco periods and their artefacts. What he had seen today had left him speechless. He now had to decide how much he should tell his client about what he had found.

Lucas looked at his watch. He had arranged to make contact in exactly one hour from now, and before then he would have to arrive at a decision. If he was clever, he might carry off a very profitable double theft — one for his client, and one for himself. He would need all his wits about him if he were to make it work, but it was too big an opportunity to let slip.

He made himself a strong coffee and sat down to think, although he already knew what his decision would be. Lucas was about to orchestrate the perfect robbery.

With his own expertise, a crack team to call on, and above all, Chaos, how could he possibly fail?

CHAPTER SEVEN

By the time the vegetation swamping the old pillbox had been cleared to reveal the entrance, it was pitch dark. Under the harsh glare of halogen lamps, Rory, along with photographer Ella, his senior technician Spike, and two uniformed constables, finally got down to work.

One of the constables, a young, powerfully built man whose exposed arms were covered in intricate tattoos, was the first to go in. 'Door's all rotted,' he called over his shoulder, 'but I've managed to force it open.'

'Okay, hold back and let the Maestro take a first look inside. I'd hate one of you flowers to pass out on me just as we're almost there,' Rory said, pulling a twig from his jacket with finger and thumb.

'Be my guest, Prof,' said the policeman, visibly relieved.

Rory edged his way forward, on the lookout for possible evidence, and shone his torch beam into the depths.

He had been told what was in there, but even so, Rory couldn't suppress a jolt of horror when he saw it for himself. Swallowing, he began to take stock of the layout.

The place had evidently been used as a storehouse, either by the farmer, or the householders of the property on which the pillbox stood. They would need to remove and itemise the entire contents of the pillbox in order to determine which it was, although he guessed it to be the farmer, judging by the heaps of old sacks. The floor was covered in rubbish — discarded tarpaulins, buckets and various rusty tools. On top of all this lay the bodies. It looked as if they had been tossed into that dark, evil-smelling prison like more pieces of rubbish.

Rory closed his eyes briefly. He was deeply offended at the brutal, callous way these poor people had been treated — no, more than that, he was enraged.

With anger came determination.

'Three bodies,' he called back, his voice steady. 'Although we may find more underneath. This isn't going to be easy, and I'm not sure it's advisable to continue working in the dark. I don't want us to miss a single incriminating thread or fibre.' He looked over his shoulder at the others. 'Spike, your opinion, please. Gird up your loins, my trusty, and take a look.'

Spike took in the scene, seeming to react with more stoicism than Rory. After a pause, he said, 'You're right, Prof. This is one for the morning. The halogens are good, but they distort things, throw shadows. We could miss something. The weather report for tomorrow says it's gonna be dry, so I think we should wait.'

Rory stood back. 'Officers! Can you make sure that this aperture is kept securely covered, and the cordon manned all night? No one at all is to come into this area until I return at first light. Understand? Absolutely no one.' He turned to Ella. 'Interior photographs to be taken tomorrow, not tonight, dear heart. Okay?'

Ella said that she understood.

'Is DI Jackman still here?' he asked.

'Yes, sir,' answered one of the constables. 'He's in the bungalow, talking to the guy who made the discovery and his family.'

'Would you be kind enough to fetch him for me? He needs to be informed of my decision.'

The officer hurried away, returning ten minutes later with Jackman and Marie in tow.

'Sorry, my angels,' said Rory. 'We've made an executive decision to abort further investigation tonight, in favour of working in the daylight. It's a complex situation, and we need to give ourselves the best chance of getting it right first time.'

'Whatever you think best, Rory,' said Jackman. 'Can you tell us anything from what you've seen so far?'

'Well, you have at least three bodies. I can't say more until that hellhole has been emptied of its contents. The main question is, why are they entwined in such a strange fashion? And I'm not even attempting to hazard a guess at this juncture. I can't even give you an estimate of when they died. It's damp and humid in there, just the kind of environment to speed up decomposition.' Unusually for him, Rory was uncertain of everything about this bizarre discovery on the edge of a peaceful Fenland field. 'Another factor is that it's unlikely that they were killed in situ, meaning that they could have been dead for some time before being entombed in this godforsaken dump. Only a detailed forensic post-mortem will give us any answers as to that. Sorry, old chums, but your redoubtable grand master of the time of death is well and truly perplexed.'

Jackman gave his shoulder a pat. 'It's okay, Rory. A single glance was enough to tell us that this isn't going to be easy. But would it be in order for us to take a look before you seal it up for the night? The protective suits have arrived.'

Rory grimaced. 'If you're not worried about having nightmares, be my guest. But be warned — pretty it is not!'

'I'll risk the nightmares, Prof. I just need to get an idea of what we are dealing with.'

'Then you needn't bother with coveralls. We checked on our way in, and there's nothing of note. Just don't touch what's left of the door . . . actually, don't touch anything. Just look.'

They were quiet when they came back out, and for once, Rory made no comment. He said only, 'I'll be up with the lark and working. Meanwhile, I and my trusty colleagues will have to formulate a plan to get those poor souls safely back to the mortuary.' He smiled sadly. 'I'm sure I have no need to say it, but this will have my full attention for as long as it takes. Now, I suggest you two dear hearts get home and pour yourselves a bloody strong drink. That's certainly what I'm going to do!'

* * *

After driving in silence for a while, Marie asked Jackman if he had any theories about the bodies in the pillbox. Jackman shook his head. 'Nothing that isn't straight from some horror story.'

Marie didn't respond. She had wanted to explain that despite all the occasions on which they had confronted death in the past — the terrible find beneath Windrush came to mind — for some reason this one had shaken her to the core. But somehow, the words failed to materialise.

After driving on in silence for a while, Jackman said, 'If it helps, I feel the same way.'

How did he know? Then she smiled. 'Ah, kindred spirits, huh?'

'Definitely. And don't ask me why this one seems to have affected us so much more than usual.' He gave her a quick glance. 'If I had to hazard a guess, I'd say it's because it was so heartless, so cold, and . . .'

'. . . Shows such utter, cruel disregard for human life?' Marie added.

Jackman smiled bitterly. 'You got it, Marie. We've come across some cruel people in our time — killers like Ashcroft — but what we've seen today is something like a death pit, a . . . a mass grave.'

'Yes, and I know we need to push past our feelings, do what you said earlier — find answers for those poor people, and make someone pay. But it's not so easy, is it?' Marie thought for a while. 'It's situations like this that make you question yourself. I mean, how long can I go on doing this? Just how hard do I have to become? Or will this be the straw that breaks the camel's back?'

It was some time before Jackman replied. 'But if we are honest, don't we always doubt ourselves? After all, we come across things that most people only see on TV. Almost every day, we confront the reality of death in all its forms. But I think it's because we *are* human, and we *do* care, that we are driven to find answers and provide them with justice. Every time we find the person responsible for some cruel act and they are made to pay for it, we find the strength to go on.' He gave a short laugh. 'And here endeth the lesson.'

Marie smiled. 'Oh, I do hope you are right, my motivational friend. And I for one can't wait to find that strength you mentioned because I'm really in need of it right now. Anyway, let's talk about something else, shall we?'

'Right. How about food? I think we missed supper, didn't we? Shall we get a takeaway?'

'Well, Ralph was picking up a couple of ready meals on his way home. Maybe I'll ring him and see if he's got that far yet.' Marie pulled out her phone.

'Praise be! He's still at work, too, so a takeaway it is. KFC? Or a Maccy D?'

Even as she spoke, she understood that Jackman had been right. Somehow that terrible moment of self-doubt had passed, and they were back on track. Back to searching for justice, fuelled by the occasional takeaway meal. Back to normality.

* * *

Lucas lay in bed going over the evening's Zoom conversation with his client. He thought he had played it well — superbly, in fact. He had drip-fed Crispin Payne with information, starting with confirmation that the rumours about Hartwood House had been correct, and that the house was indeed a

71

treasure trove. He paused, watching his client lean forward in anticipation, and split the screen. Photographs of individual items preceded video clips of entire rooms. His final shot lingered on the jewel in the crown. The look of amazed incredulity on Payne's face was worth a screenshot in itself.

Of all the items Lucas had seen, this was the most exquisite. An Art Deco stained-glass window, still perfectly intact and without a single blemish. He had spent some time just gazing at it, blown away by the clean lines, bold, geometric patterns, and above all, the colours which seemed not to have faded at all. As to its value, well, he had seen something of the same quality, albeit considerably smaller, go under the hammer in the States. It had fetched half a million. This one was far superior, and Payne knew it.

Lucas was satisfied that the plan he had conceived was the best he could have come up with. His decision not to be greedy would pay off in the long run. After all, his cut would still be considerable, and he would retain the services of his client.

Eyes closed but unable to sleep, an endless sequence of images kept running through his mind — vases, lamp stands, items of furniture. Statues, mirrors . . . and then there were the smaller items scattered throughout the house: cigarette and jewellery boxes, powder compacts, photograph frames and ornaments.

Yes, he had been clever in deciding to give everything to the client — everything Art Deco, that was. What he hadn't showed to Payne was that single Art Nouveau room. The masterpieces he had found there were for him alone.

* * *

Jackman sat facing Marie at her workstation, a bucket of chicken and fries between them. It was late, but they were too hyped up to think of going home. And they were both starving.

'So,' Marie began, raising a chip dripping with tomato ketchup, 'how do we deal with all that we've got? You're on the final stretch of the money laundering racket and I have a missing jailbird to find. We're not exactly sitting on our backsides waiting for work to come in, are we?'

Jackman took another piece of chicken from the box. 'Hardly. I'll have to run it past Ruth Crooke first, but if everything goes well with Max and his cohorts tomorrow, we can begin the process of closing that investigation down. I can leave a couple of unlucky detectives dealing with the paperwork, and put the others on this case — whatever it turns out to be. Meanwhile, you stick with your case. Continue liaising with Anna Millard and keep up the pace in the hunt for Johnny. Okay? Pull out all the stops, and use Robbie to the maximum. Frankly, until we get a whole lot of information from Rory, our macabre find will have to go on hold. As long as Ruth agrees, I'll get everything set up for when we have all the forensic reports. Hopefully by then we'll have enough people free to tackle it.'

'It's a real mystery, isn't it? And in such a peaceful location too. I have a friend who used to live there, he couldn't wait to get out. Said it was far too quiet.' Marie grimaced. 'Who knows, he could have been living next door to a psycho killer!'

'Something about that oh-so-peaceful setting doesn't seem right to me,' said Jackman thoughtfully, spooning the last of his rice from its container. 'If you consider where the entrance is, you'd have to cart your dead body along the edge of an open field with absolutely no cover on one side. That's a bit risky, isn't it? Anyone could see you from across that field.'

'Good point,' said Marie, reaching for the cartons to clear them away. 'Unless you moved your body in the dead of night.'

'Still iffy. Look at the number of shift workers there are moving about at night, anything like that would stand out like a sore thumb. And then there are the cottages, they're all along that stretch.'

Marie yawned. 'You're right, Jackman, we're going to have to know a whole lot more about those dead people — and when they died or went missing — before we can start trying to work anything out.'

'Nevertheless, after such a shocking find, your brain can't help going into overdrive, can it?' He got to his feet. 'Anyway, right now I reckon it's time to go home. It's almost eleven, and we've some long days ahead of us.' He looked at Marie. 'Are you okay now? Sure?'

'I'm good. Honestly.' She gave his arm a gentle squeeze. 'Like you said, grim as it is, it's all part of the job. We'll get to the bottom of it, and those people can have a proper burial. Until then, I'll be working my socks off for answers.'

'Nothing new there then, Mrs Enderby! You may have embarked on a new chapter in your life, but I'm pleased to see your work ethic hasn't diminished.' He laughed. 'Not that I thought it would. Once a terrier, always a terrier.'

'Excuse me, my friend, but it's Evans while I'm at work, don't forget. I'll take the bit about terriers as a compliment, and will endeavour to live up to my reputation. Right now, I'm off to rev up my Tiger and get home. See you in the morning.'

* * *

That night, and despite all their brave words, five men and a woman were all finding it hard to sleep.

One was an artist, another an aspiring gardener, along with a detective inspector, a pathologist, a forensic technician, and, finally, a detective sergeant. All linked by a brief glimpse into a vision of hell.

CHAPTER EIGHT

Daybreak found the entire Saltern-le-Fen police station working full steam ahead. Ruth Crooke, alerted by a text message from Jackman, was at her desk by seven. By eight, they had a strategy and timeline mapped out.

Jackman was busy updating his team, along with DI Jenny Deane, on yesterday's nightmare discovery at an unassuming bungalow in the tranquil village of Fendyke. Then there was the inevitable paperwork to complete, along with a review of the previous night's reports. That done, he gathered Max, Charlie and Gary together for a meeting to discuss the final details of the forthcoming raid on the convenience store.

On arriving at work, Marie sought out Robbie in order to decide how best to proceed with the hunt for Johnny Millard. Soon, Jackman was the only person left in the office. He sat at his desk and began to take stock. Surprisingly, after his restless night, he didn't feel like shit, in fact he felt remarkably energised. On some base level, he was happy to have his head crammed with disparate pieces of information and courses of action. Allowed to wander, his thoughts inevitably turned to the past — and Laura. In spite of endless sessions with Julia Tennant, the force psychologist, he still hadn't been able to overcome his grief, which at times was debilitating. He was certainly a great deal better, back to functioning one hundred per cent where work was concerned, but it was the rest of the day that was the problem. He supposed it was the suddenness of her death that had so badly derailed him. One minute they were happily looking forward to their day, and the next, she was just . . . gone. It was as if part of him had remained stuck in that moment, and he wondered if he'd ever be free.

'Boss! We gorra right problem!' Max's cockney accent always came to the fore when he was excited.

'Tell me,' said Jackman, immediately back in the present.

'My informant has just phoned me and he's shitting hot bricks! Lars Westerham has changed his plans. He's going to the meeting place this morning!'

'Time?'

'Eleven fifteen, boss. Can we reorganise everything that fast?'

'Yes!' Jackman stood up. 'Yes, we damned well can! You get your side together, and I'll get onto uniform. We'll bring the briefing forward. We discussed tactics and fail-safes last night, so we'll just have to mobilise our forces early.' He looked hard at Max. 'You're sure that's the time?'

'Yes. His mate overheard Westerham on the phone, and the owner of the shop wrote it down, so there's no doubt. As soon as he heard, Sid's mate rang him straightaway. Eleven fifteen it is.'

'Then let's get going. And stabbies for everyone — no exceptions. Westerham is a nasty piece of work, and his heavies are probably worse, so we're not taking any risks. I'll notify Ruth, we'll have a final quick briefing, and then we'll be off. Go, Max!'

Max hurried out, and Jackman rang the duty officer. They'd make it; they'd already gone over the whole thing the day before, so it was just a case of bringing the raid forward a few hours. If their intel was correct, and Westerham didn't throw any more spanners on the works, it should all go ahead as planned. Then he could draw a line under the money laundering affair and concentrate on the gruesome discovery at Fendyke.

* * *

DC Max Cohen was buzzing with that adrenalin rush he knew so well. Westerham had arrived fifteen minutes early, but Jackman had allowed for that eventuality, and they were all at their stations, ready to take out the biggest money launderer in the Fens.

From his vantage point at one of the first-floor windows of a building opposite, Max watched the big car draw up outside the front of the store. Max waited for the doors to open, seized with the terrible thought that it might drive away again. Then they did, and three men got out, Lars Westerham and his brother Giles, a thinner, older version of Lars, who did the accounts for his illegal business. The third man remained by the car. This was not good news. It had been planned that two unmarked vehicles would park in front and behind Westerham's car to prevent a fast getaway. Now that was impossible. Such a move would certainly raise the suspicions of the third man, who would undoubtedly pull his boss out before the transaction took place.

'Look!' Charlie Button nudged him in the ribs and pointed to an old van backing rather uncertainly into the space in front of Westerham's BMW.

Max stared as the passenger door opened and a rather unkempt middle-aged woman climbed out, dressed in overalls, scuffed boots and a baseball cap with a logo on it. She proceeded to open the side door of the van and remove two pet carriers which she set down on the pavement. As the sliding door partly closed, Max saw the logo on the side of the van: *MARIGOLD'S CATZ HOTEL*. Underneath, someone had added *Best Exotic*, and a cartoon of a crazy-looking cat wearing a brightly coloured turban.

'Shit man! This isn't good.'

As he spoke, his radio crackled into life and he heard Jackman say, 'Relax, Cohen. It's uniform, they're using Plan B — Dolly and Midge. As soon as they've done their thing, get down here. Our man on the spot says Westerham is in situ in the back room. Proceed as planned.'

Max gave a low whistle.

'Phew,' Charlie said. 'For a moment there . . .'

They watched as the cat lady was joined by the van driver, a larger, older, equally scruffy woman with curly iron-grey hair. They stood on the pavement in front of a mobile phone display, and then looked up at the numbers on the flats above the shops. Both women appeared confused.

Finally, the first cat lady turned to the stony-faced man at the car, who was watching them with an unblinking stare.

Max was too far away to overhear the woman say, ''Scuse me, duck! D'you know where number seventy-three is? I got two cats to collect, and I'm buggered if I can find the address.'

The man glared at them. No, he didn't know the area, he was waiting for someone, and they were parked far too close to his car.

To which she flung back that if he'd just help them find Flat B, Seventy-three, East Street, they'd be gone in no time.

Max and Charlie watched the pantomime unfold, waiting to see what would come next.

The next scene left the two detectives in two minds as to whether to laugh, or applaud.

Stoneface had evidently decided that the best way to get rid of them was to find the address, so the three of them began to check the flat numbers on the doors. Peering at a faded name plate, Stoneface found himself taken to the ground, handcuffed and bundled into the back of another vehicle. In seconds, the street was empty, the cat carriers had been put back in the van, and Dolly and Midge had reverted to PC Andrea Parton and PC Jim McUre. Andrea drove the decoy van away, while Jim joined DS Danny Page, who was ready to ferry Stoneface off to the station.

Now the fun was over, Max and Charlie hurried downstairs to take their places for the final stage of the operation. The reaction of the Westerham brothers when they discovered their associate gone was going to be a concern, but swift action on everyone's part should take care of that. Even so, Max had his fingers crossed as he and Charlie positioned themselves in the doorway of a defunct hairdressing salon.

The minutes ticked by. Max spotted Jackman waiting outside a nearby doner kebab shop, along with a couple of scruffy-looking young men in hi viz jackets. The public had been restricted at both ends of the road, but it was far from empty. Pedestrians — all police undercover — made it look like any other day. Max hoped it would appear that way to Westerham too. At least, if Westerham did decide to dodge back inside, he was in for a surprise; the moment the Westerham brothers vacated the front of the shop, uniformed officers, along with Gary Pritchard, would have entered through the rear door and barred the exit. Then it would all be over. Max's only worry was whether his voice-activated recorder had caught the whole of their conversation as they completed the deal.

'Look,' hissed Charlie. 'See that hand on the *CLOSED* sign? I think they're coming out.'

Both held their breath.

They emerged, and as expected, Lars Westerham stopped in his tracks, his expression changing from puzzled to angry when he realised there was no one at their car. He looked both ways, then realisation hit him. He turned to plunge back into the shop, but a shout went up, and policemen began converging on him from all directions.

What followed passed in a blur. Max was only able to reconstruct the sequence of events later, when it was all over.

He and Charlie were sprinting towards the two brothers when Max saw Giles's hand go to his pocket.

'No! Don't be a fool, Giles!' This was Lars, shouting an urgent warning to his brother.

There was a sharp crack. Max heard a grunt, a shocked exhalation of breath, and Charlie Button crumpled.

'Jesus! Charlie!' Max threw himself to his knees in front of his injured friend so as to shield him from a further shot. Out of the corner of his eye he saw Giles Westerham hit from the side. With the force of a runaway train, Jackman ploughed into him, taking him to the ground and smashing his face into the pavement. The gun flew across the street and landed at Max's feet.

Seeing a constable run across to secure it, Max ignored the gun and turned his attention to Charlie, who was clutching at his arm. Blood was seeping through his shirt and dripping onto the asphalt. 'Shit, that hurts,' groaned Charlie, whose face had turned white.

'Officer down!' yelled Max, pressing hard on the wound. 'I need assistance here!'

Men and women were shouting, running towards them. Then Jackman was kneeling by his side.

'How bad is it, Max?'

'Can't stop it bleeding, boss.'

'Keep up the pressure, the ambulance is on its way.' Jackman cast an anxious look at Charlie, and gave him a reassuring smile. 'It's all right, Charlie-boy, take it easy. They'll have you fixed up in no time, and you'll be the talk of the station.'

'Yeah,' muttered Charlie. 'I can hear it now, the muppet who stopped a bullet.'

'Nah, you're a hero, mate,' said Max, hoping he sounded more confident than he felt. Charlie was very pale, and he suspected that shock was setting in. This sort of thing wasn't supposed to happen in a quiet Fenland town.

'Talking of heroes, Max,' said Jackman quietly, 'your prompt action didn't go unnoticed.'

'Whatya mean, boss?'

Without taking his eyes off Charlie, Jackman said, 'I saw you place yourself between the shooter and your comrade. Now, want me to take over till the ambulance gets here?'

'I'm afraid of releasing the pressure, boss, so it's all right, I'll hang on.'

Soon afterwards they heard the sound of sirens.

'But we did get them both, didn't we, sir?' asked Charlie faintly.

'Oh yes, we got them. And thanks to that arsehole of an accountant, they'll be facing a far more serious charge than they might otherwise have expected.' Jackman made a face. 'Although I'd have preferred it if he hadn't shot one of my best detectives.'

Charlie gave him a weak smile. 'Thanks, boss. I never knew you thought that.'

Then the paramedics were with them. 'It's okay, lads, we've got him.'

Max looked down and saw that he was covered in blood. All at once, the enormity of what had happened hit him like a blow to the gut. Charlie could have died. He could really have died. The Westerham family had never been known to use weapons before. Corrupt businessmen, dangerous in a lot of ways, with some very nasty contacts, but they didn't dirty their own doorstep. Until today.

Max swallowed. If Giles's aim had been only slightly higher, it could have been a head shot, and they'd be giving Charlie's mum the news that her son had died.

Disregarding the blood, Jackman put his arm around Max's shoulder. 'Come on, lad. He'll be okay. And I reckon it's time for you to stand down.' Seeing Gary Pritchard hurry in their direction, Jackman told him to get Max back to base and help him get cleaned up. 'I'll be back for the debriefing,' he added, 'as soon as we've got this fiasco sorted.'

'Sir! The recording.' Max was almost afraid to ask. 'Do you know yet? Did . . . did the recorder work?'

Gary gave him a grin wider than a Cheshire cat. 'Like a dream, Max. Like a dream.'

* * *

This crime scene was like no other that Rory could ever recall, and so he decided to approach it differently. The first thing he did was bring in the farmer and have a discussion with him.

Donald Telford, a solidly built weatherbeaten man in his sixties, had been horrified to hear that dead bodies had been found on his property. He was able to assure them that the old pillbox, albeit straddling the boundary, did in fact belong to the Telford Farm Estate.

He was pleasant and most cooperative, immediately giving permission for Rory and his colleagues to cut back the trees and other vegetation covering the pillbox, and to cut a pathway to the entrance. He even offered them the use of a small excavator that would do the job in a fraction of the time it would otherwise have taken.

By eleven thirty, the pillbox was stripped clean of overgrowth and fully exposed. Rory then had forensic sheeting brought in and laid over the freshly cleared area. The old and partially rotted door was removed, and he was ready to start work in earnest. Given the complexity of what they were faced with, he had called upon a colleague to assist him, a highly trained forensic anthropologist by the name of Professor Jan Wallace. This wasn't the first time she'd come to the Fens to assist with a tricky investigation. She had worked with them on the terrible case at Roman Creek, and her input had been invaluable to both Rory and Jackman.

He glanced at his watch. She should be here soon, if she hadn't been held up at the university, where she was one of the faculty members. Besides Jan Wallace, he had also rung one of his oldest friends, Stuart Bass. They had been together at uni and had remained friends ever since. Stuart was a forensic archaeologist, and would have been well up for it. Unfortunately, he was currently unearthing some bones of his own, in a newly discovered mass grave in Bosnia.

Rory loosened his shirt collar. It was one of the hottest days this month, and after the previous night's rain, the air was humid and sticky.

'Professor Wilkinson! How are you?'

Striding towards him across the field was a short, stocky figure with a mass of wild grey hair surrounding her head like the mane of a lion.

'Jan! Welcome!' He gave her a hug. 'Although welcome to what, I'm not quite sure.'

'Your message was both intriguing and worrisome, but here I am, and I'm all yours for the duration. I've taken some long-overdue leave from my needy young students and booked myself into the best hotel in the area. This, my dear Rory, is what is known as a busman's holiday.'

'That's the best thing I've heard in years! So, if you are ready, I shall show you what a couple of unsuspecting gardeners had the misfortune to run across while they were fighting their way through a thicket of blackberries.'

Jan Wallace was already wearing an all-in-one suit. Now she stopped and fought for several minutes to push her mane of locks into the hood. Battle won, she gave Rory a broad grin. 'Lead on! I can hardly wait.'

'Have I ever mentioned how much you resemble the Elephant Man when you put on that suit?' said Rory sweetly.

Jan rolled her eyes. 'Many times, and I haven't laughed yet. I do wish you'd come up with a new and more complimentary comparison.'

'Oh Lord! You *and* my detective friends both calling me predictable. This is truly awful!'

Ahead of them was the grey hulk of the wartime relic. As if on cue, the sun went behind a rolling cluster of clouds and the light seeped from the copse. It felt like a warning. Rory fell silent, all humour gone.

'They're inside there, and until we extricate them, I have no idea how many bodies there even are.'

Jan Wallace nodded.

They approached the entrance, and Rory stood aside so that his colleague could look in. If she was shocked at the sight — and he presumed she had been — she didn't show it. But then bones were her speciality. They spoke to her, told her stories about themselves. Jan could examine unidentified skeletal remains and tell you exactly how much time had passed since death. She could, after tests had been done, provide information on origin, ancestry, sex, stature, age at death and how they died. Bones were her field. She wasn't interested in Rory's area of expertise. Rory called her the Bone Lady.

When she turned back to him, she simply said, 'I'm sorry, Rory dear, but there's no quick fix here. This will take time, and I'm hoping my university will be understanding enough to allow me to extend my already generous leave if I have to. I estimate five bodies of various ages, and you and I, and whichever hapless technicians you have enlisted for the task, need to take them to bits, and put them back together again.' Beneath her hood, her eyes were shining. 'This is a challenge in anyone's book.'

He gave a little bow. 'And it goes without saying that it's one we shall all rise to.' Rory put a hand to his head. 'Rats! There goes my spa weekend with David.'

'My heartfelt commiserations, but this is death, and we cannot ignore its call.'

'Perish the thought!' He sighed. 'So, what do we need in order to get started? My lovely Cardiff and Spike are waiting in the wings with bated breath for your orders. Let's do this.'

CHAPTER NINE

Marie and Robbie had barely been ten minutes at the station when her mobile rang.

'Marie? It's Kevin. I've just heard the news! Is Charlie all right?'

'Ah, Kevin, I was just about to ring you.' Marie flopped into her chair. 'We've only just come in, but Jackman's been to the hospital and says they're going to operate to get the bullet out, and do some repair work on his arm. They'd hoped it was just a flesh wound, but it seems it's a bit more serious than that.'

'Poor little sod! That's awful. I guess he'll be off work for a while, then. Is he in the local hospital or Greenborough General?'

Kevin Stoner had recently joined their team as a detective constable, and was currently on holiday in Scarborough.

'Greenborough, and they've no prognosis yet, but if all goes well, I suspect he'll be off for a good few weeks, and then he'll be on light duties.'

'I'm coming back, Marie. I've only got two more days anyway, and Alan doesn't mind. In fact I think he's secretly pleased, because it means he can watch the cricket uninterrupted — the Test Match has just started.' Kevin's partner, Alan, was a massive sports fan.

'I'm sorry about the holiday, but I can't say I'm not delighted. We've got more work than we can cope with,' Marie said. 'Want me to tell Jackman?'

'If you would, Marie. We are all packed and ready to head for home. See you tomorrow.'

Marie breathed a sigh of relief. Kevin was a good detective, and after the shooting, they were a man down. Literally. What the hell had that idiot Giles been thinking of? Knowing Lars Westerham, he'd have the sharpest crooked lawyers in the country already lined up, and Giles would have got off on a technicality. Now, thanks to one moment of crass stupidity — in front of witnesses *and* on CCTV — Giles would be facing a charge of the attempted murder of a police officer, and no one would be able to get him off that one. Well, it was one way of getting a villain off the streets, but the cost to Charlie Button had been far too high.

'We seem to have missed a high-octane shout.' The speaker was Robbie.

Marie nodded. 'Sounds like it. Gary said it came so out of the blue that everyone was gobsmacked, including Lars Westerham. Gary reckoned he screamed at his brother not to be a fool.'

'I heard on the grapevine that Max threw himself in front of Charlie to shield him from any further bullets.' Robbie shook his head admiringly. 'That takes some doing when you've a wife and two kids.'

'Instinct,' said Marie. 'He's a good bloke. He wouldn't even have considered the implications.'

'Respect. I reckon it could get him a commendation.' Robbie grinned at her. 'And I'd have loved to have seen our boss in action! Gary said he barrelled into Westerham like a charging rhino!'

'Well, you know how loyal Jackman is to his team. That idiot accountant made the worst mistake of his life in hurting one of us. I'm telling you, it's a wonder he's still walking!'

Robbie laughed. 'I'm not sure that he is! According to Gary, he face planted the kerb a treat! He certainly won't be cooking any books for a while.'

Marie had a nightmare vision of the mountain of paperwork that was necessarily involved in preparing the case for the CPS, and which could easily take months. However, most of the work would be done by civilian case officers and evidence gatherers. Most of these were retired detectives, re-employed by the force in order to allow their younger compatriots to get down to the job of apprehending criminals.

As Robbie went off to the local deli to get them some lunch, Marie turned her thoughts to Johnny and Anna Millard. In a way, she wished she hadn't taken this on. She felt a certain sympathy for Anna — it must have taken some guts to turn to the police for help — but the old pillbox and what she had seen there kept coming back to her, however much she tried to concentrate her thoughts on the missing hacker. What drew her back to the Millard case was how vulnerable Anna was. That house she was in, remote as it was, wouldn't be much of an obstacle to anyone wishing to harm her. Marie reminded herself to get in touch with Anna and ask her to consider moving somewhere safer. The Millards had money, she could take a room in a hotel under an assumed name, though Marie doubted she'd agree to that. Despite her assertion that Johnny was dead, she clearly clung to the hope that he might be alive, and she wanted him to be able to find her.

Marie had just decided to ring her when she saw Max coming out of the men's locker room. She hadn't seen him since the events of that morning, and she wanted to find out how he was. She ran towards him and gave him a warm hug. 'How're you doing, my friend?'

'I'm not quite sure, to be honest. I feel kind of like the wind's been knocked out of me.'

He looked it, too, glassy-eyed and not quite there. 'I know what you need — strong coffee, packed with sugar so the spoon stands up in it.'

'That would be good. Gary did get me one but I was talking to Rosie, and I forgot it. I didn't want her to hear about it from anyone but me.'

Marie asked Tim Jacobs, the office manager, to fetch Max a cup of coffee. 'And make sure it's stuffed to the gunnels with sugar.'

'My pleasure. Anything for our hero.' Tim gave a little bow and ran off to the vending machine.

'I'm no soddin' hero,' muttered Max, looking almost angry. 'If anyone deserves to be called a hero, it's the boss. Marie, you should have seen 'im! He was on that man like he'd been fired from a rocket — and the guy 'ad a sodding gun! 'E could'a swung round, fired at Jackman and the boss would of been history. It was like something out of an action movie!'

'Even so, it doesn't lessen your own selfless action,' Marie said. 'That lunatic could easily have fired a second time at Charlie, and you'd have been history. Let's just be thankful that neither of those things happened.'

While she was speaking, Gary had come over to join them. 'News from the hospital. Charlie's stable. He's going into theatre in about an hour. His mum is with him, as well as the super, along with a VSO and a couple of people from HQ.'

Marie considered the implications of such an unexpected turn of events during what should have been a straightforward raid. The smallest detail would be raked over with a fine-tooth comb. There would be an enquiry for sure — gun crimes are rare. However, very few take place in front of such a large number of witnesses, *and* in front of a CCTV camera that was trained directly on the assailant. Not only that, but Gary had it from one of the uniformed officers who was present that two PCs caught the whole incident on body cam, including Lars Westerham calling out to his brother not to be a fool. Now, that would be very valuable evidence indeed. It would provide a perfect opportunity for Ruth to show the police in a favourable light for once. They had been getting a really bad press lately, thanks to the actions of some senior officers in other divisions.

'We'll be organising a roster for visits as soon as it's allowed,' added Gary. 'Hopefully, he won't be in too long.'

'Put me first, mate,' said Max urgently. 'I need to see him for myself so I know the little sod's really all right. I carried off a couple of litres of his blood on my jacket!'

Marie watched Max carefully. He had always been very protective of Charlie, whom he regularly called all the names under the sun, but heaven help anyone else who dared do the same. So long as Max didn't bump into Giles Westerham in the custody suite! She dreaded to think what damage that encounter would result in.

It was a strange time. The atmosphere in the station was a mixture of wild jubilation and horrified shock. In one sense, the operation had been a success — the Westerham brothers had finally been apprehended, along with Stoneface, and the shopkeeper, who had been caught engaging in an illegal transaction. On the other hand, the shooting down of DC Charlie Button had shocked everyone to the core.

Marie kept a discreet eye on Max. He had refused to go home, and would see neither the FMO nor Julia Tennant. But the fact remained that Max had seen his best friend shot in front of him, which had to have been traumatic. At least she knew the warning signs to look out for, and perhaps Jackman could have a quiet word with him, and get him to agree to seek some professional help.

As soon as the opportunity arose, Marie took Gary aside. 'Keep a close eye on our young friend, won't you? We all know what shock can do.'

Gary smiled at her. 'Don't you worry, Sarge. He's my number one priority, and for the rest of the team too. We've got him covered.'

His words made Marie quite emotional. How many other stations could boast such a tight-knit group of officers and civilians? Even Tim Jacobs, threw regular glances in Max's direction from his desk. The only other team as close as they were was CID Greenborough. Even the team her husband Ralph was part of, albeit friendly, had none of the same feeling of camaraderie.

She fervently hoped that all would be well with Charlie, and Max would soon have his mate back. Until they knew the outcome of the operation, Charlie's career hung in the balance. An unsuccessful result would be devastating, not only for the lad himself but for all of them. And especially Max Cohen.

* * *

Jackman returned to the CID room exhausted. Marie took one look at him, and instead of following him into his office, hurried off in the other direction, to the vending machine. She reappeared a few minutes later carrying two beakers of coffee and a couple of chocolate bars.

He smiled gratefully at her. 'What a day! Talk about highs and lows.'

'Any news of Charlie?' asked Marie.

'Ruth rang me just now. They've finished operating . . .' Jackman bit his lip. 'Apparently, there was considerable vascular damage, and they're not sure how much use he's going to have in his arm and hand. They won't know for a while. Luckily, Charlie is left-handed, and he was hit in the right arm, so that's one positive. Now, it's just a case of wait and see. He could be fine, or . . .'

'Shit,' breathed Marie. 'Poor little devil. And his career—'

'We won't lose him, Marie,' Jackman said. 'I'll make sure of that. And he may not be too badly restricted, that's just the worst-case scenario.'

'I'll tell the others,' said Marie, 'but I won't dwell on any worst-case scenarios, especially with Max. He's very shaky, Jackman, which is understandable considering what he's just been through. We're all keeping a careful eye on him.'

'He will be shaky, Marie,' Jackman said, 'and what makes it worse is that our Max looks on Charlie as a sort of kid brother. I'll have a chat with him, and give him all the usual options. Oh, and half an hour ago Giles Westerham was transferred to Greenborough. Ruth considered it prudent to split up the two brothers.'

'And no doubt to prevent anyone lynching the bastard for shooting one of our own,' growled Marie.

'Oh, she's just following procedure,' Jackman said, and tore the foil off a chocolate bar. 'Thanks for this, Marie, it's just what I needed. It's been quite a morning.'

'Actually, it's well into the afternoon,' she said. 'Still, at least it's distracted us from that heap of bodies for a while.'

Jackman thought there were better ways to provide a distraction. 'True, but before we get back to all that, let me fill you in on a couple of developments following the money laundering debacle.'

'Developments?' Marie looked at him hopefully. 'You mean that the Westerham empire has fallen here in Saltern?'

'It could be even better than that, Marie. Thanks to Giles Westerham choosing to up the ante by attempting to murder a police officer, tongues have been loosened.' He raised an eyebrow. 'We've been approached by two major players, both deeply involved in the organisation, who want nothing to do with what happened today. They are giving us everything they can on the Westerhams, and not just their local activities. They know they are scuppered, and they're trying to make things as easy as possible for themselves. One says he has access to various other connections, beyond Saltern. It seems that Lars Westerham's empire wasn't confined to this area, and he was keen to take over a number of the smaller illicit operations in other towns.'

Marie grinned. 'Oh, I do love a good informant, don't you?'

'Wait till you hear the rest. The other guy dropped a hint that Lars isn't only into money laundering, but that's as far as he would go without having a lawyer present.'

Marie chuckled. 'Oh, I say, it's beginning to sound like your raid might have been far more successful than you expected — apart from our Charlie getting hurt, that is.'

'As long as he pulls through with no lasting damage, he'll come to realise that what happened to him could well have brought about the downfall of a very big criminal organisation. Those villains I told you about would never have talked if Charlie hadn't been shot. It sounds a bit callous when I put it like that, but you know what I mean.'

'I do,' Marie said. 'Let's just hope those surgeons did a bloody good job.'

They sat for a few moments in silence, until Marie said, 'Oh, Jackman, I've suddenly had a thought. This is going to mean an awful lot more hours spent on this case, while we have what could be a multiple murder enquiry waiting in that pillbox, not forgetting my missing hacker. How are we going to cope?'

'Relax,' Jackman said. 'It seems we aren't the only ones who have been watching Lars Westerham. I'm still waiting for Ruth to get back to me but there's talk of a special unit taking it over, one with a great deal of clout. I could be wrong, but I suspect Lars was using the money laundering racket as a cover for something far more serious. I'm just hoping that in the fullness of time, our little songbird down in the custody suite will decide to confirm it.' He smiled at Marie. 'After a pretty hefty debriefing, I could be handing the whole thing over to that unit, and if Max and Gary are up to liaising with them, I'll be off the case.' He smiled even wider at the relief on her face.

Marie then gave him the good news that DC Kevin Stoner was cutting short his holiday in order to come back to help them.

'Good man!' Jackman exclaimed. 'That'll make life a lot easier. I've also asked Ruth if there's a chance she might get us a couple more detectives to come in and assist. She's hoping to get hold of DS Vic Blackwell, who's due back tomorrow from secondment.'

'Excellent! Vic's going from strength to strength since he got his life back on track. He could be a massive help.' She beamed at him. 'Then as soon as Rory makes contact, we'll be ready to roll! And Robbie and I won't have to let the Millard investigation slip. Oh, happy days!'

* * *

Anna Millard's day was far from happy. She had locked all the doors and fastened the windows, which meant the house was uncomfortably warm, but she hardly felt it. She seemed to have ice running through her veins instead of blood, as if she were dying from the inside out.

She paced from room to room, pausing only to stare out of the windows, watching for any untoward movement. She had played down her fears to the detectives, but she knew just as well as Marie Evans that being alone in this house put her in danger. Johnny was strong, but what if they used torture to force him to reveal her whereabouts? For they wanted her, too, she had no doubt of that. She and Johnny had never made a secret of how close they were to each other, and they would assume she knew much, if not all, of what Johnny himself knew.

Anna stood at the window of one of the bedrooms, gazing out at a copse of trees. In fact, she knew nothing of value, but they wouldn't be taking any chances.

Yet she remained in this house, the only place Johnny could find her — if he were still alive. Anna hardly knew if she was watching for signs of approaching danger, or for Johnny to come back. Then she saw something that made her gasp. There, in the shadows of the treeline — movement. Her hands clenched tight, fingernails digging into her palms, she waited.

The young muntjac deer stepped tentatively out of the copse, glanced around, and stood stock still for a moment before reaching out for some mountain ash berries.

Anna breathed out. Suddenly, she felt very alone, and very, very afraid. What had they got themselves into? It had seemed so cool, the game they were playing — cheating the system while making money out of it. At what point had it all changed? What had started out as fun had cost Johnny seven years of his life, hers, too, in a way. Then, having been dealt a Get Out of Jail Free card, an even nastier game began. Snakes and ladders, hunters and the hunted, now they had no cards left to play. *Oh, Johnny. Where are you?*

Anna shook herself, annoyed at herself for her weakness, and went downstairs to make yet another cup of tea. Much as she hated to admit it, her best — her only hope was DS Marie Evans. Dammit.

CHAPTER TEN

Rory was grateful that their activities were so well hidden. Even a drone would struggle to see exactly what this small group of people were doing on the margins of a field in this otherwise peaceful rural setting. From where he stood, Rory looked across acres of gently swaying golden barley to where a church spire majestically rose into a blue sky.

Rory sighed, and turned back to his task. Although he was accustomed to dealing with death and its causes, he found this case profoundly depressing. Thank goodness for Professor Jan Wallace, who kept his feet on the ground and his mind on the job.

'You do come up with some complicated cases, don't you, my friend?' she called out.

'To be perfectly candid, dear heart, I'd have gladly passed this one to someone else,' he said.

'Nonsense! Think how intriguing it is, even if the field-work on the scene makes for a few complications.'

'Everything is complicated these days,' grumbled Rory. 'All the red tape, and the amount of damn forms we're supposed to fill in.'

'Oh, believe me, my grumpy little friend, the paperwork for this little lot is a doddle.' Jan peered at him over the top of her mask. 'I worked a site in a city not so long ago, and I was handed an entire booklet on the new procedures for recovering and identifying human remains. I was informed that I must take particular note of the section on retrieval and investigation. I'm telling you, it was so involved and recondite that I couldn't make head nor tail of it. You're lucky to be working in such a backwater, anywhere else this site would be heaving with officials and swamped in acronyms. How would you like to work out just what is an SERM, a SIM, a SIO, a VRTL and possibly an HSE, while being sure to place your victims in a VHAA before they can be removed?'

Rory endeavoured to look contrite. 'Oh, dear me! Put like that, this is positively old-fashioned, isn't it? From now on I shall consider myself exceedingly lucky to be working in this "backwater", as you so kindly refer to it.'

Jan grinned. 'What's more, when I said complicated I was referring to the configuration of the bodies and the difficulties with their extraction, not the ruddy paperwork. Come on, Rory, let's go play forensic detective, and fathom out what happened here.'

She and Rory, along with Spike had, with some difficulty, succeeded in disentangling the first body. It now lay in front of the pillbox on one of the forensic sheets. It was identifiably male, with a few strands of muddy-coloured brownish hair still clinging to the skull. His clothing had largely disintegrated, but there was enough of it left to discern the remains of a wax jacket and cord trousers he had been wearing. His boots had evidently been expensive leather, as they had survived the years of immolation practically intact. Jan declared that it had only been the heavy clothing that had held him together.

In silence, they stared down at the remains. Looking at this sad heap of bones, even Rory found it hard to believe that it had once been a human being with thoughts and feelings.

'This was the easy one,' murmured Jan after a while. 'I suspect I was right about there being five bodies in all, and unfortunately the rest are going to be much harder to bring out.'

'Any theories as to how they became so strangely entwined?' Rory asked.

'Only one, and it doesn't bear thinking about.'

'This theory. It wouldn't bear a terrifying resemblance to an Edgar Allen Poe story from *Tales of Mystery and Imagination*, would it?' Rory said.

'I hope not,' said Jan seriously. 'But let's wait till we've seen more before we start hypothesising on the how and the why. Which one should we tackle next, do you think?'

Rory had mentioned Poe in jest, yet there really was something of the horror story about the sight of those tangled bodies. Only when they had the first body lying out in the open did he truly feel that they were dealing with a human tragedy, and not some outdated horror movie.

Yet the sense of unreality persisted. He barely heard Jan when she spoke to him. This wasn't like him, and it worried him. He made a concerted effort and just caught the tail of her sentence. '. . . then again, it'd probably be best to tackle it by first removing all the rubbish from around them. What say you, my friend?'

He nodded, trying to pull himself together. 'We'll need to do it very carefully, in case there's any evidence amongst it. I'll get Cardiff and Spike to lay out more sheets for whatever we take out. It will all have to be bagged and tagged, and Ella will have to photograph it all.'

'Absolutely,' said Jan. 'I can't help wondering if all that junk was deliberately put in there with the intention of concealing the bodies, rather than just using the pillbox as an unofficial dumpsite.'

'Oh, I don't know. I think my money is on the latter,' said Rory. 'There is a considerable amount of old debris beneath them by the look of it. It's the sort of thing I can imagine a lazy gardener doing, rather than carting it away for proper disposal. Anyway, time will tell. I suppose we'd better get a move on, or you, dear lady, will be needing that extended holiday you mentioned.'

'I'm here for as long as it takes, Rory. It's ages since something has fascinated me like this does.' Jan smiled a little wickedly. 'Historical finds are extraordinarily interesting — it's what I spend my life on — but this is a whole new kind of challenge. I won't let it go until every single bone in those bodies has spoken to me and told me their story. I want to know what, and hopefully *who*, is behind this atrocity. Because that's what it is. It's like nothing I've ever seen outside a battleground.'

It was affecting all of them, wasn't it? Rory suddenly realised that it wasn't just him. No one on this investigation was reacting normally. Jackman openly admitted to having been shaken to the core. Even the battle-hardened Marie had been having nightmares. Ella had said that the only way she could deal with it was by looking at it through her camera lens. As for Spike, he was pretty sure that his assistant was putting on a show of machismo. And now Jan Wallace, who had spent a lifetime disinterring bones, was calling it extraordinary.

'We both work with the dead, Rory, and death comes in many forms, but occasionally it holds an element of something beyond our comprehension. Don't you agree?'

The smile Jan gave him was full of understanding. Rory shook his head. 'Jan Wallace, you are amazing! Not only are you an expert in forensic anthropology, but you can read minds too. I am sincerely impressed, dear heart. I had just arrived at that very conclusion.'

'No need for accolades, my friend. I could see it in your expression, and that of everyone involved. I've seen it in people confronted with war graves and evidence of genocide. In those situations it's the enormity of the crime, along with the inhumanity of what was done that gives rise to these emotions.

Admittedly, this is on a lesser scale, but it touches us in the same way. It's one more reason for providing our colleagues in the police with sound evidence on which to base their investigation.' She regarded Rory intently. 'Which means we must disregard our emotions . . . and pull our bloody fingers out!'

Rory laughed. 'Spoken like a true commander. Spike! Ella! Cardiff! Come! We are ready for your services. Let's sort this mess out!'

* * *

By late afternoon, Lucas had set up a face-to-face meeting and made all the necessary phone calls. He was now ready to carry forward his plan for the greatest robbery of his life. He'd also spent a considerable amount of time in conversation with his client, who was now almost as excited as Lucas himself. Almost. Unlike Lucas, he didn't have the additional thrill of a secret hoard of Art Nouveau gems to get excited about. By now, Crispin Payne had had plenty of time to look at the images Lucas had sent him, and was blown away by what he had seen. Given the number of treasures to be found at Hartwood House, he hadn't found it easy to decide which items to include in Lucas's 'shopping list'.

Lucas had his own particular way of going about a job, and he always insisted on his clients agreeing to it before going ahead. In the present case, he asked the client to list those items he wanted stolen in order of priority. Lucas must be provided with two lists — a short one including only the most valuable and desirable items, and a longer one, containing every object the client was willing to pay for should the opportunity present itself. Obviously, it would profit Lucas to appropriate as many items as possible for his client, but in this case he also had that Art Nouveau room and its contents to consider.

Needing to escape the confines of his room, Lucas decided to go for a walk. The Fens were definitely not for him, but he supposed that for a lover of solitude, they might possess a certain ethereal beauty.

However, he took little interest in the merits of the landscape. His thoughts were all on the mammoth undertaking he was about to embark on. He was good, and he knew it. He was well respected in the criminal fraternity, and understandably so. In the six years in which he had been operating, he had kept himself totally under the radar; never once had his name appeared in a single police file. He had made many rich people even richer, and in the course of his activities had gathered around him an army of helpers, all professionals in their own right, who could always be relied upon to do a good job.

Striding along a perfectly straight field path beside an expanse of ripening wheat, he went through the list of associates who had agreed to help him carry this off, adding the names of others with particular skills he might need. He was unwilling to rush the job, but it needed to happen in the very near future. His client was not the most patient of men. Even so, it had to be executed flawlessly, and to do that he wanted people with him whom he could trust implicitly. Generally, he liked to keep his operations tight, involving as few outsiders as possible, but on this occasion he was going about it quite differently. He smiled to himself. Theft on a grand scale. Theft like no one had ever seen before!

He looked up at the big fenland sky, where a gentle breeze was chasing white clouds across an expanse of blue. For once, he didn't think of home.

* * *

Home at last, Marie opened the door and was greeted by the mouth-watering aroma of something spicy. She went through to the kitchen, where she found her husband, Ralph, just about to dish up their evening meal. The table was set, and beside her plate, a large glass of wine sparkled in welcome.

'Sit! I'm allowing you two, okay three, gulps,' he pointed to her drink, 'then you tell me about your day.' He grinned at her. 'If you even know where to start. You look a bit shell-shocked.'

Marie sank down on her chair and took the prescribed swallows. 'Oh boy! Did I need that!' She closed her eyes for a moment before raising them to Ralph. 'Today goes down in the diary as one seriously shitty day. I guess you heard on the grapevine that one of our team got shot.'

'I certainly did,' Ralph said. 'The jungle drums had it round the whole division in minutes. How is Charlie?'

'He took a bullet in the upper arm. Lost a lot of blood, most of it over Max. The medics reckon he could have impaired use of that arm and hand, but it's too early to say as yet. We can only hope and pray that they've done a good job on him. He's a great kid, our Charlie, and this is the second time he's been injured on duty. Last time he tackled a group of smugglers out on the sea bank and got a couple of broken ribs and a pneumothorax for his trouble. His poor mum is probably going apeshit.'

'You going to visit him?' asked Ralph, heaping her plate with vegetable curry and rice.

'I'm down on Gary's rota for tomorrow afternoon. I must say I'll feel a whole lot better once I've seen him for myself.' She helped herself to mango chutney, looking longingly at the naan bread Ralph was just taking out of the oven. 'However did you find the time to do this, o wonderful husband of mine?'

'I ducked out a bit early. I had a witness statement to take just a couple of miles from here, and we got it over quicker than I expected, so I came straight home. I thought my wife would probably be in dire need of sustenance, so what could I do but cook!' He sat down. 'Seriously, Marie, how are you, really? You've had a rough couple of days.'

Marie tried to describe the way that their find out at Fendyke Village had affected them, and how it kept creeping into her thoughts. 'Like some horrific image flashing up on a screen.'

'It sounds like that is one investigation that you really do need to solve as fast as possible, and move on.' Ralph reached for the lime pickle. 'You need to stop thinking of how weird and spooky it all is, and start seeing it as a crime. You aren't going to find some demonic entity lurking in the marshes somewhere, but a brutal killer. I think you guys are egging each other on, and blowing it out of proportion. I know it sounds harsh, my love, but you must get your copper's head on, and do what you do best.'

Marie stifled a giggle. 'I consider myself duly chastised, Dr Ralph. Seriously, you are right, but I'm sure we'll all be back in gear by tomorrow. It's probably the shock of our Charlie being shot, along with a missing computer genius and an unknown runaway with one handcuff and blood on his face. Throw in a concrete bunker full of bodies, and it's no wonder we're all reeling!'

'That is one serious overload,' admitted Ralph. 'But on the positive side, I hear that by arresting Lars and Giles Westerham, you've managed to make a whole lot of police officers very happy indeed. Is it true that there's a Serious Crime unit heading your way to take that one over?'

'Hellfire, Ralph! That grapevine does work well, doesn't it? I only heard about it myself just before I left, and yes, it's true, so at least the team will be free of all that money laundering crap, thank heavens.'

'And in the meantime you'll be sticking with your missing techie, until the forensics from Fendyke Village comes in.'

Marie thought it rather fortuitous having a fellow detective sergeant for a partner. For a start, there was little she needed to explain in the way of basics and procedure. 'I sure will. Robbie and I, with some help from Orac, are going to try to make some headway with Johnny Millard before that happens, because sure as eggs is eggs, he'll get relegated to the back burner as soon as our Pillbox Killer investigation takes off. That one will mean a whole lot of media hype, and I'm dreading that part of it. I can see the headlines now. The public will be devouring every word, the phones will start ringing, and every nutter in the county will have a field day. At our expense.'

'I expect you'll be needing extra help, won't you?' Ralph said. 'My team is snowed under right now, but I'm betting my boss could let you have a couple of our pool detectives, or maybe a uniformed crew. Tell your superintendent to contact DCI Barclay at Fenchester.'

Marie drank her wine, more slowly now. 'That's good to know. I'll get Jackman to speak to her first thing.'

They ate in silence for a while. 'Would you do me a favour, Ralph? Can you see if any of your recent cases have some computer wizard somewhere in the background? Our missing man, Johnny Millard, was a shit hot hacker, yet he got wiped out by someone who knew a whole lot more than he did. He finished up serving seven years for something he didn't do, courtesy of that someone.'

'Not in anything I've handled, but I'll speak to my boss, if you like. He's been watching a few heavyweight cases recently, not on our patch, and mainly linked to the big cities rather than here, but they do involve cybercrime.'

'Sounds good,' said Marie. 'This anonymous person would not have come cheap, so someone paid a packet to stitch up Johnny Millard. Problem is, we have no idea why. He's a bloody clever man, but not big league, so why they found the need to remove him from the scene is a mystery.'

'And now he's disappeared,' mused Ralph. 'By choice, as in out of fear, or was he taken?'

'If only I knew,' said Marie. 'And I'm left with a wife who is pinning all her hopes on me to find out.'

Ralph smiled at her. 'And she couldn't have anyone better on her side. Most coppers would run a mile rather than stick their neck out for a villain's wife.'

'Yeah, well, I'm not exactly hot on his heels yet, and frankly I'm doing it because it took a lot for her to walk into the nick and ask for help. Oh, and bottom line is that she loves him, plain and simple.'

'And you're a big softie, Marie Enderby!' He stood up and cleared the plates away. 'Now, let's not talk shop anymore and talk puddings instead. I bought a lemon meringue pie to cool us down after the curry. Any takers?'

'Do you really have to ask? And don't stint on the portion size either, think of the day I've had!'

* * *

He tried to ease himself into a sitting position. He had the mother of all headaches and felt nauseous. They'd moved him somewhere, and by the smell of the place, it wasn't a garage. He couldn't make it out in the pitch dark, but it seemed larger than where he'd been before.

Struggling to sit up caused him to groan out loud. Every part of him hurt, and from the way his head was pounding, along with his dry mouth, he was sure he'd been drugged. He'd been given a bottle of water, which he'd drained. It had tasted strange, but he was so desperate for liquid he didn't care. He recalled very little after that, just an impression of being somewhere horribly uncomfortable, possibly the back of a van.

Nothing made sense, his confusion resulting partly from the drugs he'd been given, but mainly because he had no idea where he was or what these people were planning to do with him. The main question was why. What was the reason for his abduction? Okay, he was no saint, and he'd been pretty wild as a teen, but he'd done nothing to deserve this — had he?

He had to find out what the hell was going on. Or get away. Ha, fat chance of that, not when he was tied up and woozy from the drug.

As he sat trying to straighten out his head and fathom out where the hell he was, the man glimpsed a tiny ray of hope. If their endgame was to kill him, surely they'd have done it in the smelly old garage? But they hadn't. Instead, they'd taken the trouble to drug him and transport him to this place. The glimmer of hope died. Would he ever be let go? Would he ever see . . . ? He swallowed, hard. For the first time since he'd been taken, he allowed himself to think about her. She'd be frantic with worry, and she'd already suffered so much.

The image of her face clear in his mind, he lowered his head and wept.

CHAPTER ELEVEN

It was the popular belief around the station that Orac never left her underground domain, probably never slept or ate and existed in a kind of technological homeostasis. Humorous as it was, there was an element of truth in this depiction of the mysterious Orac. She had faced many dangers in the course of her career. Having been deliberately blinded in one eye, it was decided that she should be spirited away to a place where her skills could still be of use but where she would be relatively safe from harm. Which was why Orla Cracken, former highly skilled security operative, was now ensconced in the basement of Saltern nick. And no, she didn't live there, but resided in a small flat a few steps from the police station car park.

She spent most of her time alone, routinely leaving work late and arriving early, partly engaged in police business, but also working on tasks assigned to her by 'other' sources. These tasks, designated classified, were generally labelled 'Top Secret'. Only the higher echelons of the service were aware that the computer system used by Orac was far more sophisticated than the needs of an unremarkable Fenland Constabulary station would normally warrant. The limited number of people who did know happened to include DI

Jackman and DS Marie Evans. This was due to an incident that had involved Orac's personal life, in which Jackman and Evans had been involved. Everyone else believed they were simply lucky to have such a well-equipped IT department, with a real whiz of a computer specialist at the helm. And that was as it should be, because the fewer people who knew that what they actually had was a government controlled Secure Isolated Network the better.

Now it was five in the morning, and Orac was sitting at her desk completing an unofficial check on the background of her newest recruit, Coral McIvor. Naturally, given the unorthodox situation, the woman had been carefully vetted before she came to Orac's notice. The authorities had given Coral the all clear, but Orac was taking no chances, so she looked into areas that they might have considered irrelevant. Finally, she pushed back her chair with a satisfied smile. Good to go!

They had agreed that Coral would start work early, at seven, and leave at three, unless longer hours were called for. She was happy with that, as it gave her more time to spend with her father. He was now quite frail, and although he tried to be independent, Coral knew that he valued and enjoyed her company. It also meant that she could do some of those jobs that he was no longer able to do for himself. Orac had an idea that, other than her father, Coral didn't have many friends, and was reserved with those she did have. This was all good in Orac's book. Above all, she demanded absolute dedication of her assistants, and she had a feeling that Coral McIvor was going to provide that in spades.

Orac went to the communal kitchen area, made herself a strong coffee, and took a high-energy granola bar from the jar. Despite the received mess-room wisdom, she did in fact eat, but she did tend to treat food as medicine. Her one vice was coffee, of which she consumed far more than was wise. Apart from eating well, she subjected herself to a gruelling exercise regime. She was fully aware that sitting at a computer for hours on end was not good news as far as the body was concerned, thus her one stipulation on arriving in the Fens was that she must have a fully equipped gym room attached to their workspace, plus a shower and personal water cooler. She thought this was the least she could expect, given her value to the service.

She checked the time, and decided to spend an hour working on Marie Evans's mystery man, Johnny Millard. Then a twenty-minute workout, a shower and she'd be ready for Coral's arrival.

Orac was justifiably proud of the way she'd managed to extract the Millard man's hardware from the secure evidence storage facility at the Cybercrime Unit. However, finding anything of value on it was a different story. Whoever had hacked it had done a bloody good job. Nevertheless, her department was known for working miracles. Maybe, Orac thought as she lifted weights and pounded on the treadmill, she ought to pray for one. Orac the scientist firmly believed in miracles.

* * *

Besides Orac, Johnny Millard was on the mind of someone else. Harry Barnham, stuck at home after breaking his wrist, was not sleeping well and thus was spending far too much time with his thoughts. It was great to see Robbie Melton again, but his news about their old friend Johnny had been terribly disturbing. Harry was feeling guilty, wishing he had taken the trouble to visit Johnny again before his release from prison. Who knew, Johnny might have told him something, dropped a hint about what was going on with him.

It was a fact that Harry probably knew Johnny better than anyone, other than his wife, Anna. He had kept it to himself, but Harry had known quite a bit about the extent of Johnny's criminal activities. Over time, technology had become the epicentre of Johnny's world, and Harry was pretty much the only friend he still kept in touch with. Hence, when he needed a sounding board, someone to run over his plans with, those plans often ended up in Harry's lap. He had told Robbie that he hadn't ever condoned what their friend was doing, and that was true, but while imploring Johnny to stay on the right side of the law, he couldn't help being in awe of Johnny's brilliance and the sheer temerity of some of his schemes.

There being little point in lying in bed unable to sleep, Harry got up and went into the kitchen to make himself a coffee. He couldn't stop wondering if there was something he could do to help Robbie and the police find Johnny Millard. Was there anything that he'd said in the course of those disquieting visits to the prison? After so many years inside, Johnny had become a changed man. The visits were awkward, painful encounters with none of the banter they used to indulge in. So much so that Harry had occasionally left early, and the time between visits grew longer and longer. Then Harry's conscience would kick in, he'd request a visiting order, and the whole process would begin again.

As he attempted to spread butter on his toast with his left hand without sending it flying onto the floor, he tried to recall some of those prison conversations, but nothing that had been said seemed relevant. The one thing that did emerge was Johnny's bitter resentment over what had been done to him. 'And who could blame you?' Harry muttered to the empty kitchen. Even so, there was something about Johnny that was so profoundly unlike the happy-go-lucky chancer of before that Harry was filled with apprehension, almost fear. Only on that last visit, when he'd heard that parole had been granted, did Harry detect a thaw in his icy determination to obtain revenge, though he was still nothing like the Johnny of old. Harry had stepped out of the prison gates convinced that his friend was lost to him for ever.

Then came the visit from Robbie Melton.

Was Johnny out there somewhere? Had he gone to ground in order to plot his revenge? But that would mean breaking the terms of the parole he'd fought so hard for. Surely, it was too big a risk to take. And what about Anna?

Johnny would never just disappear without telling her what he was up to. No, it looked like Johnny could well be in grave danger, even . . . Harry shuddered.

He turned his attention to his toast, now cold and unappetising, given that marmalade was a step too far for a one-handed man to tackle. Slowly, Harry chewed on his breakfast and again tried to recall those prison conversations.

According to Robbie, Anna feared that Johnny had indeed been killed, yet she refused to give up on him. Well then, neither would he. After all, back in the day, Johnny had been one of the best mates a man could ever have. Harry smiled reminiscently. There was something very special about Johnny, and he deserved their help, even though the silly arsehole had got himself in far too deep.

Harry dabbed at a blob of butter that had fallen on his pyjama top, only succeeding in making it worse. This bloody arm was a curse . . . Or was it? His brain still functioned, his only problem was that he had too much time on his hands — or hand. Plenty of time to try and help Robbie find Johnny. Okay, he couldn't drive, but he had a phone and a computer, and if he desperately needed to go somewhere, his dad would take him. His dad had always had a soft spot for bad boy Johnny Millard, and unlike most people who knew him had actively encouraged Harry to visit his friend in prison. His father was firmly convinced that just because a friend of yours has taken a wrong turn in life, that was no reason to abandon them.

Harry got to his feet. A shower, and then down to some serious thinking about those prison conversations.

Taking a shower was not an easy process. It involved releasing his arm from the sling, negotiating it into a waterproof protective sleeve and then trying to wash himself one-handed. After what seemed an age, he was finally dressed and ready for action. For the first time since that ill-advised rugby tackle, Harry felt positive about something. Johnny needed him, and he'd follow his dad's wise counsel and not let an old friend down.

Three quarters of an hour later he had a sheet of A4 paper covered in scribbled notes. He would normally have used his computer, but typing with one finger was excruciatingly slow. He sat back and read through what he had written. Then he read it again.

Thoughtfully, he took a red pen and marked one paragraph:

> . . . JM referred to some very interesting people that he'd met inside. He mentioned one man in particular, although he denied that they'd become friends. George Rider, also in for cybercrime. JM said that if he decided to continue in a life of crime after his release, he'd go straight to see George. He said George could appreciate his skill, and had already offered him one or two tasty opportunities which could bring him some serious money.

Harry squeezed his eyes shut and summoned an image of this Rider, whom Johnny had pointed out during one of his visits. Rider had looked ridiculously out of place in the prison visiting room, where he seemed more like a visitor than an inmate. His hair was stylishly cut and he wore dark-rimmed designer glasses and a royal blue, long-sleeved shirt and denim jeans. He gave the overall appearance of someone highly intelligent, self-assured and perfectly composed. Harry remarked that prison must be treating him pretty well, to which Johnny had shrugged. Rider was due out in six months, he said. He added that Rider was said to have taken the rap for someone else, a family member who was a key member of his organisation, this being preferable to having his long-term 'investments' go down the pan.

'He's clever, all right,' Johnny had whispered. 'He's the boss of a large criminal network, but unusually for someone in that position he's also a good, solid bloke. He actually has high moral standards, and sees what he does as fighting against a corrupt ruling class. I like him, he's a man after my own heart.'

Harry remembered Johnny giving a dry laugh. 'What's more, his presence here is a cover — you know, an alibi — while others carry out his plan.'

Remembering how impressed Johnny was with this Rider, Harry wished he'd paid more attention to what Johnny had said about him. At the time he had been far more concerned about what Johnny would do when he got out, and whether he'd go off the rails again, than hearing about some wannabe Robin Hood-type villain. When he asked Johnny, his friend had said that of course he wasn't about to jeopardise his freedom, but it was nice to know that he was still in demand. It meant a lot to him, he said, that someone believed that he'd been set up, especially when that someone was as highly placed as George Rider. 'Besides, Harry-boy,' he had added, 'I've got more important things to attend to when I get out.'

From the narrow, flinty gaze Johnny turned on him, Harry had had no doubt that he was talking about revenge.

Harry went over and over every word on that page, and kept coming back to the name George Rider. He was sure that the two of them had been closer than Johnny had admitted. Did this mean that George might know something about Johnny's plans for after his release?

He leaned back in his chair and stretched out his legs. As far as he could see, he had two choices. One, tell Robbie and get him to go and see Rider in prison. Or, two, ask Rider for a VO, and go and talk to him himself.

Harry hesitated for a good ten minutes, then reluctantly picked up the phone. Calling Robbie wasn't his first choice — he was sure he'd have better luck with Rider, being a close friend of Johnny's, but he knew he would have a hard job convincing Rider to add him to his visitor list. Not to mention how long it would take — and Johnny might not have that much time.

'Robbo? Harry here. Look, this might be a wild goose chase, but I've been thinking over my prison visits to Johnny, and . . .'

* * *

112

Jackman could not recall ever having been so happy to hand over a case. He had walked into the CID room much earlier than usual, to find Superintendent Ruth Crooke talking to two stern-looking strangers. He had no need to ask who they were, everything about them screamed 'Serious Crime Unit'.

'Ah, Rowan. These officers are working with EMSOU, the East Midlands Special Operations Unit, heading up a team gathering intelligence about cases such as that of the Westerham brothers . . .' At that moment, a number of detectives entered the room. 'Let's go to my office. We have a lot to talk about.'

An hour later, Jackman returned to his office and began to gather up all the reports of the raid, which he had been instructed to hand over forthwith.

He looked up to see Marie at his open door, a broad smile on her face. 'You're looking pleased with yourself, boss.'

'Ecstatic,' he said. 'And I'm not joking. You should have heard those EMSOU blokes on the subject of the Westerhams — talk about cagey!'

'So, what are they after the brothers for?' she asked.

He shrugged. 'You know as much as I do. Whatever it is, it's serious, all right, and a humble DI in an even humbler Fenland town is apparently not considered worthy of being taken into their confidence.'

'Oh right.' Marie looked positively furious. 'Correct me if I'm wrong, but wasn't it you who caught and arrested the buggers, *and* handed over several others prepared to sing their hearts out in order to have their own sentences reduced? I'd have thought the least they could do was give you a bit of hint as to what the Westerhams were up to.'

Jackman laughed. 'It's all right, honestly! I'm quite willing to let this one go. We've got a pillbox full of dead people to worry about, and I'm sure Ruth will fill us in at some point. The most important thing is that we have rock-solid evidence where the Westerham case is concerned. Police body cams, CCTV, a video recording of the transaction, and more reliable witnesses than there are supporters at the Cup Final. They can't possibly fault us. Naturally, I've offered every support, but EMSOU seem to want us well away from their investigations, so I'm pretty sure that once I've handed everything over, we'll be free of it.'

'I still think it's bad sportsmanship,' muttered Marie. 'But, hey-ho, at least it means we can move on with matters that really do belong to us. Which reminds me. An update on the Millard affair. Robbie's mate, Harry Barnham, thinks Robbie might do well to talk to a man Johnny Millard was friendly with while he was inside. Robbie's setting up a trip to HMP Marshfield right now.'

'Are you going with him?' Jackman asked.

'No. We decided that he should take Harry. This other con saw him when he visited Johnny, so he'll know he was a friend, especially as he was possibly one of the only people, other than Anna, to visit Johnny in the slammer. It could help break the ice and persuade the guy to open up a bit more.'

'Good thinking,' Jackman said. 'So, what are you working on, as I'm going to be busy all morning with the handover?'

'I'm going to take a quick trip out to see Anna. She's worrying me, out there all alone, and I'd like to have another shot at convincing her to get out of there and find herself a small hotel or guesthouse somewhere to lay low in.'

'Worth a try, I guess,' said Jackman. 'Although if that house is the one place she believes Johnny will head for to find her, I can't see her budging, can you?'

Marie shrugged. 'I guess so. Still, it's worth a try. Now, I'd better leave you to get on. I'll get Gary to bring you a coffee, and I'll let you know how things go at HMP Marshfield and with Anna. Good luck with the offload!'

'It will be a labour of love, believe me,' breathed Jackman. 'There really are more pressing things right now, and when we hear from Rory, it will be all systems go — and I dread to think where to.'

CHAPTER TWELVE

There was just one person whom Lucas completely trusted, other than himself. Her name was Nina Hagen, and she had been involved in all his more innovative heists. A tall, athletic, dark-haired Norwegian, she spoke perfect English. More importantly, she was the most single-minded person he'd ever met. Nina was the only person he could trust with the details of his daring double theft. More than that, he was going to ask her to lead the team that would strip the Art Nouveau room of its treasures and ferry them to a different destination than the main bulk of the stolen goods.

He had arranged to meet her in a small restaurant in town, and after lunch, they took a walk through the backstreets of Saltern-le-Fen, discussing his plan.

'So, what do you think?' he asked.

She thought for a moment. 'Audacious, but doable.'

'Naturally, I shall make it worth your while. The size of your bank account will be enhanced after we complete.'

She linked her arm through his. 'Always appreciated, Lucas. You know how expensive my tastes are.'

'So you accept the job?' For a moment he had been afraid she might say it was too risky. He should have known better, of course.

'Most certainly. Needless to say, I shall want to see the videos, and the layout of the house and its surrounds. I'd like to bring in my own team as well. I assume you will be going ahead?'

'Once I am certain that the plan is foolproof, and that everyone involved knows what is expected of them, we'll proceed.' Lucas looked pensive for a moment. 'I want it completed this week, so I can be back in London by the weekend. The client isn't someone to want to wait too long for results.'

'You are using the same team?' Nina asked. 'Because if you are, I'd advise that you drop the HGV driver you used on the last assignment. I've been told that he's drinking rather heavily, so better to be safe than sorry.'

He thanked her for letting him know, as he hadn't heard about that. Fortunately, he had already decided to use a new man, someone who had been recommended to him as having experience in transporting rare artefacts and museum pieces. 'Apparently, he's a real professional, and could be a massive asset, considering the value of the items we'll be moving.'

They were now approaching Nina's car. Lucas regarded the gleaming BMW i7 with some amusement. The lady did indeed have expensive tastes. 'Come to where I'm staying this evening, Nina, and I'll show you the shots I took of the house and the items we'll be acquiring. I have an idea that even you will be impressed by this particular little hoard. Make it seven, and I'll cook dinner.'

Nina regarded him sardonically. 'I'll eat before I come, thanks, Lucas. I've eaten some of your healthy meals in the past. In the absence of a Michelin-starred restaurant in the locality, I'd really rather plump for a pizza and coleslaw.'

Lucas widened his eyes in mock horror. 'Philistine! Then make it seven thirty, *after* I've consumed my vegetables. And prepare to be amazed.'

* * *

Infected by Jan Wallace's furious energy and enthusiasm, all Rory's previous ennui had vanished, and he was as eager as she was to uncover the mystery of what had led to the presence of a collection of unclaimed bodies in sleepy Fendyke Village. His newly found fervour had galvanised everyone around him, and the morning had been far more productive than he had expected. At one o'clock, he called for a break, and distributed the sandwiches and other sundry snacks he'd sent out for earlier.

He and Jan strolled back to where his beloved Citroen Dolly was parked, and took stock of where they'd got to.

'We've had good results this morning, and I'm sure this afternoon will see even more,' said Jan, biting into a chicken and bacon sandwich as if she hadn't eaten for a week.

'Those two experienced SOCOs I drafted in from Fenchester have been a great help,' Rory said. 'And now all that detritus has been removed from around the bodies, it will certainly make the extraction of the remaining ones considerably easier.'

They had already disentangled a second body, this time a woman, but had found it difficult to determine her age, since she was in a far worse state of decomposition than the man. Jan had put her at around forty, but this was only a guess.

'Three more to go,' she said, 'and then the real work begins.'

'Ah, yes, listening to the bones and the stories they tell,' Rory mused.

'We will rebuild their lives, Rory, so that your friends in CID can begin *their* work. And, knowing them, they'll move heaven and earth to find the person responsible.'

'Oh, you can rest assured on that score, dear heart.' He was silent for a few moments, and then slowly said, 'I know why the bodies are in a tangle.'

Jan nodded, apparently unsurprised. 'So do I, Rory, although I can hardly bring myself to admit it.'

'It makes what was done to them all the more callous, doesn't it? Rory said, gazing out across the sleeping fields. 'But

117

we have to accept the fact that one of the victims was still alive when they were consigned to that pillbox.'

'Ghastly,' said Jan quietly. 'They were probably unconscious when they were thrown in, and would have awoken to find themselves . . . Oh, Rory, can you imagine anything worse?'

'In darkness. With no way out. Fighting to free themselves from the cadavers heaped on top of them. Wrenching arms and legs this way and that in a frenzy of blind panic. No, Jan, you're right. Nothing could be worse than ending your life like that.'

'I seem to remember you mentioning Edgar Allen Poe at one point,' Jan said. 'Well, the comparison has turned out to be singularly apt. This is indeed Gothic horror. Horror at its worst.'

'And somehow, this peaceful, mundane location makes it all the more shocking. There's no build-up in the form of a sinister castle, ill-lit corridors and damp, rat-infested cellars. Finding something like this in a small, well-kept country village amid acres of rural farmland, it brings you up with a jolt. It's almost beyond comprehension.'

'It makes me feel very sorry indeed for your police colleagues,' Jan said. 'All we have to do is examine the bodies and pass on the results. All very scientific. Those poor lambs will have to delve into the mind of the creature who brought this about. And to do that, they will be entering a dark and evil realm.'

Rory winced. 'Well, I must say, you do have a way with words.'

'I also have a way with reconstructing lives from old bones. Now, I think we should get on, don't you? One more chocolate bar, and I'll be ready to hear what they have to tell me. We are going to do our damndest to help the police as much as we can. Agreed?'

'With knobs on, dear lady! Kit Kat or Mars Bar?'

* * *

118

Orac watched Coral McIvor from her bank of screens. She seemed to be blending in well with the rest of the team. Of course, Coral already knew Leon Barras, who had told her about the job and suggested she apply, which made it easier for her to integrate. At thirty-four years of age, Coral was attractive in a Tinseltown sort of way. Slim but shapely, she had abundant hair of a rich brunette colour, and very dark brown eyes. In short, she was as different from Orac as it was possible to be — in looks, that is. Underneath, the two women shared a passion for technology and an unquenchable thirst for knowledge.

In fact, Orac thought with some amusement, Coral bore an uncanny resemblance to that star of the golden age of the screen, Hedy Lamarr. Orac recalled that, unlike the usual run of celluloid beauties, Lamarr had a brilliant mind. Despite a series of romantic scandals — Lamarr had been married six times — her real passion was science, invention in particular. She had once said that she never had to work on her innovations, they came to her of themselves. It was she who laid the foundation for Wi-Fi and Bluetooth. Many of her inventions only came to light following her death in 2000, and included technology to help guide torpedoes underwater without being detected, using frequency hopping and spread spectrum. Armed with equipment given to her by the eccentric billionaire, Howard Hughes, while on set, Lamarr spent hours in her trailer, experimenting and developing her theories. Lamarr had been a revelation and an inspiration to Orac, and Coral's resemblance, however tenuous, to her idol had struck her immediately. Whether or not she would prove to be a genius, she was indisputably brilliant in her field, and would be an enormous asset to the team.

'Got a moment, chief?'

It was David Serlin, standing next to her desk and looking anxious. 'Sure. How can I help?'

'I've been going over the transcripts from Johnny Millard's trial, and the more I read, the more I think there has been a serious miscarriage of justice. Mind you, I can't see how it could ever be proven. Most of it's suspicions and a vague uneasy feeling that something's not right.'

'You felt uncomfortable with the verdict from the outset, didn't you?' Orac asked.

'I did, but with nothing to support Millard's claim that he'd been framed, we were stymied.' David shook his head. 'If that bloke served seven years for something he didn't do, I'm going to feel pretty shit about myself.'

'You were only an expert witness, David. If there had been anything to indicate a setup, you'd have acted upon it.' She flashed him a metallic smile. 'You're not the only one who felt like that, and was thwarted by lack of evidence. What we *can* do now, however, is take his hardware apart, and use all the knowledge we have at our disposal to try and find something even Cybercrime missed.'

David puffed out his cheeks. 'Tall order, chief, but I'm game.'

'Good. I thought we'd work on this in tandem. I've already had a brief look, and I'm clearing up whatever else I had pending before hitting this hard. Millard is missing, David, and Marie is very anxious to both find him, and discover who wanted him sent to jail to get him out of the way.'

'But why? What was going on that necessitated his removal?' David's frown deepened. 'Johnny Millard was bloody clever, chief. Okay, he wasn't in the all-time top ten, but who knows what he might have been capable of if he'd had the chance to up his game and show his true colours?'

'Exactly.' Orac waved him away. 'Now, bugger off and clear your desk. Offload anything outstanding to Philip or Leon because you and I have work to do.'

* * *

Having contacted HMP Marshfield in the vain hope of obtaining a visitor's pass, Robbie, much to his surprise, was informed that he was down for a short visit with George Rider that very afternoon. On explaining that the visit concerned an ongoing enquiry into a missing man who had broken his parole, the response was that he was welcome to try, although he had about as much chance as a cat in hell of getting anything out of a con like Rider.

He and Harry went through the lengthy security procedures, and were conducted to the visitors' lounge, which was empty, this not being the normal visiting hours. Two bored-looking prison warders stood off to the rear, showing scant interest in either prisoner or visitors.

Looking exactly as Harry had described him, Rider was regarding them with a slightly amused smile.

'Thank you for agreeing to see us, sir,' said Robbie politely, introducing himself and Harry. 'I believe you may have seen my friend Harry before. He used to visit Johnny Millard.'

George Rider nodded to Harry. 'Johnny told me about you. Said you were good friends. I'm curious as to why you are back here now, seeing that Johnny is a free man. And I'm definitely curious about why you have a detective with you.'

'Because we need your help, Mr Rider,' said Harry.

'Johnny has gone missing,' Robbie said, looking Rider straight in the eye. 'He's broken the terms of his parole, and we fear for his safety. It's true, I am a detective, but I also knew Johnny when we were younger.'

Several different expressions passed over Rider's face. 'I see. I didn't know that.'

Robbie was very good at reading people, and he could tell that the news had genuinely shocked Rider. Rider thought for a moment or two. 'I'll be frank, DC Melton, I agreed to this interview with the idea that I might have a bit of fun with the police. And now . . . Let's just say I'm not laughing.'

'I don't have to tell you how badly Johnny wanted that parole,' Harry said. 'I'm absolutely certain he would never have jeopardised his freedom to simply do a runner.'

'Neither would he leave his wife Anna unaware of what has happened to him,' added Robbie. 'I've spoken to her, and she's distraught.'

George Rider said nothing for a while. He seemed deep in thought. Finally, he said, 'You know he didn't commit the crime he was convicted of, don't you?'

Both of them nodded.

'I like Johnny a lot . . .' said Rider, as if he were thinking aloud.

'We were good friends at school,' said Harry gravely, 'and I really want to help him. So does Robbie, but we have no idea of what he got himself mixed up in.'

'Sadly, neither did he,' said Rider. 'And it was eating him up. I watched him over the years, saw him change, and I didn't like it one bit. Someone took him out, and although I could be wrong, that someone could well be behind a lot of the serious crimes in this area.' He paused, looking from one to the other of them. 'I can see you really are concerned about him, so here's what I'm going to do. As long as you keep my name well out of it, I'll speak to my contacts and find out what the word is on the street. That's the best I can do, gentlemen, because I know sod all about why Johnny's been targeted.'

Robbie agreed to return in two days' time to see if Rider had had any luck with his contacts.

'It doesn't look good for Johnny, does it?' said Rider as they stood up to leave. 'I am grateful to you for taking this seriously and not dismissing Anna's pleas for help. Most rozzers would just have laughed their heads off and sent her packing.'

'You have our DS to thank for that,' said Robbie. 'She's always had reservations about that trial, and like you, she could see the extent of Anna's concern. Now we've taken up the gauntlet. We'll find him, Mr Rider.'

George Rider sighed. 'But will he be alive?'

None of them knew the answer to that.

* * *

Marie flopped down at her desk and bit her lip. By rights, she should be relieved after her trip out to see Anna Millard. Instead, she was left with a niggle of discomfort.

'In a world of your own, Sarge?' It was Gary, staring down at her.

'Don't you hate it when a situation seems all hunky-dory, but you're still uneasy about it?'

'Oh yes,' Gary said. 'Really bugs you. What's the problem?'

'Anna Millard. I went to see her. All seemed well, a bit too well, in fact. She appeared more relaxed than before, although she did say she was desperately on edge — you know, watching out of the window, being paranoid about locking the doors.' Marie frowned. 'She said she'd seen something move in the bushes and almost died of fright until she realised it was a bloody deer. It just seemed that what she said didn't match her expression.'

'Maybe she was paranoid, but your visit allowed her to relax,' suggested Gary. 'In a situation like hers it's reassuring to see someone you trust, isn't it?'

'I know you're right, Gary, but even so . . .' Marie drummed her fingers on her desk. 'I tried one more time to get her to move, and would you believe it, she agreed! She's always been dead set against it, but this time she just said I was probably right, and did I have any suggestions about where to go.'

'Well, surely that is good news,' exclaimed Gary.

'Of course, but even that made me twitchy. It was such a sudden about face.' Marie frowned. 'I'll be honest, Gary, I wondered if she might have heard from Johnny.'

'Surely, she would have told you, Sarge?' insisted Gary. 'After all, she came to you for help. I'm certain that if she had heard from Johnny, she'd have let you, of all people, know.'

'I want to believe that, but I'm just not sure.' She pushed back her chair. 'Oh, take no notice of me, Gazza, I must be getting neurotic in my old age.'

'Never!' he said. 'I know from bitter experience it doesn't pay to ignore DS Marie Evans.' They both laughed.

Marie looked around the office. 'Max at the hospital?'

'He'll be back soon, and hopefully the poor little sod will be a bit happier once he's seen his old mucker.' Gary shook his head. 'It really knocked him sideways, didn't it?'

'It's pretty scary when you see someone you care about injured like that, but at least the early reports of Charlie's condition are encouraging,' Marie said. 'If Max sees his friend looking relatively chipper, he'll start to get some perspective.'

'And it's your turn as soon as Max gets back,' said Gary. 'I'm going tonight after work, as long as he's up to it. We don't want to tire him out with too many visitors.'

'Jackman says they're bending the rules about visiting hours, because of the nature of our work,' said Marie. 'It's easier to do that since he has a room to himself.'

Gary laughed. 'I hear he's being given special treatment all round. He's quite the little hero, especially among the nurses.'

'Good for him! It's about time our Charlie got himself a steady girlfriend. Maybe he'll find one while he's there.'

Not long after this exchange, Robbie Melton arrived back, and headed straight for Marie's desk.

'How did it go, Rob? Wasted trip?' she asked.

'Surprisingly, no.' He flopped into a chair opposite her. 'Looks like we've now got a con on our side. He was well rattled when he heard Johnny'd gone missing. He was genuinely surprised when we told him. He's got no idea who is behind it, and he swears Johnny wouldn't have risked bailing on his parole. He also intimated that someone's masterminding a lot of the criminal activity round here.'

'Who is this helpful jailbird, Robbie?' asked Marie, hoping he wasn't a clever conman who was feeding them misinformation.

'Guy called George Rider, another cybercrime man Johnny got friendly with in prison. He's the big daddy of a lucrative family business that earns its money through corporate fraud.' Robbie gave a dry laugh. 'He said he'd have hired our Johnny if he hadn't been so determined to get his own back on whoever framed him. He said he liked him a lot, and he did, too, you could see it on his face. Fact is, I liked the bloke. Anyway, he said he'd send out some feelers through his contacts about Johnny and this anonymous Mr Big. I'm going back the day after tomorrow to see if he's had any luck.'

This was unusual. Villains didn't usually offer to assist the filth. But neither did villains' wives come to them for help, and Marie trusted Robbie's judgement. This was no ordinary case, that was for sure. 'Okay, Robbie, what's your gut feeling on what happened to Johnny?'

Robbie hesitated. 'You got me there, Sarge. I really can't make up my mind. Sometimes I think he's been abducted by the people who had him put away in the first place, but then I think, well, he badly wanted revenge. I mean, wanted it enough to keep his beloved wife in the dark while he went about it.'

'Yeah,' sighed Marie. 'Ditto. And your latest foray into HMP Marshfield has done nothing to tip the scales, has it?'

'Nothing whatsoever, other than make me very uncomfortable. Rider mentioned how Johnny changed while he was inside, and then there's what he said about some shady figure behind the criminal activity in the area.'

Marie straightened up. 'As soon as Max is back from delivering grapes to his little mate, I'm off to do my bit at Greenborough Hospital, but before I go, let's take Orac this information about some creepy Einstein directing the local villainy.'

'I think we should.' Robbie stood up. 'We believe he exists, because of what happened to Johnny, but now we have corroboration from the other side of the fence, so to speak, which makes it all the more possible that Johnny's case wasn't an isolated one.'

They hurried out of the office and down the stairs to the IT department. There, they found Orac in deep conversation with David Serlin and a strikingly beautiful woman Marie took to be the latest recruit, Coral McIvor.

Robbie's mouth dropped open, which was funny enough in itself, but what really made Marie want to laugh was the contrast between the two women. The white-blonde Mohican and the luxurious brown curls — the very epitome of chalk and cheese.

Introductions over, Marie, suppressing a fit of giggles, told Orac what the prisoner in Marshfield had said to Robbie.

Orac nodded sagely. 'Coral here has a number of rather interesting stories from her previous job that she's just been telling us about, one of which concerned the hunt for a cyber-crime "Wunderkind". Everyone assumes them to be a kid because of the sheer audacity of what they pulled off, but frankly, it could be anyone. I've just told her about Johnny Millard's case, and . . . Coral?' She gestured for the other woman to continue.

'Fits the MO perfectly. Whoever it is, they'll go down in the annals of cybercrime history as a legend. Even the top brains in the Met are quietly tearing their hair out over him — or her.'

Coral had a rather cutglass accent, which her quiet voice and unpretentious manner softened and made her pleasant to listen to.

'Oh, deep joy,' murmured Marie. 'Just what we need. I don't suppose you have anything on this, er, person?'

'Unfortunately, all we have is a name,' Coral said. 'And that's only because they gave it to us. It's Chaos.'

CHAPTER THIRTEEN

A hush fell over the group gathered around the pillbox, all gazing down upon the last person to die. For some reason, the fact that it was a woman made it so much worse, although Rory couldn't help wondering why. In his experience, women were a great deal stronger than men, especially in a crisis. In this case, however, no one, man or woman, should have had to endure what this woman had.

They had found her crouched in a foetal position, with her face close to the wall, and her back to the gruesome contents of the pillbox. Rory imagined her trying desperately to distance herself from the horror. She had even managed to drag some of the old plastic sacks around her, forming a barrier between herself and the others. He hoped that for her sake, her original injuries had been serious enough for her to have died relatively quickly. His post-mortem would answer that, and part of him was dreading the outcome.

He glanced around at the silent people around him. Each one seemed deep in thought. There was none of the dark humour they generally employed as a means of distancing themselves from the stark fact of death. Indeed, what this woman had suffered was beyond words, let alone some humorous quip. He cleared his throat. Time to rally the troops.

'Okay, my cherubs, I personally think this poor lady has spent far too long in this loathsome place, and it's time we got our arses into gear and freed her from it. Chop, chop!'

As if a display from Madame Tussaud's waxworks had come to life, people began to move, and work resumed. Rory heaved a sigh of relief. It wasn't a very nice experience working a case that affected his staff so deeply, and this one was doing that in bucketfuls. Still, Jan had been right, it was going to be even worse for his dear friends Jackman and Marie. And thinking of them, he realised he ought to report on their progress. Time for DI Jackman to see for himself what they had found.

Stepping aside for a moment, he rang the DI. 'Time you graced us with your presence, dear heart. And there is something I need to tell you, preferably face to face, *if* you can drag yourself away from that gorgeous office of yours, and trudge through the mud of my less-than-cosy field?'

Saying he'd been in the office all day, handing over a complex case to another division, Jackman told Rory he'd be glad of some fresh air. Marie was visiting Charlie, but he could be with him in half an hour.

'Good,' said Rory. 'But prepare yourself,' and hung up without explanation.

* * *

Nowadays, Jackman tried not to drive alone. He was used to the presence of Marie beside him, and when, like now, she wasn't available, memories of Laura came flooding back, and threatened to overwhelm him.

Trying to push them away, he turned his mind to what Rory might have meant when he told him to prepare himself. For what? How much worse could that case get, for heaven's sake?

After a few miles, an inexplicable calmness came over him. He heard the words, 'It's bad, my darling, but you'll find who did this. You will, I promise.'

It was as if Laura were sitting next to him, her reassuring hand on his leg. Jackman wasn't a fanciful man, far from it. But those few seconds of her presence had given him courage, and he arrived at the village with renewed determination. Yes, this case was bad, one of the worst he'd handled, but for that very reason he needed to find the perpetrator, and fast.

Approaching the bungalow, he saw that the press had got wind of some sensational bit of news in Fendyke Village, and were beginning to gather at the cordon. Jackman flashed his warrant card and was directed to where the other cars were parked about a hundred yards from the field, but seeing the crowd of reporters and nosy neighbours, Jackman decided that Rory and his bad news could wait for a few minutes while he had a word with the Smith family. They were probably feeling beleaguered, and he thought he might offer them the alternative of moving out for a few days, until the furore died down.

He was welcomed in by the son, Bryson, whom Jackman was pleased to see had stayed on rather than beetling back to the Smoke. Bryson was obviously a cultivated man, and Jackman thought it was a pity they'd met in these difficult circumstances, as he would have liked to spend some time in conversation with him.

'How are your folks holding up, Mr Smith?' he asked, as Bryson ushered him into the lounge.

'Call me Bryson, please,' he said with a smile. 'Surprisingly well, but then they are Yellowbellies, after all, and a more stoic group of people would be hard to find. Dad is in his element. He can't wait to get back to the pub, where he will be the star attraction. Mum, too, is taking it in her stride. She has converted the kitchen into a twenty-four-hour refreshment hub for the workforce. It's given them a new lease of life, but then they don't know the full details, do they?'

'Thank God! But in the light of what you just said, I guess I'd be wasting my breath in offering you alternative accommodation for a while?' Jackman said.

'You would. In fact, it'd probably take one of your tactical units to remove them.' Indicating a chair, Bryson asked him to sit down.

'I won't stop now, as I need to get down to the scene of the crime. Will you be around for a while? I foresee a bit of a siege when the media discover what this is all about.'

'I've put all my assignments on hold for the duration. I can't leave my parents while all this is going on. Work can wait,' he smiled, 'and since it concerns masterpieces that have been kicking around for centuries, it's not exactly urgent.'

'I appreciate that, Bryson, and I'll keep you updated. When the practical business is complete and the area made safe again, we'll be needing your help with some of the background to the place, its history and that of the people who live, or lived, here.'

'We'll do all we can to assist, I assure you, Detective Inspector.'

'Forget the title, Bryson, just call me Jackman.'

As he made his way to the field, Jackman went over his conversation with Bryson Smith. He admired the way he had not forgotten his roots, which, having made a name for himself in the big city, he could so easily have done. He'd already looked him up on Google, where he read that he was a well-respected and highly regarded figure in the art world. Jackman appreciated integrity and kindness in people, and concluded that Smith had both in abundance.

Rory greeted him enthusiastically. 'And here's the man himself! I have a lot to tell you, my angel.'

Jackman listened carefully while Rory explained why he and Jan Wallace thought the bodies were entangled in that way. He had now had time to prepare himself for the horrors to come, and was able to confront them with a certain degree of detachment. Basically, his job was straightforward — he must catch a callous killer. Of course, the perpetrator might be long deceased, since he had no idea of exactly when the crime had been committed, but he had to be absolutely certain that there was no further danger to anyone. Ever. Dead or alive, finding who had done this terrible thing, was paramount. And now that the Westerham case had been handed over, the Pillbox Killer was all his. Jackman was determined not to let it rest until he could write the words *CASE CLOSED* across the top of the file.

Aware that the gruesome task of retrieving the bodies would have badly affected everyone concerned, Jackman had a quiet word with Rory before he left. 'How's morale, my friend? Everyone seems to be working flat out, but what's going on behind the masks?'

'Dear heart, we all seem to be yo-yoing rather spectacularly from high to low, thank you for asking.' Rory gave a little bow. 'However, yours truly made the masterful move of engaging the services of the inimitable Professor Jan Wallace. That woman has been a veritable rock, and has even managed to whip my scrambled brain cells into some semblance of order. Yes, this one has even got to me, Rory Wilkinson, the most stoic and level-headed of pathologists.'

Jackman smiled. 'Hardly surprising, is it? I mean, you are only human after all, er . . . You are, aren't you?' He asked Rory if he was able to give him a rough estimate of when the last victim died. 'I can't even begin my investigation until I know that.'

'I thought you might ask,' said Rory. 'And it will be our first job. Jan already has some ideas, and as soon as we're able to get down to the post-mortems, we will prioritise establishing the date of death. For once — and I say this with a certain modicum of regret — I shan't be requiring you, or the lovely Marie, to beg for the usual snippets of my vast knowledge.' He sighed dramatically. 'Much as it pains me to say this, we have agreed that we will proceed as speedily as possible to bring this ghastly case to a conclusion. So there will be no, ah, Rory-isms.'

'I shall miss them,' said Jackman, 'though doubtless you will revert to the status quo as soon as this case is over.'

'Oh yes, my friend. You may rely on that!'

* * *

Nina arrived at Lucas's rented cottage promptly at seven thirty.

'Mmm, good choice — modest, unremarkable and just far enough off the beaten track for convenience.'

'I miss the city desperately, but I admit this place does have its attractions. I might even go so far as to say that if Hartwood House is the source of riches I expect it to be, the Fens could well become my second home,' Lucas said.

'Well, *I* miss the fjords, but they don't provide me with the appropriate lifestyle, so I stick to where the money is, thank you very much.' She smiled at him. 'And talking of money, if you've finished your terribly healthy meal, perhaps you could show me your Aladdin's cave.'

An hour later, nursing cups of strong coffee, they got down to business.

Astounded at what Lucas had been showing her, Nina bombarded him with questions. 'So. The owners of the house. Who are they? I assume you'll have done the research.'

'Brothers Derek and Norman Greene,' he said. 'Fifty-nine and sixty-one respectively. Born in Saltern-le-Fen to wealthy parents who had made their money, quite legitimately, in the rag trade. From an early age, the brothers exhibited signs of the obsessive-compulsive disorder that would dog them for the rest of their lives. They were close, and almost friend-less, becoming ever more reclusive as they grew older. Over the years, they hopped from one obsession to another, until they finally settled upon their true passion — the art of the 1920s and 30s. After their parents died, within six months of each other, they sold off most of the family businesses, retaining only the most lucrative ones to keep them in funds. The brothers then embarked on a spending spree. They purchased

Hartwood House and began transforming it into the perfect setting for their rapidly expanding collection. They haven't stopped, by the way, and continue to identify and collect precious items from the era they are so fond of.'

'So, how come nobody knows about these obsessive collectors?' asked Nina, frowning.

'Because they are very, very clever. They are compulsive about keeping their identities hidden, using every trick in the book, from never having anything delivered directly to their place of residence to using bogus names whenever they attend a viewing. They have even gone so far as to disguise themselves as a couple of old country locals. Over the years, people have made up all sorts of stories about who they really are.'

'And you have found them.' She sipped her black coffee appreciatively. 'I am assuming that, apart from your client, you and I are the only people to have seen inside Hartwood House?'

'Correct.'

'And your client has *not* seen the Art Nouveau room?'

'Once again, correct.'

'Would it be presumptuous of me to assume that you wish me to use my special expertise with regard to that particular room?' She raised an eyebrow.

'It would not. You have a very specific part to play in this, er, heist, and that room is at the heart of it. No one else but you will know about it, and I can guarantee that it will be worth your while.'

'And my usual little, er, perk?' Nina tilted her head to the side.

Lucas laughed. 'Oh, that still stands, don't worry.' Right from their very first job together, Nina had insisted on retaining a keepsake, a small memento of a particular undertaking. 'One stipulation, though. It must come from the secret room. Naturally, it can't be something the client has seen in the videos and images I've shown him.'

'No problem. I prefer Art Nouveau anyway. It suits my taste more than Art Deco.' Nina set down her cup. 'So. Strategy. How do we proceed?'

Lucas ran through the steps, one by one. 'Broadly, it's as follows. The Greene brothers will be lured away on the promise of an extremely rare and beautiful Tiffany table lamp some distance from the house. This will give us two hours. Chaos will get our full team safely inside Hartwood House, where we will relieve the brothers of all the items the client requests. We exit. Chaos reactivates security. We leave in our separate vehicles, to reconvene that same evening in the place where our acquisitions are to be stored. Twenty minutes after the others have left, you and your two chosen associates will return to the house. Chaos again deactivates the security system, and you remove everything I have listed from the Art Nouveau room. You have thirty minutes to complete the job before Chaos reinstates the alarm system. And that's it.' He looked at her. 'Think it's doable?'

'Tight, but, yes, doable. One thing — and it might not be possible, but it would ensure that the second part of the operation ran smooth as silk.'

'You want to see inside the house, don't you?'

'I don't want to risk jeopardising the operation, but a quick walk-through would give me an idea of any possible pitfalls. We can do a virtual one from your video, but it isn't the same as being inside the venue itself. If you're there in person, you can feel in your bones whether something might present a problem.'

Lucas understood what she meant, and had pre-empted it. 'Be here at ten thirty tomorrow. The brothers have an appointment in Lincoln. I have arranged a thirty-minute slot with Chaos. I'll give you some overalls to wear, so come in strong boots, okay? I have a vehicle ready in the barn next to this place. We are lucky in that Hartwood House has no immediate neighbours and is very well concealed by hedges and trees, but even so, we must take all the necessary precautions.'

Nina smiled at him. 'I do like working with you, Lucas. Not only do you pay well, but we think alike too. I might even go so far as to say we're kindred spirits.'

Lucas surprised himself in feeling a little thrill of pleasure at her words. There was nothing sexual about it, it was more a sense of satisfaction at finding such a compatible partner to work with.

'I presume,' she said, 'that your client has a pretty extensive shopping list. Yes?'

'He has. It will be stretching us to full capacity, but he'll reward us generously for our efforts.'

'And I imagine he'll be wanting that stained-glass window.' Nina gave him a wry smile. 'Because I would, in his place. Even I can see its value, and I'm only a logistics expert.'

'He wants that window more than all the rest put together.' Lucas sighed. 'And whatever the client wants, the client gets. When we go in tomorrow, I will confirm the measurements, and by nightfall, a plain-glass replacement will have been made and loaded onto the lorry ready for the following day. The original will be made ready for transportation as a matter of priority. We will divide those who will be assisting us into two teams. I will be leading Team A, and you will take charge of Team B, dealing with the movable items. Is that satisfactory?'

Nina nodded. 'Perfectly. And when all those precious artefacts are well on their way to oblivion, we will work our way through your list, assuming you have your own preferences?'

'You assume correctly.'

'And you will be hoping to garner as much as possible from your personal list,' she said. It wasn't a question.

'Only in so far as it doesn't jeopardise the operation,' he said. 'I'm not about to get greedy at this juncture.' He gave her a significant glance. 'This is a trial run, Nina. It could lead to a whole new modus operandi, to the benefit of us both.'

Nina leaned forward, chin in her hands. 'I'm listening.'

'Let's see how this assignment goes first, shall we?' Lucas said. 'Then you and I will be in a better position to weigh up the pros and cons of working for ourselves. That is where your logistics expertise will come into its own. It will have to be a good deal more profitable than working for a client, otherwise it's not viable.'

Nina sat back. 'You're right. We mustn't get ahead of ourselves. Concentrate on the job in hand, and then we'll talk about the future. Any chance of another one of those delicious coffees?'

* * *

Charlie Button was starting to find the endless stream of visitors exhausting. He was grateful to them for coming, but now he was just pleased to have a few minutes to himself so he could close his eyes and relax. He had soon learned that you were never left alone for long in hospital. Even when there were no visitors, the nursing staff seemed always to be around, taking samples of this and that bodily fluid, checking your blood pressure, or adjusting some monitor or other.

'Sorry, Mr Button, can I do your obs?'

Charlie opened his eyes. The voice belonged to a young Filipino nurse — Jasmine, according to her name tag. 'Carry on. After all, I'm not going anywhere.' He indicated to the drip stand and the tubes running into his arm.

It took her a moment, then a smile spread across her round face. 'Yes, you are my prisoner.'

Charlie decided he didn't mind being kept prisoner by this particular nurse. Privately, he thought of her as a sweet little thing, though that was probably politically incorrect. Whatever, she was always pleasant and cheerful, in stark contrast to Sister, who had been decidedly unsympathetic after the embarrassing incident with the catheter earlier in the day.

Securing the blood pressure cuff, Jasmine beamed happily at him. 'I've never looked after a hero before.'

'What, me?' Charlie said. 'I'm no hero. Quite the opposite. I'm the prat who couldn't duck fast enough to dodge a bullet.'

She frowned. 'Prat?'

'Erm, idiot. You know, stupid person.'

'You are too modest, Mr Button. We all know what happened. Now, open your mouth, I want to take your temperature.'

Charlie was only too glad to be able to sit and admire the pretty young woman. When she took out the thermometer, he said, 'You have a lovely name, Jasmine.'

'I'm honoured to be named after the national flower of the Philippines, like my grandmother,' she said proudly.

'Well, it suits you,' said Charlie. 'Oh, and by the way, I wouldn't try calling anyone a prat. It's not a good word. Stick with "stupid", it's much safer.'

Jasmine laughed. 'Okay. Now, you rest, Mr Button. We'll do your blood pressure again in two hours.'

'Please call me Charlie. I was named after my grandfather, too, so we have something in common. Could I have some more painkillers, please? My arm's hurting again.'

'Sorry, Mr . . . er, Charlie, not for another hour, but I'll have a word with the ward sister for you. Now, you rest.'

Charlie closed his eyes again, and was immediately assailed by a series of flashbacks. Oddly, the most persistent image was Max's eyes, and the anguish in them. He had still looked haunted when he came in that afternoon, so much so that Charlie barely recognised him for a moment.

In contrast to Max, Marie had been upbeat and positive. She was able to reassure him that no matter how things panned out with his recovery, his job would still be there waiting for him when he came out. This was an enormous relief, especially after he'd been told by the surgeon that regaining full use of his arm could not be guaranteed.

Then Gary, who had been, well, Gary. Having dispensed with the usual queries, he proceeded to tell a series of hilarious stories, leaving Charlie in much better humour than when he'd arrived. His friends were the best, Charlie thought. And he dozed off, happy at the prospect of being back in the CID room with them again . . . as an active member of the team.

CHAPTER FOURTEEN

The following morning, Rory was back in his mortuary. Macabre as it might sound, he felt as if he'd come home. He was just so pleased to be out of that field, and a long way from the awful pillbox.

Apart from Spike, Jan and the others had remained at Fendyke. Rory and Spike had returned to the mortuary to prepare for the unusual number of bodies they would soon be receiving. The mortuary consisted of a sterile area — access strictly controlled — surrounded by thick glass panels and entered through electronic sliding doors. With its own heating, ventilation and air conditioning system, Rory thought of it as a microcosm, a world within a world. Because of the risk of contamination, outsiders wishing to observe proceedings stood looking down on it from a viewing gallery, communicating with Rory and his assistants through speakers.

Of the five mortuary tables occupying this little area, only three were as yet occupied. By the end of the day, all the victims of the Pillbox Killer would be in situ, ready for examination.

Rory looked at the body bags containing the remains of the two men and one woman, and wondered grimly if there were really only five bodies. Could there be more victims, lodged elsewhere? What were they looking at? He sincerely hoped that the Fens wouldn't gain the dubious notoriety of being home to one of the worst serial killers the world had ever known.

'Get a grip, Wilkinson,' he muttered to himself. 'Allowing your fertile imagination to run riot is not exactly advisable right now.'

'Sorry, Prof?' Spike looked up from one of the empty tables that were being prepared for occupancy.

'Giving myself a little bit of advice, dear boy,' Rory said. 'I only hope I'm capable of listening to reason.'

Smiling, Spike shook his head. He was used to Rory by now. 'You know, Prof, I can't help wondering if this is it. I mean, what if this raging nutter has other dumping grounds? Doesn't bear thinking about, does it?'

'You too, eh? Oh dear, it looks like I need to give you the same advice as I gave myself. Let's deal with what we have, Spike, as if that wasn't enough, without indulging in morbid conjecture. We need to give the police all the help we can, and let them catch this demon. Only then will we find out the extent of his hideous activities.'

'Point taken, Prof, but—'

'Spike! Shut up.'

* * *

Marie stared at her phone, and then handed it to Robbie. 'What do you make of this?'

Robbie Melton read the message:

Marie — you were right. I am not safe here. I'm taking your advice and moving to a quiet B&B. Meanwhile, don't use this number. I'll contact you. Please, just find my husband. Anna.

He handed back her phone with a frown. 'I'm not at all sure about that. Sounds pretty iffy to me.'

'That's what I thought,' said Marie. 'You up for a swift dash across, to see if she's left yet? I need to talk to her.'

'Sure. It's still early, so with any luck she'll still be packing.' He hurried back to his desk and grabbed his jacket.

Marie called after him. 'I'll tell Jackman, so he's aware of where we've gone, but we should be back in time for the morning meeting.'

Marie drove as fast as she dared, and they arrived at just after eight. Even before they got out of the car, Marie knew they were too late. The house had the air of abandonment of a place whose occupants have left in a hurry.

Three rings on the doorbell produced no response.

'I'll hop over the side gate and check the back of the garage,' said Robbie. 'There should be a window, then I can see if her car has gone.'

Marie's head was full of unanswered questions. Why hadn't Anna told her where she was going? Why didn't she want her to ring her on the phone that was supposed to be specifically for them to stay in contact? Had she really been afraid, or had she been forced to send that message? Had she been taken too?

'Garage is empty, Sarge,' said Robbie, climbing back over the gate. 'Your bird has flown.'

'I need to see inside, Rob. I want to check that there's no sign of a struggle.'

They peered in through the front windows. It all seemed okay, but Marie still had a distinct feeling that something at Ambleside House was very wrong. Robbie again vaulted the side gate, returning a few minutes later to say that he'd looked in all the rear windows, and the rooms were tidy and undisturbed.

'Maybe she simply followed your advice, and took off,' said Robbie. 'Perhaps something spooked her. Wasn't she going to ask you to suggest somewhere? The odd part is not telling you where she's gone. Even so, maybe we are reading too much into this.'

'And your gut feeling?'

Rob pulled a face. 'Considering what happened to Johnny, my gut is screaming that this isn't right at all. On the other hand, my rational mind is saying that Anna is strung out tighter than a bowstring, ready to flee at the slightest thing. Remember what she said about that deer in the garden.'

'Yes, but what about the phone?' Marie queried. 'I'm the only number on that phone, it was our one means of contact, so why tell me not to use it?'

Robbie thought for a minute. 'She knows that we have the means to track a cell phone, even a burner. If, for some reason, she really does want to keep her new hidey-hole secret, she might have temporarily decommissioned the phone.'

Marie sighed. 'And you believe that?'

'Not really.' Robbie looked at her miserably. 'Just looking at the possibilities.'

'My gut feeling says something happened here last night. Whatever it was, it means we now have two Millards missing, and one of them is the most important link to the other.' She turned away from the silent house. 'Well, it's no good hanging around here. Let's get back to base.'

'At least we have my friend Harry and our new ally, George Rider. Let's hope George can find out something from his network that we'd never get to hear about,' Robbie said as they got into the car. 'Roll on tomorrow's prison visit. Ah, and don't rule out Orac. If there is anything at all on that computer of Johnny's, she'll find it. If we can understand why he was targeted, and by whom, we have a chance of finding him.'

Marie appreciated his positive attitude, but it didn't lift her spirits. She knew from bitter experience that she wouldn't be able to rest until she knew what had happened to Anna. She decided that as soon as they got back to the station, she'd get someone to check the traffic cameras at the junctions where the back roads met the main thoroughfare. It was an outside chance, but they might get a sighting of Anna's car, and the direction it was travelling in. And, more importantly, whether or not she was alone.

* * *

Given their reputation as a couple of unfriendly recluses, plus the absence of immediate neighbours, the Greene brothers were unlikely to be receiving visitors. Much as he disliked it, the isolated fenland setting played nicely into Lucas's hands. No one would be peeking over the hedge, no one would engage him in conversation. It seemed the place did have its advantages after all.

'Those overalls suit you,' he remarked to Nina as they approached the van.

'Thank you. Not really my colour, but they do have a sort of industrial chic to them. Nice touch with the pest control company logo, by the way. I should think rats are prevalent round here.'

'Indeed, but we are after wasps today, should the unthinkable happen and we are forced to speak to anyone.' Lucas took up his iPad, tapped something into it, and checked the other small device. 'We're in. Chaos has worked his magic, and it's time for you to see what Hartwood House has to offer.'

Nina wandered through the rooms like a woman in a dream. Her voice hushed, almost reverent, she told Lucas she had never seen a house like it.

Lucas was ridiculously proud of himself for his discovery, although he managed not to show it. 'We have twelve minutes to be clear of the place. Anything else you need to check?'

'No, if you've got your measurements, I'm done, so we can disappear.'

As they drove away, Nina let out a long breath. 'Thank you, Lucas. I appreciate that. To be frank, if we hadn't come today, I'd have found it hard to concentrate when we do carry out the job. It's all so much more impressive than it appears on video.'

'That's why I arranged for this little preview,' Lucas said. 'It will be different for the others, they aren't connoisseurs. Neither will they appreciate the value of what we are about to appropriate. I could almost see you totting up the profit in that calculating brain of yours.'

Nina laughed. 'Fortunately, like you, I can resist the temptation to become greedy and carry away too much. A perfectly executed job reaps more than adequate rewards, and it also ensures that I remain free to enjoy the fruits of my labours.'

'Like you said — kindred spirits.' Lucas gazed through the windscreen at the expanse of fields. She was right, freedom was paramount. What use was wealth if you were trapped in a cell? So far, they had both managed to stay ahead of the law. Lucas himself had started out as a scout for a small-time gang. He was young and athletic, and a talented gymnast, able to squirm his way into the smallest aperture. He had no fear of heights, and relished a challenge. He would find a way for the gang to enter a property, but never took anything for himself. Job done, he disappeared, collecting his cut from the bossman the following day. It hadn't taken long for him to rise in the ranks before striking out on his own. Now, he entered his chosen venue through the front door. He had his own network of professionals, of whom the crème de la crème was Chaos — and Nina, of course. And there was no reason why this satisfactory situation shouldn't continue. Thankfully, Nina felt the same way.

'Right, my friend. Back to my fenland retreat for more coffee, and we'll discuss the finer details. How does that sound?'

'Perfect,' she said. 'Does life get any better than this?'

He chuckled. 'Oh yes it can. Once we get this little gem of a job out of the way, the world will be our oyster, as they say.'

Nina clapped her hands. 'Then bring it on, Lucas! Bring it on!'

* * *

DC Kevin Stoner sat with Jackman and listened to him summarise the events of the past week. Life never stood still in the CID office, but it seemed that he'd missed a lot more than usual while he was away on holiday.

'I'm going to get you to work on the pillbox investigation with me, Kevin. Word of warning, lad, it's gruesome, and despite the possibility that it occurred years ago, we're treating it as a current case. The perpetrator has to be identified as fast as possible — you'll see why in a moment.' Jackman stood up. 'Ready to see the forensic photos? Then I'll get you to drive out to the site and get a feel for the location. Okay?'

Kevin jumped to his feet. 'Ready, boss.'

The images were more shocking than he'd expected. Jackman had warned him that they'd be grim, but the inhumanity of what had been done to the people in those photos was sickening. When he'd finished viewing them, Kevin experienced a sudden urge to talk to his father. Dad was the diocesan bishop for the area, and Kevin often sought his advice regarding issues he confronted in the course of his work. He wasn't able to discuss specific cases because that would be breaking the Official Secrets Act, but he could ask more general questions about morality, and what might cause people to behave in ways he found despicable.

Suddenly, he heard Jackman say, 'It's okay, Kev, we all felt the same. Actually seeing that hellhole shook the life out of Marie and I.' He paused. 'Mmm, not the best way to put it, but you understand my point, I'm sure.'

'I've seen the horrific pictures of mass graves following a genocide, but for this to have happened in a village in the middle of the Fens, it's . . . well . . .' Kevin's voice trailed away as he struggled to express his emotions.

'Incomprehensible?' offered Jackman.

'Yeah, I guess so.' Kevin sighed, and then cleared his throat. 'But, hey, I'm a detective, and I need to be able to cope. I'll go over the implications in my own time, but for now, I should go and check out this pillbox.'

Jackman laid a hand on his arm. 'Don't let this get to you, Kevin. Talk to us, don't bottle it up. When I said we were all affected, I meant it. Every single one of us was shaken — including Prof Wilkinson, and that's never happened before. So, you're not alone.'

'Thank you, boss,' Kevin said, greatly relieved. 'I'll take your advice. Now, I'd better go and see the crime site.'

'And while you're there, perhaps you'd call in and check on the Smith family. I'm not sure how they're taking the fact that their dream of creating a peaceful wild area for birdwatching has gone rapidly down the pan. The son, Bryson Smith, is being a real rock, and Mum is busy running a veritable soup kitchen for all the workers, but I still can't help feeling concerned for them.'

'I know what you mean, sir. The reality of it could kick in at any time. I'll certainly go and introduce myself to them.'

At least, thought Kevin as he drove towards Fendyke Village, the victims had been removed from the pillbox, and some were already at the mortuary. He pictured again the tangle of limbs and protruding bones, and shuddered. Jackman had been right, it was hard to believe that a human being could have done this. This was one of those times when he wished he didn't have such a vivid imagination, as strange and macabre scenarios kept flashing into his brain. Over and over, he kept asking himself why were those people there? And what had they done to deserve such a terrible fate?

Kevin knew the area fairly well, and took a short cut to the village along a back lane. It was narrow and rutted, with a deep ditch running the length of one margin. As long as there were no tractors using it, it enabled him to avoid the village roundabout, and a set of temporary traffic lights that had sprung up a week before, and which showed no sign of being removed.

He rounded a tight bend and spotted a figure up ahead, a tall woman walking her dog. The animal, he saw, was off the lead, and Kevin muttered, 'Irresponsible,' to himself. Suppose a tractor suddenly appeared and spooked the . . . dog? Kevin squinted at the creature. That was no dog! The woman was walking a bloody fox!

He drew up beside her, and the little fox crept behind the woman's legs and sat down. He was just about to wind the window down and comment upon her pet, but one look at the woman's angry glare made him change his mind, and he accelerated away.

'Well, I've seen it all now,' he muttered to himself. 'These Fens really are the strangest of places.'

It was difficult to find a place to park, so Kevin turned back and left his car a short distance away and walked back, heading first to the bungalow. An older constable who had been briefly teamed up with Kevin when he was still in uniform waved at him from the doorway.

'Hi, Kev!' called out the constable, whose name was PC Chris Elliott. 'Looks like you and me both drew the short straw.'

'Looks that way,' said Kevin ruefully.

'Still, it could be worse. Betty Smith, who owns the house with her husband, is providing us with an endless supply of tea and biscuits.' Chris gave Kevin the wide, toothy grin that was his trademark. 'I'm on my way to the kitchen right now.'

'I need to have a quick chat with Mr and Mrs Smith before I head down to the pillbox, so I'll come with you and you can introduce me.' He stopped. 'Chris, you're a local here, aren't you?'

'Sure. Me and the missus live in the next village.'

'Well, I drove here via Back Lane, and I came across this really tall unfriendly-looking woman walking a fox, of all things.'

Chris's grin widened even further, if that were possible. 'Oh, you've just had the pleasure of meeting Mad Sally. And it was a fox. It joins her every day for a walk around the lanes.'

Kevin shook his head. 'But a fox? Bit weird, isn't it?'

'They don't call her Mad Sally for nothing,' said Chris significantly.

'Does she live in Fendyke Village?'

'She lives in an old farmhouse out in the fields, slap bang between here and Bartoft Village, where I live.'

'With family?' asked Kevin.

'Alone. I've no idea if she even has any family, either here or elsewhere. She's a rum one, all right.'

'What's the story with the fox?' asked Kevin.

Chris shrugged. 'No idea, mate.'

'Hasn't she told anyone?'

Chris gave another toothy grin. 'Mate, Mad Sally doesn't talk to anyone. Ever.'

'And no one's asked her?' Kevin persisted, intrigued by the story of this odd woman. 'After all, it's not exactly something people do, even out here.'

They were now at the back of the bungalow, where a number of people could be seen coming and going from what Kevin assumed to be the kitchen.

'Oh, they've asked her — well, they've tried at least. Like I said, Sally doesn't talk to anyone.'

'Is there something wrong with her, then? Maybe she can't speak,' Kevin said.

It was Chris's turn to look thoughtful. 'Oh, I think she can, she just chooses not to. I say that because I've noticed a telephone wire going to her property, so why have a phone if you can't talk?'

'Maybe it was already there when she moved in,' suggested Kevin.

'Sally has been living in that place for donkey's years, mate. I reckon she had it installed.' He shrugged. 'Now. Tea!' They went inside where they found a woman with a broad smile handing two steaming mugs to a uniformed sergeant. 'Morning, Betty. This is my friend, Detective Constable Kevin Stoner, and he's keen to try one of your special brews.'

'And a quick chat, if you have a moment,' Kevin added

'Of course,' said Betty. 'Bring your tea, my duck, and we'll pop through to the lounge. Trade's a bit slow right now.'

'It's very kind of you to do this for us, it's a lot more than we usually get,' said Kevin. 'I hope you're going to be reimbursed, we must be consuming vast quantities of milk and tea.'

Betty dismissed this with a wave. 'It's a pleasure, really. It's the least we can do.'

Taking a seat on a comfortable-looking sofa, Kevin's eyes were immediately drawn to a large, framed picture hanging on the opposite wall. 'Oh wow! That is powerful. And what an unusual style.'

'It's the work of a war artist who served in the Royal Army Medical Corps in the First World War. He became an Associate of the Royal Academy in 1939. Do you like it?'

Kevin turned to the speaker, who was standing in the doorway regarding him. 'Um. I'm not sure if "like" is the right word, but it's so incredibly striking. Who is the artist?'

'Christopher Richard Wynne Nevinson, a Futurist. He was a friend of Wyndham Lewis, the Vorticist, but subsequently fell out with him, though his work is similar. Check him out when you have a minute. Many believe him to be one of the most important British artists of the twentieth century. Anyway, I won't bore you with any more lectures. I'm Bryson, Betty's son.'

Kevin took to him at once, and it didn't take him long to perceive that both Bryson and his mother were dealing pretty well with the situation they had found themselves in. The Smiths came from solid farming stock — people who got on with things, and were far from being fanciful. Even Bryson, who had seen what was in the pillbox, had recovered — or seemed to, at least — from the shock. He referred to the example of his beloved war artists, who had witnessed a great deal worse. He expressed his willingness to do whatever he could to help the police.

Kevin finished his tea, and accepted Bryson's offer to accompany him to the pillbox.

As they made their way through the garden, Bryson said, 'I haven't told my parents precisely what I saw in the pillbox. All they know is that there were a couple of bodies inside it. I think it's better that way. And I am keeping an eye on them, don't worry. I've cancelled all my engagements for a while, and I'll be staying on here until I know they're all right.'

'Yes, my boss, DI Jackman, told me, and he appreciates it. He is always concerned for the people who get unintentionally involved in these situations,' Kevin said.

'That's good to know,' Bryson said. He showed Kevin the pillbox from their side, saying they had discovered it while he and a helper were clearing the surrounding area to create a wild garden to attract insects and small animals and birds. Then he led him to the gate into the field, where he left him to go on alone. 'It's cordoned off now, and besides, I've seen more than enough of the scene.'

Kevin went through the gate and into the field, feeling somewhat trepidatious about what he would find.

The first person he met was Professor Jan Wallace, who was smiling at him over her mask. 'Ah, a new face! And who are you, young man?'

When he gave her his name, her eyes widened. 'Not the Right Reverend Michael Stoner's son?'

Kevin nodded. 'Seems everyone knows my father.'

'I wouldn't be surprised,' said Jan. 'He's on more committees than anyone I know. Pleased to meet you, Kevin. So, how can I help? I'm afraid our delightful Rory isn't around at the moment, having skived off for a couple of hours.'

Kevin explained that he had been assigned to the case by DI Jackman, and needed to familiarise himself with the scene of the crime.

'Well, Kevin, we've just extracted the last of the five victims, so if you come with me, I'll show you our final unfortunate victim, or what's left of him. Then you can see the place where they were so heartlessly deposited.'

Taking a deep breath, Kevin followed her.

CHAPTER FIFTEEN

PC Simon Laker had been heading out to talk to some disgruntled villagers who had complained about kids vandalising the local bus shelter, when a call came over his radio. Immediately, he turned the car round, and returned to the station. As he pulled in, he saw another squad car flashing its lights at him.

'Park up, Simon! You're with us, and make it fast!'

He did as he was told, and hurried across to where PCs Stacey Smith and Jay Acharya were waiting for him. He climbed in the back of their car, and they took off out of the station gates at speed.

'What's occurring?' he asked.

'We thought you should be in on this shout, mate,' said Jay. 'It might be nothing, but—'

Behind the wheel, Stacey took over. 'A man who owns some units in a small industrial park just outside town has reported hearing noises coming from a vacant one that's awaiting renovation. It's locked from the outside, but he thinks he heard . . . well, he reckoned it was someone crying.'

'It could well be an animal that got accidentally shut in,' added Jay, 'but knowing you've been hunting for that kid with the handcuff, and half the force are on the lookout for that missing hacker Millard, we thought we should take you along.'

'Thanks, you two, much appreciated,' said Simon. 'I had that retired copper — the one whose house the lad turned up at — on the phone earlier, asking about him.'

'Well, we'll soon know. The manager and the owner are waiting for us, hopefully with a spare key,' said Stacey, turning off the main road and making for the industrial park.

Jay grinned. 'If he doesn't have a key, I've got enough jemmies and bolt cutters to fill a hardware store, and an enforcer to boot, so no sweat there.'

The Saltern Enterprise Park consisted of some ten units housing a number of small independent businesses. Stacey drove past a car repair shop, a cleaning company and a sign maker's before they caught sight of two men waving to them from a unit that stood a little away from the rest at the far end of the park.

One of the men, a tall, anxious-looking individual was tapping his foot impatiently. 'I'm Gerry Lennox, the owner, and I swear it's no animal in there. It's gone quiet now, but it was definitely a person. Thing is, the damn spare keys have gone missing. I had to evict the last people who rented it, who left it full of crap. The people I got a quote from to gut the place never returned the keys.'

'Then if you've no objection, we'll have to force the doors.' Jay was already opening the boot of their car.

'Got no option, have I?' replied Lennox grimly. 'If some plank has got himself locked in there, he needs help. I can always bill him later.' He added a hopeful, 'Or maybe I could bill you guys?'

While Stacey spoke to the owner, Jay and Simon checked the unit doors. They were made of heavy wood in the old style, whereas the newer ones all had metal roller or sectional electric doors. A chain and padlock made it doubly secure.

Jay used the bolt cutters, and shortly afterward the chain fell to the ground with a clank. 'Right,' muttered Jay, 'that's the easy bit. Now for the lock.'

Simon listened, but could hear no sound coming from within. He was beginning to think they would find a terrified and hungry cat perched on a shelf and ready to make a dash for freedom as soon as the doors opened.

Jay was now jemmying the door, trying to do as little damage as possible, in case this was a false alarm. 'Got it!'

The door swung back and they stared into the gloomy interior.

No cat flew past them. The interior was dim and evil smelling, but nothing moved. Not at first.

As the three police officers entered, there was a distinct moan, followed by a plaintive whimper. Simon flipped the light switch, but nothing happened.

'Sorry. Electric's off,' stated the owner.

Stacey hurried back to the car and grabbed a torch, while Simon produced a pocket Maglite, and they moved further inside, the thin beam of light cutting through the gloom as they tried to locate the source of the noise.

Lennox had been right. It was full of crap. Simon picked his way between pallets, boxes, buckets, duckboards and untidy heaps of packing materials.

All at once, Stacey's voice rang out. 'Over here!'

The three of them stood looking down at a huddled figure, lying on an old sleeping bag, his knees drawn up in a foetal position and his eyes squeezed tightly shut. Simon thought he heard the words, 'No more. No more,' though it could have been something else.

Stacey knelt down beside him. 'It's all right, fella. We're the police. Hang on in there and we'll soon get you some help.' She looked up. 'He seems drugged to me, and he's in a bad way. Get an ambulance, Jay!'

'Drugged, but not by choice. He's no addict,' added Simon, looking at the single handcuff hanging from one wrist. 'At least my retired copper can stop worrying. We've found our missing runaway.'

While Simon rang it in, Stacey informed Gerry Lennox that this was a crime scene, and no one was to enter until forensics had swept the area. He should either submit the bill for the damaged door to the police, or they could get someone out to fix it for him. To his surprise, Simon heard Lennox say gruffly, 'Forget it. I'll deal with it when I clear this place out. I should never have left it empty for so long in the first place.'

Jay attended to the young man while they waited for the ambulance to arrive. Stacey explained to Lennox that they'd be needing the names of the people who had last rented the unit, and that of the man he suspected to have walked away with the keys. They'd also need to talk to the other businesses, to see if anyone had noticed any recent activity around the empty unit.

Lennox held up his hands. 'Do what you must, we'll help all we can.' He looked down at the pathetic figure still curled up on the floor. 'Poor little sod. Just get whoever did this to him, right?'

'That's the plan,' said Stacey.

* * *

Jackman received the news of the young man's discovery with mixed feelings. Naturally, he was relieved that the young man had been rescued, but, even though the case had been given DI Jenny Deane, it added to CID's workload.

As he turned the implications over in his mind, there was a knock at the door, and Jenny herself entered.

'Have you heard the news?' she asked.

'I've just been told,' he said, pointing to a chair. 'Any news on his condition? Do we know who he is?'

'As to his condition, he's out of the woods, but he's terrified — of us as well as whoever did this to him. I've got Simon Laker with him, and I'm hoping he can reassure the lad that we are on his side, then maybe he'll open up. As to his identity, we have no idea,' she said. 'We've taken a DNA

153

swab and run it through the system, but no hits. He looks clean, but who knows? Maybe he's a wrong 'un that hasn't yet been caught.'

'Have you notified Huntingdon about him?' asked Jackman.

'Yes, and they'll be getting someone down here before the end of the day.' She hesitated. 'I know this sounds stupid, Jackman, but I rather wish they'd leave this one with me. Usually I'd be delighted to chuck it to another county force, especially when we are so busy, but for some reason I, well, I want to keep it.'

He smiled at her. 'Yes, that *is* an unusual reaction. I've just offloaded the money laundering case to a special unit, and I'm practically breaking open the champagne.'

'Hardly surprising, with the investigation you've just taken on!' said Jenny. 'But I've got a kind of feeling about our Handcuff Boy. Anyway, he's going to be in hospital for a few days, and they don't want to move him, so I'll use the time to dig around and see what I can find.'

'Fair enough,' said Jackman. 'I'd probably do the same if I had one of those niggly feelings.'

Jenny stood up. 'I'll keep you posted, Jackman. It's certainly a mystery, if nothing else.'

It was that! Jackman assured her he'd be very interested to hear who the kid was and why he'd been abducted, but even as the door closed behind her, his thoughts were back with the sinister pillbox.

Before he could do anything else, there was another knock at his door, and Kevin Stoner came in, looking pale.

'Oh dear! You've obviously been to see the pillbox,' Jackman said. 'Sit down, Kevin, and I'll get you a cup of coffee.' He went out in search of Tim, his office manager. Not seeing him, Jackman went down to the vending machine himself and got two coffees.

Back in the office, he placed one in front of the young detective. 'Have they retrieved all the bodies yet?'

'Yes, sir. They'd just got the last one out when I got there. Young chap, apparently — well, that's what Professor Wallace said. I wasn't quite sure what I was looking at. He was wearing jeans, and he had a few scraps of other clothing clinging to what was left of him.' He swallowed. 'The professor said that they were correct in their assumption that there were no more than five victims. She said that they hadn't been completely sure because of all the rubbish that was in there with them. She said to tell you she believed that they were all deposited there over a period of eighteen months to two years, but not to hold her to that. They'll need to carry out a lot more forensic tests before they can say for certain. She said she's sorry, and she's aware how vital it is for you to know when the murders occurred, but she's unwilling to speculate. She promised it'll be their first task when they get back to the lab.'

'And we badly need that timeline,' Jackman said. 'We can't begin checking out missing persons or reports of disappearances until we get it.'

'I gathered the Prof himself was already back at the mortuary with the first three victims, sir,' said Kevin. 'And I think bringing in a forensic anthropologist like Jan Wallace will speed things up considerably.' He smiled for the first time since his return to the station. 'She's a real character, isn't she? It was a bit like asking your favourite auntie a complex forensic question on microbiology along with her recipe for chocolate brownies.'

Jackman laughed. 'I know just what you mean, Kevin. The first time I saw her, way back during the Windrush affair, I was reminded of my auntie Hilda, and it was all I could do not to refer to her as "Auntie".' He took a sip of his coffee. 'But don't underestimate her. She's got a brilliant mind, and we are really lucky to have her on board.'

Kevin nodded. 'Between her and our Rory, I reckon it'll be no time at all before we have everything there is to know about those victims.'

They drank their coffees in thoughtful silence. Then Kevin said, 'Um, sir? I know I should remain practical, but when I saw that place, and the two bodies with all that rubbish that had been put there with them, I couldn't help wondering what kind of person would do such a callous, inhuman thing. Maybe it's my religious upbringing, but it bothers me, terribly.'

Jackman smiled at him kindly. 'As I said earlier about it affecting everyone, it's also forced us all to dwell on that exact point. What kind of person are we dealing with? It's not you alone, lad, it is all of us.' He leaned forward. 'Here's my advice, Detective. Talk the morality of it over with your father by all means — as you know, I have nothing but admiration for Michael — but while you are at work, make sure you grab this case by the throat and concentrate solely on the practical aspect. If we do it as a team, we'll get justice for those five poor souls. Okay?'

Kevin drained his beaker and stood up. 'Got it, boss! Sorry for the wobble, but I'm back on track now.'

'Nothing to be sorry for, it's just the process. Now you can move on.'

'So, what's my first job, sir, now I'm up to speed on the background?'

Jackman grimaced. 'Well, it's really a waiting game until we get a timescale and the preliminary report from forensics, but you could take a trip back to the village and get a word with the farmer whose land that pillbox is situated on. His name is Donald Telford, and apparently he's been more than helpful to Rory and his people, even clearing some of the copse with his own JCB. Sound him out on anyone who either knew about the pillbox, or showed an interest in it. Ask him if any of the men or women he's had working for him over the years have ever bothered him in some way, or caused trouble. You know the kind of thing to ask, Kevin. And that'll be it for the day, as it's almost four now, so do that, then get yourself home. Oh, and one last piece of advice. When you do get home, pour yourself a good strong drink.'

Kevin left with a smile on his face.

* * *

Marie looked at Orac hopefully. 'I know it's too early to say yet, but I was wondering if you could tell me whether you think you'll be able to retrieve anything from that hard drive of Johnny Millard's.'

Looking slightly amused, Orac said. 'Ah, Marie! Like you said, it's early days yet. You see, the thing is, the longer ago the files were deleted, the less chance we have of getting them back.'

Marie wondered why, if that was the case, Orac was wearing what, for her, was a distinct smile on her face.

'However, no matter how cleverly the files were wiped, if you have specialised tools and a technician with a superlative brain, even corrupted, damaged and apparently dead hard drives can be made to work. Well, some can. With very large files, like videos, forget it, I wouldn't even try — unless it's absolutely crucial to the investigation.'

Marie was almost dancing in her seat. 'I suppose you couldn't just give me a straight answer, could you?'

Orac laughed. 'Oh, all right, if I must. We *are* getting there, Marie, but we've found nothing of importance so far. The Met did a good job, but our unit here, with our access to the higher echelons . . . Let's just say we have the capacity to go deeper, but don't tell the Met that.'

'As if!' Marie said. 'We are just so grateful to be able to benefit from it.'

'One thing I can say for sure is that the data still exists if you know how to find it. Okay, the operating system may have been removed, but—'

'Whoa! You are talking to a woman who struggles to operate her own TV set! I'll leave the technicalities to you, but I'm well happy to know there's been some headway.' Marie met Orac's metallic gaze. 'Thing is, Orac, Anna has fallen off the radar. She's moved from the house where she was hiding and I've no idea where she is. Even the burner phone we gave her to keep in contact with us seems to be unavailable.'

At once, Orac became serious. 'Give me the number. I'll do what I can.'

Marie took out her own phone and handed it to Orac. 'Her last message is still on there.'

Orac read it and frowned. 'Mmm, doesn't look good, does it? Leave it with me. It might only be possible to trace the last location where it was still switched on, but even that might help, if she used it after she left the place where she had been staying.'

'Thanks, Orac. Give me a bell if that's the case?'

'Of course.'

As Marie took her phone back, she received a call from Robbie.

'Marie, got a possible breakthrough here. The super has just had a call from the governor at HMP Marshfield. George Rider, that prisoner I made contact with, has asked to see me as a matter of urgency. He has some information for me and thought I should hear it before tomorrow. Okay if I go straightaway?'

'Absolutely!' exclaimed Marie. 'I'll come with you.'

'It's okay, Sarge,' said Robbie quickly. 'No offence, but if it's all right with you, I'll take Harry. Not being police, he kind of smooths the way with the prisoner, and we've already established a kind of rapport with this Rider.'

'Sure, if you think that's best,' agreed Marie. 'I'll wait to hear what he has to say.'

'I'll ring you as soon as we've spoken in case it's a wasted trip, then you can go home,' said Robbie. 'I'll get away immediately.'

Marie pocketed her phone. She was pretty sure that Rider wouldn't have bothered to request an urgent visit if it wasn't bloody important.

'Good news?' asked Orac.

'I really hope it is. I'll tell you later. But I'll be crossing my fingers until Robbie gets back from HMP Marshfield and has any news from his talkative inmate.'

'He trusts a con? That's interesting,' said Orac, frowning.

Marie nodded. 'For someone on the wrong side of the fence, our Johnny cultivated some strange friendships. I mean, a detective *and* a prisoner, who even though he's a big fish in his own pond, is prepared to help us help Johnny.'

'Want some background on that prisoner?' suggested Orac. 'Just for a bit of enlightenment should it be needed?'

Marie grinned at Orac. 'Yes, please. His name is George Rider.'

When Marie got back to the CID room, Robbie had already left and the others were packing up to go home. She went to Jackman's office and saw him talking on the phone. She turned to go back to her desk, but he beckoned to her. His hand covering the receiver, he whispered, 'Sit down, Marie, I won't be a minute.'

'I'll get us some coffees,' she whispered back.

Call over, he sat back and eyed the beaker of coffee gratefully. 'That's the third call in a row. The last one was Rory. He said, and I quote, "*All are safely gathered in, now the experts can begin.* Shakespeare — or was it Bacon? Act Three, Scene One. Can't remember the play."'

Marie chuckled. 'Well, at least he's back on form, thank heavens.'

'I don't think he has much choice with that force of nature Jan Wallace working with him, do you?'

'Probably not,' said Marie. 'So, he has all the victims back at his necropolis?'

'Yes, and he's promised a prelim report for tomorrow, with the full report following as swiftly as is humanly possible. He reckons he and Jan will start work on Victim One this evening, and both Spike and Cardiff have volunteered to assist, so I think we can safely say that we are out of the

159

starting blocks at last.' Jackman regarded her seriously. 'But you are far from happy about your case, are you?'

'Damn right I'm not!' growled Marie. 'Anna has really put a spoke in the wheel by buggering off, *if* that's the case, of course. I have no idea what to believe. Still, on the positive side, Robbie is back at HMP Marshfield — his caged bird says he has some information for us. And Orac is having some success with that trashed computer of Johnny's.'

'So, not all bad news, then. And add to that the fact that DI Jenny Deane has that other missing man safe and under close protection in the local hospital, it means things are moving in the right direction.'

'I guess that must have broken while I was with Orac,' Marie said, surprised. 'Hell, I was certain he wouldn't turn up alive. Is he okay, Jackman? You said he's in hospital, is he injured?'

'He'd taken a fair old going over, but nothing life-threatening. They'd drugged him to keep him quiet.' He looked puzzled. 'What bothers me is why were they holding onto him? If he was a real danger to someone, or a high risk to an upcoming job, why not just get rid of the guy?'

'Sounds a bit like Johnny Millard, doesn't it?' mused Marie. 'We kept asking ourselves why Johnny was only made a scapegoat and incarcerated when they could have removed him from the scene.'

'True,' said Jackman. 'But they're very different people. Johnny is a smart, good-looking, well-heeled and well-educated man from a moderately affluent family, or so I'm told, and Handcuff Boy is a scruffy little oik who is terrified of everything and everyone.'

'And a complete unknown, Jackman,' Marie reminded him. 'We have no idea of his background. Who knows, the clothes he was wearing might not even be his. Even a rich kid can be scared shitless. And no matter where he comes from, someone badly wanted him out of circulation, just like Johnny.'

'You do make a good case, Marie, I'll give you that.' Jackman nodded. 'So let's hope Simon Laker can get him to start talking. It might not be our case, but Jenny's right, it is a mystery, and one I'd like to see solved.' He drained his beaker. 'You getting away now?'

'No. I said to Robbie I'd hang on until either he gets back, or rings me to say he's learned nothing of use to us.'

'I'd stay on with you,' Jackman said, 'but I've promised Sam and Julia I'd take them out for an Italian meal tonight, and it's all booked.'

Marie beamed at him. 'Heavens! You go. I'm delighted to hear you are doing something that's nothing to do with work for once, even though I bet the three of you end up talking shop over the tiramisu!'

Sam Page had been Laura's dear friend and mentor. He was an eminent psychologist, and Marie knew that he and Julia had formerly been married. After Laura's death, Sam had moved from a remote cottage on a bird reserve out in the marsh to Jackman's converted mill. Sam and Jackman had supported each other as they tried to come to terms with losing the most important person in their lives. After that turbulent period, the two of them had settled into a very amicable living arrangement, with Julia using Laura's rooms for private consultations. Gradually, she came to spend more and more time at the mill, often working with Sam, than she did in her own home. It seemed the two of them had come full circle, and Marie secretly hoped that they would get back together properly, especially as Sam had told her that they had only split because they had married too young, at a time when they were just starting out on their careers. Neither had married again, and they had never fallen out of love. Life just got in the way, taking them in different directions. Marie thought it unbelievably romantic that the tide of life had swept them back together again.

'You have a lovely evening, Jackman, and give Sam my love. We must all get together for a drink one evening. Oh, and warn Julia to expect a stream of visits from traumatised police officers involved in the pillbox case.'

Jackman retrieved his jacket, assuring her he'd pass on both messages.

'And I'd better ring Ralph and tell him I'll be late for dinner. Again. It's lucky he's a detective, too, or we could be in deep shit before too long.'

Car keys in hand, Jackman said, 'Seeing you two together, I sincerely doubt that. Your Ralph would walk over hot coals for you, no matter how many delayed dinners you threw at him. And that's a certainty!' He paused at the door. 'As would I. But in a slightly different way, of course.'

Then he was gone, leaving Marie feeling all warm and fuzzy.

Robbie was back within two hours, and from the look on his face, his journey had not been wasted.

He flopped into a chair and regarded her with a frown. 'Well, what he told me doesn't help us much regarding Johnny, but it's extremely worrying nevertheless. There's something serious beginning to develop in the criminal world, so bad that even George is disturbed. It seems that a major player — a man George believes to be a trafficker in any and everything illegal, but mainly arms — disappeared a week or so ago, and yesterday turned up dead.'

'We never had any intel on that,' murmured Marie. 'Not a whisper.'

'George says we won't either. He's not known to us. He's not really known to George either, or any of the other major local villains, and by all accounts, he was extremely dangerous.'

'And now he's dead, you say?' Marie's frown deepened. 'So where's the body? And where was it found?'

'George says it was discovered outside the home of another villain, left on the doorstep, apparently. It's been secretly dealt with, and if not for George, we wouldn't have known a thing about it.'

162

'So it was a warning?'

'George isn't sure,' Robbie said, 'but it looks that way. Thing is, it isn't the first disappearance to have occurred, and George suspects that Johnny Millard could well be another. The difference in Johnny's case is that we —the police — are involved.' He leaned forward. 'And listen to this. It's making a lot of bad guys extremely twitchy indeed, and could well be the reason why Giles Westerham was carrying a gun. He's never carried before.'

'And George Rider really has no idea who is behind all this?' Marie asked.

'Not an inkling, and I'm certain he was being straight with me. He's now climbing the walls worrying about his family's safety while he's banged up inside.'

Marie's head was spinning. This was the last thing she'd expected. Was this another bad guy wishing to extend his empire? Or was this guy a psycho who believed he was an avenging angel quietly cleaning villains off the streets?

'I'm guessing you are asking yourself the same questions Harry and I were asking,' said Robbie quietly. 'All it does is fry your brain.'

Harry. Oh shit! Marie suddenly wondered if it had been wise of Robbie to involve a civilian friend. 'Sorry, I have to ask you, but I'm concerned that Harry was with you when George told you all this. You said Harry was close to Johnny, so is he sound? I mean, do you really trust him, Rob?'

'Harry's okay, Marie. I trust him. And he knows the score. He's always disapproved of Johnny's decisions and has tried to get him to keep to the straight and narrow, but despite that he's stuck by his friend. I've had a serious chat to him, Marie, and I've sworn him to secrecy. He won't talk. And should he ever hear from Johnny, he'll be onto me like lightning.'

'Okay, that's good, but maybe he shouldn't go on any more trips to Marshfield. I know I agreed that he could go with you today, but perhaps from now on, police business remains with us.'

Robbie nodded. 'Yeah, I was thinking that myself. Sorry if I overstepped the mark, I probably didn't think it through, but he has been a real help with Rider.'

Marie smiled at him. 'It's my fault, Robbie, and let's face it, you had no idea Rider was going to hit you with a bombshell like that. I'd expected a possible sighting of Johnny, or a bit of gossip from the bad boys' network.'

'So did I,' said Robbie. 'I wonder what Jackman is going to say when he hears.'

Marie thought of Jackman enjoying a rare night off with his friends. 'Telling Jackman can wait till tomorrow, then you can come with me and hear what he says for yourself. Time to get off home, I reckon.' As Robbie got up to go, she said, 'And, Rob, you did a good job making that contact with George Rider. Well done. Without that, I'm pretty sure we would never have got to know what is happening in the criminal underworld.'

And what did it all signify? Marie wondered to herself. Just how dangerous was that piece of knowledge?

CHAPTER SIXTEEN

PC Simon Laker had tried everything he could think of to get Handcuff Boy to open up — or at least give them his name. Hours of sitting at the lad's bedside and talking calmly to him had yielded nothing, and now Simon was seriously worried. What on earth had he been threatened with to make him so afraid to speak? It was now a whole day since Handcuff Boy had been rescued, and still he remained silent. Simon had left two constables with him overnight, both amiable and unthreatening, but the injured young man had refused to say a word to either of them.

Now it was eight in the morning, and Simon was back at his bedside trying to fathom a way to coax something out of the still cowering young man. In his report to DI Jenny Deane the previous evening, he had asked her about the possibility of getting the force psychologist to have a look at the patient. To his surprise, at a quarter to nine, the door opened and Julia Tennant stuck her head in and beckoned to Simon.

'Can I have a word, please, PC Laker?'

Outside in the corridor, he told her about how they had found the young man, and the terrible state he had been in.

'According to the report, he turned up on someone's doorstep asking for help, but ran off before the police got there,' said Julia. 'Would you mind if I had a little time alone with him, so I can get an idea of his mental condition?'

Simon said he was grateful for her help. He didn't say as much but he appreciated the way she'd asked if he minded. Most officials of her rank would not have been too interested in a humble constable's opinions.

He waited outside, almost certain that she would emerge successful. But her expression when, after half an hour she joined him in the corridor, said otherwise.

'It's fear, as I'm sure you already realise, PC Laker. He's terrified of what the repercussions will be if he talks, and nothing I said was able to reassure him. He wouldn't even give me his first name.' Julia sighed. 'It's not what you wanted to hear, I'm afraid. I'm certain we'll get there in the end, but it's going to take time.'

Trouble is, thought Simon, time is what we do not have. He had a strong feeling that what Handcuff Boy could tell them might save others from suffering the same fate.

He looked into the professor's kindly eyes and decided to risk making a suggestion. 'I was thinking about it last night, Professor, and, well, I'm not sure if this'll work, but the man whose doorstep our lad in there ended up on is a retired policeman. His name's Bob Ruston, and he's very concerned about the lad. I think he feels guilty about not allowing him inside the house, which is perfectly understandable, anyone would have done the same. Anyway, I gave him a ring last night to tell him the lad had been found and he asked if he could see him, to apologise, like. Well, it suddenly dawned on me that Bob is the only person that our young man has ever uttered a word to. So I just wondered . . . I mean, he's not a copper anymore, so he won't present a threat. Maybe Bob could get him to talk?'

Julia was silent for a few moments. 'If he's willing, then it's certainly worth a try. And having been a police officer, he'd know what, and what not to say.' She smiled at Simon. 'Why not give the man a ring?'

Simon rang him there and then. 'He'll be here in half an hour, and he's more than willing to assist.'

'Excellent. I'll be around for a while, so I'll have a swift word with him before he goes in.' Julia regarded Simon intently. 'It could work, and I sincerely hope it does, but don't get your hopes up too high. That young man is seriously traumatised, and it might just have to come down to patience and professional help, I'm afraid.'

Simon said he realised that, but he was afraid for the safety of whoever this young man was trying to protect.

'In that case, we'll just have to keep our fingers crossed that your Bob Ruston is persuasive. I've a few things to do now, so I'll come back in half an hour. See you then.'

Simon knew it was a long shot, but he liked Bob Ruston, and he had a feeling that Bob's air of solid dependability might lead the young man to confide in him. Well, that was the plan, anyway.

* * *

Marie and Robbie got hold of Jackman before he took the morning meeting, and brought him up to speed on the revelation from HMP Marshfield, for which he was grateful. He told them to keep it to themselves until he'd had time to talk to the super about it. It could affect them in a big way, or, with no bodies and no names and only the word of a con to go on, it could have no impact at all. It was one of the oddest things he'd come across in a while.

His initial gut feeling was that Rider had spoken the truth, and they either had a major criminal organisation moving into the area who was dispatching the competition before they could oppose him, or it was a ruthless dark crusader out for rough justice. On further reflection, he wondered if this tale was a smokescreen intended to distract them from what was really going on. He trusted Robbie's judgement, and he believed George Rider was on the level, but perhaps Robbie's liking for Johnny Millard was colouring his judgement. In addition, maybe Rider himself had been fooled, and had himself been fed dubious information. Had anyone actually seen this supposed dead man whose body had been left on someone's doorstep?

Jackman decided that this was beyond his remit, and was one for Ruth Crooke and the higher echelons to decide on. They had five bodies in the morgue, and finding what had happened to them was far more important than playing Chinese Whispers with some nameless villain. Jackman was even having his doubts about Marie's missing hacker and his vanished wife, though he would never say so to Marie. It had to be investigated, but he couldn't help wondering if Johnny hadn't engineered his own disappearance.

He pushed these thoughts aside. He would need Marie with him as soon as Rory's forensic reports were in. When that happened, Johnny would just have to take a back seat. He wouldn't pull the plug on it, though, as he knew how worried Marie was about Anna.

By the time the morning meeting was over and Jackman was making his way to Ruth Crooke's office, his doubts about George Rider's information had dissipated. As he knocked on her door, he realised he'd come full circle, and was back with his original gut feeling.

He told her what Rider had said and waited for Ruth's reaction.

Her thin lips little more than a tight, straight line, she seemed to be calculating what she was allowed to tell him.

She began slowly, measuring her words. 'Yesterday, we received intel from a neighbouring force which ran along the same lines as what you've just told me. Nothing is proven as yet, but people higher up the chain than I have decided it should be treated as authentic. Something is indeed going on within the criminal underworld, and it is being closely monitored.'

Although her words had been intended to reassure Jackman, they had the opposite effect. He became filled with apprehension. Not because of the wider consequences, but because of Robbie and his connection to the criminal who had provided the information.

He remained silent for a few moments.

'Well, Rowan? My news should have you grinning from ear to ear,' said Ruth. 'Instead, you look as if I've just told you your house is sinking into the marsh.'

'It's not the information itself that's bothering me, but the source. DC Robbie Melton has been cultivating a . . . how can I put it, a rapport with a certain inmate of HMP Marshfield, who passed on this information in the hopes of assisting us to discover what happened to our missing hacker, Johnny Millard. It was given to our DC on the understanding that his identity — the informant's — is to remain confidential. You will have to report this upstairs, I realise that, but do you think you could keep the details under wraps for a while?'

'As in, unsubstantiated confirmation from "the streets" perhaps?'

'Uh, yes, ma'am.'

'I hate it when you call me that, Rowan. It always ends up with me telling porkies to someone in gold braid.' Ruth took a deep breath. 'I assume you think that if the department conducting the investigation get hold of it, they'll put the thumbscrews on your incarcerated convict, which will screw up the "rapport", as you put it, between him and your DC Melton.'

'That's the crux of it, and the knock-on effect will be to lose our only pair of ears on the other side of the fence regarding what may have happened to Johnny Millard. Oh, *and* his wife, who has just slipped off the radar as well.'

'Jesus,' muttered Ruth, 'this just gets better and better. Okay, okay. I'll tell them there are similar rumours doing the rounds in Saltern-le-Fen and the surrounding area, but we have no names as yet, only that the criminal fraternity is on edge.' She glared at him. 'That satisfy you?'

'Perfect,' he said, and chanced a grateful smile. 'Thank you, Ruth. That will buy Marie and Robbie some time, while the rest of us get down to tackling the pillbox murders. On that score, Rory has promised us a prelim report today, and then we will be able to move forward. We are all prepared and ready to go, and—'

'All right, Rowan, I get the message. Now, I suggest you sod off and do some work, while I prepare the tissue of lies I'm to pass upstairs.'

Jackman responded with alacrity, and was out of the office and breathing a long sigh of relief before Ruth could pick up her pen. It was probably only a stay of execution, but it would have to do for now.

* * *

Lucas and Nina had been working on their plan all morning. Now, as lunchtime approached, they took a break and assessed their progress.

'I'm still hesitating about which is the best way to lure the brothers away from the house. That Tiffany table lamp is gorgeous, but unless I offer them something of real value and scarcity, they won't take the bait.'

He passed Nina two glossy photos of a couple of the Art Deco items from his own private collection.

'Not my bag really,' she said, 'but that second one is stunning. Where did you get it?'

Lucas regarded the photo wistfully. 'A legitimate purchase made years ago. It's one of my favourite pieces. It's designed by Maurice Ascalon, whom some consider to be the father of the modern Israeli decorative arts movement. The brothers have nothing like it in their collection, so it could do the trick. *If* I manage to steel myself to sacrifice it.'

'Really, Lucas, if you could see your face! As you English so quaintly put it, it's a sprat to catch a mackerel, and look what it will be providing! A room full of unique and beautiful pieces.'

The object in question was an extremely rare solid bronze and brass container, hand enamelled inside, and with a Verdigris patina lid. Lucas hated the thought of letting this lovely piece go even for a minute, let alone forever, but he knew it would take something rare and very special to tempt these avid collectors to leave their retreat.

'Go with that one,' urged Nina. 'It will work. Who's going to take it to the dealer?'

'Jean-Paul. He's staying at my London house while I'm away. I'll ring him shortly and get him to pack it up and drive it down to Artie's place in Bristol. Artie and his sons are all prepared to receive our "buyers", and to detain them long enough for our purposes.'

Jean-Paul was Lucas's cousin, and had worked with him for years. He kept Lucas's personal affairs running smoothly while he was away 'on business'. He was family, and therefore Lucas trusted him implicitly. Artie was a reputable dealer whom Lucas had cultivated in the course of many years. He and his two adult sons were not averse to doing a little private work for Lucas if he made it worth their while — which Lucas always did. Furthermore, the Greene brothers had dealt with Artie in the past, so they would not be surprised to receive a call from him about a new and exciting acquisition coming in.

'So, if everything's in place, I suggest we have a quick lunch. I'll ring Jean-Paul, and then we'll go over the whole thing again just to make sure.'

Nina raised an eyebrow. 'And what little delight do you have in mind for lunch?'

'Considering your aversion to healthy food, my dear, I called into the supermarket before you arrived, and bought you a chicken, bacon and mayo sandwich, a packet of crisps, and a Double Decker.'

She grinned. 'Now, that's what I call healthy food. Thank you. What are you having?'

171

'Miso roasted tofu with power grains, broccoli, peas and edamame, if you really want to know.'

Nina rolled her eyes. 'I might have known. Serves me right for asking.'

Lunch over, they took their coffee to the dining room and took their seats at a table covered in notes, printouts, maps, diagrams, and photographs, along with two top-of-the-range laptops.

After an hour of intense concentration, they sat back in their chairs. Barring a few last-minute phone calls, they were ready to go. Lucas had been careful to ensure that everyone involved knew exactly what they had to do, including what to wear, the routes to be taken, and when they were to link up. Overnight, the vehicles had been procured and marked with the logos of various trades. Nina had memorised all the pieces on the client's two wish lists, along with where they were distributed around the house. Nothing else was to be removed. It was a tight schedule, but if they kept strictly to plan, the operation would go like clockwork. The team Lucas had assembled had worked with him on eight successful jobs, and had proved to be trustworthy and reliable. The new man, in particular, had been recommended to Lucas by one of the biggest art thieves in the world.

He received the call he'd been waiting for. Turning to Nina, he said, 'Bingo! The replacement window is ready and loaded onto the lorry. All the tools required for exchanging it with the stained-glass one have been double-checked and are in the cab. They've also loaded a roll of special fleece wrap to both protect and conceal the Art Deco window once it's in.' He chuckled. 'I asked James how long he predicted it would take, and he compared it to an FI pitstop tyre change. He said that if I blinked, I'd miss it.'

'And then we all drive off into the sunset,' said Nina.

'Only, some of us will return,' he said.

'We certainly will. And we'll start all over again, but with no client to worry about.'

172

Lucas felt a thrill of anticipation. 'Now we have everything in place, there's no point hanging about. I'll ring Artie and tell him to contact the Greene brothers. We go tomorrow.'

An hour later, the call came back. 'They have agreed to be there at two p.m. tomorrow afternoon. Artie told them he had another client eager to see the Ascalon box, but he wanted them to have first option.' Lucas ran his tongue over his top lip. 'They almost bit his hand off for it. Nina! We are on!'

* * *

By lunchtime, Marie and Robbie had phoned every B&B in the area. None had a guest answering the description of Anna Millard. They extended the search to small hotels, with the same negative response. Marie then moved on to the bigger hotels, thinking that Anna might have decided she'd have a better chance of passing unnoticed in somewhere with a larger number of guests. All to no avail.

'I give up,' muttered Robbie, and sat back. 'We're just going to have to wait until she contacts you.'

'*If* she does.' Marie was beginning to wonder if Anna would contact her at all. That message had not rung true, and the thought of it rankled. Orac had informed her that the last call from their contact phone had been made from the area around Anna's friend's house, and no calls had been made since. So, had that message been sent under duress, simply to get Marie out of the equation for a while? Or, had Anna been scared enough to decamp in a hurry? There could be another reason behind it, of course, which was that Johnny had turned up, and they were both now running scared.

'So, what's next?' asked Robbie.

Marie sighed. 'Damned if I know. The traffic cameras have recorded no sign of Anna's car on the roads leading away from Dowdyke End, so that's the end of that. I guess all we can do is wait it out and keep our ears to the ground while we pitch in and help the boss with the Pillbox Killer investigation.'

'Sounds like a plan,' said Robbie. 'I'll keep in close contact with Harry, and do a daily check of possible sightings. Other than that, we are stumped, so rather than sit and stare at a blank screen, we might as well be doing something useful.'

Marie pushed back her chair and stood up. 'I'll go and update Jackman, and get a status report on their case, and we'll take it from there.'

She entered Jackman's office just as he was putting down the phone. He smiled at her grimly. 'That was forensics. We have a timeline on the victims from the pillbox, Marie. At last we can move forward!'

'And if you like, you can have two additional detectives to help you.' She dropped down into a chair, 'We've run up against a blank wall, and have been forced to press the pause button on Anna Millard.' She went on to explain that there had been no sightings of the fugitive woman.

Jackman's face said it all. 'Oh, that's great, Marie. I'll be very glad of your help, especially as we now know approximately when the deaths occurred. Other details are sketchy so far, but Rory and Jan are pushing hard to get us some answers. All the victims died within an eighteen-month period, Marie. The oldest body has been dead for nigh on three years, and the most recent died around one and a half years ago. Eighteen months of continuous killing. Forgive the glazed expression, but I've just had one of Rory's lectures, this one having to do with the rate of decomposition and skeletonization being dependent on the cause of death, the weight of the deceased, and environmental factors. And so on and so forth.' He gave Marie a somewhat exasperated smile.

'Wow, so we are looking for people who went missing during or just before the year 2023. Kind of depending on whether they were killed immediately, or possibly held prisoner somewhere before being killed,' said Marie.

'Exactly. And thank heavens it's not any further back in time, or our job would be a whole lot harder,' said Jackman. 'When we first saw those bones, I was expecting an historic crime, which would have made it really difficult to solve. At least people can recall what happened a couple of years back with some degree of clarity.'

'So, what would you like us to do, boss? Robbie and I are ready to rumble.'

'If you would round up the others, we'll meet in the CID room and I'll give everyone the news from forensics. After that, I'm off to meet with Rory. How about you come with me, and Robbie joins the rest of the team when I've allocated jobs?'

'Sounds good to me. I'll be happy to have something to take my mind off Anna,' Marie pulled a face, 'even if it is five dead bodies.' She hurried off, and soon everyone was gathered for the briefing, with the exception of Kevin, who was out trying to track down one of the farmer's former employees whom he — the farmer — had found a bit strange.

After the briefing, Jackman told the team to head for Fendyke Village and start asking questions. As soon as Kevin returned, he and Gary would start by talking to Bryson Smith and his family, to find out as much as they could about the inhabitants of the village, particularly the previous owners of the bungalow. Max and Robbie were asked to prioritise people like the vicar, the landlord of the Ruddy Duck pub, and any of the more prominent figures, such as the chairman of the Women's Institute and the bowling club.

'Note down the names of everyone you talk to, and record their accounts of any disappearances, as well as people who have suddenly upped and moved away. You're going to have an awful lot of flannel and gossip to sift through, I'm afraid, but don't forget there's often a grain of truth in the wildest rumours. Oh, and anyone who bothers you in some way. I'd like a separate list of those.'

'How much do we tell them, boss?' asked Max.

'Well, they are going to see the whole thing blasted across the headlines tomorrow morning, so we have to tell them something. Not the gory details, as they haven't been released, but tell the villagers that it is a murder enquiry.' Jackman glanced at his watch. 'I need to get over to the morgue, so you guys move out as soon as possible. And, Gary, ring Kevin and see where he is, would you? If he's still out Fendyke way, tell him to wait for you there, and you can join him.'

'You got it, sir.' Gary pulled out his phone and called Kevin. 'He's still there, so I'm going to meet him at the Smiths' bungalow.'

'Off you all go, then.' Jackman turned to Marie. 'Prepare yourself to face yet another edifying tutorial on death and its multiple causes — our much-loved pathologist is obviously back on form.'

'Can't wait,' said Marie. 'You driving, or shall I?'

CHAPTER SEVENTEEN

Bob Ruston pulled his chair closer to the hospital bed. 'Hello, lad. I'm Bob. I'm not sure if you remember me, but it was my door you knocked on the other morning, and . . . well, I just wanted to say I'm sorry for not letting you in.' He gave a rueful smile. 'Boy, did my wife read me the riot act after that! So, anyway, apart from apologising, I also wanted to explain the reason why I made you wait outside.'

Bob went on to describe the extraordinary lengths thieves went to to gain entry to a house. He said he'd been concerned about his wife and son's safety. He finally told his silent companion about the two cars that had drawn up outside the house after he'd disappeared. The young man's jaw tensed, but he remained mute.

'Come on, lad, I can't keep calling you "lad", can I? It makes you sound like Wallace's dog, Gromit. Surely you can tell me your first name, there's no harm in that, is there?' Bob fell silent, while he tried to think what to say. 'Truth is, I feel responsible for what happened to you after you left my garden. It must have been bad, or you wouldn't be here.'

The young man merely shifted slightly in his bed.

'So, I'd like to help you if I can,' finished Bob.

His voice little more than a croak, the patient said, 'Craig. My name's Craig.'

Feeling like giving a loud "hurrah", Bob said evenly, 'I guess you're keeping mum to protect someone. Thing is, that doesn't work with villains. The police are very worried that whoever this person is could be in danger. All they want to do is make sure they're safe, and if necessary get them out of harm's way. They don't suspect you of anything, and you're not in any trouble.'

'I—'

Craig bit on his already split lip, and winced.

Then Bob got it. 'You really don't know why you were taken, do you?'

Craig shook his head, and his eyes filled with tears. 'I'm no angel, but I've never done anything criminal in my life. I was just on my way to my gran's house when they took me.'

'So, is it your grandmother you're so worried about?' Bob asked.

The tears were falling freely now. 'She's my best friend, my gran is. When my mum and dad split up it was her took me in, even though she's had such a rotten life herself. I'll never forgot what she did for me. I'm really frightened about what's going to happen to her. They said they'd kill her!'

'So they knew about her, then,' Bob said. 'Did you tell them?'

'No,' Craig said. 'I never said a word.'

'Well, if they knew about *her*, they must've known about you, so it was not a case of mistaken identity. But why abduct you, that's what doesn't make sense.'

Craig shrugged.

'You say you've done nothing illegal, but do you know anyone who has? Maybe you witnessed a crime, and the guys involved saw you watching,' Bob asked.

'No, and don't think I haven't racked my brains trying to remember. I've had enough time in the past few days to practically go over my whole life,' Craig wailed.

Bob leaned forward and patted the young man's arm. 'You're safe now, Craig, and when you're better they'll get you some counselling, which will help. But right now, the most important thing is to make sure your gran is safe, we can think about why you were taken later. So, how about giving me her address? Then I can pass it on to the police.'

Craig sank back against his pillows, evidently torn between his trust of Bob and fear of his captors, and the threats they had made.

After a while, he seemed to come to a decision. 'If I do, can someone go who doesn't look like a copper?'

'That's no problem at all,' Bob assured him. 'They'll send a plainclothes officer who'll be very discreet. They'll make sure that she's safe, but they won't frighten her, I promise. I expect she's worried sick that you haven't been round to see her as usual, so someone needs to tell her you're okay.'

Craig looked up at him. 'Would you go, Bob? She wouldn't speak to a copper, but I think she'd trust you.'

Bob thought about his wife and son. He never left them for longer than a trip to the shops, a pint in the local or a dog walk along the sea bank. What if Troy had a bad day? What if . . . ? Then he heard himself say, 'Does your gran like dogs?'

Ten minutes later, Bob left the room clutching a piece of paper bearing an address in Huntingdon. By doing this, he'd be discharging his responsibility, and his good-hearted Daisy would approve. He just had to convince the police that this was the best move. Maybe that nice PC Simon Laker would be able to swing it for him.

As soon as Bob emerged into the corridor, the constable hurried towards him. 'Any luck?'

Bob gave him a thumbs-up. 'I have his name, and also the name and address of the person he's protecting.' Bob hesitated. 'Now I have a big favour to ask.'

Simon looked delighted, relieved, and then suspicious in quick succession. 'What kind of favour?'

'Well, it's like this . . .'

It hadn't been easy for Marie to push aside her concern for Anna Millard, especially because with every hour that passed with no word and no sighting, Marie became increasingly convinced that something had happened to her. Having found the courage to walk into the police station and ask for help, and then provide a secure way of keeping in contact, why on earth would Anna suddenly go off the radar?

The problem with Anna had been playing on her mind all the way to Rory's laboratory, until the moment when she stood in the observer's gallery, looking down on Professor Jan Wallace working on Victim One from the pillbox.

Standing next to her, Rory noticed her expression.

'I cannot tell you how grateful I am to that magnificent woman,' he said, pointing at Jan. 'Apart from having a brain the size of a pumpkin, she's one of the most level-headed people I've ever met. That woman, dear heart, has a rare ability to use her reason, even when faced with such a case as this. She would have none of my flights of fancy, and certainly wasn't going to stand for any maudlin sentimentality on the part of yours truly. I'm positively rejuvenated, thanks to our Jan.' He regarded them both thoughtfully. 'And you'd do well to remember that she's just as capable of putting anxious detectives back on the right path. Now, let's go to my office. I'll bring you up to speed, and then I must get gowned up and back to work before said lady gets her whip out.' He winced. 'I'm a lot of things, my cherubs, but a masochist is not one of them!'

They followed Rory back into more familiar terrain, entering his office to find Spike placing four fancy beakers of coffee on the desk.

'I thought you could do with a bit of caffeine to revive you after your stint on the viewing platform,' he said. 'I even went so far as to go out for some of the real stuff. There's a new coffee shop opened around the corner, and their coffee is crazy good!'

Indeed it was, and Marie started to finally unwind.

Rory leaned back in his chair. 'Here's the plan. Today, I shall give you a general description of each victim — gender, height, approximate age, hair colour, and anything that marks them out as unusual. That should help you to sketch an initial outline of these people. Following that, Jan and I will take each victim in turn, and run all the relevant tests. As soon as they are in, our redoubtable Jan can give you a more detailed account of her findings.' Rory sniffed appreciatively at his coffee. 'And I think you'll be amazed at just how much that lady will be able to tell you from their remains. Do you know,' he leaned forward, his eyes shining behind his glasses, 'from a pathetic heap of bones, she is able to reconstruct where a person lived, how far they travelled, and even what they ate. Everything leaves a trace, dear hearts. Anyway, starting with the obvious, we took each one's DNA and had a look at what it shows. If that proved insufficient, we then brought in Jan, our secret weapon.' He took a long drink of his coffee. 'Thus far, we have ascertained how long ago these people died, and the order in which they were killed, although two victims seem to have died in a single year, so further tests will be necessary in their case. The first to die was a man whom we believe was in his forties, around five feet ten inches tall with grey hair. His clothes were mostly nylon, so had not decomposed, and indicated that he hadn't been very well off.'

'His shirt still had the logo of a discount warehouse store on it,' added Spike, 'and that and the other garments suggest he may have been an agricultural labourer — field worker to you lot from the Fens.'

'Between our facility here, and Jan's university, we have the very latest technology available to us — more than you could ever dream about. The science of forensics is moving forward at the speed of light. Meaning that Jan is no soothsayer reading bones around a campfire, but is a veritable fount of cutting-edge diagnostic techniques.' He glanced at Marie. 'I told you she had a brain the size of a pumpkin, and I wasn't joking.'

'That's one awesome lady,' said Spike, and turned to Rory. 'Can we show them our new toy?'

'Indeed! If you've finished your coffee, we shall adjourn to the conference room.'

'You have a conference room?' Jackman said. 'That's new, isn't it?'

'The excellence of our work has finally been recognised, dear hearts — and not before time, I might add. At last I have some long-overdue new equipment installed, and a very nice room in which to show it off.'

Five minutes later, they were all seated in padded chairs around a semi-circular conference table facing what appeared to be a blank wall. Rory dimmed the lights, and the wall revealed itself as a massive screen. He tapped on it. 'You are about to see an automated record of all our findings regarding our victims. And . . . using AI, it will interpret those findings for us.'

'We've given them names until you guys find their real ones,' whispered Spike. 'The Prof likes to personalise them. He reckons it makes them seem more like people, and not just objects.'

Marie knew this of old, and totally understood it.

'Victim One is "Eamonn", as the Prof is certain he's of Irish descent,' Spike whispered.

'And here we have him — our Eamonn,' Rory touched the screen again.

Marie's eyes widened. An image of the dead man as he had been found filled the enormous screen. A few more swipes and taps from Rory followed, as if he was scrolling through a giant mobile phone, and the victim's skeleton appeared.

'And here's our most interesting find so far.' Rory zoomed in on the skull, then rotated the image to show the back of the skull, which was badly fractured. 'Blunt force trauma, to the most vulnerable spot on the head.' He turned to look at them. 'All your victims were killed in the same fashion, my friends. All struck from behind with enormous force.' He grimaced. 'One thing I will say is that your killer is immensely powerful.

182

One single blow, and this poor man died almost instantaneously from brain stem herniation.'

'And that is?' asked Marie.

'I can do better than merely tell you. With our magic wall, I can show you,' said Rory, obviously delighted to be able to show it off. 'Oh, how I love this thing!' He tapped the screen and the image of a skull appeared. 'And this, my cherub, is what happened . . .' As Rory went through his description of what happened — that the skull protected the brain from damage, but that should a bleed occur, the solid carapace is unable to expand causing pressure to build up — the image on the screen showed the bleed spread through the brain and push downwards.

'First, the increasing pressure shuts down brain function,' explained Rory. 'Then it forces the brain material down to the foramen magnus, which is the only opening, and where the spinal cord is joined to the skull.'

So this is what had happened to one of the people she was working to get justice for. Marie found this whole state-of-the-art experience quite disturbing. She glanced at Jackman, whose expression said he felt the same way. Knowing about it and actually seeing how it happened added a whole new dimension to what had been done to their victim.

'. . . And then consciousness is lost, breathing stops, and death occurs, which, following such a severe injury, would take minutes. In the case of a less punishing blow, the process can take hours, even days.' Rory swiped at the screen, and the image disappeared.

Marie thought about the last woman to die. Had she too died in this way? Had it been a less brutal blow? And if so, had she remained alive in that pillbox for many hours? She shivered.

'Any thoughts on a murder weapon?' Jackman was asking.

'That's my next job,' said Spike. 'We know that whatever hit him was very heavy, and had a flat surface but with possibly a ridge in it.'

'We do know that's it's not a hammer, or the like, because of the nature of the fracture,' added Rory, 'but we'll let you know the minute Spike comes up with something.' He gave a little bow. 'Presentation over, dear friends, and thank you for joining me on the bridge of the Starship *Enterprise*. Beam me up, Scotty!'

On the journey back to Saltern-le-Fen, Marie kept saying how amazed she was at the new developments in Rory's domain.

'I'm not surprised,' said Jackman. 'We tend to think of Rory as a colourful character, a bit of a comedian, but he has quite a reputation in the forensic world. He's full of praise for Jan Wallace's brilliance, but he's way up there in his own right.'

'He certainly deserves it,' said Marie. 'It's just with so many cutbacks these days, I found it rather surprising.'

Jackman gave her a sideways look. 'Think about it, Marie. It's a bit like Orac. The additional work she does for the various services calls for top-of-the-range equipment. Rory is often called upon as an expert witness and a consultant on high-profile cases well beyond the sleepy Fens. Lucky old us, we get to benefit from the facilities they're accorded.'

'I can't disagree with that,' said Marie. 'But I can't help feeling a little left behind.' She was reluctant to admit it but the recent advances in technology frightened her. AI was suddenly everywhere, and whereas in areas like medicine it could only be beneficial, in others, particularly the media, she no longer had any idea of what was true and what false. It left her feeling helpless.

'I think we need to accept that it's here to stay, and that all we can do is make use of it, because it's beyond our understanding,' said Jackman. 'It will speed up our investigations, that's for sure. Like actually seeing a blunt force trauma and what it does. I mean, Spike will probably have identified the weapon used by the time I'm parking up at the station.'

'I guess you're right. What else can we do but use it to our advantage,' said Marie. 'Although I'm not yet ready to embrace it.'

184

Jackman laughed. 'Just don't be scared of it, because there's no going back.'

'Ain't that the truth!' she said. 'Even for a Welsh dinosaur like me.'

* * *

'So, how are things going with our newbie?' Orac asked Leon as he laid some printouts on her desk.

'Good,' replied her top technician, 'Actually, very good. She's fitted in with our little team perfectly. She will be an asset, I know it, and her expertise is undeniable.' He smiled at her. 'And she's very much in awe of you. I don't mean you personally — she hasn't got a crush or anything —but of your skills and ability.'

Orac inclined her head. 'That lady has plenty of skills and abilities of her own. The Met were pretty pissed off when she decided to relocate. It was mentioned several times in her references. They weren't happy bunnies at all.'

'She asked me if I'd like to meet her father,' said Leon. 'So I'll be popping in after work, just to say hello. Coral said that he's lived in Kirby Fenside for more than twenty-five years. He lost his best friend recently, so he's a bit low. She thought meeting a new face might cheer him up.'

'She said he's not in the best of health,' said Orac.

'No. From what she says, it sounds like some form of arthritis. Apparently, he's not very mobile, and being inactive doesn't sit well with him. He must be delighted that she's decided to move here and he can see more of her.'

'And we benefit too. Win-win all round,' said Orac.

She didn't tell Leon that her vetting of Coral had also included her father, William McIvor. Leon had been right, he did suffer from osteoarthritis, and several other health problems that impeded his movement. In fact, there was little that Orac didn't know about Coral. Not that she was so very interested in her on her own account, but the sensitive material

185

they had access to meant that her staff had to be absolutely trustworthy.

As Leon turned to leave, Orac said, 'Ask Coral to come and see me when she has a free moment, would you?'

'No need, chief, she's heading this way now.'

'Everything okay, Coral?' asked Orac.

'Absolutely,' replied Coral, 'except that I'm quite astounded to find myself working on the same issues as I was in the Met. Who'd have thought that friend Chaos would be so active out here in rural Lincolnshire? It's bizarre.'

'I suppose distance and location mean nothing to a hacker, but you're right about his presence in the Fens. Surely, we're pretty small potatoes compared to what goes on in the Smoke.'

'Maybe he just likes it here. And who's to say he was even in the city in the first place. No one has ever managed to pin him down to a specific location.' Coral made a face. 'I keep referring to this person as a "him", but they could just as well be a woman.'

'Me too,' said Orac. 'For some reason I see him as a man, but I have nothing other than instinct to go on.'

Coral smiled. 'Maybe we'll get a surprise when we finally take the mask off. They were running a book back at the Met, and the odds were definitely in favour of a woman. But the Met is predominantly male anyway, and they probably fancied having a gorgeous Mata Hari as their adversary.'

Orac wondered how many of them fancied the gorgeous Coral McIvor, but she kept that to herself.

'Well, no matter what gender they are,' Coral said, 'I still believe they've worked either for the State, or some really big corporation. He's way beyond being some nerdy kid in their bedroom. He's a pro, and he's really . . . well, causing chaos.'

'Aptly named then,' Orac said.

'Oh, very,' said Coral. 'It's a funny thing, you know, but after I decided to move here and be closer to my dad, I was relieved that I'd no longer be having Chaos to deal with. Then, when I did leave the Met, I found I couldn't forget him.

I'm actually delighted to be back hunting him again. I've a feeling I would have ended up spending my nights trying to track him down from home.'

'And all your background knowledge will save us from going down rabbit holes and into cul-de-sacs.' Orac's mirror-eyes flashed at her new recruit. 'Stick with it, Coral. Between us, we'll get him.'

'God! I do hope so.' Coral hesitated. 'There's just one thing you should know. Back in Cybercrime, I started noticing a small anomaly that cropped up from time to time in our efforts to track him. It's my belief, and it's entirely unsubstantiated, that he's not working alone.'

Orac stared at her. Nothing she had come across pointed in that direction. For a start, hackers were invariably loners.

'Don't get me wrong. He works alone, but occasionally there seems to be input from another source.' Coral frowned. 'On two separate occasions, I was on the verge of making a breakthrough when all of a sudden, I was blocked.'

'But that must have been Chaos himself, surely. He must have an impenetrable firewall,' Orac said.

'That was my first thought, but no, it came from somewhere else, I know it did. It got me thinking about another job I worked on, years ago. I won't bore you with the details, but in a nutshell, the person under investigation was a first-class hacker working with a criminal organisation. Well, this guy had what's called a "guardian", another operative who watched his back during risky undertakings.'

'And you think Chaos has a guardian?' asked Orac.

'I do.'

Orac immediately recalled how Johnny Millard's computer had been mysteriously wiped while in secure storage deep in the heart of the Serious Crimes Unit. They had believed the person responsible to be whoever framed Johnny, but what if it was a guardian?

'It's either that, or there's another scenario,' said Coral gravely. 'Something even more scary. What if someone else is tracking Chaos, and they want him as badly as we do? And they close us down if we get too close.'

Orac drew in a long breath. It was all too horribly possible. 'As in, they're not protecting him, but seeing us off?'

Coral nodded. 'I know which of those two possibilities I'd prefer.'

'No contest,' murmured Orac with a shiver. 'Oh my, that makes things really messy.'

Coral turned to leave. It was three o'clock, and the working day was over for her.

Orac watched her go. Their latest recruit was unaware of the full capabilities of the unit she had just joined, and had no inkling of Orac's connection to higher powers outside that unit. And until Coral McIvor had served her probation, it would stay that way.

Coral had given Orac a lot to think about, and she needed time alone. Decisions would have to be made as to where to go from here, and who to let into her confidence. It wasn't going to be easy.

CHAPTER EIGHTEEN

The team met back in the CID room at five, when the day would normally be ending. No one was clock watching. They had a killer to find.

'I won't keep you long tonight,' said Jackman, 'but don't get used to it. We could be having quite a few very late ones from now on.'

Jackman stood with his back to the wall beside an empty whiteboard that he had had to fight to hang onto. These days most other stations used digital ones. He wasn't averse to those, but he knew Marie and Gary were more comfortable with the old version. Naturally, the younger detectives were itching for a new one, but they'd just have to wait. Keeping his two senior officers happy was more important.

He reported what Rory had said about Victim One, and attached photos of him and his injury to the whiteboard.

'This man was the first to die. Rory has given him the name of Eamonn.' Jackman pointed to the second image showing the massive fracture to the back of his skull. 'Note that this is how all of them died — blunt force trauma to the back of the head. Although, until Rory and his people have completed their tests it's all we have so far.'

'Has the weapon been identified yet?' asked Gary.

'Not yet, but I'm expecting a call from Spike to tell me precisely what we're looking at. Apparently, it's an unusual shape and he needs to look at a few possibilities.' Jackman turned away from the board. 'Now, did any of you find out anything interesting from the villagers?'

Gary stood up. 'We've just been comparing notes, boss. As you'd expect, there was quite a lot of talk about people who'd left the village at around that time, but nothing to make anyone's antenna buzz.'

'Well, sifting through rumours and gossip isn't an easy task. Better luck tomorrow, guys. Now get yourselves off home.'

As the rest of the team trooped out of the room, Kevin hung back. 'Um, sir. Have you got a few moments? There's something bothering me.'

Jackman sat down and pointed to a chair. 'Of course, Kevin. What's the problem?'

'It's about the work we've been doing interviewing the villagers . . .'

'Go on.'

'Two of the people Gary and I talked to mentioned someone who knows everything about what goes on in that village. They said she never misses a thing. The thing is, I don't know how to approach her.' Kevin told Jackman about his encounter with the woman and the fox.

'And she never speaks at all?' asked Jackman. 'Most people who know all the gossip can't be stopped.'

'Not Mad Sally, sir,' sighed Kevin. 'At first I thought maybe she had something wrong with her and couldn't speak, so I spoke to the local GP. But he said she has no physical impediment, she can talk if she wants, but chooses not to. So now I'm a bit stuck. I've no idea how to go about it. Nor does Gary, and that's never happened before. She's . . . well, she's pretty intimidating, sir. You should have seen the look she gave me when I stopped to ask her about the fox. I'm telling you, it could have frozen hell over.'

Jackman barely managed to keep a straight face, although Kevin was obviously really concerned. 'You know what these out-of-the-way villages are like — they have at least one oddball, and we usually find a way to get something out of them. Maybe you could get Marie to go with you? She has a way of getting people to talk. If anyone can get this Mad Sally to speak, it'll be her.'

Jackman recalled a past case involving a tough and belligerent Fen woman — Marie had been awesome with her. 'If this woman really is disturbed in some way, I think another woman would likely have more success with her than a male plod.' He looked at Kevin. 'A fox, you say? Sure it wasn't a dog? My mother looked after a little Japanese hunting dog once, I forget the breed, Shiba something, but it looked exactly like a fox with red fur and the same pointy nose.'

In a tone of somewhat weary patience, Kevin said, 'It was a fox, sir. An old crewmate of mine who lives around there said it walks with her every day.'

Jackman raised his hands in surrender. 'I stand corrected. Sorry.'

Kevin broke into a smile. 'It does sound ridiculous, doesn't it, sir? It made me wonder if I was seeing things. I'll certainly get Marie to go with me tomorrow.'

'If I were you, I'd stay well in the background, and let Marie approach her on her own,' suggested Jackman. 'You and Gary can be nearby in case she needs any help.'

Kevin stood up. 'Got it, sir, and thank you.'

When Marie joined him, Jackman told her about Kevin's problem. 'There's always one, isn't there? How many oddballs have we come across in the course of our investigations, I wonder?'

'Too many!' she said. 'But it doesn't pay to overlook them, does it? People often let down their guard in the presence of someone they consider to be the village idiot.'

'And as we've discovered in the past, they are far from being country bumpkins, and often turn out to be a lot more savvy than people realised.'

'I wonder what this Mad Sally's story is? People don't just decide not to speak to anyone unless they've a damn good reason,' Marie said.

'Ah, good,' Jackman said with a smile. 'I'm pleased to see your interest has been piqued, Sergeant Evans, because it's your first job tomorrow. See if you can get this woman to talk.'

'I accept your challenge, Detective Inspector Jackman, but right now, I'm off home for a leisurely dinner with my husband while I still can.'

'Sensible move. As for me, good old Hettie Maynard has promised to leave me one of her famous beef hotpots, plus some of my favourite herb dumplings.'

'Mmm, tasty!' Marie licked her lips. 'At least I never have to worry about you starving while Hettie's around to look after you. It's Ralph's day off, so I'm hoping I, too, have a culinary delight awaiting me.' She pulled her leather jacket from the back of her chair and turned to go. 'Oh, by the way, I forgot to tell you, Ralph said if we need outside help with this murder investigation, Ruth can contact DCI Barclay at Fenchester. Ralph is sure he'll be able to raise a few volunteers if we need them.'

'Good to know, Marie, especially as our DS Vic Blackwell has been detained for at least another day on his secondment, and who knows where this case will take us? Thank Ralph for me, won't you? We might very well need some extra help.'

Alone in the CID room, his words came back to him. Where exactly would this case take them? His gaze drifted to the image of the skull fracture on the whiteboard, and he considered again the rage that must have impelled the killer to inflict such a devastating injury. For a second, he could almost feel the impact on his own skull. Jackman shuddered. Time to go home.

* * *

Lucas and Nina sat facing each other across the table going over the final plans for the following day. Nina had even condescended to share Lucas's meal, and much to her surprise, had enjoyed it. In future, she said, she would cut him a bit of slack regarding his healthy diet. It made Lucas feel good to hear her say 'future'. The two of them made a good team, and with her at his side, and Chaos's expertise, they couldn't possibly fail to pull off some spectacular heists, becoming, in the process, very rich indeed.

Nina sat back. 'As far as I'm concerned, it's foolproof. Now, I should get home and rest. It's a big day tomorrow, and I want to be on top form.'

Lucas could not imagine Nina being anything other than on top form. She never seemed to tire, her attention never flagged and her commitment was absolute. 'Of course,' he said, 'and I shall do the same. And do you know, tomorrow is not just a big day, it could well prove to be the biggest of my life.'

Nina stood up. 'And we'll enjoy every minute of it, Lucas, especially when we drive away for the second time.'

Much to his surprise, when he saw her off at the door she gave him a light kiss on the cheek.

'I'll see you as arranged. And tomorrow night, we celebrate.'

And then she was gone, leaving Lucas feeling utterly bemused. In all the years he had worked with Nina, she had never been anything other than completely professional. The kiss, little more than a slight touch of her lips, had caught him unawares.

He returned to the kitchen and sat thinking for a while. As long as the brothers went ahead with their trip to Bristol, the job should run like clockwork. Artie was going to ring him as soon as the deal was done. If the job was taking more time than expected, the Greene brothers would find themselves 'delayed' by a broken-down vehicle blocking the exit from the antique dealers' car park. Lucas didn't think this would be necessary, but it was always good to have a contingency plan. Expect the unexpected, he thought, and you won't get caught out. Thinking of things unexpected, he thought of the touch of Nina's lips on his cheek. That was unexpected, all right, and so out of character. For some reason, it worried him. What did it mean? Was she trying to get something out of him? More than her agreed share? She was certainly avaricious enough.

Lucas stood up abruptly, his chair legs squealing on the tiles. This was not how he should be spending the night before a job. He needed to be in the zone. He needed sleep. He couldn't afford to waste his energies worrying about a little kiss, for God's sake. 'Concentrate!' he said, his voice sounding unnaturally loud in the silence. There would be plenty of time for such things when the robbery was over, and he had his precious treasures safely in his hands.

* * *

Unable to sleep, Bryson Smith heard noises downstairs in the kitchen. Evidently, his mother couldn't sleep either, or was it his father? With a sigh, he raised himself off the pillows and sat on the edge of the bed for a moment, before getting up. He hoped it was only their arthritis keeping them awake, and not the murders playing on their mind.

He padded down to the kitchen in his bare feet to find his mother standing by the kettle, waiting for it to boil.

'Make that two, Mum,' he said softly, so as not to startle her.

'Three, actually, son. Your father can't sleep either.' She took another mug from the cupboard. 'I think it was having those two detectives here. It really brought the whole thing home to us. I — we — can't stop thinking about how we've been living alongside a killer. And who knows, maybe we still are. Now we don't know who to trust.'

'Oh, Mum, I'm so sorry this has happened. I feel responsible somehow, since it was me that found them,' said Bryson. He gave his mother a hug.

'Well, I'm jolly glad you did. Think of those poor souls lying in that cold, awful old bunker. People will have been fretting about them for years, wondering where they are, not knowing if they are dead or alive.' She hugged Bryson back. 'It's horrible, but it's a good thing you found them.'

Taking the milk from the fridge, Bryson said, 'There's no guarantees that the killer lives or lived around here, Mum. He might easily have brought them here from somewhere else. You know what they say about not dirtying your own doorstep.'

Looking both amused but reproving, she said, 'It's good of you to try and protect your dear old mum's delicate sensibilities, but do you honestly believe that? No, son, he was right here among us when he killed those people. What's more, I believe he still is.'

Bryson had no answer for this.

'I'll just take your dad his cuppa, and then we'll have a talk.'

She was back in seconds.

'Typical! I make him a brew, and now he's fast asleep,' she said. 'Well, good luck to him, I'm far from sleepy myself.'

They sat at the kitchen table nursing their mugs of tea in silence for a while.

'I was thinking about what the detectives asked us, you know — if there was anyone we considered a bit strange, or who bothered us in any way. It's made me look at the people in the village with different eyes.' Betty stared into her drink. 'And that's not a nice way to be, is it?'

'It's unavoidable, Mum. The seed has been sown. I don't like it any more than you, but it's human nature. And we aren't the only ones, I'm sure. Everyone will to be looking at their neighbours and wondering if they really know them at all.'

Betty sighed. 'Sad to say, but you're right. I'm just worried that some people might take it too far, like get an idea in their heads about someone in particular and make their lives hell.'

Bryson frowned. 'Surely no one would be that vindictive, would they? You make it sound like people will be engaging in witch-hunts!'

195

Betty shrugged. 'Well, that's not so far-fetched. There are a few very old families still living around here, people whose ancestors lived in the area when it was little more than a few scattered dwellings around a swamp. Without being unkind, many of them have very little learning, and some are bordering on . . . Oh, you know what I mean.'

'I do. The results of generations of inbreeding.' He sipped his tea. 'But there can't be many people like that left. Most are incomers, people who've moved here in the last couple of decades.' Bryson reached forward and touched her arm. 'Come on, Mum, you're one of the most sensible people I know. Don't let this get to you, and don't be swayed by what other people say. It's a horrible thing to happen, but sadly bad things do. And the police will find who did it, I'm sure.'

'I know,' said Betty, and smiled at him, looking more like her stoical self. 'Things always seem worse at night, don't they? I'll be fine again by tomorrow. Anyway, technically it's not even on our land. Donald Telford freely admitted that the pillbox is on his side of the boundary.'

As if that made any difference, thought Bryson, but it was a good way to distance herself from both it and the killings.

She drained her mug. 'And what's more, there are five villages in this locality, so it's more than possible that he's from one of the other ones.'

'Makes sense,' said Bryson, finishing his drink. 'And another thing. DC Stoner told me that the murders took place ages ago, none recently, so there's a good chance that either something happened to him, or it got too hot for him here and he's a hundred miles away by now.'

His mother merely shrugged.

'Anyway, Mum,' he said, 'I think it's time you tried to get some sleep now, don't you?'

'And you too, son. Don't worry about me, I'll be back smiling again tomorrow, and running my soup kitchen, never fear.'

Bryson kissed her goodnight, knowing that in her heart, she believed that the killer was still here in the village. And his mother was rarely wrong about anything.

Back in his room, he realised that sleep was going to be impossible. With a grunt, he pulled on his jog pants and a sweatshirt over his pyjamas, found his trainers, and, quietly as he could, unlocked the back door and went out, careful to lock it behind him. Nobody in the village had ever locked their doors before the bodies were discovered, and Bryson was sad that people now did so as a matter of routine. He had come out without the slightest idea of where he might go, but knowing there was still a police presence at the pillbox, he headed out in the opposite direction, into the fields that belonged to Donald Telford.

It was a beautiful night, with a brilliant glowing moon that dazzled if you dared to stare at it. He had heard earlier on the weather report that it was a supermoon tonight, and that was certainly the case. For a while, the tranquillity and the sheer beauty of the scene across the fields allowed him to forget the dreadful goings-on of the last few days, and he saw the vista as a nightscape painting. The brilliance of the moon and the deep dark shadows from the trees that edged the field caused a dramatic effect that in art is called chiaroscuro, which translates literally as 'light-dark'. Thinking of this, and of some of the artists who had mastered the technique to such perfection, Bryson suddenly missed his work and being in the city. He loved his parents to distraction, but suddenly he wanted away from the reality of what he'd discovered in that pillbox, and to be back in the world of creativity, imagination and art.

Sadly, that wasn't going to happen for some time. Not while his mum and dad's property was the hub of a murder enquiry.

He rounded a bend in the path and stopped, catching his breath. Just feet away from him, the pale and ghostly form of a barn owl was sitting on a tall fencepost. They regarded each other for what seemed an age, and then, very slowly, Bryson moved on, the bird turning its head to follow his progress. He turned back for a last look, and saw the magnificent bird flap its wings noiselessly and fly away into the night.

Still smiling at the brief, magical moment he'd been granted, he was brought up short by a movement in his peripheral vision. He turned abruptly, and peered. Whatever it was had been close to the boundary between his parents' and the farmer's land, in the copse of trees that hid the pillbox from view. A deer? For some reason he didn't think it was an animal. It seemed more, well, human.

Bryson stared hard at the point where he thought he'd detected movement. A tall figure emerged and hurried along the perimeter of the field. One of the police officers — it had to be. Laughing at himself for his stupidity — must have been the sight of that ghostly owl in the moonlight, he nevertheless went back to the police cordon.

The lone policeman on duty regarded him suspiciously as he approached. 'Couldn't sleep,' Bryson said. 'PC Chris Elliott, isn't it?'

Chris's expression cleared. 'Oh, it's you, Mr Smith. I didn't recognise you in the dark. Well, I'm not surprised you can't sleep what with all this going on in your back garden.'

'It's my mum and dad I'm worried about,' Bryson said. 'I can stay on for a bit longer, but not forever.'

'Don't you worry, sir, we've got the whole shebang onto it now. The detectives will be all over the village tomorrow, questioning everyone, and forensics are identifying the victims, so hopefully they'll get some leads soon, and find the bastard who did this. 'Scuse the language.'

'Don't apologise,' said Bryson, and started to move away. 'Oh. Fancy a cuppa? I can make you one if you like. I'll be a stand-in for my mum, though I can't promise to make tea like she does.'

Chris laughed his big laugh. 'No, sir, you're all right. I brought a flask with me, and Freddie, who's on duty with me did too. There's only us here tonight. Freddie's camped out at that creepy old pillbox. There's not much need for a full crew now they've taken the bodies out.'

Bryson frowned. 'He's at the pillbox, you say? He's not on patrol, then?'

'Yeah, poor old Freddie drew the short straw, and he's stuck there all night. Someone has to remain at that pillbox until forensics gives us the all clear. Why d'you ask?'

'I saw someone over by the copse, they were walking round the perimeter of the field under the trees. I thought it was one of you guys.'

'Bloody wasn't!' exclaimed Chris, and raised his radio to his lips.

The response was a crackle of static.

Calling back, 'Stay here!' Chris was already racing down the rutted track towards the pillbox.

'No way!' called Bryson. 'You might need a hand.'

'Well, watch your footing, then. It's lethal in the dark. Don't want a broken ankle.'

Unheeding, Bryson ran after him as fast as he could. He kept seeing that furtive figure moving towards the pillbox, and a single bored constable, alone by the copse.

At least the halogen lights were still on but the clearing in front of the pillbox was empty.

'Oh shit!' cried Chris, and began yelling, 'Freddie! Freddie!' He tried his radio again, and again the only response was static. Then he contacted the crew in the nearest squad car.

Soon the other two police officers had joined them. It formed a bizarre scene, the four of them, crashing through the tangled copse, in and out of deep shadow like a manic version of Bryson's beloved chiaroscuro.

He heard a noise coming from a spot close to the field edge. It was faint, but it sounded like a cry for help. 'Chris! I think I heard him. He's over there, and it sounds as if he's hurt!'

Bryson got there first. He saw the indistinct shape of a figure huddled beneath a tree, but without a torch, he couldn't make out much more. The others weren't far behind him, and their torch-beams lit up a young man, half-sitting, half-slouching on the ground.

'What took you so long,' PC Freddie Copeland whispered hoarsely. 'Rotten buggers. I . . . I've . . .' and his voice trailed off.

'There's blood on his collar,' said Bryson. 'And from the way he's slurring his words, I think he might have a concussion.'

One of the officers immediately rang for an ambulance, while Bryson and the others tried to keep the man awake.

Chris knelt beside his crewmate, and urged him to try and tell them what had happened. From what they understood from his disjointed account, it emerged that Freddie had heard a noise, and suspecting an over-zealous journalist, had gone to investigate, and had been struck from behind. The next thing he knew, he was lying in the bushes with the headache from hell. He hadn't seen his assailant.

'By the looks of it, the bloke who did it gave his radio a going-over, too,' remarked one of the PCs, pointing at the battered device that lay half-hidden under Freddie's arm.

'I don't get it,' said Chris, looking around. 'What the devil were they after? There's nothing here apart from a couple of bags of crap from the pillbox.'

Bryson had his own ideas, and none of them were pleasant. He shivered, wishing he didn't have such a vivid imagination. The old adage kept playing in a loop inside his head: the killer invariably returns to the scene of the crime.

CHAPTER NINETEEN

It was just after six in the morning, and a thick mist blanketed the Fens. It will soon burn off, Jackman thought, looking out at the blurred shapes of the shrubs outside the window. Thank goodness for that. Rain, plus fields and trampled ground equals mud, which hampers investigations and makes for bad-tempered detectives.

He noticed that Julia Tennant's car was still parked outside the mill, and smiled, pleased for his old friend Sam. Jackman had been afraid that coming to live in the place that had been Laura's would only make Sam's grief that much harder to bear. Now Julia was often around, he was in markedly better humour and had regained his zest for life. At first, seeing them together seemed to intensify his own grief. Now, however, it gave him hope. Since that strange episode in the car when he had felt Laura so close to him, he had begun to come to terms with her loss. He realised that not so very long ago he would have found the morning mist depressing. This morning, however, he saw it as a prelude to a good day.

* * *

Rory arrived at work early. He had not seen the mist as a good omen. His partner David had returned to work after a whole year at home since retiring from a highly stressful job as a water resource engineer in underdeveloped countries. David had now become a recruitment manager for his old company, and although this would not take him to some of the most dangerous places in the world, as his last position had, it did mean that he was away from home for days at a time. Waking up alone made Rory remember the times when David had been out of touch in some dreadful war-torn area, or far too close to an uprising, and Rory had learned the meaning of anguish. No matter how hard he tried to tell himself that there was little threat from sitting in a conference room in Sunderland, he still found himself watching his phone for the next message.

Spike was already working when Rory arrived at the mortuary. He and Cardiff had agreed on an arrangement whereby he started two hours early, while she spent a further two hours after the end of the day. As for Rory, David was away for three days on a consultancy, so he could work as many hours as he cared to, meaning that they could push on and provide the police with results sooner than they might have done.

In his office, he took stock of the current position. Yet again, he marvelled at what their expert forensic anthropologist had brought to the table. Rory was no slouch himself, and with all the technology now at their disposal, they no longer had to wait weeks for results to come back. Jan Wallace, however, was in a different league altogether, plus she was able to call on the resources of her department at the university. By end of the previous day, she had taken all the necessary samples. Tests were running, and she had produced a preliminary overview of the man they called Eamonn. Furthermore, while she awaited the results of the tests on Eamon, Jan had moved on to Victim Two.

Spike stuck his head around the door. 'Morning, Prof. If you've got a moment, I've found something interesting I thought you might like to see.'

Rory stood up. 'For you, dear heart, I have all the time in the world. Lead on.'

Spike had been working in the main part of the lab, examining the victims' clothing. He led the way to a long bench where the pieces of cloth had been laid out. 'It's Victim Three, Prof. I've found something that might make identification a whole lot easier.'

'Good news indeed,' said Rory, feeling his earlier rather miserable mood somewhat alleviated. 'Reveal all.'

Spike picked up a clear evidence bag, and laid it carefully on the bench. 'It was in a small pocket in the lining of the gilet he was wearing. The other pockets were empty, but I guess this escaped the killer's notice.'

Rory found himself looking at what first appeared to be a loyalty card. He stooped to look closer, and saw that it was in fact an electronic key card.

'It's an RFID card,' said Spike, 'a radio frequency identification card, and it's a door key. The best thing about it is that there's a logo on it, not of a hotel as I first believed, but a business. There's a good chance that if we locate the company's premises, they should be able to give us a list of key-holders. Then we look for any of them who's gone missing.'

Rory beamed at him. 'Who's a clever boy, then? Do you feel like tackling that, or shall I pass it onto the detectives?' As Rory knew he would, Spike said he'd get straight onto it, although if it turned out to be taking too long, he'd give it to the police.

'Let me know how it goes, dear Spike. I have to admit it would give me a great deal of pleasure to be able to casually say, "Oh, by the way, that partially skeletonised body that's been dead for over a year is Fred Bloggs, of twenty-three, Railway Cuttings, East Cheam."' He looked at Spike. 'I might even renounce that moment of joy and give you the honour of bearing the glad tidings to Fenland Constabulary's finest. Anyway, see what you can do to earn yourself some Brownie points.'

Back in his office, Rory finished some paperwork and checked the computers for the latest results. It was a slow trickle, but the information was coming in.

'Good morning to you, Rory.' Jan Wallace came in and sat down beside him. 'I've managed to talk my delightful hotelier into providing me with an early breakfast, so I'm here and ready to go. Would you care to assist me with Victim Two? She's that poor soul who didn't die before she was thrown into the pit, and then inadvertently caused such a tangle of bodies for us to sort out. Oh, and provide her with a suitable name, as is your wont?'

'My pleasure, dear lady. Let's get scrubbed up.'

It took Rory a full hour to decide upon a name for this unfortunate woman. He called her Violet, since her ravaged body — or what was left of it — had been cloaked in a purple anorak, with a purple fleece scarf around the bones of her neck. Together, he and Jan measured, took samples, examined every bone, and carefully recorded the details, especially any anomalies they found. In Violet's case, one of those was a slightly deformed wrist, which they agreed was the result of a fracture, probably sustained in her early teens, that had been poorly reduced. It must have been painful and inconvenient for poor Violet, but would be of great benefit to them when it came to identifying her.

They were still busy with Violet when they heard Spike, speaking to them from the gallery via the speaker system. 'I've had a stroke of luck, Prof! I haven't got a name yet, but I've found which division of the company uses those key cards. The premises are just outside Peterborough. Best of all, I've been given the name of a guy who's been working there for years and knows everyone. The receptionist is getting him to ring me back.'

Rory looked at Jan. 'Looks like I may not need to invent a name for Victim Three. This is exciting!'

'Indeed,' she said, looking up from examining Violet's lumbar vertebrae. 'And if they can identify our man, they might well be able to discover why he was in that particular area, *and* who he had dealings with.' Her eyes sparkled. 'This could be the breakthrough they need.'

'Updates all the way, please!' Rory called back to Spike, and smiled as he received a double thumbs-up from his top technician.

As he returned to matters anatomical, Rory decided his day wasn't turning out bad at all.

* * *

Spike was finding it hard to concentrate on the decaying piece of cloth from Eamon's trousers. At the same time he was waiting for a match between the head injury and a comparable weapon to flash up on his computer screen, but even more importantly for the promised phone call from someone called Andy Parsons. Parsons was the distribution manager for the company that used the key card he'd found, an import—export business was involved in the importation of various goods from abroad, and whose Peterborough depot housed mainly high-end furniture and some more decorative items such as expensive ornamental vases and unusual lamps and light fittings.

The sound of his ringtone made him jump, almost dropping the tweezers he'd been using. He introduced himself to his caller, explaining that he was working with the Home Office pathologist, Professor Rory Wilkinson. Sounding somewhat bemused, Parsons asked how he could help.

Spike explained, without going into the gruesome details, that they wished to identify a body on whom the key card had been found. 'I'd like to know if you have a list of key-holders, or if you know of someone working with you who suddenly disappeared around a year ago.'

'Well, I'm damned! He's dead, you say?' Parsons said, sounding shocked.

'You know him?' Spike asked, crossing his fingers.

'Well, yes. If it's who I think you're talking about. It's like this. There was a bit of a row between him and one of our drivers — more like a fight really — and after that he just buggered off. Never said a word to anybody. Bloody hell, I should have followed that up, shouldn't I?'

'Can you give me his name, sir, and his address if you have it in your records?' Spike hunted around for a pen.

'It's Gino. Gino Lombardi. I'll need to check the address.'

'Italian?'

'From what he told me, his grandparents were Italian, but both his parents were born in the UK. He said it was like a tradition to keep the Italian names, however long they'd been here, but Gino was a Yellowbelly, born and bred in Lincolnshire. Look, can you hold on for a few minutes while I go to the office and see if we still have his records on the computer?' Andy heaved a sigh. 'He was a good bloke, Gino. Bit of a temper, but only when he was in the right.'

Spike waited, positively elated by what Parsons had told him. They now knew who Victim Three really was, and could furnish Jackman with some vital information. Then he told himself not to jump the gun. Even if it had been in his pocket, there was nothing to say the key card had belonged to Gino Lombardi.

'Got it.' Andy Parsons was back on the line. 'Sandilands, Fourteen Windsor Close, Lower Thorndyke, Lincolnshire. And here's the number we had for him. It's a mobile.'

Spike duly wrote it down, knowing the number would be useless. None of the victims had mobiles on them, and as far as Spike knew, all their pockets were empty, other than that tiny inside one in Gino's gilet. 'You don't happen to know where Thorndyke is, do you, Andy?'

'It's on the outskirts of Peterborough, off the road that heads out to Crowland.' Parsons cleared his throat. 'I don't suppose you know what happened to Gino, do you? Or maybe you can't say.'

'Unfortunately, it's an ongoing enquiry, so I'm afraid I can't give you any details. The police will be taking it from here,' said Spike. 'The man Gino's key card was found on might not even be him, in which case I'm sorry if I caused you unnecessary distress.'

'That key card never left his possession,' said Andy quickly. 'Gino was the only staff member in this section with a card that opened every door, you know, like a kind of master key, and he always kept it on him. He lived alone, so why would someone else have his key?'

Why indeed? thought Spike. Their man had to be Gino. He thanked Andy Parsons and hung up. At that very moment the magic word, MATCH appeared on his computer screen. They had their murder weapon. He ran to the viewing gallery.

'Victim Three is Gino Lombardi,' he said, trying to keep the elation out of his voice. 'No confirmation as yet, but I was told that key never left him, so ten to one we have an ID. And, Prof, he was killed, using a particular type of heavy-duty, ground-breaker spade.'

Rory grinned up at him. 'Go on then, Spike, dear heart. Make your call, and make Jackman's day!'

* * *

'I've had another message from Anna,' Marie said quietly to Robbie. 'And I'm even more anxious now. Read this.' She passed him her phone.

Robbie read it, and bit his lip. 'Ah, shit. I see what you mean. And do you think *that*,' he pointed at a word on the screen, 'is a typo, or a deliberate mistake?'

'Jury's out on that, Robbie, but my guess would be that she's trying to tell me something.' Marie stared at the word 'Maria' and wondered. Of course, it could always be predictive text butting in and the sender hadn't noticed, or it could be one of two other things. Either Anna was trying to make

Marie understand that the text was not to be believed and she was in trouble, or . . . someone else sent it. She read it again.

I'm okay and I'm safe. Please don't worry about me. I know I asked for your help, but that was a mistake, so Maria, please forget about me and Johnny and get on with your other work, as you have plenty more serious things to deal with at the moment. I'm sorry to have wasted your time. Anna.

Marie closed her eyes and tried to decide how to proceed. Her whole being said not to ignore Anna's message, but what the hell could she do?

'Tricky one, Sarge,' said Robbie softly. 'And what with everything else, the boss will probably say to take it at face value. After all, her car hasn't been sighted, the phone only pings near Ambleside House, and we know for sure that she's not there, so what can we do?'

'That's the trouble with written messages, they can so often be taken the wrong way — you read so many different meanings into them. If you hear someone's voice, or watch their body language, you can interpret what they want to say without them even uttering a word, but when you can't see them . . .' She sighed. 'You're right, Jackman will tell us to leave it on the back burner, and we've done all we can.'

'But you don't think we have, do you, Marie?'

'If that,' she held up her phone, 'is a cry for help, and I've ignored it, well . . . Okay, Rob, we carry on as we were, but I'm not giving up on Anna Millard — or Johnny. If we get the slightest hint as to where either of them might be, we act. Is that all right with you?'

'Absolutely,' said Robbie. 'And I'll continue to keep in touch with Harry, as well as following up on the information George Rider passed on to us.'

'I'm going to assume that that message was either written under duress, or someone else sent it, so I'll alert uniform to keep their eyes open for any indications of someone being held captive. They're already doing so where Johnny's concerned, so if I throw Anna into the mix I'm not giving them extra work. Meanwhile, we get on with the hunt for the Pillbox Killer. It's the best we can do.'

'Gotcha, Sarge, and for what it's worth, I think you're right. I'll ring Harry now, and then we'll plough on with pillbox case.' He glanced at the clock. 'Bloody hell, it's nearly lunchtime already, time's really flying today.'

'Isn't it just. I'd better tell Jackman about this message, but assure him we're not letting it divert us from the job in hand. Then this afternoon we hit the road and carry on in Fendyke Village. One way or another I've got to get hold of Mad Sally, who wasn't around this morning. Jackman also wants me to go with him to speak to Bryson Smith about last night's incident at the pillbox, so when you're through, you can join up with the others and continue interviewing the locals. We'll tie up at clocking-off time.'

She hurried off in the direction of Jackman's office, almost colliding with him on his way out.

'Glad I ran into you, Marie,' he said with a grin. 'We've just had a massive breakthrough, courtesy of our Spike!'

'He's identified the murder weapon?' asked Marie.

'Yes, but that's small potatoes compared to what else he's identified. One of the victims has a name! We need to confirm it, naturally, but he's pretty sure he has the right man.'

'Already! That's incredible!' exclaimed Marie.

Jackman told her about the key card Spike had found, and his subsequent discovery.

'We should get him to join CID,' Marie said.

Jackman was practically bubbling over. They never got a break this early, especially in the case of murders committed several years ago.

'Come into the office, and I'll give you the details,' said Jackman, 'and show you the kind of murder weapon used.'

A few moments later, Marie was looking at a picture of a hefty-looking garden spade. The weapon, according to the forensic report, was a heavy-duty, stainless steel, ground-breaker spade with an ash shaft. It was a good quality tool, and would not have come cheap, but was nevertheless widely available. This was valuable information, and would help narrow the search, since few people would be willing to shell out fifty quid for a garden spade when B&Q could supply a decent alternative for half that price. It also gave them something specific to look for, rather than bringing in half the garden implements in Fendyke Village for testing!

'And the victim?' she asked, as Jackman printed off the details of the spade.

'The key card Spike found in the clothing belonged to a man called Gino Lombardi, store manager for an import company based in Peterborough. It was assumed he had walked out following a dispute with a fellow employee, and when the company failed to contact him, they posted his P45 to his home address, and that was that. Forensics ran his DNA through the system, and he was not on the national database. However, fourteen months ago a man with that name was reported missing in the Cambridgeshire area. Since he wasn't vulnerable and had no mental health issues, it wasn't brought to our attention, and the details were passed on to Missing People and the Missing Persons Agency. And that's where we'll start. We need to find out who reported him missing, and trace his family and friends.'

'And find out why he was in Fendyke Village, and what he did to get himself killed,' added Marie.

'Precisely. So, in the light of that, we'll postpone our visit to Bryson Smith. Uniform are working on the attack on PC Copeland last night. I suggest you get hold of Kevin and reschedule your interview with Mad Sally. This is a real lead, we're not just chasing people who may or may not know something. But Kevin is not to talk to her himself, and nor must any of the others. I want *you* on that one, but it can wait until we have a positive ID on Gino, Spike's Victim Three.'

He threw her an excited look. 'We are on the move, Marie! So let's keep up the momentum!'

* * *

As soon as the Greene brothers were safely on their way to Bristol, Lucas's plan swung into action. Their timing was flawless. Everything on the client's list had been secured, including the stained-glass window. It could not have gone more smoothly. Now, Lucas, Nina and her two chosen assistants were back at Hartwood House.

Having deactivated the alarms, Chaos politely reminded them of the limited time they had in which to complete this second phase. Lucas needed no such reminder, being always well ahead of schedule. He took no chances, especially with a job like this.

At last, he was back in the Art Nouveau room, and once again, the contents took his breath away. He found himself transported to another, finer era, and it was hard to concentrate on the practical aspects of the operation.

A nudge in the ribs from Nina brought him back to earth, and the next fifteen minutes proceeded like a military manoeuvre. It was easy to see why Nina had chosen Shaun and Valerie for her collaborators. All the items from his wish list were carefully removed, packed in special protective material, and carried in boxes to the hall, ready for evacuation. Sculptures, lamps, vases, pictures, posters, mirrors, the occasional small piece of furniture, all disappeared from the room like magic.

'This one is mine,' whispered Nina, showing him an exquisite silver and enamel necklace.

'Wise choice, it's quite beautiful. But we have eighteen minutes left, so it's time to load up.'

It took precisely eight minutes to load the goods into the lorry, after which Lucas allowed himself to relax.

'Nina, you and the others check that everything in the vehicle is secure, and get ready to leave. I'll do a final walk round to make sure we've left nothing incriminating. I'll see you in the car.'

He made his way from room to room, and when he was satisfied, hurried down the stairs. As his foot hit the hall floor, the sound of the alarms froze him to the spot. Chaos had mistimed their exit! He whipped out the device and stared at it, and, yes, it read 00.00 minutes. Immediately, he called the emergency number Chaos had given him, but to his horror, was informed the number was unrecognised. Then his screen went blank.

Lucas raced to the front door, but it was locked. Overcome with panic, he ran into the lounge whose window overlooked the front drive. Nina was standing outside, her face ashen and her mouth slightly open.

He rapped on the sealed triple-glazed window. 'Nina! I can't get out! This place is a fortress! Chaos has cocked up the timing! Ring him on that emergency number I gave you! There's something wrong with my phone! Tell him to get me out of here!'

She pulled out her phone.

'It's connecting!' she cried.

'Thank God,' he murmured. 'Listen! As soon as he answers, you and the others get away fast. Leave me the car, and I'll follow as soon as he lets me out. And, Nina! This is important! Go to my rented cottage. If I'm not there shortly afterwards, get inside and take my laptop, and anything else that could identify me. If you don't hear from me by five o'clock, you know what to do with the haul from the previous robbery, then use our emergency procedure and go to ground. Got it?'

Nina nodded, still staring at her screen. 'Lucas, he's typing!'

He waited, amid the deafening shriek of the alarms. 'Well? What's he said?'

Nina looked up at him, her expression blank. 'Nothing. He's said nothing, Lucas. He's just left a whole line of emojis. He's laughing at us.'

CHAPTER TWENTY

'So, Leon, what was Coral's father like?' asked Orac, swivelling her chair round to face him.

Leon pursed his lips. 'We chatted for hours. He's obviously very intelligent. I liked him a lot, but I couldn't help feeling sorry for him.'

Orac pointed to the chair beside her. 'Oh? Why?'

'It's just such a shame seeing the way a combination of age and bad health stops someone doing the things they love. He wasn't self-pitying, not at all, and he made light of it, but I could see how unhappy it made him.'

'It's true, age does take some things away from you, but it often leaves others in its place. Things like wisdom and empathy, and sometimes you discover new passions and interests, things you *are* capable of doing. Maybe Coral's dad hasn't yet learned acceptance.'

Leon grinned. 'Oh my, chief! We are getting deep!'

Orac sniffed. 'Just an observation. And, no, it doesn't come from personal experience — not yet anyhow. So, back to work. Anything to report?'

'Ah, yes. Work. Well, by the end of the day, I'll have sorted everything that's outstanding, and I'll be able to pitch in with the Millard/Chaos investigation, if that's okay with you? Philip is going to deal with anything else that comes in, unless it's something that needs both of us to deal with.'

'That's good, Leon. David and I are beginning to realise what a tangled web the Met, *and* Coral, have had to unravel. Thank heavens she's here, or we'd be following the same red herrings that had the Met spending months running down blind alleys.'

'Stroke of luck, that,' remarked Leon. 'And how is the work on Millard's computer coming on?'

'It's arduous and time-consuming, but we are making headway. Trouble is, it hasn't yielded anything particularly useful to the search for Millard, or this shadowy Chaos figure.' Orac grimaced. 'Frustrating, to say the least, so another brain — i.e. yours — will be very welcome.'

Leon departed, to be replaced by David Serlin. David was the only person she had told of Coral's suspicion that Chaos had a guardian. His expression was grave.

He sat down with a groan. 'I'm stiff as a board! I've been staring at my screen for three whole hours, and I swear I've hardly blinked. I've found something a tad disturbing.'

'Should I be reaching for the Valium?'

'Not yet, but who knows what tomorrow might bring?' He sat back in his seat. 'I've been sounding out a couple of people we trust in other IT units outside this area. One of them has been tracking Chaos for some time now, in the belief that at some point he's got to make a mistake. The thing is, before I'd even mentioned it, he suggested that Chaos might have a guardian, and what's more, he had proof. And then there's these mysterious deaths of certain prominent villains whose bodies haven't been found. My counterpart reckons it's not some new gang trying to muscle in on the old guard, but someone making trouble on a grand scale.'

'But murdering people with no cause or motive other than to stir up trouble?' Orac shook her head. 'It doesn't make sense.'

'We don't actually know if there were any murders, do we?' said David. 'What if that's all part of the charade? Maybe one of the so-called victims is behind it all and is living the life of Riley in Brazil or somewhere? But whether or not any deaths have occurred, there have been threats, and it's scaring the shit out of some of the lowlifes, so if the intention is to cause chaos, then it's working.'

Orac looked slightly amused. 'Cause chaos, David? Did you use that word deliberately?'

'No, but now you mention it, given that the criminal fraternity is in complete disarray, I might well have. It literally is chaos.'

'I wonder,' mused Orac. 'What are the chances that our Chaos is behind all that too?'

'It's possible, I suppose,' said David, 'but Coral and I were wondering if it might be a massive clear-up job on behalf of some really big criminal organisation that's ready to extend their empire.'

'But Chaos could still be doing the prep work for them, couldn't he? Oh hell, don't you hate suppositions?' muttered Orac. 'I think we should stick to what we are good at, and leave our friends upstairs to deal with the guesswork. Our job's dealing with the technology. Anyway, forget all that for the time being, and think about Johnny Millard's data. I'm beginning to understand why everyone says he's so brilliant. He's clever, very clever, and if he's still alive, he must be eaten up with rage over what happened. I'm pretty certain that it was Chaos who framed him, which makes him a very dangerous adversary.' She lowered her voice. 'As you know, David, we are one of the best-protected agencies in the country, but even so, I've upped our security to the highest level.'

'You think there's a chance he might target us?' asked David incredulously.

'I can't afford to think otherwise,' said Orac. 'So, make sure you're extra vigilant. All we can do is expect the worst, and hope for the best.'

'I've been to this area before,' said Marie, looking out of the window as they drove towards the outskirts of Peterborough. 'Ralph's old crewmate lives around here somewhere. We visited them a while ago, and his wife helped us with the background to the Solace House investigation. Considering its proximity to a sprawling city, it's a lovely area with some gorgeous houses.'

Gino Lombardi's house, however, was definitely not gorgeous. It was a small, semi-detached that might once have been neat and tidy, but now it was a shambles. The front garden was an overgrown mass of nettles, out-of-control plants and long grass. The path to the door was hardly visible beneath a dense mat of weeds.

'Nice,' muttered Marie. 'Think it's time to meet the neighbours, don't you?'

There was no answer from the adjoining property, but on the other side, an elderly man answered the door and peered at them suspiciously.

'I'm not buying anything,' he stated before Jackman could open his mouth. 'And I'm not looking for God either. I found Him years ago.'

Jackman smiled. 'And we aren't selling anything — products or religion. I'm Detective Inspector Jackman and this is Detective Sergeant Marie Evans. Could we have a word with you, sir? It's about Gino Lombardi.'

The man seemed taken aback. 'Oh, have you found him at last? Is he all right?'

He looked genuinely concerned. 'Did you know him well, sir?' Marie asked.

The man seemed to deflate. He stepped aside. 'You'd better come in. Sorry about the mess. My daughter usually comes once a week and sorts me out, but one of her lads is poorly, and, well, I haven't got around to tackling it myself. Shall I put the kettle on?'

Marie smiled at him. 'That would be lovely, sir. Can I help?'

He looked at her reprovingly. 'I may be well over eighty, but I can still make a better cuppa than most I know.' With that, he disappeared into the kitchen.

Marie stifled a giggle. 'Oops! That told me.'

'And this is hardly a pig-pen, is it?' said Jackman, looking around. 'It's tidier than Mill Corner before Hettie Maynard gets the Hoover revved up!'

The man, whose name was Stan Berry, returned from the kitchen carrying a single mug of tea, which he placed carefully on the coffee table. He repeated this procedure twice. Marie didn't dare offer to assist.

'How can I help?' asked Stan, when they all had their tea in front of them. 'I suppose your visit means I've lost my neighbour permanently.'

'We can't be certain, sir,' said Jackman, 'but we believe that's the case. A body has been found, but has not yet been formally identified. We're trying to trace Gino's relatives and friends so we can be sure it definitely is him.'

'You'll have no luck with any relatives, Officer. You can tell that from the state of his house. No one ever comes to tidy it up.' Stan shook his head. 'Big family he had at one point, too, but he lost both parents, and his brothers and sisters all went their own ways and he never kept in touch.' He frowned. 'As far as I could gather, there was a falling-out over money, need I say more?'

'And friends?' asked Marie, sipping what was indeed a very good cup of tea. 'Did he ever mention a woman called Alice Benson?'

Stan smiled reminiscently. 'Sweet girl, Alice, and she was so cut up after he disappeared. I miss seeing her come to visit. Lovely nature she had.'

'According to the Missing Persons Bureau, it was Alice who reported him missing,' Jackman said.

217

'Wouldn't be surprised,' Stan said. 'I only saw her a couple of times to talk to after he went, then one night I saw her standing in the street and staring up at the house, looking as if her heart would break. And that was that. She never came again.'

'Do you know if she's local, sir?' asked Jackman.

'Yes. Unless she's moved, she lives in a flat in a big, old converted house on Brick Lane. Bideford House, it's called, so Gino said.' Stan looked mournfully at Jackman. 'How did this man, the one you believe to be Gino . . . how did he die?'

Jackman said quietly, 'It appears to be a suspicious death, sir.'

'Murder?'

'Too early to say, sir, but we need all the help we can get to identify him, so we'd very much appreciate anything you can tell us.' Jackman took out his notebook.

After about twenty minutes, they thanked Stan, complimented him on his tea-making and went in search of Alice Benson. It didn't take them long to learn that she had moved out six months ago, leaving no forwarding address. That left them with one more person to contact. Stan had given them the number of a local gardener who looked after both his and Gino's gardens. According to Stan, Gino and this man had some hobby in common and had become friends. His name was Arthur Brownlee, and he was their last hope. If that failed, they'd have to resort to technology for clues.

To Marie's surprise, Arthur Brownlee answered almost at once. He told her he was working in the area that day, gave her the address and said he'd see them in ten minutes.

She had expected someone older, but Arthur was in his mid-thirties, tall and fit-looking with a ruddy face that suggested he spent all his time out of doors.

'I was afraid that's what had happened,' said Arthur sadly. 'He just wasn't the type to bugger off and say nothing. And, okay, it wasn't a mansion, but he loved his house; he would never have left it to go to rack and ruin.'

They had met Arthur in the grounds of a nursing home. From the well-maintained stretches of lawn and flowerbeds, it was clear that Arthur was good at his job. He led them to a wooden bench between two tall trees that he said were Norway maples, and they began to question him about his friend.

'Have you any idea why Gino would have been in the vicinity of Fendyke Village?' Marie asked.

'Is that where he was found?' Arthur said, a spark of recognition in his eyes.

'If the body really is Gino, then, yes,' said Marie.

'That's an easy one,' said Arthur. 'We used to go there once a month. You see, we shared the same hobby, which is why we became friends. We were both ghost-hunters, and our group used to meet in a house in Fendyke Village.'

When Arthur mentioned ghosts, Marie glanced at Jackman and hoped his sardonic expression wasn't too obvious. But whatever the nature of Gino's hobby, they now had a reason for his presence in Fendyke.

Arthur had indeed noticed Jackman's reaction. 'I know. You think it's a load of rubbish, and I don't blame you. It's more a social thing, really, and the club members are a proper mixed bag. Some are looking for the source of old folktales, some are firm believers, while others come in order to disprove the existence of ghosts altogether.'

Marie didn't like to ask which camp Arthur was in, but said, 'And what was Gino's take on ghosts?'

'Alice's grandmother was in a care home over Fendyke way.' He looked around at the gardens and the large modern building behind them. 'Nothing on the scale of this one. It was an old house with a chequered history. He sometimes went with Alice to visit, and while she was with her gran, he would chat to the staff about the history of the place. Several of the nurses told him it was haunted, and when he laughed, they told him he should come over one evening and see if the apparition turned up. And that's where it all started.'

Marie's eyes widened. 'He saw the ghost?'

'No, but the atmosphere had a strange effect on him, and it kept drawing him back. He went several times after that, and although he never saw an actual ghost, there was something about it that convinced him of their existence.' Arthur looked at them both. 'Listen, I know he has — had — no family around here, so I'd be prepared to identify him for you if it would help.'

'That's very kind of you,' said Jackman. 'Unfortunately, it's not as easy as that. You see, he's been dead for a long time. Although you could take a look at what's left of his clothing. We could send you some photographs to save you a trip to Saltern. Would you be able to do that?'

'For sure,' Arthur said.

'Excellent. As soon as we get back, we'll contact you. We'll be going into his house to pick up traces of his DNA, but it will take time to obtain the results, so it'll be much faster if you can identify any of his clothes.'

After obtaining the address of the house in Fendyke where the ghost-hunters group met, and taking the names of some of his fellow hobbyists, they thanked Arthur and went back to the car.

'It's him, isn't it? It's Gino,' said Marie.

'Ten to one,' said Jackman, his hand on the car door.

'Excuse me! Hold up, officers!'

Arthur Brownlee was running towards them.

'I've just had a thought! Was that dead man wearing a wax Barbour-style gilet?'

'Yes, he was,' Jackman said.

'He wore that gilet all the time,' Arthur said. 'Check the right-hand flap pocket. If there's a tear in it, it's Gino's. He did it while we were out one night looking for ghosts. I remember it so clearly because he swore, which was unusual for Gino.' Arthur drew in a breath. 'From the look on your faces, I have a sinking feeling you recognise that gilet.'

'Well, thank you for that. We'll let you know one way or the other,' Jackman said.

They were barely out of the nursing home grounds when Jackman received a call from Ruth Crooke.

'Rowan, this is a big favour to ask, but I've no choice. We've had reports of an incident in one of the outlying villages, and it's a weird one. I need you to divert from whatever you are doing and give me a situation report. DI Deane has had a family emergency and is out of action for a day or so, but you don't need to follow it up. DS Vic Blackwell will be here in the morning and will take the lead until Jenny Deane is back. Here's the address.'

'Can you give us a brief outline of what has occurred? And what makes you say it's weird? I'm not sure I like the sound of that,' Jackman said.

Ruth gave one of her rare laughs. 'I'll leave you to find that out. All I'm saying is that a certain art thief might never live this particular heist of his down. Goodbye!'

Jackman rolled his eyes. 'Oh deep joy! Just what we needed right now.'

'Aren't we the lucky ones,' Marie said with a chuckle. 'Though it does sound intriguing. At least it's not too far from here, so let's go see what it's about.'

* * *

The driveway to Hartwood House was mayhem, filled with various vehicles attempting to get as close to the front doors as possible.

'Blimey! That's what I call a circus,' said Marie. 'And why are they all grinning like that? What can have happened?'

'I dread to think,' muttered Jackman, 'but I keep hearing Ruth say "weird". Let's see if we can find the officer in charge of this melee.'

An amused-looking constable told them the officer in charge was Inspector Unsworth. 'He's right out front with Stacey and Jay. They were the first to respond to the call.'

Newly promoted Inspector Allen Unsworth greeted them warmly. 'Nice to see you. You're going to love this one!'

'So, what's the score?' Jackman asked.

'Right, well. Turns out this place is as well alarmed as a nuclear weapons depot. We got a call from several locals, and from the security company that installed the system. PCs Stacey Smith and Jay Acharya took the shout, and as they were heading towards the place, we got a further call from the owners.' He indicated two men in animated conversation with a uniformed sergeant. 'Derek and Norman Greene. They were on their way back from Bristol when their security service alerted them to the break-in.' He lowered his voice. 'Turns out they are collectors and the house is chock-a-block with rare antiques and valuable art pieces. According to them, a serious amount of it has gone.'

'Okay, so why am I going to love it?' Jackman asked, with a glance at Stacey, who had just joined them. She too had a broad grin on her face.

She answered for Unsworth. 'Because when we arrived, the thief was locked inside, hands over his ears, almost deafened by the alarms!'

'He was yelling for us to get him out,' added Jay Acharya. 'Screaming like a banshee, he was.'

'No kidding, sir,' chuckled Stacey. 'It was like one of those comedy programmes where everything goes wrong for the hapless villain.'

Marie and Jackman were beginning to see the cause of all this hilarity.

'So where is he now?' Jackman asked.

'In the back of our car,' said Jay. 'Still partially deaf.'

'Okay, we'll just have a word with the property owners, and then speak to your unlucky thief.' Jackman frowned. 'I still don't get it, though. I mean, if he was the thief, where's all the stuff he nicked? Is he the fall guy, and his mates have taken off with the booty?'

'That's what we believe, sir. There are the tyre marks of a heavy vehicle just in front of the house,' said Jay. 'We reckon it must have been a gang, and they left our man behind for some reason.'

Jackman asked the inspector what procedures had been put in place. An all-forces alert had been issued for a vehicle believed to be carrying a fortune in stolen antiques, and they had already checked the traffic cameras for vehicles seen leaving the area shortly after the alarm went off. Officers had been sent to knock on the doors of the few scattered dwellings in the vicinity, although even the nearest of these was so far from the house that their enquiries weren't expected to yield any positive results.

They made their way over to where the sergeant was trying unsuccessfully to calm the two distraught householders. After a few moments of everyone trying to talk at once, Jackman held up his hand. 'One at a time, please.' He indicated one of the brothers, who introduced himself as Norman Greene. 'Right, Mr Greene. Can you tell me, *briefly*, please, what you believe to have been stolen.'

A look of positive anguish spread over the man's face. Almost sobbing with rage and despair, he began to list the items. The list was long, and after a few minutes, the sergeant interrupted.

'We accompanied the gentlemen on a swift walk-through, sir. It seems that a fortune in valuable collectibles has been stolen — oh, and that includes the removal of a stained-glass window. They did a really professional job on that, sir. The original was taken out, and a plain-glass replacement installed, along with the security sensors.'

Marie looked at Jackman. 'How the hell did they achieve all that without activating the alarm sooner? It doesn't make sense.'

Jackman shrugged. 'Vic Blackwell and DI Deane are going to have fun sorting this one out.' He turned to the two brothers. 'I'm afraid I'll have to ask you to come down to the station with us and give us a full description of everything you believe to have been taken. Your house is now a crime scene and will have to be thoroughly examined for possible evidence.'

'We can't possibly have people traipsing all over our home. There are still some priceless items here, and we're certainly not leaving.'

Jackman was growing less and less able to see the humour of the situation. He could envision them having a bugger of a time interviewing these two brothers. They were a couple of obsessives, who would do nothing but throw up obstacles at every turn.

Marie decided it was time to throw a bit of oil on waters that were growing more troubled every second. 'Why don't you go and talk to the man in the car, sir? I'll have a word with these two gentlemen and explain the need for their cooperation.'

Jackman smiled at her gratefully. If anyone were to calm these two, it would be Marie. So, leaving Stacey with her, he took Jay with him to their car and the unfortunate robber.

'His name is Lucas Corbin, sir,' said Jay. 'His story is that he came here to talk to the Greene brothers about some antique or other, and found the front door open. He went in, the door slammed shut behind him, and the alarms went off. He's adamant he had nothing to do with any theft, and says it must have happened before he arrived.'

'Do you believe him, Jay?'

'Not for a minute, DI Jackman.'

'Have the Greenes seen him yet?'

'No, sir. They were mad as hell, so for the poor guy's sake, we decided it wasn't the right moment. They'd probably have torn him limb from limb.'

'So, is this art collection, or whatever it is, really worth all that much money, Jay?' asked Jackman.

'A fortune, sir,' said Jay. 'The Greene brothers seem to be complete recluses. As far as I can ascertain, they have no friends and their whole world revolves around their priceless collection. That's where they were today, viewing some artefact they wanted to purchase. It's their whole life, hence the hysterical reaction.'

As Jay spoke, Jackman had a flash of inspiration. Of course! Bryson Smith. Okay, this wasn't his speciality, but his overall knowledge of the subject could be invaluable. And he was right here, on the spot, saving them the endless delay of getting someone in from the Met's Art and Antiques Unit. The last time something like this had happened, they had been told to handle it themselves, as there weren't enough qualified officers to attend cases outside London.

When they reached the car, Jackman asked Lucas Corbin to get out so that he could introduce himself.

Corbin was a rather handsome man, with the body of someone who took care of himself. He looked to be in his late thirties, with neat, nicely cut hair. He was wearing a pale blue Oxford shirt and navy chinos. Nothing about him marked him out as a thief. But who could say what a thief looked like?

He listened to the man repeat his story. It sounded genuine enough, except for the fact that people didn't just call on the Greene brothers. Jackman had learned from Stacey and Jay that the reclusive brothers never gave their address to anyone.

'Okay, Mr Corbin, how do you come to know where the Greene brothers live?' asked Jackman.

Lucas Corbin smiled. 'Years of hunting, Detective Inspector! Everyone in the art and antiques world had heard tell of these mysterious collectors, but no one knew their exact whereabouts. I'd been looking for them for months until I got a whisper of them being here in the Fens. Then I overheard a dealer talking about two men who were purchasing a small piece of Art Deco furniture from him that they were collecting that afternoon.' He shrugged. 'I admit it was wrong of me, but when they left his premises, I followed them here. I didn't approach them immediately, as I wanted to make sure that these men were indeed the mysterious collectors. I made a few enquiries, and when I was absolutely certain, I decided to introduce myself as a fellow aficionado, and ask if they would let me see their fabled collection.'

He's convincing, and he speaks well, thought Jackman, but it doesn't ring true.

'And you are a collector too?' asked Jackman.

'Oh yes. Have been for years. I have some nice pieces at my home in London.'

I bet you have! Jackman wondered how many were legally obtained. 'So it was total coincidence that you chose to visit on the one day the Greene brothers were out, and you picked the very time a gang of robbers had just broken in, stolen a fortune in precious collectibles and got away without activating the alarm system, only to get trapped inside yourself.' He raised an eyebrow. 'I'm sure you can understand my scepticism, Mr Corbin.'

The man looked angry. 'Of course I can see how it looks. But it's the truth, the whole thing was pure coincidence.' He looked straight at Jackman. 'Check me out. You'll find I have never been found guilty of wrongdoing. I have receipts and invoices for every purchase I've ever made — I have to, for insurance purposes. I'm an honest man, Officer, who happens to have a passion for the Art Nouveau period. One thing I am not is a thief!'

This man was clever. Jackman was in no doubt that if they were to check at his home, they would find only items purchased legitimately. 'Oh, we'll be checking you out, sir, never fear. Right now, we'll get you down to the station and process you.'

Corbin opened his mouth, but Jackman had already turned to Jay. 'Get two officers to accompany Mr Corbin to the custody suite, please. Oh, and I want him well out of the way by the time the Greene brothers come in to make their statement.'

That done, Jay followed Jackman back to where Marie and Stacey were still talking to the Greene brothers. Jackman was relieved to see that the two men were now considerably less irate.

Marie turned to him. 'Norman and Derek will come back to the station with us, and they've assured me they'll help us as much as they can. I've said that I'll accompany them back to the house so they can collect what they need for an overnight stay in a hotel, and that we'll get them home as soon as forensics have examined it for evidence.'

Jackman doubted that they'd find a single shred of evidence, but you never knew. After all, every move we make leaves a trace. 'That's good. I see that the SOCOs and Ella Jarvis have just arrived, so I'll go and have a quick word with them before we leave.'

Jackman hurried off, conscious that the less time he spent around the brothers the better. Marie was clearly working her magic, and it would be wise not to interfere.

'This makes a pleasant change from the last case,' said Ella. 'Beautiful works of art as opposed to decaying bodies. No contest!'

'I'll suit up and come in with you,' Jackman said. 'It's the room they found Lucas Corbin in that I'm most interested in seeing. He was pretty desperate by the time we turned up — climbing the walls, according to uniform.'

'So you think that if he was one of the thieves, he might have been careless?' asked Ella.

'Either that, or as soon as he understood the position he was in, he got cunning.'

'How do you mean?' asked Ella.

'It was a very professional heist, Ella, including the removal of a whole window, so he'd have worn gloves, but there were none on him when uniform got him out, so he must have stashed them somewhere.' Jackman's eyes narrowed. 'And there's something about his clothing that doesn't make sense to me. It's nothing obvious, but it's definitely there. Just keep your eyes open, and I'll tell the SOCOs to do the same.'

'Will do, sir,' Ella said.

They pulled on coveralls, shoe covers and masks, and Jackman had his first look at Hartwood House. He noted the empty spaces where objects had obviously been removed, but it was still immensely impressive. Again, Jackman thought of Bryson Smith. He had an idea that a fellow enthusiast might be of help when the Greene brothers compiled their list of missing items. At very least, Bryson could act as mediator between him and the unhappy brothers.

Walking through the house, he began to understand something of what Norman and Derek Greene must be feeling. He could hear Laura's voice urging him to be more compassionate. These men had spent years of their lives building up this shrine to the Art Deco movement, and in a matter of a few hours their dream had been shattered.

'Okay, Laura, I hear you,' he whispered to himself.

'Sorry, sir?'

'Just talking to myself, Ella. It's quite a house, isn't it?'

'I've never seen anything like it in my life,' Ella said. 'It's like I've wandered into a film set. And considering what they left behind, it makes you wonder what the things they took were like. They must have been really exceptional, or very rare.'

'Mmm, shopping list thieves,' said Jackman.

Ella looked at him. 'Shopping list?'

'It's where thieves act on behalf of someone. The client gives them a list of what he wants and they take only those items. It's a quick job and they get out fast,' Jackman explained. 'Except on this occasion something went very wrong.'

They walked slowly from room to room, careful not to touch anything, while Ella took photographs. After fifteen minutes, Jackman gave up. He could see nothing obvious, and as he daren't touch anything, he could only stare at the objects he passed. He thanked Ella and went outside to find Marie.

'I've parked them in the back of the car,' she said. 'And I've warned the desk sergeant to get them straight into an interview room as soon as they arrive. They are much more amenable now, but I don't want them bumping into Lucas Corbin.'

'In that case, there's nothing more we can do here,' said Jackman. 'Forensics have already begun their sweep, and once they've finished, we'll need a list of the valuables taken, and their provenance.'

Marie threw him a quizzical look. 'This is beginning to sound a bit more than the sit rep Ruth asked for.'

Jackman smiled a little sheepishly. 'Oh, just getting everything in place for Vic. Don't want him discovering that the first on scene, i.e. us, have missed something, do we?'

'Uh huh, and that's all, is it? Just Jackman's sense of propriety?'

'Damn it, Marie! I honestly wish that this really was our case. It's bloody fascinating. I'm getting all these vibes about different aspects of it that I won't be able to follow up. It's so frustrating.'

Marie chuckled. 'Thought so. I've seen that look before.'

'I think I might burn the midnight oil on this tonight, before Vic comes back. After all, if Spike confirms that there is a tear in the dead man's gilet, we can be more or less certain that he's Gino Lombardi, and then there's little more we can do until the additional forensics reports come through. And we have every officer and his dog out in Fendyke, questioning anything that moves about missing people. So I think I can spare a few hours on Hartwood House.' He gave her a narrowed look. 'And I'm betting you won't want to miss the interview with Lucas Corbin either.'

'Oh, that's a given, boss.'

'Then we'll get those two gentlemen interviewed, find them some accommodation and go talk to the handsome Lucas. All right?'

'I'll say! Let's go, Cisco!'

CHAPTER TWENTY-ONE

Kevin looked at his watch. It was well after clocking-off time, but he was starting to get a sense of the dynamics of the population of Fendyke, and the more people he spoke to, the more interested he became in the village hierarchy. He supposed that all small rural communities ran along similar lines, but this one fascinated him. A real bonus was the fact that the villagers loved to talk, although this meant heeding Jackman's instruction to weed out the chaff from whatever he was told.

'You planning on staying all night then, lad?' asked Gary, stifling a yawn. 'Only I promised my Gilly that I'd take her out for a fish supper tonight, and time's getting on.'

'You head back, Gary.' Kevin looked at the list of names in his hand. 'I'll just do another couple of visits. I'm more likely to find people at home in the early evening.'

'If you're sure, lad, only I don't like leaving you out here banging on doors on your own. We can catch up tomorrow, surely?'

'It's okay, Gazza. You go. The late shift will be on soon, so I can ask them if I need a hand.'

Reluctantly, Gary left him, and Kevin set off for the house of someone who was purported to know everyone in

Fendyke going back three generations. He had been wondering what Dudley Nailer would be like, as the comments about him were rather varied, but he hadn't bargained for the man who answered the door.

The rotund little man peered short-sightedly at Kevin's warrant card and exclaimed, 'Ah! It's an officer of the law, as I live and breathe! How delightful!'

Kevin suddenly wished he'd asked Gary to stay with him.

'Come in, come in! I was just sampling a dear friend's homemade elderberry wine. Can I pour you a glass, young Detective Constable Kevin Stoner?'

Kevin was impressed that the man had remembered his name after a single brief glance at his warrant card. 'Er, thank you, sir, but not right now. I've got a few more people to call on, and I've heard what homemade wine can do to you.'

'And it's all true! But, please, follow me to the kitchen, and I will do my very best to help you.'

With a theatrical bow, Dudley Nailer ushered him into a big country kitchen and pointed to a carver chair with a multi-coloured cushion on the seat. 'Right. What did you want to know?'

Kevin had the impression that he'd just walked into his favourite childhood book, *The Wind in the Willows*, and was now seated in Badger's kitchen. An enormous fireplace was home to an Aga multi-fuel cooker, bundles of herbs and copper saucepans hung from wooden beams in the ceiling, and an ancient Welsh dresser displayed an array of china and porcelain tableware. The old wooden table had been scrubbed clean so often that it was almost white, and above them, running the full length of the room, a plate rack was lined with colourful old china plates. That, and the bookshelves crammed with old books, gave the impression of somewhere from a different world.

'If I can't tempt you with Alf's wine, maybe a warming beverage?' Dudley asked solicitously.

'A cup of tea would be lovely, sir,' Kevin said.

'Lapsang? Gunpowder? Earl Grey? Darjeeling, maybe?'

'I suppose you don't have good old builders', do you?' Kevin asked tentatively.

'Of course,' said Dudley, looking disappointed. 'Although I prefer to call it English Breakfast Tea.'

A few minutes later Kevin was nursing a mug of strong tea, and Dudley was sipping elderberry wine from an engraved fine crystal glass. They had already established that the enquiry concerned people who had left the village suddenly, apparently having disappeared.

'Ah, but people do come and go, don't they?' mused Dudley. 'Mrs Ames's son, for example — he had a job offer in Leeds and was gone in a day! A dear boy, too, and we all miss him. But let me think . . . Over a period of up to two years, you say?'

As Dudley pondered, Kevin was left to drink in the tea and the atmosphere, and appreciated both immensely.

'Very well, young Detective Stoner, get your pad out. I have a few names for you.'

Kevin put down his mug and took his iPad from his bag.

'Dear me!' exclaimed Dudley. 'Times have changed. Oh well, so be it. Here goes.' And he gave Kevin three names: Shelley Kershaw, Gino Lombardi and Jeremy Logan. 'And only one of those three was a local,' he added. 'That was Jeremy Logan, who had what people like to call serious learning difficulties, so he might well have been magicked away by his family to a home of some description. Whatever, they never referred to his departure, or where he went. His parents still live here, but on the outskirts of the village, and they are, shall we say, less than friendly. Their names are Edith and Patrick Logan. Oh, and just for the record, I, and many of the other villagers, doubt that he ever went into any home, although we've never been able to come up with any alternative suggestions as to where he went, other than the sublime and the ridiculous, of course.'

Kevin made careful note of everything Dudley told him, pleased to finally have something to take back to Jackman. 'And Gino Lombardi?'

'Nice man. I met him several times in the local.' Dudley chuckled. 'He belonged to the Fendyke Ghost-hunters Club, if you can believe such a thing even exists. I think he lived down Peterborough way, but he was a regular visitor here. He often said that if it wasn't so far from his place of work, he'd have happily moved here to this village. He was popular, too, and not just in the club, then all of a sudden he stopped coming.'

Now, that was interesting. And they'd be able to trace him much more easily than the Logans's son.

'And Shelley Kershaw?' Kevin said.

Dudley looked sad. 'Poor Shelley. She had a reputation, I'm afraid.' He have a discreet cough. 'Some of the coarser elements in the public bar referred to her as "the local bike". As for me, I think she was maligned. All that was wrong with Shelley was that she was too trusting of men who abused that trust. Mind you, I've no proof. It comes from reading between the lines. I have pretty keen shrewd observational skills, even now.'

'So, what happened to her, Dudley?'

'She was last seen walking towards the bus stop a few moments before the last bus into Saltern was due. She was never seen again.'

'Was she reported missing?' asked Kevin.

'I doubt it. It's over a year since she disappeared, and frankly, nobody knew she'd even gone for a good while. She rented a room in a ramshackle old house close to the church from an old woman who lived there. Old Jeannie always reckoned Shelley got fed up with all the names people called her, and buggered off to try her luck somewhere else.'

Kevin finished his tea, and said he'd better go. He'd enjoyed his visit to this *Wind in the Willows* kitchen and was quite reluctant to depart. It had been well worth staying on for, and not because of the delightful kitchen. Now, he finally had some names to go on.

Just as he was about to leave, Dudley put a hand on his arm. 'I don't know if it's even possible, but if you can find a way to get Mad Sally to talk to you, you'll find it most useful.

That woman knows more about this village and what goes on here than any of us, including yours truly.'

Kevin frowned. 'I met her once, in one of the back lanes.'

'With the fox, I suppose.'

'That's right. I've been wanting to talk to her, but my boss thinks my sergeant, DS Marie Evans, might have more luck with her, and unfortunately she couldn't come today.'

'Well, give your sergeant my deepest sympathies. Still, it's definitely worth a try. Tell her to bear in mind that Mad Sally is anything but mad. She seems to have a sixth sense for trouble, because no matter what is going on, you'll find her there in the background, watching. The villagers like to say, and I quote, "She do 'ang abaht like a bad smell!" But to my mind she's more like a dark wraith, a harbinger of doom.' He smiled sheepishly. 'Listen to me! Now you know why I got my reputation for being overdramatic.'

Recalling the stony face of the woman with the fox, Kevin decided that on this occasion, Dudley was probably not over-dramatising at all.

* * *

The interview with the Greene brothers turned out to be less heated than Marie had feared. Initially, they had flatly rejected any suggestion of bringing in an art expert, but when they learned that he was a well-respected London-based profes-sional, they finally gave in. Jackman had already contacted Bryson Smith, who said he'd be delighted to assist. It would be a welcome distraction from the pillbox, and provide an opportunity to get back to his own world for a while.

When the brothers had finished giving their statement, Stacey and Jay drove them and their few meagre possessions to a new Travelodge that had just opened on the Fenchester Road just outside Saltern.

As soon as she returned, she and Jackman went over what the Greene brothers had said, in preparation for the first offi-cial interview with Lucas Corbin.

'It's getting late, Marie, and you told me Ralph was on a couple of rest days. Are you sure you want to come with me? I can easily speak to Corbin on my own,' Jackman said.

She gave him a withering glance. 'I'm not missing this, not for anything. And as Ralph's off work, he will have dinner ready for me when I get home, so I'm all good, thank you for asking.'

'In that case, we'll get on with it, and you can get home to whatever tasty morsel Ralph has rustled up for you,' said Jackman, 'And before you start nagging me about not eating, I'm having a takeaway brought in.'

But before they could set off for the interview, Jackman received a call from Spike. He listened, and thanked him, and turned to Marie. 'As we thought. Our victim's jacket has a tear in the flap of the pocket. It's Gino Lombardi.'

'Better ring our friendly gardener then, and put him out of his misery.'

Jackman made the call, and then came yet another interruption. Robbie Melton stood at the office door.

'I thought you'd want to know this before you interview your thief, boss.' Robbie checked his notes. 'That antique dealer in Bristol the Greenes were visiting when the robbery occurred, well, he checks out. It's a bona fide business, he's been in the antiques trade for donkey's years. He's verified that the piece of Art Deco he was offering the Greene brothers came from a private collector, and he has all the paperwork, so it doesn't seem to have been a decoy. Plus, and this is more important, there is nothing anywhere to suggest Lucas Corbin is anything other than what he says he is. His London address checks out, and he's been a prolific buyer and seller of antiques for several years. No indication of any previous illegal dealings.' Robbie turned away to leave, and then stopped and looked back at Marie. 'And there's nothing new on the other front — Anna and Johnny — so if it's all right with you, I'll be heading off.'

Marie thanked him and said she'd see him tomorrow.

At last, they were able to go to the interview room, where Lucas Corbin was waiting, looking considerably more composed than he had done at the house. Evidently he'd had time to get his story straight.

And he had. When the introductions for the recording had been dealt with and the interview proper commenced, Lucas presented a convincing portrait of a person caught unawares by circumstances beyond his control. Surely, they could see that the robbery had absolutely nothing to do with him, he said. When it seemed that nothing they tried could shake him out of his attitude of wounded innocence, Jackman adopted a more aggressive stance, homing in on the timing of his entry into Hartwood House.

'What? You expect us to believe that you turned up for a cosy chat with a couple of recluses who talk to *no one* just as their house has been burgled? According to you, the door was wide open, yet the alarm wasn't tripped until you went in. Forgive me, Mr Corbin, but that is a load of bullshit!'

Lucas Corbin met his gaze, unruffled. 'Sorry, but that's exactly what I am expecting you to believe, because it happens to be the truth. For a start, I had no idea they were so reclusive. As far as I knew, they were two men with a very impressive collection of Art Deco memorabilia whose whereabouts they weren't keen to make known, no doubt because of its value.' He raised an eyebrow. 'If you were a fellow collector and had finally traced this almost legendary pair, I'm sure you'd think it worth a punt at getting to see their fabled collection.'

Ignoring this remark, Jackman pressed him on his story about the open door closing behind him, thus activating the alarms.

'Sorry, Detective Inspector, but I have no idea how it happened. I'd have thought it was something for you to investigate, not for me to speculate about.' He assumed a pained expression. 'Look, I've had an awful experience, and now I want to go home. Why should I be treated like a criminal when I haven't done anything wrong?'

He's good, thought Marie, and he's not dropping the cover story for one moment.

Jackman's phone, which he'd muted, buzzed softly in his pocket. He took it out and glanced at it, his expression going from bewilderment to shock. Abruptly, he stood up and announced that the interview was suspended.

Outside the room, he ran along the corridor, Marie in hot pursuit, and dived into the first empty room. Only then did he accept the call, putting the phone on loudspeaker.

The disembodied voice rang out, echoing around the bare room. 'Don't let dear Lucas fool you, DI Jackman. And should his silver tongue have begun to convince you of his supposed innocence, have a listen to this, and I suggest you save this message . . .'

The loud clamour of an alarm issued from the mobile, causing both Marie and Jackman to jump. As they wincingly listened, they heard someone shouting, faint above the din.

Nina! Ring Chaos on the emergency number I gave you! Something's wrong with my phone! He's cocked up the timing! Tell him to get me out of here!' There was a short interval in which nothing could be heard but the blare of the alarm, and then the same voice — Lucas's — saying, *'Listen! As soon as he answers, you go with the others, and get away fast. Leave me the car. As soon as he releases the lock, I'll come after you. But Nina! This is important! Go to my rented cottage! If I'm not there shortly afterwards, get inside and take my laptop, and anything else that could identify me. If you don't hear from me by five o'clock, you know what to do with the haul from the previous robbery, then use our emergency procedure, and go to ground, got it?'*

The alarm abruptly fell silent, and the caller softly laughed. 'Clever, huh? I'd like to see him talk his way out of that. I'm sure your IT department can minimise the background noise, and voice recognition will do the rest. Soon it'll be, "Lucas Corbin, I'm arresting you for the theft of . . ."' Chaos laughed again. 'Anyway, I'll leave that with you. And should you have trouble locating the stolen goodies, I might just throw you another tasty hint. Bye now!'

'Chaos,' whispered Marie.

Jackman nodded. 'Chaos. And I'll not even begin to suggest tracing that call.'

'Total waste of time,' Marie said, 'as would be asking how the hell he got hold of your personal mobile number.'

The two of them remained speechless for almost a minute, floored by the realisation that their mysterious hacker was involved in even this seemingly unconnected art theft.

Marie was the first to come to her senses. 'Jackman! You need to get that recording to Orac, right now! I'll go and terminate the interview and meet you in IT.'

But Jackman needed no telling. He was at the door before she'd even risen from her seat.

* * *

Unaware of all the drama at his place of work, Charlie Button was sitting in a chair next to his hospital bed trying to come to terms with the news he'd just been given. His surgeon had popped in to tell him that the operation had been successful, and that as long as he kept up his physiotherapy exercises, he would be almost certain to recover most, if not all, of the use of his hand and arm. Soon after the surgeon had left, the ward sister came in with news of his impending discharge. He would be going home the following day.

This was good news, yes? So why wasn't he happy?

The fact was, Charlie Button was in love. If he went home tomorrow, he might never see Jasmine again, and the thought of that was unbearable. But could he find the courage to ask her out? Charlie had little experience of girls, and he found himself all at sea. What if all patients fell in love with their nurses? He'd look pretty stupid making such a big deal of it.

Charlie got up and wandered aimlessly about the small room. No, it was more than that. What he felt for Jasmine was more than a passing fancy, and he wasn't going to let it go. But how to approach her? What should he say? Charlie was in uncharted territory and had no idea how to proceed.

He spent the best part of the next half hour agonising about what to do, and came to the conclusion that he needed help. But who to ask? Suddenly, his expression cleared, and he reached for his phone.

'Max, old buddy, I *really* need some advice.'

* * *

When Kevin arrived back in the CID room, he was surprised to see so many people still working. The atmosphere was charged, clearly something had occurred.

'That Chaos bloke has contacted DI Jackman,' one of the night shift detectives told him. 'Looks like the bastard is everywhere.'

As he spoke, Kevin saw Marie emerge from Jackman's office and beckon to him. 'I thought you'd have gone home by now,' she said.

'I stayed on in Fendyke to do a couple more interviews, Sarge, and I've got some names for you. They're all people who disappeared suddenly during the last eighteen months or so.'

'Excellent,' Marie said, 'and we've managed to ID one of our victims from a keycard that Spike found in his clothing.'

'It wasn't either Gino Lombardi or Jeremy Logan, was it?' Kevin asked.

'Yes, it was Gino Lombardi. So, he was on your list too?' she said.

Kevin nodded. 'The old guy who gave me the names is pretty shrewd, so I'll take a very close look at the other two.' He looked around. 'But that's not what all the activity is about, is it? It must have to do with Chaos contacting the boss.'

Marie frowned. 'You've heard already?'

'Buzz just told me, but he didn't give me the details.'

Marie filled him in, then raised a finger. 'Picture this, Kev. We're in interview room three. Jackman's phone rings. We suspend the interview and go outside. The caller then plays a recording made *inside* the crime scene of our thief yelling to his sidekick, who we now know to be someone called Nina, to tell Chaos to get him out!'

'Bloody hell, Sarge! That's weird.'

'IT are now running a comparison between the voice on the recording and the man in the interview room, although we already know it's the same person. Our biggest worry is Chaos, and what the hell he's up to.'

Kevin exhaled. This was getting complicated. It sounded like what Buzz had told him was right. That bastard really was everywhere.

'But that's not the end of it,' Marie said. 'To top it all, when Jackman and I got back up here after that call, PC Simon Laker was waiting for us. That retired detective, Bob Ruston, had been in touch. You know who I mean, the man whose doorstep that abducted kid first turned up on.'

'Yes, I heard about that.'

'Well, the kid was so traumatised he was refusing to speak, so Simon had the idea of bringing Bob in to try and get something out of him. Turns out it was a smart move, and we now have a name for him. He said he'd been going to his grandmother's place when he was taken, which has now been verified. Bob Ruston himself went to Huntingdon with one of our constables and spoke to the old lady. Not only did she confirm that her grandson Craig had never been in any serious trouble, but she also gave Bob a very interesting piece of information.' Pausing for effect, Marie said, 'What would you say if I told you that young Craig is a computer wizard? According to his teachers, he was streaks ahead of any of his fellow students, and could have had a glowing career in that field, but for some reason, he didn't want to go that route.'

Kevin squeezed his eyes shut and considered the implications of what he'd been told. The two — apparently unconnected — men who had gone missing — Johnny Millard and this other lad, Craig, both had exceptional IT skills. Add to that Chaos's sudden explosion of activity wherever you looked, and . . .

'Technology. Chaos,' Kevin said quietly.

'A very apt name, wouldn't you say?'

'Can't think of anything more appropriate,' murmured Kevin, then something occurred to him. 'Doesn't that put young Craig in a very vulnerable position, Sarge? After all, Johnny Millard is still missing, and can't help us trace Chaos, but we actually *have* Craig, and if he can tell us what he was doing that got him kidnapped, we could have a lead.'

'That's just what Jackman thought. So, Ruth Crooke is right now trying to get Craig moved to an undisclosed medical facility where he'll be under round-the-clock protection. It's likely that if Chaos is behind this, he'll already have wiped all the data from the lad's computer, wherever it is, but something necessitated his removal from the scene, and as you rightly said, that means he's in grave danger.' Marie checked the time. 'Kevin, it's late. You get off home. We'll tackle all this in the morning.'

'I'm just going to do a quick search on the other two names that old man gave me, and then I'll call it a day,' he said.

'Well, make sure you do,' said Marie firmly. 'Looks like things are hotting up around here, so get what time you can at home. In fact, leave those names till tomorrow. There's nothing you can do about them tonight, anyway, and I know what happens with those searches, you go down a rabbit hole, and you'll still be here at midnight. So do what your dear old sarge tells you, and bugger off.'

After a moment's hesitation, Kevin threw up his hands. 'Okay, I give in. 'Night, Sarge. See you in the morning.'

''Night, Kevin, and well done getting those names.'

Kevin made for the door, feeling quite chuffed. It felt good to be appreciated, and it made him want to work harder.

Indeed, he could hardly wait to get back to tracing Shelley Kershaw and Jeremy Logan.

* * *

'Tomorrow morning at nine, Rowan. The upstairs conference room. Extraordinary meeting. And I want you and Marie there to present the facts as we know them, and also to point out any potential threats to security. I've already notified my uniformed counterpart, and Orla Cracken will be there too.'

Ruth was in full superintendent mode, and Jackman knew there was no point even asking who else would be attending this 'extraordinary meeting'. Possibly the chief constable, along with a few unfamiliar men and women from shadowy departments who tended to drive cars with bullet-proof windows.

'We'll be there, Ruth.' What else was there to say?

With a brisk, 'Thanks,' the line went dead. Well, if this was what Chaos was aiming for, he was succeeding brilliantly. But sod bloody Chaos, right now, he, Jackman, was going home, where hopefully Julia would have saved him some of the dinner he'd missed. He grabbed his jacket, picked up his car keys and strode out into the CID room.

'Marie! Home! Get that husband of yours to feed you well, and make you a packed lunch for tomorrow, as heaven knows when we'll find time to eat. Oh, and have a good breakfast. I'm working on Napolean's theory that an army always marches best on a full stomach. We have a meeting at nine, and it sounds like it's the prelude to a major hunt for a very clever, and most probably exceptionally dangerous hacker.'

CHAPTER TWENTY-TWO

At just after nine the following morning, as Jackman was briefing a roomful of sombre, high-ranking officers on one of the most serious situations of his career, Rory was going about his work, humming contentedly.

'Do you know what I love about this job? It involves nothing but concrete facts. In a world of misinformation and fake news, I find that *so* satisfying. Thanks to AI and our politicians, we have no idea what is and what is not real, or even whether what we are constantly fed by our leaders is even true. I mean, look at this woman's intestines. What they show us is indisputable, no one can possibly say it's not real. Isn't that the most wonderful thing?'

'Only you could wax lyrical about someone's stomach contents,' said Spike laconically.

'But they are such *revealing* stomach contents, dear boy. Just think, within them lies the whole story behind this poor woman's death. It's so, well, beautiful.'

Spike regarded him with a long-suffering expression. 'But we still have no idea if she ingested the poison by accident, design, or whether it was administered by a person unknown, so maybe it's not so perfect after all.'

Rory waved this aside. 'Forensically, it is complete, dear heart. Now we can inform the correct authorities, and it's up to them to find out how it occurred. However,' he raised a finger, 'they have unarguable proof of the cause. Our work is done. So, if you would kindly finish up here, we can return to Professor Wallace and the anthropological nightmare of the pillbox.'

Jan Wallace looked far too happy to be in the grip of any form of nightmare. She beamed at Rory when he entered the lab. 'We now have the biological profiles of all five, and as one is already identified, we are doing well. So it's down to waiting for the test results to come back while we press on with finding any anomalies our victims present. Speaking of which, I've found a very interesting bit of dentistry on our Violet. No doubt a dentist somewhere will have her records, and if she's local, we might be able to find her that way. I must say, it's all most positive this morning.'

Rory smiled at her enthusiasm, although Cardiff looked less than exhilarated. She knew, as did he, that a biological profile was only the first step in identifying a victim. All it really told them was whether they were male or female, approximately how old they were when they died, and how tall, and where they came from. This was all vital information, but there was still a long way to go. They could extract DNA and check dentition, but the bodies were in such a state of decomposition that they had no fingerprints left on which to base a search. And DNA, amazing as it was, was only of use if the deceased person had come to the attention of the police or Interpol. They had to know who the person was in the first place before they could obtain a sample from a family member.

Today, however, Rory was on Jan's side. It was all very positive indeed. 'I was just thinking that should our precious wards offer no leads, we might resort to technology, and plunge into computerised 3D modelling for facial reconstruction. What say you, dear Jan?'

'My thoughts precisely.' Jan positively purred. 'And it's growing more accurate by the minute. It's one of my little favourites — a magnificent combination of technology and art. Okay, it doesn't yet produce an exact replica of the living person, but the likeness is certainly close enough to prompt recognition.'

'Then since we have both technology and your unsurpassable skills, I suggest we use them sooner rather than later. If our detectives' initial enquiries fail to produce any result, we'll go for facial recognition. Agreed?'

'Absolutely, and since some of the bone analysis tests should be back soon, we've plenty to occupy us meanwhile. Come on, troops! Liven up! Let's crack on!'

Cardiff's attempt to stifle a laugh ended in a snort. 'Yes, ma'am!' she said, and saluted. 'Ready for duty.'

'Then fall in, girl. There's a very interesting upper thoracic vertebrae I'd like you to take a look at . . .'

* * *

Back in the CID room, an anxious group of men and women had gathered for a meeting with Jackman.

'The bottom line is that Chaos is living up to his name. In the meeting I attended earlier, it emerged that he is targeting locations right across the Midlands and the East Coast, and as far south as London. He is seemingly picking crimes at random and obstructing the criminals carrying them out; yesterday's art theft is a prime example. The rumours that some villains have died or disappeared are still unsubstantiated and we think it's some sort of malicious rumour intended to have the same result, but we cannot rule them out. The thing is, although he's focussing on the crimes themselves, the fact that he has access to our systems and our mobile phones is a major cause for concern. Orac has upgraded our security to the highest level, and everything incoming, digital or not, is being scanned prior to being opened. We are lucky to have a new member of staff in the IT section, Coral McIvor, who has had previous dealings with this hacker while she was in the Met Cybercrime Unit, and she's been able to give us valuable information about his MO.' Jackman shrugged. 'Basically there's no better way of describing what he's up to than chaos.'

'But what's his motive, boss?' asked Max. 'Is he some kind of "Taxi Driver" figure like in the movie, clearing the bad guys off the streets?'

'No one has the slightest idea, Max. Theories range from roughly what you just said, to his being a super-cybercriminal preparing the way for some massive new organisation to take over. We're assuming he's doing it for big money, but he could just as well be out for revenge. Or it's neither of those, and he's doing it simply because he can, for the fun of it. We simply don't know.'

'Could he be Johnny Millard, out for revenge?' asked Gary. 'Johnny lost years of his life for something he didn't do, and the people who met him inside all said that he'd changed.'

'He has the skills,' added Robbie, 'but unless he found a way to kick all this off while he was inside, the timing doesn't fit.' He shrugged. 'And okay, I knew him slightly, but I'm not biased, and I seriously can't see that being the case.'

'There is one other factor, too,' added Jackman. 'Orac and her new colleague, Coral, are of the opinion that Chaos isn't acting alone.'

There was a murmur of surprise.

'If that's the case, we don't know what this other person's role might be. The name they have for him — or her — in IT is "guardian". It's something I'd never come across before, but I'm assured they are often used by spooks and the government to ensure that certain operatives are kept safe, kind of covering his back, cyber-style. IT has seen small indications that a second party is tidying up after Chaos's operations.'

'Bloody hell, boss! This is all a bit out of our league, isn't it?' said Max. 'It's like a movie. I'm half expecting Tom Cruise to swing through the super's window on the end of a wire attached to a helicopter!'

Jackman was grateful for the ripple of laughter that ran around the room diffusing the heavy atmosphere that had descended on the gathered officers.

'You're right, Max,' he said with a grin. 'I'm not sure about Tom Cruise, but it's certainly out of our league. All we can do is press on with our own investigations and trust that Orac and her cohort of cybercrime experts manage to expose Chaos. Just be hyper-vigilant when you're using your phones and devices, send no sensitive information without running it past IT and report even the slightest hint of something not being right.'

Having issued their daily orders, Jackman went on to say, 'Just before this meeting got underway, we received a memo from forensics. As promised, they have sent the biological profiles of the five victims from the pillbox. One, a male, we now know to be called Gino Lombardi, and DNA samples are being collected from his home this morning. The other four are as follows: two males and two females. The male, who's been given the name Eamonn, was white, approximately five foot eleven inches tall, and aged between fifty and fifty-five at the time of his death. He had brown hair and wore "country-style" clothes, including an expensive wax jacket. The other male, whom Rory has named Anton, is five foot ten inches in height, with grey hair and was between forty-two and forty-five years old. Professor Wallace believes that he might be of Eastern European origin. DNA from the bones will confirm or deny that hypothesis. His clothes suggest he might have been a field worker.' Jackman drew in a breath. 'Now, the two females. The first, "Violet", is quite short, being only five foot one or five two inches tall. At time of death her age was in the mid-twenties — probably twenty-four to twenty-five. She had almost black hair, and had a bony deformity to her wrist. Unusual dental work has been noted, too, and she was wearing a purple anorak and a purple scarf. Finally, the last victim is an older female who died at between the ages of fifty-seven and fifty-nine. She was five foot six or seven inches tall. Sadly, most of her clothes were made from natural fibres and have decomposed, but she was wearing an old wedding ring and an expensive gold bracelet. Rory has named this woman "Juno". He assures us that the test results on these bodies will start to roll in very soon. So, bear these details in mind when you are talking to the villagers. We'll give you the finer details as they filter in.'

He put aside the memo and looked at the team. 'I'm sure I don't need to tell you that these people might not be local villagers at all. Moreover, although we've had an incredible stroke of luck in identifying one of them, we may never know who the others are. I'd like to ask one of you to get the ball rolling with the Missing Persons Bureau and with Missing People. I've already contacted the National Crime Agency and they will alert Interpol to issue a black notice. As you know, these notices are issued when a body is found that cannot be identified. It is hoped they might tally with the yellow notices that are posted when someone is reported missing, but that takes time, and we need to make quite sure that these unfortunate souls are not some of our own from right here in the Fens. Any volunteers?'

Max put his hand up. 'Well, some poor sod has to do it, so it might as well be me.'

Pleased that Max was sounding far more like his old self, Jackman thanked him. 'By the way, Max, have you heard from Charlie?'

Max smiled happily. 'I have, and I can report that he's feeling pretty good, considering. Mainly because he's going home, and also because he's got the hots for some gorgeous nurse, and he needed Uncle Max's advice on how to proceed.'

'Oh, dear Lord!' Marie said, looking horrified. 'I dread to think what your advice was.'

'Naturally, I gave him the benefit of my vast experience in such matters, but, er, delicately.' He gave a roar of laughter.

'Come on, Sarge, this is Charlie Button we're talking about, not Casanova!'

It took Jackman a minute or two to rein them all in after this last remark. When the laughter finally subsided, he said, 'One last thing — and this is being handled by uniform at present. I'm sure you've all heard about the attack on PC Freddie Copeland while he was on night duty at the pillbox. Well, you'll be glad to hear he's back in action with no more than a couple of stitches, a big bruise and severely wounded pride. No evidence was found in the vicinity, and although there were plenty of footprints, the ground had been trampled by our and the farmer's people. PC Copeland is starting to believe he was right in his original assumption that it was someone from the press, who panicked and hit him. It certainly wasn't intended to do serious harm or kill, and the weapon used was a tree branch, not the spade used on the dead victims, so he may well turn out to be right. However, this doesn't mean we should relax our vigilance, plus, if I'm to be honest, I don't quite buy the journalist theory. Anyway, we'll see. Now, any questions?'

There being none, the team dispersed.

'So, what are we up to?' asked Marie. 'Anything specific, or shall Robbie and I pitch in with the others?'

Jackman thought for a minute. 'Get Robbie to go out to the village with the others, while you arrange with Kevin to interview Mad Sally this afternoon. When you've done that, you can join me. Bryson Smith will be here shortly, and I want him to meet the Greene brothers prior to doing a walk-round at Hartwood House. Oh, and DS Vic Blackwell is back and is being briefed by the super, so he'll be joining us as soon as she's finished with him.'

'Okay, boss, I'll be back in five, and I must say I'm relieved that Vic's back. We can't waste a minute where that case is concerned. The slightest delay on our part, and I swear those brothers will clam up on us. Vic needs to keep the ball rolling and never take his eyes off either one of that weird couple.'

Jackman decided she was probably right. The Greene brothers were a strange pair, polar opposites in appearance, Norman being gaunt and tall, while Derek was shorter and rotund. They were stiff and oddly tense, and he found them hard to like, so he wouldn't be sorry to hand them over to Vic Blackwell. Notwithstanding the brothers, the case itself intrigued and fascinated him, and the sudden eruption of Chaos onto the scene threw a whole new light on it.

* * *

Having spent years as a uniformed officer, Kevin Stoner thought nothing could surprise him anymore. He'd been inside every sort of dwelling, from disgusting squats to luxury apartments, but Laburnum House was something else. Dudley Nailer had called it ramshackle, but it could be better described as a disaster area.

'Bloody hell, Kev,' muttered Gary. 'Do you think it's even safe to go inside?'

Located a few hundred metres from the church and set in extensive grounds, in its heyday Laburnum House must have been a very desirable residence. Now, the grounds were an impenetrable forest of overgrown shrubs and unkempt trees. The path to the front door, although thankfully clear, looked as if someone had attacked it with a machete. The house itself was falling to bits — missing tiles, crumbling brickwork, peeling paintwork, decaying timbers and windows that were cracked. If Dudley hadn't told him that old Jeannie, the owner, was the only person who might know something of the whereabouts of Shelley Kershaw, he would have suggested to Gary that they give the whole thing up as a bad job.

It took her a while to answer their knock, which wasn't surprising given her age and obvious infirmity. She stood behind her walking frame peering at them suspiciously until Gary introduced them. Then, she relaxed slightly, and said they'd better come in.

She turned, and with no little trepidation, they followed her retreating back down a narrow corridor with faded wallpaper that still miraculously clung tenaciously to the damp walls, and into a kitchen.

Kevin, who liked clean lines and tidy surfaces, stared about him in horror. The kitchen, though big, seemed small and cramped because of all the clutter it contained. In the centre of the room was a massive old pine table, every inch of it covered in, well, *stuff*. Boxes, bottles, empty milk cartons, plastic containers, balls of string, piles of unopened junk mail, cat food and plastic bowls of rancid milk.

They both hastily declined her offer of tea, and after clearing old clothing, a tea cosy, a stack of plastic bags and a large ginger cat from the kitchen chairs, she asked them to sit down.

And this woman took in lodgers? How could anyone live here? Kevin thought. Were the rooms she let out like this? Surely not.

Gary took the lead, for which Kevin was grateful. He was still reeling from the state of the place.

'So you see, Mrs Roberts—'

'Call me Jeannie, everyone does.'

'All right, Jeannie, we are trying to find out about a young woman who has gone missing. We believe she stayed with you for a while. Shelley Kershaw?'

Kevin watched as several conflicting emotions passed across the old woman's face. She said nothing.

'Was she with you for long, Jeannie? Can you tell us anything about who she was and where she came from?' Then, responding to Gary's gentle, almost chatty tone, the old woman seemed to relent.

'She was a rum 'un all right, but I liked the girl. I felt sorry for her. I'd stopped taking lodgers years back, when me legs got too bad to get up the stairs. But Shelley had nowhere to go, so I let her have a room at almost no charge.'

'How come she ended up in this village?' asked Gary. 'She wasn't from round here, was she?'

'She came from somewhere up north, but she never said where, and I only knew that from her accent. She'd been in retail, she said, worked in a big store, but something happened and she had to leave. She came down here to stay with someone, though she never said who, but that didn't work out either. After a bit, she got a job in the pub in the next village, but it didn't pay much, so finding a place to stay was a problem.' Rubbing hard at a painful knee, she looked up at Gary. 'She had a bad reputation hereabouts, but I reckons it weren't her fault. She was a sweet little thing when you got to know her.' She sighed, and then said angrily, 'All that girl wanted was someone to take care of her. I reckoned she'd had too many bad experiences with men in her short life. I'm not saying she were soft in the head or anything, but she was — what's the word now — sort of innocent. *Naïve*, that's it, especially for her age.'

'How old was she?' asked Kevin.

'Ooh I've never been good at ages. Twenty-three, twenty-four? Could've been a bit older, I'm not sure. She was very pretty, I can tell you that, very pretty indeed. Lovely dark hair she had, and lovely smooth skin.'

Kevin straightened up. Not Violet! Could they be that lucky, twice in a row? 'Did Shelley own a purple anorak by any chance?'

'No idea. I'm colourblind. I mix up my colours something awful. Runs in my family.'

'How about a problem with her wrist? Sort of knobbly as if she'd had an injury at some point?'

'Well, if she did, I never noticed.'

Kevin knew his next question was going to be about as useful as a lead parachute, but he had to ask. 'I suppose you don't have a picture of Shelley, do you? Or know of anyone else who might have one, maybe a friend? Young people these days are always taking selfies of their mates.'

'Lord, no. I never had no picture, and she didn't have any friends. I suppose there might be one in her room. You can look if you like.'

'You've still got her things? In her room?' Kevin asked.

'I've always had this feeling that one day she'd walk back in, large as life,' Jeannie said wistfully. 'So, they ain't mine to throw away, are they?'

'Yes, we'd like to take a look, if you don't mind,' said Gary.

Kevin guessed Gary felt the same as he did about opening up a room that had been unused for eighteen months. 'Well, we won't ask you to accompany us, unless you want to, of course.'

'Not with these knees! Haven't been up there for many a month.' Jeannie glared down at the offending legs. 'It's the first door on the left off the landing.' She got to her feet with some difficulty, opened an old-fashioned wooden key cupboard and took down a modern Yale key. 'It was a nice room,' she said a little sadly. 'And Shelley looked after it too. Not like some. When I first took in lodgers, we, that was my husband Bernard and me, always made the rooms comfy, but most of them didn't respect them. Then when Bernard died, sudden-like, and the money ran out, I lost interest. That's when the place started to go to rack and ruin.' She looked around vaguely. 'Still, it'll see me out, I suppose.'

Kevin wasn't too sure about that. Now he understood why what had once been a lovely property had been left to deteriorate so badly. Jeannie clearly had no one to help her.

They mounted the wide staircase, trying not to worry about the ominous creaks. On the landing, they took a breath and opened Shelley's door for the first time since she went missing.

To Kevin's surprise, Jeannie had been right. It was a nice room, simply furnished with a circular table and a chair, a bed, a chest of drawers, a narrow pine bookcase and a small single wardrobe. A wall-mounted basin doubled as a sink, and a short counter held a plug-in electric hob with two hot plates, a small economy microwave oven and an electric kettle. There were two sash windows, the casements now swollen and jammed shut, that looked out over the garden and across to the church. The room had the musty smell of disuse, and a film of dust covered every surface, but you could see how pleasant it had been. Even the wallpaper, although faded, was unmarked by damp and still smooth. It had a pretty design of soft blue and lavender wisteria that gave the appearance of blossoms filling the room.

Gary whistled. 'Kev! All her things are still here! Clothes, magazines, cosmetics, all her personal possessions untouched. Poor girl. No one bothered to report her missing, and no one came looking for her. That's awful! A pretty young woman goes out one day to catch a bus, and not only does she disappear, but no one even cares!'

'Do you think she's Violet, Gary?' Kevin asked.

'Well, we'll know soon enough, won't we? Even if we find nothing in her belongings, this room must be heaving with her DNA. And look! Photos!' Gary went over to the dressing table. 'Mostly old snapshots, but we'll get Jeannie to confirm if any of them are Shelley. And then the Prof can do a facial recognition comparison. We need forensics here.'

Back downstairs, Jeannie immediately pointed out a dark-haired young woman in a picture with two older women. 'She's a lot younger in this, but that's Shelley Kershaw all right.' She stared wide-eyed at Gary. 'Is she dead, then? She's not one of the bodies from that damned pillbox in Teddy Smith's garden, is she?'

So the news had reached even as far as this old house. 'We really don't know, Jeannie,' Gary said gently. 'That's what we are trying to find out, and you've been very helpful. I'm afraid we'll have to get some of our forensic colleagues in now, to go over Shelley's room, but we'll try not to cause you too much inconvenience.'

She sighed. 'I wish I'd done more to find her when she never came back. It was just . . . what with all these men being attracted to her, like, I thought she must've run off with one of them. She once said that if she met Mr Right, she'd walk right out of her present life and never look back.' She swallowed. 'Even though she left owing a month's rent, I always hoped she'd found her Mr Right.'

Gary patted her arm. 'I promise I'll come back and tell you what we find out. Then, well, even if it's bad news, at least you'll know one way or the other.'

As they said their goodbyes, Jeannie said, 'One thing, Detectives, don't slam my front door when you go out, and tells your mates the same. I don't want anyone hit by a falling roof slate, and the bit above the front door is the worst. Ask the postman!'

Noting the three shattered slates on the ground, he and Gary went out, closing the door, very gently, behind them.

CHAPTER TWENTY-THREE

Bryson Smith greeted Jackman's story of a bungled robbery in which the thief had been trapped inside with a roar
of delighted laughter. Jackman omitted to mention Chaos's
involvement, leaving Bryson to believe that Lucas had somehow triggered the security system himself.

'Hilarious as it is, his cohorts pulled off a massive theft,
which is why I thought of you,' Jackman said. 'Your assistance
in providing a description of the stolen items would speed
things up considerably. All forces, along with Interpol, must
be told exactly what it is they are looking for as quickly as
possible. My colleague, DS Vic Blackwell, will liaise with you
as soon as he's free.'

'Sounds like it was a pretty daring raid, Jackman,' commented Bryson, 'and well thought out, until that last catastrophe.' Bryson was evidently puzzled that an obviously adroit
criminal had allowed himself to become ensnared in that way.

'Ah, we think he either got greedy and outstayed his welcome, or accidentally reactivated the alarms. Whatever, he's
equally secure now, but in one of our cells.' Jackman smiled
and moved on quickly. 'It's very good of you to assist, Bryson.
I can only imagine how long it would have taken one of our

officers to describe such items. You are also in the unique position of being able to tell how accurate the Greene brothers have been in evaluating their worth.'

'Well, that's what I do,' Bryson said. 'My job consists of appraising and evaluating works of art for auction. And it so happens that Art Deco and Art Nouveau are particular favourites of mine. I've been itching to get back to London and my studio, so having something like this to do is a real blessing.'

'You might not think so when you meet Norman and Derek Greene,' said Marie grimly. 'Not only are they eccentric, but they're bloody rude with it.'

Bryson laughed. 'Oh, this trade attracts them by the dozen, believe me. I must have met them all by now. Some are quite paranoid, and squirrel their treasures away so only they can enjoy them. Others are quite the opposite, and think they're really something because of what they possess, even if their treasures were only inherited. One thing they have in common is that they are all, every single one of them, totally obsessed.'

'Well, you are about to meet two more obsessives,' Jackman said. 'Forensics hope to be out of Hartwood House by early afternoon, since there was no violence involved.' Jackman checked his watch. 'I'll introduce you to Vic Blackwell, then Marie and I will accompany you both to the local Travelodge to meet the Greene brothers, after which we'll leave you in Vic's tender hands.'

'Sounds good to me. And don't fret over the eccentric brothers, I know how to handle their type.'

Jackman didn't doubt him for a moment.

Vic Blackwell met them in the foyer. Seeing Marie, the big man beamed, and at once came over to give her a friendly hug. Relations between the two of them had been stormy, to put it mildly, but over time they had become firm friends.

'Vic,' said Jackman. 'Glad to see you back. This is Bryson Smith. He's the art expert I was telling you about, so if you're ready, we'll go and see the Greenes.'

An hour later, Jackman and Marie were on their way back from the hotel, once again thankful for Bryson's assistance. It had been hard to convince the brothers that the theft of their precious possessions was receiving the police's fullest attention, and that they were not being fobbed off with less important personnel. However, Bryson had saved the day, and by the time Jackman and Marie had left, the three of them were practically best buddies.

Jackman turned into the road leading to the station. 'Right, Marie! All formally handed over. Now Vic and Bryson can take it from here.'

'So it's back to the Pillbox Killer, then,' Marie said. 'Kevin and Gary should be finished with their interviews by around two, so I'm driving out to Fendyke to meet them and we'll try and track down Mad Sally. Meanwhile I'll do a bit of research on that woman so I don't put my foot in it out of sheer ignorance.'

'Good idea. People don't get a reputation like hers for nothing, so forewarned is forearmed. What do we already know about her, Marie?'

'Very little. Kevin's been asking around about her but nobody can tell him much. Her proper name is believed to be Sarah Nugent. She lives in a small farmhouse — two old cottages that were joined together way back, and it's a bit of a time warp, apparently. The address is Rivendell, Fourth Drove, and it's right out on the edge of the village. Someone told Kevin that the house itself is in Fendyke, but the garden is in neighbouring Bartoft Village. Apart from that, I know sweet Fanny Adams, and I'll be needing a whole lot more than that before I attempt to get her to speak to us.'

Jackman pulled into the station car park. 'Well, I'll have to leave you with that, Marie. I need to report in to Ruth, and then I have to check on progress in IT — oh, and also speak to Rory about the possibility of using facial recognition on the girl he calls Violet, so we'll tie up again at close of play, if that's okay with you?'

'Gotcha, boss. I'll do my best with Mad Sally, but from what we've heard, I can't guarantee I'll have much success.'

Strangely, Ruth Crooke seemed newly galvanised when Jackman met with her.

She fixed him with one of her stares. 'I know this is no longer your baby, Rowan, but we all need to be aware of the machinations of Chaos, every step of the way. I've had a memo from DI Nikki Galena in Greenborough, copied to Orac. It's a report from their IT consultant, Sarah Dukes.'

'Ah, Spooky,' said Jackman. 'Quite a whizz, that one.'

'Er, yes, Spooky.' Ruth gave him a slightly mystified look, 'Tell me, Rowan, is it part of the head of IT's job description to be known by a weird nickname?'

'It's no different to coppers,' he said with a grin. 'I mean, we have "Nobby" Clark, there's "Swifty" Fleet at Fenfleet, not to mention my favourite, "Rusty" Gates. Even Rory calls Erin Rees his technician "Cardiff", after her hometown. It's what we do.'

Ruth shook her head. 'Anyway, this, er, "Spooky" person has been looking into a case for DI Galena, and it's clearly one of Chaos's little pranks that he's playing on another criminal gang. This time it was a daring hit on a security company van that was delivering money to cash machines. Two hours before it took off, DI Galena received a text with a set of coordinates and a message telling her it might be to her advantage to be at this particular spot at a certain time. Luckily, she didn't dismiss it as a hoax, and her team nailed three armed robbers just as they were about to ram the armoured van.'

'Nice one!'

'*Very* nice one, Rowan. And as you might expect, Spooky's traces on the sender of that text message went halfway round the world before disappearing into a black hole. However, she got hold of the thieves' phones and discovered that the van's computer system had been hacked, and at a certain time, just moments after the van was to be run off the road, the doors would have automatically opened, allowing the thieves access without violence.'

259

'Ah, I get it. Chaos was paid to do that, and then he dobbed the gang in it! Just like Lucas.'

'Just like Lucas,' said Ruth. 'But what Spooky, and now Orac, are trying to find out is how these ill-fated criminals paid Chaos, in the hope of finding a weak point somewhere in the transfer of funds from them to him. If nothing else, it proves that Chaos is working independently, offering his services to the criminal fraternity, no doubt at a price.'

'In light of that, couldn't we lean on those armed robbers, or Lucas, and get them to tell us how they first heard about Chaos, and what means they used to contact him?' asked Jackman.

'I've already spoken to Vic Blackwell about that, and he's willing to give it a try. DI Galena is also pursuing that route, but she reckons that by now Chaos will have closed that door very firmly. He's too damn clever to leave himself open to anything like that, don't you think?' Ruth said.

'Yeah, you're right, far too clever. Meanwhile, he's handing us bad guys, right left and centre.' Jackman smiled. 'Maybe we shouldn't be complaining?'

'Our arrest rates have never looked better, that's for sure. Trouble is, we don't know what his end game is, because I'm pretty damn sure it's not to make the Fenland Constabulary look good.' Ruth glanced at the memo. 'Oh, and another thing. He seems to have left the Met alone since he started targeting our area. They've had nothing their way for weeks. His attention is all on the Fens.'

'Lucky old us,' murmured Jackman. 'But we have Orac and her team, and Nikki Galena has Spooky; even the Met doesn't have people with their level of expertise to call on.'

'And those in power are aware of that, Rowan, as you must have gathered from the meeting. Because no one knows the extent of Chaos's capabilities, they are considering him a clear and present danger and we've been put on high alert. Currently, Chaos is concentrating on villains, but what if he targeted us, or he got bored with the bad guys and thought he'd have some fun with,' she shrugged, 'take your pick — airlines, maybe? Train companies? Energy providers?'

'Communications? Banks? The Stock Exchange?' Jackman had recently read the annual report on cyber-attacks and breaches of data security. The report had said that there had been over nine thousand publicly disclosed incidents in the year under review, so how many others might there have been? He groaned. 'I don't even want to dwell on that one, thanks. I've got to keep focussed on what's happening in our patch, and especially in and around little Fendyke.'

'Indeed you do. But be prepared. From now on, I'll be giving you daily updates on the situation regarding Chaos. And for your part, please pass on to me immediately anything you hear on the grapevine, even some vague rumour, concerning the criminal sector.'

'Of course.'

'Right, then. Back to the real world. Where are you with your pillbox deaths?'

Jackman filled her in on their progress, telling her about the man who had been identified, and that they might soon have a name for the younger of the two women. 'I'd like you to know that DC Kevin Stoner's commitment to the case has been exemplary. He's shown himself to have a very strong work ethic. For example, he cut short a holiday when he heard Charlie Button had been injured, he's worked well over his hours and has already made some useful contacts in the village. I'm very impressed with his performance and I felt you should know what an asset he's turned out to be.'

'Duly noted, Rowan. Thank you.' She glanced at the clock. 'And now I have to throw you out, I'm afraid. Like it or not, the media are hungry for more information about the Pillbox Killer. So far I've managed to keep it low key, but now I think it's time for the full story to come out — well, as much as I'm prepared to divulge. So be prepared for a storm. This is exactly the kind of case that the broadsheets and mass media love to pounce on. Naturally, I won't be giving them all the details. They'll come out later, that sort of thing always does, but I'll do my best to buy you some time before the whole thing turns into some dark tale from the Middle Ages, and you become the Witchfinder General!'

'Appreciated, I'm sure.' Jackman stopped halfway to the door. 'It's just struck me that we are working at both ends of the spectrum at the moment. At one end, we have a hi-tech cyber hacker, and at the other, a Gothic charnel house full of decaying bodies. It beggars belief, doesn't it?'

'At least you can't complain police work is boring, can you?' said Ruth with a wry smile. 'Now, you'd better hurry up and sort out your charnel house before that pillbox becomes a Mecca for sickos trying to get a photo to put on Facebook!'

* * *

'So how do we play this, Sarge?' asked Gary. 'It's just that I'm really not happy about you going it alone.'

'Don't be such an old woman, Gary,' said Marie, nudging him from the back seat of the car. 'She's quite harmless, just eccentric, and hellfire, we deal with those every day of the week. And if she refuses to talk to me, it could be a fruitless mission anyway.' She had scoffed, but Gary's concern for her gave her a warm feeling, which went some way to mitigate her lack of success in finding out anything at all about Mad Sally. 'I just wish I knew what made her stop talking to people.'

'Dudley says she's always been taciturn, then all of a sudden, she stopped saying anything at all. Only once did she speak, when the driver of a tanker come to empty her septic tank backed into her gatepost. She certainly spoke then, and by all accounts used some pretty choice language! Dudley reckons something bad happened to her, but he has no idea what.'

'Could well be,' said Marie. 'Trauma often does have that effect, and if she's mistrustful of people as well, that could explain it.'

'I was thinking that, too,' said Kevin, negotiating a sharp bend in the lane. 'Dudley said she always seems to be on the scene whenever anything happens . . . like she's looking for something, or watching out for someone.' He glanced at Marie in the rear-view mirror. 'It's not the same, I know, but when I was in uniform there was this one time when we had a stalker out on the streets, and he'd apparently frightened this woman called Becky really badly, so what did she do? She started to follow *him*. And I mean, followed — she haunted the guy. We warned her off for her own safety, but she wouldn't let it go. One day, the stalker followed a young girl, eventually making a move on her. Immediately, Becky appeared out of nowhere and started laying into him with this rounders bat she was carrying. She knocked seven bells out of him, she did.'

'Good for her,' Gary said. 'So where is this Rivendell place?'

'I think we're nearly there,' said Kevin. 'See where the lane curves round by that thick stand of trees ahead? Well, if it's where Dudley told me, the house should be about five hundred yards further on.'

It was a lonely spot to live in. No neighbours for miles, and no other buildings either, not even a barn.

'How depressing is this,' said Gary. 'Solitude is all very well, but you'd think she'd at least have chosen somewhere a bit pretty. This place looks, well, forgotten.'

The house itself was weathered but not derelict. The front garden was overgrown, but not a jungle like Gino Lombardi's had been. Marie thought it had an odd dormant quality to it.

Kevin parked outside the gate, from where a wide gravel drive led to a garage. 'Dudley said she drives an old army Land Rover Series 111, a seventies model, he thinks. Those old things go on forever, and she'd need something like that living out here.'

Marie took a breath. 'Okay, lads. You wait here, and I'll go see what I can do. If I need help, I'll come and get you, or give you a call. I can't say I hold out much hope, but we have to try.'

She got out of the car and started up the driveway, hearing car doors open and then close behind her. Gary and Kevin were clearly not happy about her going solo, and were ready to leap into action.

She could see no bell, but there was an old cast-iron door knocker, so she gave it a hearty hammering, and stood back.

The woman who opened the door matched her in height, which was unusual. Few women were as tall as her. But that's where the similarity ended, for Marie was solidly built, whereas this woman was lean and wiry.

'Hello,' Marie said brightly. 'Sarah Nugent? I'm DS Marie Evans, Fenland Constabulary, based at Saltern-le-Fen. We are calling on everyone in the area, to reassure you about the recent happenings in the village, and also to ask for your help. Could you spare me a few minutes, please?'

Mad Sally eyed her up and down in a manner clearly meant to be intimidating. Marie held her gaze steadily. 'I'd really appreciate your help, Sarah, as we're dealing with a very serious matter here. We've been told you live alone out here and we are concerned for your safety, so I think it's only fair we put you in the picture. One or two of the other residents who live in remote places like this one are making arrangements to stay with relatives, or to go away for a few days while our enquiries are underway.'

Marie wasn't sure, but she thought she saw a flicker of amusement on Sally's face, but it was gone almost at once. Without a word, she turned, leaving the door open, and walked back inside. Taking it to be an invitation to go in, Marie followed. She closed the door after her, giving her two anxious-looking colleagues a quick thumbs-up.

The narrow hallway was bare of furniture, and devoid of pictures or other decoration. The solid wooden parquet floor, which showed signs of wear, appeared to be oak.

At the end of the hall, the woman turned in through a narrow doorway, again leaving the door open for Marie, who found herself in a large kitchen. Marie uttered a little gasp of surprise, suddenly struck by a memory. She had been in just such a kitchen in the house of her grandparents, in another part of the Fen, a lifetime ago.

'This is amazing,' she whispered. 'You have an incredible home, Sarah.'

And it was, but it was also like a museum dedicated to country life centuries ago. Marie wondered how on earth this woman managed to live here in the modern age. There was no mains drainage, no gas supply, no central heating system, no modern appliances. There was electricity, but when Marie looked, she noticed that the sockets were the old type that took plugs with round pins.

It took her some time to focus on the purpose of her visit. The room was cluttered and untidy, but there was no dust or marks, and when Sarah shifted a pile of washing from a chair so that Marie could sit down, she noticed that although it hadn't been ironed, it was clean and neatly folded. There were no bookshelves, but that didn't mean there were no books. Piles of them had been stacked by a chair near the old stove. Glancing at the bindings, Marie saw Chekhov's short stories, George Orwell's *Nineteen Eighty-Four*, and a beautiful leather-bound copy of *Titus Andronicus*.

A silence descended, broken only by the logs spitting in the open range. It seemed that the woman was waiting for Marie to deliver her message, and then leave. Yet she hadn't been openly hostile, having even gone so far as to offer Marie a seat.

Sarah, however, remained standing, which Marie assumed was intended to put her at a disadvantage. Meanwhile, she was racking her brains for something to say that would persuade this woman to speak. As nothing helpful came to mind, she decided to proceed as she would with any other villager.

'I'm sure you've heard about the discovery of a number of bodies in the village of Fendyke?' Marie didn't wait for a reply

265

as she knew none would be forthcoming. 'I'd just like to assure you that this isn't a recent occurrence, and we are hoping that the perpetrator is long gone from the area. However,' she said, looking deep into the woman's piercing dark eyes, 'the fact is, we cannot guarantee that he — or she — is not still here among the local community. Of course, that is only the worst-case scenario, but on meeting you, I have the impression that you'd prefer me not to minimise the importance of something as serious as murder.'

She waited. It was hard going, but Marie wasn't about to be beaten. Her eyes never left Sarah's.

'Sally. I don't answer to Sarah.'

You don't answer to anything much at all, thought Marie, quite elated at this small victory. 'I beg your pardon. Sally. While we are worried about you living out here all alone, we were also wondering if you might be able to help. We'd greatly appreciate it if you could tell us about anyone you have seen behaving oddly, or who you find disturbing, even as far back as three years ago.'

Sally stared at the floor, and shrugged. 'Can't help you.'

'Can't? Or won't?' Marie said quickly but gently. 'Come on, Sally. You see things, I know you do.'

The eyes flashed. Was it anger? Or derision? 'I see you've been talking to those nice people over in Fendyke.' She sniffed. 'They would say that, wouldn't they: *Mad* Sally sees things.'

This wasn't getting her anywhere. Suddenly, Marie said, 'Why don't you talk to people?'

Abruptly, Sally sat down. 'No one worth talking to.'

'In an entire village? That's a bit harsh, isn't it?'

'You don't know them! You come into the village asking your questions, and they fill you with all the rubbish they've been telling each other for years. Rumours, the lot of it. Idle talk. Gossip and slander. All those people ever do is lie.'

This outburst, from someone who supposedly never spoke a word, came as a bit of a shock. But this woman was beginning to intrigue Marie more and more. Sarah — Sally — puzzled her. Called mad by everyone in the village, Sally had revealed herself to be of what they called 'good stock' in this part of the country. Marie had an idea she was intelligent — the books she read were testament to that — possibly even cultivated.

But Sally hadn't finished. 'Most are damned incomers anyway. What do they know of our ways? They come into the villages and take over. Form committees. Hold meetings. And slowly, insidiously, they insert themselves into the local councils. And they change things.'

'Were you born in the Fens, Sally?' Marie asked.

'Born and bred. This is my home, this is my land, and I don't need incomers to tell me how to live.'

'That might be true, but plenty of people say that if it weren't for the incomers, the villages would have died. The young people have moved away, and new blood is needed to keep them alive. Youngsters are no longer interested in working the land, they want more these days.'

'Some villages would be better left to die,' Sally retorted. 'Like this one. And what would you know about it anyway? You're Welsh.'

'And born not twenty miles from this cottage,' Marie said. 'Okay, I went away to school, but I spent every school holiday here with my dad, who was a Yellowbelly through and through, his family had been here for generations. And where did I choose to train and work? Right here, in the Fens. So, as it happens, I know plenty about it.'

Marie fell silent, slightly embarrassed by her emotional response. Sally was certainly talking, but they'd gone way off-piste in terms of the enquiry. She'd need all her skills as an interviewing officer to get them back on track. From the way Sally chose to live, without a single modern amenity, it was clear that she hated and resented change. Time to throw her a curve ball.

'Any idea who might have killed five people, Sally?'

'What? Other than me? I'm the obvious suspect, aren't I? Antisocial, uncommunicative. Alienated. Why look any further?'

Marie gave a little laugh. 'Well, not many people I talk to offer themselves up as the guilty party. But seriously, Sally, you are obviously a very astute woman, so answer me honestly. In the last few years has anyone here, resident or visitor, made you anxious about them or their actions? I don't mean trivial things, I'm talking about real apprehension.'

There was a long silence. Then Sally said, 'Like I said before, I can't help you. And it's can't, not won't.'

Marie stood up. This wouldn't be her last visit, but right now, it was time to walk away. 'Give it some thought, Sally.' She took a card from her pocket and laid it on the kitchen table. 'Five people are dead, and I need your help. And, if you ever need *my* help, ring me, understand?'

Sally gave her no answer, but she understood all right.

CHAPTER TWENTY-FOUR

The team gathered for a late meeting at just after five o'clock. There was a lot to cover, but the most important piece of information was that a second victim had been identified. 'Violet' was Shelley Kershaw.

'Rory phoned a few minutes ago,' said Jackman. 'He fast-tracked a test on some of the personal items retrieved from her room in Laburnum House, which gave a positive DNA match for the younger of the two female victims. Professor Wallace ran a facial recognition test even before they received a photograph of Shelley, and it came up positive. So, we have another identity confirmed. It appears that Shelley never caught that late-night bus.'

'In that case, we need to look for anyone who saw her that evening, and whether they noticed anyone else hanging around,' suggested Gary.

'That's your first job tomorrow morning, my friend,' said Jackman. 'Then, you take Shelley's life apart, because she really upset someone. Badly enough to get herself brutally murdered.'

'Or stumbled on something the killer couldn't risk becoming common knowledge,' added Max.

'True. Oh, and see if she had any dealing with that ghost-hunters club, the one Gino Lombardi belonged to. There's a good chance there's something that links all the victims, so we might as well start there.'

'In which case, when we get the facial recognition pictures of the other three, perhaps we should take them to that club as well, in case they were members, too,' suggested Kevin. 'It's a long shot, but people do come and go with groups like that, so maybe someone might recognise one of them.'

'It's worth a try. Rory says the images should be ready tomorrow morning, so do that, and also spend some time trying to find out if Gino knew Shelley. It's a small village, and if she was a bit, well, free and easy with her favours, there's a chance their paths may have crossed.' Jackman looked pensive. 'Something links those five victims, apart from their killer, but going by their ages and general descriptions, they couldn't be more different. We have a lot of work to do.'

'I suppose that we can't ignore the fact that there might not be a link,' added Marie soberly. 'They could have been random acts of violence on the part of some psychopath.'

'Let's hope that isn't the case,' said Jackman. 'It would make our job even more difficult than it already is.'

'Just playing devil's advocate,' said Marie. 'And for what it's worth, I think there has to be a link, too, but—'

'Don't assume anything,' Jackman finished. 'Now, Max. Dare I ask how the Missing Persons search is going?'

Max rolled his eyes. 'Well, the notices are now all recorded, but there's so little to go on. I mean it's bloody daunting when the database coughs up over a thousand potential identities for the first bloke, the one Rory calls Eamonn. Facial recognition will be a great help. We might get somewhere if we can start putting up a few images.'

Jackman knew there were people out there who constantly scanned the latest reports on missing people in the hopes of seeing a loved one's face. 'Keep at it, Max. We've been lucky so far, let's hope that luck holds out, and you find a match.' He turned to the others. 'Now, I don't want to keep you any later than I have to, but if you could all just make a few calls tonight and set up appointments with as many people in the village as possible, we can hit the ground running tomorrow. We'll skip the morning meeting and plough straight in. Uniform are going to do a house-to-house search for a ground-breaker spade of the same design as the murder weapon.' He smiled grimly. 'And you'll be delighted to know that your lives will be made even more difficult from now on, because the media will be gathering. Ruth is giving a press briefing tomorrow. Finally, young Craig Sharpe has been moved to a safer location, and with the aid of Bob Ruston, he's cooperating with us, as far as he can. So, do what you can to prepare for tomorrow, remember what I said earlier about being "Chaos-aware", and then get yourselves off home. I hope to see you firing on all cylinders tomorrow morning.'

* * *

Bryson Smith sat down to eat supper with his parents, but his mind was elsewhere. He couldn't stop thinking about the Greene brothers, whom he'd taken an instant dislike to. He'd put on a good show, with a fair amount of success — in fact, he'd had them eating out of his hand by the time he left their hotel — but he couldn't help finding them almost repellent. He'd had a similar reaction to some of the more avaricious collectors he'd met in the course of his work. It was as if they were prepared to stop at nothing to get hold of a coveted artefact, and when they did, they made sure no one else would ever set eyes on it. They gave him the odd piece of useful information, such as the names of galleries and antiques dealers, but nothing of much value. So, Bryson decided that after supper, he'd contact a few people he knew in the trade, and make some discreet enquiries about the reclusive and obnoxious brothers. He would start with a London auction house Norman had mentioned, where Bryson happened to have a close friend.

'The village was crawling with police officers today, Bry,' said his mother, handing him a second helping of her home-made bread and butter pudding. 'And the media! Lord! The police are having quite a struggle stopping them getting to the pillbox, and your dad even caught a couple of the nosy little blighters sneaking into our back garden. Didn't you, Ted?'

'Gave 'em a right earful, I did,' said his father. 'This is private property, I said. Bugger off!'

'Good for you, Dad,' said Bryson. 'DI Jackman warned me that it was bound to happen when word of the bodies got out. Perhaps we should sell them tickets and make a bit of money out of them.'

Meanwhile, his thoughts remained with that morning's conversation with the men who had been robbed. He found DS Vic Blackwell as easy to like as the brothers had been hard. He seemed like a solid, down-to-earth man, and he liked the way Vic deferred to his knowledge of the art world. Vic candidly admitted that he didn't know a thing about it, but he showed genuine interest in what Bryson had to say. In addition, Bryson strongly suspected that Vic felt the same way he did about Norman and Derek Greene.

Lost in his thoughts, he hadn't been listening to what his parents were saying. They were now discussing how, if they were the police, they'd approach the search for the killer.

'If I was them,' his mother said, 'I'd look at the quiet ones, those who never push themselves forward. Meek and mild can often conceal a devious mind.'

'Oh, I dunno, love. I think I'd look at the ones who make the most noise,' added his father. 'The ones who point the finger at others.' He looked at his son. 'What say you, lad?'

'I think you're both right,' said Bryson. 'Either of those types are known to be capable of murder. We've all read those true crime stories about seemingly very unassuming people who commit horrific crimes, but also of very outgoing people who do the same. I'd be hard put to say which ones they should look at, really.' He finished his pudding and leaned back in his chair. He knew all about the 'devious minds' his mother had spoken of. And it wasn't just criminals who presented a face to the world that was very different to the person inside. He thought of the tormented genius, torn apart by feelings of inferiority and lack of self-worth. Some artists descended into madness. 'Fact is, what you see isn't always what you get.'

'Any suspects in the frame?' asked his dad, sounding like a character from a bad cop movie. 'I mean, working with the police, you're bound to come across things we won't get to hear about.'

Bryson shook his head. 'They don't talk about that kind of thing in front of a someone like me, Dad. And anyway I'm helping them with a completely different case.'

His dad winked at him. 'No harm keeping your eyes and ears open, Bry. We are. Trusted members of the community like us, you never can tell what we might hear. We can keep each other informed, can't we?'

'Stop it, Ted!' Betty said. 'It sounds like you think this is all a joke. Well, it's not. It's horrible the way things are now, no one trusts anyone anymore, and you'd do well to remember that. And don't forget, those poor souls were found on our property, so who do you think people will be looking at for the killers? We are no more trusted than anyone else in Fendyke.'

Bryson went and put an arm around his mother's shoulders. 'Hey! No one suspects you, Mum, I can tell you that for a fact. You're one of the most caring people I've ever met, and everyone knows it.' He nodded towards his father. 'I'm not so sure about that old codger over there, although I very much doubt his arthritis would allow him to murder anyone.'

His mum relented, and gave him a weak smile. 'Sorry, but I never thought something so, well, *heinous* could happen in a little village like ours. Sometimes I wonder how we will all come back from it. I love this place, and I'd hate it to get labelled as dark and blighted.'

Frankly, Bryson couldn't see his parents wanting to keep on living here after all this. Maybe they'd move to another rural village, well away from Fendyke. They weren't city people and would hate to live anywhere near him. A twice-yearly weekend at his apartment was more than enough for them, and by the end of it they were always itching to get back to the big open skies and the never-ending fields. It would be sad, they'd invested a lot of time and hard work in getting this bungalow how they wanted it. But who would want to live with such a macabre legacy at the bottom of their garden? Time would tell, he guessed.

Satisfied that normal service had been resumed in his parents' kitchen, Bryson went to his room and rang his friend.

'Hi, Alex. It's Bryson. Got a few minutes?'

'Hello, you old sod! Where the hell have you been? Jocelyn had a drinks party last week and you were sorely missed. Just wasn't the same without you.'

Bryson laughed. 'I've been staying with my parents for a bit — I'll tell you all about it when I get back. I'm calling you now because I want to pick your brains.'

'You're welcome to try. What's the problem?'

In reality, Alex Black was nothing like the image of the casual man about town that he liked to project. He and his wife Jocelyn came from old money, and were well known in those sorts of circles, but in his professional life Alex was a well-respected lecturer on Medieval Art and Architecture, while Jocelyn specialised in English pottery and ceramics. Both provided their services as consultants and valuers whenever their specific talents were required, and had, over the years, become two of Bryson's closest friends.

Bryson told him about the Greenes, and the robbery at their house, saying he'd be going there the following day to start listing the stolen items.

'Must be a fair old haul, then, if the police brought you in,' said Alex.

'They say it's one of the biggest heists on record. The thieves even took a bloody great window out of its frame, but I haven't told you the funny part yet.' And Bryson told his friend the story of the robber locking himself in when the security alarms reactivated a bit too soon.

To his surprise, Alex didn't laugh. 'You should talk to Jocelyn, my man. The Met were at the auction house only last week, asking her to keep her eyes open for anyone trying to move some rare Charles Rennie Mackintosh pieces. They told her one of the thieves had been trapped inside the showroom he was in the process of robbing. Either that's a remarkable coincidence, or the Met didn't want to reveal too many details.'

'I'll pass that on to the police up here, although they probably already know about it. But, talking about Mackintosh, would you ask Jocelyn if she's ever come across Norman and Derek Greene before? They are collectors of Art Deco/Art Nouveau art, and there's definitely some Mackintoshes among the stolen items.'

'Hang on. I'll give her a call, and you can speak to her right now.'

Moments later, Jocelyn was on the line. 'Yes, as it happens, I dealt with them earlier this year. There was an antique Moorcroft Flaminian vase come up which they showed an interest in. I'd seen them before at the auction house previews for potential buyers. Rather an odd couple, as I recall.'

'Would you say they were . . . how can I put it — above board? I mean, was there anything suspicious about them?'

'They paid up at once, and there was nothing untoward in the transaction. They definitely had money. In fact, they've used us several times, and I know that because I always check the records if it's a client I haven't dealt with before.'

'I sense a "but" coming,' Bryson said.

'Not really . . . Oh, I don't know. It sounds silly, but you know what it's like when you're selling something truly rare and beautiful. You want it to go somewhere it can be appreciated and cared for, don't you?'

'I know what you mean,' Bryson said. 'We feel responsible for them. They're not just commodities to be bought and sold, they mean something to us.'

'Well, I did not want those men to have my beautiful Moorcroft vase! I knew they wouldn't cherish it, to them it was just one more *thing* to be added to their collection. I could almost smell it on them, that greed.'

Her words came as a relief at having his own feelings confirmed. Nevertheless, he wondered how he was going to work with them at close quarters, possibly for several days.

He thanked his friends and ended the call. Then he fell to thinking about Norman and Derek Greene. He was looking forward to getting inside Hartwood House, because it sounded as if there were many interesting and valuable items still there, but he would have preferred not to see it in the presence of its creepy owners.

Back in the kitchen, his mother had made herself a cup of tea, and his dad had opened a beer. Bryson accepted the glass of wine she offered. He wasn't a great drinker, but the prospect of spending the following morning in the company of the Greenes made a large glass of red seem very attractive.

* * *

Jackman was also enjoying a glass of wine, courtesy of Sam and Julia. He had been accosted by his old friend as he got out of his car, and hustled into Sam's kitchen. There he found three places set for supper, and a delicious aroma coming from the stove.

'Julia found an old recipe of her mother's,' Sam said. 'And as she wasn't working this afternoon, she decided to try it out. Be warned, it's a rib sticker, she says, but if it tastes as good as it smells, we are in for a treat.'

As soon as Jackman walked into the kitchen, he knew what it was, and was overcome by a sudden poignant memory of his grandmother in the kitchen preparing that self-same meal. He beamed happily. 'Bacon, onion and sage roly-poly. Granny used to call it "Clanger pudding".'

'It was always a favourite of mine,' Julia said, 'but I lost the recipe, and for some reason I didn't want to get it online. Nothing would do but Mum's own handwritten recipe. I was overjoyed when it turned up in an old photo album. I just hope I can do it justice.'

She had, and an hour later, Jackman declared that the Clanger pudding was every bit as good as his gran's, which was a great compliment. Now, all feeling delightfully replete, they sipped their wine, and the conversation inevitably turned to work.

'I spent several hours with young Craig Sharpe this morning,' said Julia. 'I must say, that nursing home you've put him into has more security than Buckingham Palace.'

'So Ruth said. And I understand that we owe it to that retired copper, Bob Ruston, for getting the chap to talk at all,' Jackman said.

'That's right. I feared it would take Craig a lot of time and counselling before he'd trust anyone, but he took to Bob like a substitute dad. Bob even drove all the way to Huntingdon to pick up Craig's grandmother so she could be near Craig and also be kept safe from whoever abducted him. Bob and his family have put her up in their spare room — although naturally, that's not public knowledge.'

'Isn't that a bit risky?' asked Jackman. 'We have no idea what's going on, or why Craig was taken, other than that he's a geek. He said they threatened his grandmother, so I hope Bob knows what he's doing. He has his own family to think about, and someone told me his son is disabled.'

'Apparently, it was a decision the whole family took, not just Bob,' said Julia. 'And it's been kept very quiet. Seeing her safe and well has certainly perked Craig up.'

'Has he managed to come up with a reason for his abduction? We're assuming it's connected to his computer skills, but he must have done something to cause someone to dish out such appalling treatment.' Jackman emptied his glass. 'Hell, I think they intended to kill him.'

Julia shook her head. 'He's more frustrated than anyone about that, Jackman. He swears he's done nothing illegal — no hacking, no use of the dark web, and hasn't been involved with any suspicious characters. He really can't think of a thing.' She narrowed her eyes. 'There's no chance it was a case of mistaken identity, is there? He's just so, well, ordinary. He's not rich, has no dubious friends, and his only relative is a loving grandmother, who, frankly, is living on the breadline. It just doesn't add up.'

Jackman sighed. She was right. Nothing about this incident added up.

'Has anyone asked if he's done any private work for anyone recently?' said Sam. 'I mean, techies like him are always getting roped in to sort out people's problems with their computers, aren't they? What if he was helping someone and stumbled on something he shouldn't, even if he was unaware of it at the time?'

Jackman looked at Julia and raised an eyebrow.

'Not to my knowledge,' she said. 'I know. Bob was going to spend an hour or so with Craig this evening.' She looked at her watch. 'He should be there now. Shall I give him a ring and get him to ask?'

'Absolutely,' Jackman said. 'You could be on to something there, Sam. If Craig went into someone's house to work on their computer, even if it had nothing to do with the computer itself, he might have seen, or overheard something.' They'd been so sure it was his skills with computers that had got Craig abducted that they hadn't even looked at the simpler possibilities. He may just have been in the wrong place at the wrong time. 'Julia, if you do get hold of Bob, can I have a word with him, please? I think our Sam might have opened up a different line of enquiry altogether.'

CHAPTER TWENTY-FIVE

A thick, early morning mist shrouded the Fens, making everything seem strange and ethereal. Such mists were common, and often heralded a lovely sunny day, but Marie wasn't going to risk getting drenched on her way to work. She was no fair-weather motorcycle rider, but finding somewhere to dry her gear in the police station wasn't all that easy.

When she walked into the CID room, she found Kevin and Gary already hard at work, and from the empty coffee mugs on their desks, they'd been there for some time.

'Don't tell me you pulled an all-nighter, lads? It's only seven thirty now, and you look like you've been at it for hours!'

Gary looked up from his screen. 'Morning, Sarge. Oh, I couldn't sleep, so I came in an hour ago, and I found our Kevin already here.'

'Couldn't sleep either,' said Kevin ruefully. 'And every time I did drop off, I dreamed of bones!' He shuddered. 'Ugh. I can see them now! All trying to crawl out of that pillbox like in some zombie movie. It was horrible.'

'Well, guys, it sounds like we need to make today count,' said Marie. 'We can't have you losing out on your sleep and getting nightmares. Anyway, this is not a horror film. We have a very real, sadistic killer to find, so let's get out to that village and do what we do best — ask questions, and most of all listen, even to the gossips and scaremongers. There has to be somebody in that small community who knows something about what went on. We need to find that person. They may not necessarily be the killer, but they could lead us to his door.'

'Nicely put,' said Jackman from his office doorway. 'Ever thought of a career as a motivational speaker?'

'Sod that for load of cobblers!' she said with a grin, but quickly became serious. 'We can't afford to lose perspective, can we, boss? It's not just us either, there's a village out there full of genuine, decent people, who are currently living in fear and eyeing their neighbours with suspicion. For everyone's sake, we need to find the person responsible and give all those innocent people their lives back.'

'And that's exactly what we are going to do,' said Jackman. 'So, what's the plan for today? Kevin? Gary?'

Kevin looked down at a handwritten list on his desk. 'I've arranged three calls for this morning, all villagers who won't be there later in the day. I'm about to leave shortly, if that's okay? Then when Gary's free, we'll be working our way through all the members of that ghost-hunters club that Gino Lombardi belonged to. I'm hoping we'll have the facial recognition images from forensics by then.'

'I'll chase them up on that,' said Jackman, 'so you can get away as soon as you like. Just keep in touch, okay? Oh, and anything that bothers you, even the smallest thing, ring either Marie or myself. We'll be in Fendyke a bit later. I just have a few things to do here first.'

Kevin stood up. 'Okay, boss, I'll be hitting the road.'

'And I'll continue making enquiries about Shelley and try to find the last person to see her alive,' said Gary. 'I've already got a lead, so I'll pursue that, then go ghost-hunting with Kevin.'

As Kevin left the CID room, Robbie hurried in looking flustered. 'Bloody press! You can't get near the station for cameras and mics. I've just warned Kev that he'd better go out the back way.'

It was inevitable, but it did nothing for tempers or for the smooth running of the investigation. 'I expect we'll find that Fendyke's even worse than here,' said Marie. 'Uniform are going to have their hands full trying to keep them away from that pillbox.'

'Indeed,' said Jackman and disappeared inside his office.

'What's my first task today, Sarge?' asked Robbie, throwing his jacket over the back of his chair.

'I'm wondering if you might have more luck than I did with Mad Sally's background,' said Marie. 'I know for a fact there's no point asking her, and I badly want to know what her story is. She lives in this house like a museum of life back in the twenties or thirties, without a single modern amenity, including running water. It was actually quite creepy.' She gave a little shiver. 'Kevin was telling me about this old guy he's been talking to called Dudley Nailer?'

'Oh, yeah, that must be the guy who sent him and Gary to see another old house, the one our Violet was lodging in when she got killed.'

'That's him, and apparently his house is also old, and full of things from the Victorian era, but Kevin said it was really cosy and welcoming. Mad Sally's house was anything but welcoming — in fact, it felt kind of dead. It's hard to put it into words, but it was like the house had no soul.' She frowned. 'And now I come to think about it, I never saw a single ornament, or picture, or photograph — nothing decorative or personal at all.'

'Sounds really eerie,' said Robbie. 'Anyway, give me what you have on her, and I'll see what I can find.'

'Thanks, Robbie. I have this odd feeling that her past might tell me why I'm so convinced that she's either seen or heard something that could be useful to us. I really don't have the time or the energy to try to prise it out of her, and I don't think she'd tell me even if I did.'

'Why not have a word with Kevin's old pal Dudley?' suggested Gary. 'He did suggest that we try to talk to her, and that she wasn't as mad as people believed, so perhaps he knows more than he was letting on to Kev.'

'I was thinking that myself. As soon as Jackman's free, I'm going to suggest making him our first port of call.'

'Sounds like a plan,' said Robbie. 'Who else have you got on your list of people to interview?'

'While I wait for Jackman, I'm going to do a bit of digging into that couple who used to live in Bryson Smith's parents' bungalow,' Marie said. 'They sounded distinctly unpleasant, and whereas they wouldn't fit into the timeline as the killers, what if they had an equally nasty family member or friend?'

'Good point, and although I hate to say this,' Robbie pulled a face, 'we ought really to run a check on the Smiths themselves, including Bryson.'

'You're right, of course. We can't leave anyone out, but if it turns out to be one of those three, I'll ride Tiger naked to Skegness and buy everyone on the beach an ice cream!'

Robbie roared with laughter. 'Now, that really would be something to see! It would certainly spice up the local TV news programme!'

'Since that ain't ever going to happen, sonny-boy, you'd better get your head back into Mad Sally, while I hunt down Mr and Mrs Barking Mad of Fendyke.'

* * *

Lucas had never felt so alone, or so shocked. He had been flung from a life of order and control into another world altogether, and he was all at sea. Not once in his entire life had he ever set foot in a police station, and now he was being propelled through the judicial system like a leaf caught in a whirlwind. Being thrust into the back of a police car, then into a cell, and then into a grim interview room had been bad enough, but what followed was much, much worse. He had been taken to court, and to his horror, bail had been refused as the judge considered him at risk of absconding with the artefacts stolen from Hartwood House. He had been placed on remand awaiting trial, and told he was lucky to be interred in HMP Marshfield.

Lucky! Lucas sat on his bed in the small cell and stared at his feet. Nothing about his life right now could be considered even slightly lucky. Not that he'd ever relied on luck. His jobs had all been carried off successfully because of careful planning and scrupulous attention to detail. He left nothing to chance, never. Even this godawful situation wasn't due to bad luck, it had been a deliberate betrayal on the part of Chaos. He still couldn't understand why it had happened. He had paid a fortune for his expertise, had worked with him many times in the past, and now he cursed himself for his complacency in assuming that his hefty payments would buy him loyalty as well as a free pass into security-protected establishments.

Lucas sighed. Thank God he had a cell to himself. He was a fastidious man, and the prospect of sharing a confined space with a stranger filled him with horror. Because he was on remand, he had certain privileges, which included not being obliged to share a cell with a convicted prisoner. Though that seemed to be where his privileges ended. Things like having your own clothes, books to read, writing materials and other personal items all depended on having a relative or a friend to bring them for you. Who did he have, other than his cousin, Jean-Paul, and he was in London? He had phoned Jean-Paul, and told him of his arrest, throwing in a few random remarks that would have made no sense to an outsider. Some time ago he and Jean-Paul had devised a series of encoded messages as a contingency measure, which had come in very useful in his present situation. He had managed in this way to instruct Jean-Paul to make contact with Nina, and depending on her reply, contact their client as well. Nina was perfectly capable, with Jean-Paul's help, of seeing the job through, thereby securing the payment. Unless Chaos stuck his oar in again, the police would know nothing about the gang, or the whereabouts of the stolen goods. As long as they worked fast, Crispin Payne could receive his precious treasures on time, without any complications, and Nina and Jean-Paul could squirrel away Lucas's own Art Nouveau items until he came out. If the worst happened and he was incarcerated, at least he'd have a considerable nest egg to look forward to when he came out. But did he even trust Nina? After the way Chaos had betrayed him, he wondered if he'd ever be capable of trusting anyone.

Lucas paced the cell. He wasn't even going to consider the prospect of long-term incarceration. His lawyer had flown back early from a vacation in Barbuda and would be seeing him later that day. Gareth Rock was an influential and clever man, if anyone could get Lucas off, it would be him. Right now, Lucas needed to concentrate on finding a means to keep in contact with the outside without giving anything away. At least he could still trust Jean-Paul — he was family, and besides, he depended on Lucas to provide him with the means to pursue his extravagant lifestyle. Lucas really wanted to believe that Nina would remain loyal too, but when it came down to it, she was as much a money-loving crook as any of them. And right now, she was sitting on a fortune in art treasures. Would the temptation be too great? How would he act in her place? He honestly didn't know. Would he do the honourable thing and not head for the hills with the stolen goods? The trouble was, the haul was worth so much.

He dragged his mind back to the privileges he'd been accorded. He'd been made to understand that they would only be extended to him if he complied fully with the rules. Well, he'd see about that. Once he got his head around this alien environment, he would do his best to manipulate it to his advantage. If he were to survive this ordeal, he'd need to muster all his considerable skills to gain as much control of his surroundings as possible. At least he was in a Cat C prison, which meant that he was less likely to be subjected to threats or intimidation from other prisoners. He knew very little about what went on in prisons, but he'd been informed that this one housed criminals involved in non-violent offences like theft, fraud, and other white-collar crimes, and was heavily invested in rehabilitation. Even so, he was no fool — there would be drugs, and he'd come up against some nasty characters, so he'd have to keep his wits about him and use his intuition as to who he could trust — if anyone.

'Corbin! MO wants to see you. Come on, I'll take you to the infirmary.'

The warder didn't look unfriendly, just harassed, and Lucas got up at once and followed him out into the main corridor.

'It's an assessment, as you're a newbie,' said the warder over his shoulder. 'You're lucky. We have decent healthcare here, unlike some other prisons.'

Great, thought Lucas, someone else telling me how lucky I am.

The prison infirmary came as something of a surprise. No ward, no line of beds, just a small waiting area with two doors leading off, and that was it.

'Doc will see you in a few minutes, Corbin. I'll be back in half an hour to collect you and give you a guided tour of your new home.'

'New but very temporary home,' said Lucas smugly.

The warder snorted. 'I've heard that one before. So you're another innocent man, are you, just like everyone else in here?'

Lucas sat down. No, he wasn't innocent, far from it, but he was here through no fault of his own. 'I won't be staying. You can rely on that.'

'You hang on to that thought, Corbin. We'll see who's right in a month or so.' With a chuckle, he left, closing the door behind him.

Lucas swallowed. He was close to tears. All he could think about was how much he hated Chaos for what he had done to him.

'It does get better.'

Lucas jumped. For a moment he thought this tall, well-dressed man was the medic, until he flopped down into the chair next to him.

'I'm George, and I know just how you feel. The first few days are always rough. It's a real culture shock. You won't believe me, but there are worse places to be in than this, even if there aren't enough staff and we don't get the support we should.'

'I shouldn't be here at all,' Lucas said.

'Neither should I, but what can you do?' The man smiled, revealing even, white teeth. 'Anyway, if you need anything, ask me. I've been here long enough to know all the ins and outs of this place. I can explain how things work and how to earn yourself more IEPs — that's incentives and earned privileges, by the way. Meanwhile, keep to the rules and take part in whatever activities they offer you.' He winked and stood up. 'Be a good boy, Lucas. It pays, believe me.'

'How come you know my name?' Lucas asked.

George looked amused. 'News travels fast in these places. I know quite a lot about you, Lucas Corbin. Listen, why don't you drop by my room later? You are free to come and go within the main areas during association. We can have a bit of a chat.'

One of the doors opened and a nurse beckoned to him. 'Doctor is ready for you now.'

Lucas cursed to himself. He wanted to know exactly what this stranger knew about him, and more to the point, how.

'See you later.' With a fleeting smile, George turned and left.

The assessment was over in no time. All his observations were good, and he was pronounced fit and healthy. He could have told them that. The only thing wrong with him was injured pride. As he was about to leave, the doctor informed him that he would be allowed access to the gym, and time to exercise. At last, something positive. He knew that the food was going to be abysmal compared to his usual diet, but the chance to work out was immensely cheering. It would help keep his mind healthy as well as his body, which would be important if he were to get out of this place.

After fifteen minutes, the warder returned. The name on his ID tag was William Weaver, so Lucas smiled, and said, 'Okay, Mr Weaver, I'm ready to be shown the delights of the Establishment.'

'That'll have to wait, Corbin. I'm taking you back to your wing. I've got other duties to carry out first.'

Weaver looked even more harassed than before, which brought to mind George's remark about staff shortages. It meant, too, that he could go directly to George's cell. He had a lot of questions for that man.

George Rider turned out to be easy to talk to, nothing like Lucas's idea of a convicted prisoner. He was well-spoken, intelligent, and obviously looked after himself. Looking at George, Lucas could see what he might be like in a few years' time. It didn't take long for him to open up to this man, and instead of the questions he'd wanted to ask, he found himself telling George Rider exactly what had happened to get him arrested.

He had expected George to either laugh or express shock at what had been done to him, but George merely looked troubled. After a while, he said, 'We old lags make it our business to find out what our new fellow prisoners are like, and what brought them here, so I already knew something about Lucas Corbin and the kind of man he was.' He smiled briefly. 'So forgive me for that, but forewarned is forearmed. Not everyone who comes here is what they seem. But you, Lucas, interested me particularly, and now I see I was right.'

Rider looked distant. He seemed to be turning something over in his mind.

'You are worrying me,' said Lucas. 'I'm at a disadvantage here. Why would I interest you?'

George Rider considered him for a long moment in silence, then seemed to come to a decision. 'I had a friend who spent seven years in here, framed by a faceless computer hacker. Your situation is very similar to his. In fact, I'm pretty certain you were both incarcerated through the machinations of the same person. The one you call Chaos.'

Lucas gazed at Rider in horror, fear flooding every part of his body. Seven years! In this place? He would never survive.

'Hey! Don't go into meltdown, man. First, I could be way off the mark, but even if I'm right, I might be able to help.' Rider lowered his voice. 'Now, listen to me. The bottom line is that you are a master art thief, yes? And after years of pulling off successful jobs, your luck suddenly ran out.'

Lucas opened his mouth to object, but relented. 'Not because of bad planning, or shoddy execution, but because I trusted a wrong 'un who stitched me up tighter than a rugby ball, so like it or not, I guess it's *mea culpa.*'

'In that case, you need to get your head around the fact that you are going down.' George looked at him steadily. 'Now. Think. Do you have anything in your possession, either at home or elsewhere, that could have been illicitly obtained?'

Lucas frowned. 'No, nothing. I've never kept anything I stole. I always worked on behalf of a client and everything went to them. Plus, I have an accountant, who ensures that whatever I'm paid is well concealed.'

'So, if the police had a good look into your background, really delved deep, what would they find?' asked George.

'A successful dealer in art and antiques. All purchases and sales documented and declared to the HMRC.'

'You're totally sure about that?'

'Absolutely,' said Lucas. 'My accountant is the best there is, and he's scrupulous about the paperwork.'

'You've got a good lawyer, I presume.'

'Gareth Rock.'

George looked impressed. 'You must have been extremely successful if you can afford him.'

'And I've always made sure never to put a foot wrong in my licit business dealings. I've become well respected among the big auction rooms and galleries. But that's not what interests me, it's my private work that I love—' Lucas swallowed. 'Even if I do get off, which from what you say is doubtful, I'll be watched like a hawk. I'm finished, thanks to Chaos.'

'Not necessarily,' George said. 'True, it won't ever be the same, but you can adapt. You're clever, you just need to be smarter than whoever is watching you. You won't be a person of interest for long, believe me. The police are stretched to capacity, and they have far bigger fish to fry than some guy knocking off a few trinkets. Now, listen carefully. Here's what I have in mind.'

How long had he known this man — a convicted criminal, by the way? Not even an hour. Nevertheless, Lucas listened. Twenty minutes later, he was back his cell, pacing the floor, deep in thought. What George had proposed was risky, but considering the amount of shit Chaos had dropped him in, it was worth a try. Now he just had to wait for Gareth Rock to arrive.

CHAPTER TWENTY-SIX

Bryson Smith and DS Vic Blackwell arrived at Hartwood House at around ten thirty a.m. Neither were looking forward to spending the morning in the company of the Greene brothers, but notwithstanding the repellent pair, Bryson eagerly awaited the chance to see inside this fabled temple to art.

He stepped from the car and gazed up at the front of the house. It was rare to see architecture from that era so well-preserved. And if the exterior was anything to go by, the interior had to be truly impressive. Vic warned him to expect something of a mess following the forensic sweep, meaning that they would be subjected to a tirade of angry complaints from the occupants.

The Greenes did not disappoint, but even their whining wasn't enough to dampen Bryson's delight at what he saw. It took him an effort to remind himself of why he was here, and with the detective's help he was able to deflect the brothers' attention from the state their home had been left in — which really wasn't bad at all — and embark on compiling a list of the stolen items. Once that was done, they would then have the laborious task of going through years of the Greenes' paperwork in order to confirm the various objects' provenance. It would be painstaking work, but Bryson was good at it; he was in familiar territory, and each piece brought with it a small thrill of excitement.

In spite of his dislike of the pair, he couldn't fault their meticulous record-keeping. Not only was each item described with full details of its purchase, but every object had been carefully photographed. These records formed a near perfect catalogue of the collection ready to be distributed to dealers, auction houses and genuine collectors throughout the world.

As he worked, Bryson began to think of people he either knew or had heard about who might possibly be offered some of the stolen items. He even went so far as to wonder if one of the more 'driven' collectors might have been behind this theft. He had once visited a client in a very upmarket private estate in Surrey, who was reputed to have a locked room in his house containing some very rare seventeenth-century master-pieces. Sadly, he hadn't been permitted to view them, having been told that the paintings were kept in a special windowless storage room at a strictly controlled temperature and relative humidity. He heard later through the auction rooms grape-vine that some of these treasures had been acquired through various unorthodox means, and that the locked room con-tained a lot more than a few well-protected canvases.

Bryson found Vic a pleasure to work with. He was quick on the uptake, and well used to wading through reams of paperwork, so the inventory of stolen goods was coming along well. Much to their relief, the brothers took themselves off to another room to go over what he and Vic had done so far. Bryson waited a moment to make sure they were out of earshot, and then said to Vic, 'Do you by any chance get the feeling that those two are holding something back? They seem shifty somehow, and why keep muttering so that we can't overhear? There's no need for that. After all, we're supposed to be working together on this.'

'You're right, Bry,' said Vic. 'And they definitely want rid of us. If their paperwork wasn't so authentic, I'd have been feeling their collars by now. Something definitely isn't right with that pair. I suppose all we can do for now is keep our eyes peeled for any irregularities in this lot, and keep our ears open.'

'I guess so,' said Bryson. 'And while we've been working, I've had a few thoughts about the man behind this heist. Remind me to tell you about them once we're out of here.'

Vic raised an eyebrow. 'Interesting. I certainly will. Now, where were we? Item Seventeen: Tiffany iridescent blue Egyptian onion-flower form vase, purchased at auction in 2020 from Pearl and Swithin, auction house, London SW1.'

'God,' exclaimed Bryson. 'Those really are rare! If you like, I can check its authenticity right now. I've a friend who works there.'

Vic told him to go ahead, so Bryson pulled out his phone. 'Hi, Margaret, it's Bryson Smith. If you have a minute, I'd like to pick your brains, It's on behalf of the Fenland Constabulary.'

Call ended, he told Vic the purchase had been completely above board. 'It received the highest bid in the auction, and given the amount of interest from both here and abroad, the brothers paid top whack.'

'Pity. Another legitimate purchase,' grumbled Vic. 'Wouldn't you just love to find something iffy in among this lot?'

Bryson said he certainly would. This whole thing was a bit too perfect. As he thought about it, the more convinced he became that the brothers were hiding something. When they first met at the hotel, they had been impressed with his knowledge and seemed pleased to converse with a fellow aficionado, but now he was in the house with them, they seemed distinctly ill at ease and uncomfortable with his presence.

With difficulty, he brought his attention back to the job in hand. 'Okay, what's next?'

Sighing deeply, Vic said, 'Item Eighteen: a circular enamelled copper wall plaque with a floral decoration, purchased in 2009 from . . .'

* * *

Alone in the CID room, Jackman gazed at the five portraits pinned across the top of the whiteboard. They were startlingly lifelike. It was hard to believe that they had been generated by a computer program, helped along by Professor Wallace.

Five dead people.

Looking at these pictures had suddenly brought the whole case to life. What's more, they helped to dispel the sense of creepy Gothic horror that seemed to have infected everyone involved.

'This is bloody well real,' he whispered. 'Damn it, you are real! Two of you already have names, and the other three will soon, no doubt. That's a hard fact.' He hadn't heard Marie come in, until she murmured, 'Well, hello to you.' She was not speaking to him.

'Real people. A real murder case,' he said quietly.

'Exactly,' she said. 'These images are going to be so much help. Okay, they might not be totally accurate, but they look familiar enough to jog the memory of anyone who either knew or had met them. Looking at them now, they could be genuine photographs.'

'I've already sent the file to Max, who's passing them on to Interpol and the other relevant departments such as the Missing Persons Bureau. Added to the black notices, they could bring us some hits. They can be compared with photographs relatives provided for the yellow misper notices, which could result in some of them being named, especially in this man's case.' He pointed to the younger of the two unidentified men. 'Test results from his bones have confirmed that the man Rory's calling "Anton" came from Albania, and worked outdoors, so it's pretty well guaranteed that he was a field labourer.'

'Shall I get his picture over to uniform? They can show it around the local employment agencies, as well as the gangmasters who ferry the workers out to the fields,' said Marie.

'That was the first thing I did this morning, and I asked them to take them round the Baltic shops and money transfer outlets too. The plan is to flood the villages of Fendyke and Bartoft with these likenesses, and see what comes back. I've sent them to Kevin, so that he and Gary can take them to that ghost-hunters club.' Seeing those faces had infused Jackman with a new energy. 'At long last the ball is rolling. I'll just tie up a few loose ends here, and then we'll head out to Fendyke ourselves. Twenty minutes max, okay?'

* * *

Marie was both surprised and encouraged by Jackman's new-found energy. There had been times in recent months when he had seemed lost, as if he were in another world altogether. Now, all at once, he was again fully engaged and totally committed to their various investigations, despite all the complications that arose.

Marie knew more than most how grief can affect a person. What she couldn't account for was his sudden change of attitude. Had he at last found peace? He certainly seemed less conflicted. But it had all happened so fast.

Marie shook her head. She would just have to wait for the right moment to ask him, which was definitely not now. First, they had a killer to find.

'Sarge!'

Robbie came hurrying towards her. 'I've just had a message from HMP Marshfield. George Rider has requested a phone conversation with me in ten minutes. Want to listen in?'

'You bet I do,' said Marie.

'It's coming in on the landline, so come to my workstation, and we'll see what he's come up with this time.'

'More inside information from an anxious underworld, I should think,' said Marie.

'Probably. But it has to be important if he's requested a call to us.'

'I'm thinking the boss might want to listen in, too. I'll go and get him.'

Jackman followed Marie out of his office, and perched on Robbie's desk.

The ten minutes seemed to stretch on for hours, and they all jumped when the phone suddenly began to ring. Robbie switched on the loudspeaker, and they waited while the call connected.

The voice of George Rider finally rang out. 'Officers, what I am about to tell you could be of great importance for your hunt for Chaos.'

They all held their breaths.

'Go on, George,' Robbie said.

'You will receive a call from a lawyer named Gareth Rock, whom I am sure needs no introduction. His client, Lucas Corbin, wants to talk to you regarding the art theft at Hartwood House. He assures me that this was a first offence, which your records will confirm, and in exchange for certain shall we say, considerations, he is prepared to reveal the means by which criminals get in contact with Chaos. He will also explain how the payments are contracted, although we suspect that Chaos will have that sewn up too tightly for even your IT experts to trace. Even so, his information is sound — as long as he's assured of the aforementioned considerations, taking into account the worth of his information and his willingness to assist you with your enquiries.'

Robbie glanced at Jackman, who nodded. He said, 'We appreciate your heads-up on this, George. You must be aware that we do not make deals. However, if the information is genuine, his compliance will certainly be given due consideration.'

'Forewarned is forearmed, as they say,' George said. 'It will be to everyone's advantage that this renegade is taken out of the equation for good. Much as it pains me to say it to a policeman, in this case we wish you success.'

'No pressure, then,' said Robbie dryly. 'Thank you for your help, George. Believe me, we want this person out of the equation every bit as much as you do.'

'Just let me know if there's any news about Johnny. That's all I ask.'

'I'll do that, I promise,' said Robbie.

'Appreciated.' The line went dead.

Jackman laughed incredulously. 'Wonders will never cease. We seem to have a working alliance with the villains. Nonetheless, if that heist was a first offence, I'll eat my hat!'

'Gareth Rock, eh?' muttered Robbie. 'I've only seen him in action once, and he was terrifying. I wouldn't want to get on the wrong side of him, that's for sure. Talk about take no prisoners! He wiped the floor with the prosecuting counsel!'

'That's okay,' Jackman said. 'We can use that to our advantage if we box clever. We'll wait for him to contact us, and then I'll update Ruth.'

'We'd better let Vic know, too,' added Marie. 'It's basically his case until Jenny Deane gets back.'

'Why don't you text him, Marie?' suggested Jackman. 'Heaven knows how long he and Bryson Smith will be holed up in that museum of a house.'

'Rather them than me,' muttered Marie, as she pulled her phone from her pocket. 'Imagine having to spend days on end with the Greene brothers. It would be like purgatory!'

'Luckily, Bryson has met their sort before, and he's such a calm and intelligent person I'm sure that will help,' said Jackman. 'Vic, on the other hand, will only take so much crap from them. Who knows what he'd do after that — probably read them the riot act!'

Vic answered, sounding relieved at being able to talk about something other than expensive glass vases. 'Now I know why working with the Art and Antiques Unit never appealed to me. If I didn't have Bry with me, I'd have been climbing the walls.'

Marie told him about the phone call from HMP Marshfield.

Vic took a moment to respond. 'Look, as my DI isn't back yet, I'd appreciate it if DI Jackman would sit in on any interviews that are arranged with that man Rock. I've crossed swords with him once before, and he's a bloody Rottweiler! I don't want to be either intimidated or talked into doing something that isn't acceptable in a senior officer.'

Marie said that she was sure that would be no problem for Jackman, and added, 'This could be the first break we've had in the hunt for Chaos, and don't forget you'll have the support of Orac and half the country's IT units in following it up.'

Vic laughed. 'I'll settle for Orac, thanks.'

'Don't blame you,' Marie said. 'Anyway, I'll let you get back to your stained glass and table lamps.'

'Oh, how kind of you.'

Marie passed on Vic's request to Jackman, who assured her he'd be there, unless Jenny came back early.

'Any light on the couple who lived in Bryson's parents' house before them?' Jackman asked.

She shook her head. 'Not really. They certainly had a finger in every pie. They seemed to have belonged to every committee going, from the bowling club to the patients' participation group at the local doctors' surgery. He was on the local council, and she was a big noise in the WI, but I don't see them as anything other than self-opinionated busybodies.'

'Were they anything to do with the ghost-hunters club?' asked Jackman.

'No, that was the one thing they hadn't joined. They were fiercely opposed to it, apparently. One woman I spoke to, the former secretary of the village community group, told me they considered it tantamount to heresy, rather than just a bit of harmless fun.'

'I wonder if it really is just harmless fun, or whether there's more to it,' said Jackman ruminatively.

'Well, Gary and Kevin will soon find out, but from what that nice gardener chap — you know, Gino Lombardi's friend — said, it was nothing but a diverse mixture of people looking for answers, or indeed ghosts, or who just liked wandering around old houses at night scaring themselves to death—' She put a hand to her mouth. 'Not the most appropriate expression, but you know what I mean.'

'So you are drawing the line under the village know-it-alls, then, Arthur and Avril Self?'

'For the time being, boss. And as they are both now deceased, I think there are more profitable people we can interview — ones that are still breathing.'

'So, who's first on your list?'

'I'm thinking we should talk to the elderly couple whose son disappeared very suddenly, the one with supposed learning difficulties. Their names are Edith and Patrick Logan, and their son was, or is, called Jeremy. I was hoping to get a photo from them, so we can see if it resembles our Eamonn.'

'But don't they believe Eamonn was in his fifties when he died?' said Jackman.

'That's right, and it fits, as the Logans are in their late seventies, and they married young. I've already checked that out in the parish register. Jeremy was an only child and never left home, and as far as I can make out, they managed his mental health condition — or whatever it was — alone, refusing all offers of help.' She grimaced. 'Word of warning, Kevin's fount of all knowledge, Dudley Nailer, told him that they are very unfriendly, and to tread warily if he attempts to interview them.'

'So you want us to go and see them, and not Kevin and Gary. How nice of you. They sound like a real barrel of fun.'

Marie smiled innocently. 'Well, given your considerable charm and tact, I thought that if anyone could get them to ask us in for a cuppa and a friendly chat it would be you, boss.'

Jackman shook his head. 'Thanks. Charm and tact indeed, I don't know. Still, we'll give it a try, although I think the cuppa will probably be a step too far. If you are ready, we might as well get out there and see if we can get some answers.'

'One last thing, Jackman,' Marie said. 'You'll most likely think it's irrelevant, but I'd like to visit Dudley Nailer. I know Kevin thinks he's the best thing since sliced bread, but I can't help wondering if Dudley isn't being a bit too helpful?'

'Good thinking, Marie. After all, we've come across some very charming killers in the past.'

'Ah, those people who are *so* eager to help the police and divert them off course.'

'Yes, those. In fact, let's visit him together. I wouldn't mind seeing Mr Dudley Nailer for myself.'

'Well, according to Kevin, he makes a really good cuppa.'

'Then lead on, Sergeant! Let's see what we make of the village's most helpful man.'

CHAPTER TWENTY-SEVEN

It was almost lunchtime, and Max was still hard at it trying to trace the three remaining victims from the pillbox. Normally, he would have been itching to get out of the station and back at the sharp end, but Charlie's shooting had shaken him loose from his moorings, and for once, he was grateful to have been given the job of desk jockey. He'd get back on his horse one day, but only when he was ready, and he had a strong suspicion that the boss knew how he felt. After all, Jackman could easily have farmed it out to a civilian officer.

He pushed back his chair, stood up and made for the vending machine. His wife Rosie had sent him off with a nourishing packed lunch that morning, but right now he needed caffeine, laced with as much sugar as possible, and a chocolate bar.

Back at his desk with his bad coffee and snack, he received a message from Charlie on his phone:

Great news, mate! Back home! Mum in full nurturing mode, and I'm here if you happen to be passing. Mate, I need your help, I want to know what's happening with you lot. I'm

quietly going stir-crazy doing nothing all day but watching
daytime TV. The one bright spot is that Jasmine is coming to
visit me at the weekend — her digs are only three streets away,
it turns out. And thanks for your advice, mate. It worked!
As soon as I'm good to go again, we are going out for a meal
together. Result! Stay lucky! Charlie.

Max read the message again and realised he was grinning broadly. 'You little sod,' he whispered to himself. 'You frighten the shit out of me, and then walk off into the sunset with the girl of your dreams. Jammy little git!'

He returned to his work, still smiling, and before he'd finished his coffee saw the magic word 'MATCH' flash up on his screen. He stared at it for a moment, and then punched the air in delight. His Interpol black notice had married with one of their yellow missing person's notices. As he watched, a photograph appeared on the screen that almost exactly replicated the facial recognition image supplied by forensics. This was the real Anton.

Max read out the name. 'Dalmat Tabaku. Yes! We've found you, my friend!'

After much toing and froing of phone calls and messages, Max had obtained some of Dalmat's backstory from the relatives who had reported him missing. Dalmat had left Albania for England with his brother some four years ago. They were both in possession of university degrees, but poverty had forced them to seek manual work. Dalmat's brother had returned home in despair, but Dalmat had stayed on. Then, eighteen months ago he had abruptly stopped communicating with his parents, and the remittances he sent them ceased. They contacted the Albanian police, who didn't want to know, then Missing Persons, who, after making some enquiries and realising that his disappearance was suspicious, finally notified Interpol.

'And you end up in a pillbox on the edge of a farmer's field,' murmured Max. 'Poor bloke.' He frowned. Perhaps it was time for Jackman to pay another call on their friendly farmer, Donald Telford.

'Boss! Good news. I've identified Anton. He was a migrant labourer, apparently, so you might have a word with Donald Telford, the owner of the land where the pillbox stands. Ask him whether he ever hired a man called Dalmat Tabaku.'

* * *

'I said the ball was rolling, didn't I?' exclaimed Jackman. 'Three out of five victims have names. Now, as soon as the relevant departments, relatives, and loved ones have been notified, we can try and find out what these people had in common. There has to be something that caused those particular people to get themselves killed.'

Marie had lain awake all the previous night before trying to work out what that was. 'My best guess is that for some reason they all either did something, or went somewhere that the killer couldn't stomach for some reason, and he saw the red mist.'

'Like what?' Jackman said. 'Trespass on his land? Went into his home? I can't see how that would make someone kill not one person, but five.'

'Or maybe they invaded what the killer considered their sacred space — you know, somewhere really, really special to them.'

Jackman nodded slowly. 'Makes sense. Because as things stand, I can't see a connection between a ghost-hunting store manager, a good-time girl, an Albanian immigrant farmworker a well-dressed older woman and a middle-aged man dressed for the countryside.'

'Why don't I get Robbie onto their backstories? Maybe he can find out why they were in this area at the time of their disappearance,' suggested Marie. 'He's good at that sort of thing, and if Max has no success with identifying the remaining two victims, he could give him a hand.'

'Fair enough. Get him on that first thing tomorrow, and we'll tell Max he can give up on the other two victims if he's getting nowhere. Speaking of Max, I've just heard that he's to be awarded the Chief Constable's Commendation for an act of bravery. He deliberately placed himself between an injured colleague and the man who had shot him. That's something that needs recognition, and I'm thrilled to bits it's been acknowledged.'

'Me too!' exclaimed Marie. 'But I think we'll find we have a reluctant hero in our Max. He thinks it's you who deserves the medal, not him.'

'Me?' Jackman looked horrified. 'It wasn't even a very good rugby tackle. My sports coach would have been ashamed of me. And no one was pointing a loaded gun at me.'

'Come on, Jackman, you know very well that that idiot Westerham could have swung round and fired at you. Still, I guess we can allow Max to take the limelight this time, huh?'

'We certainly shall. The lad deserves it. Now, how far are we from this old couple's house?'

Marie smiled. Neat change of subject. 'Half a mile? Something like that. It's somewhere along Tollberry Lane, the one that meanders along the fields on the outskirts of the village. There's a scattering of houses along that road, and theirs is the farthest.'

They only located it because someone had nailed a piece of wood attached to a fence post at a junction on the lane with an arrow and the number six painted on it.

Number six, Tollberry Lane was an austere property that had nothing of the character of the cottages normally found on the Fens. Flat and square, it looked a bit like a child's drawing of a house, and though not actually neglected, looked tired and almost dispirited, if that were possible in a house. It also had no name, which was very unusual for houses in far-flung areas like this one. A name would have helped people find it, but maybe that was the point. If the Logans were as inhospitable as Dudley Nailer had said, they were probably happy not to be found.

They walked up the short path to the front door, and Jackman knocked, saying under his breath, 'Here goes nothing.'

The man who answered was tall, and held himself surprisingly erect for someone of his advanced years. Despite his shock of grey hair and shaggy beard, he did not look unkempt or dirty.

'What do you want?'

'A few minutes of your time, sir,' said Jackman, introducing himself and Marie.

The man's face creased into deep lines of suspicion. 'We've done nothing wrong, so why the visit?'

'We aren't accusing you of anything, sir, we're simply asking for your help,' said Jackman evenly. 'I'm sure you've heard about the disturbing find in the village recently — well, we're visiting everyone who lives in this area in case anyone has seen or heard anything that might be of assistance to the police.'

'Well, you've wasted your time coming here. I don't know nothing about no find. And I'm not having the likes of you upsetting my wife, either, so go away.'

He started to close the door, but Jackman stuck his foot in the gap. 'Mr Logan, you can speak to us here, or at the police station. Whichever you prefer.'

The man made a movement as if to object, then conceded defeat. 'What do you want to know?'

'We are trying to identify two people, Mr Logan, a man and a woman. The man was aged fifty to fifty-five years. He was approximately five foot eleven inches tall and was found wearing a wax Barbour-style jacket.' Jackman showed him a photo. 'Do you know this man, sir?'

The man's slight intake of breath was almost imperceptible.

'We believe he may have been Irish, although that hasn't as yet been confirmed,' added Jackman.

'Never seen him before,' muttered Logan. 'And why ask us? We rarely go into the village, and we don't know what goes on there.'

Jackman sighed. 'I have no wish to upset you, sir, but this man was brutally murdered, and several people have told us that your son Jeremy may have gone missing or moved away at the time it happened. Mr Logan, is this your son?'

Logan appeared to shrink as the fight went out of him. 'You'd better come in. But please, be quiet. My wife is resting upstairs and I don't want her troubled. She has serious health issues, and a shock of this kind could be catastrophic.'

They followed him into a comfortable lounge, and closing the door, pointed to two sofas facing each other, while he seated himself on a chair.

'When you showed me that picture I thought for a moment that it was Jeremy. It wasn't, though. You see, Jeremy was starved of oxygen at birth, something they called HIE, or hypoxic-ischemic-encephalopathy. He survived, but he was severely disabled. He suffered from brain damage along with a number of other problems.'

'I am so very sorry to hear that,' said Jackman gently, while Marie nodded sympathetically. 'It must have been terrible for you and your wife.'

'Not nearly as terrible as it was for Jeremy, Officer.' He looked away for a moment. 'Our son is dead. He ran away a couple of years ago, and we later discovered that he had taken his own life. For a long time my wife was unable to come to terms with it. She was on the verge of a breakdown, and the nosy villagers didn't help. So I had to invent a story that would keep both her and them happy. She believes he's in a very nice care home, close to the sea, where he will spend the rest of his life happily.'

He swallowed, and Marie blinked back tears.

'There are times when she talks about it that I start to believe it myself, like when you showed me that photo.' He sighed. 'That was not our boy. I just wanted it to be.'

Marie cleared her throat. 'He must have been very brave to deal with so much for so long. I suppose you don't have a picture of Jeremy that we could see?'

Patrick went to a row of framed photographs on a windowsill and selected one. 'Here he is, with his dog, Cully. They were inseparable. I think her passing was what started his downward spiral.'

Marie saw immediately that the young man was not Eamonn. She passed it to Jackman, who handed it back to Logan and got up to leave.

'Thank you, sir. And I'm truly sorry to have upset you like this. We'll leave you in peace now, and you won't be troubled again.'

'Fifty per cent of the time, he was the bane of our lives, but I'd go through it all again for the other half. Then he could be the sweetest boy imaginable. He never deserved to suffer like he did, but he's at peace now . . . in the care of angels, in a lovely home by the sea.'

Marie and Jackman returned to the car in silence, both feeling rather chastened. They had gone to that house prepared to do battle with a couple of bad-tempered old codgers, and instead had found a tragedy. Jackman started the engine. 'I'm always saying we should never make assumptions about people. I'd do well to heed my own advice. Remind me of that man if I ever sound like a judgemental prat, won't you?'

'Ditto, Jackman. Ditto.'

* * *

As Jackman and Marie wound their way back through the fen lanes, Kevin and Gary were attempting to extricate themselves from a discussion of the paranormal that was fast becoming rather too esoteric. They were in the club's unofficial headquarters, the home of its founder and secretary, Jonathon Bush.

'Well, explain this if you will,' Jonathon was saying. 'How on earth could Iris know so much about the Denby family of Cardington Hall if not through the spirit world? She went into that house knowing no more than the rest of us did, then on the way home, she all of a sudden starts spouting out the whole of their history. She wasn't even speaking in her own voice! You heard it, Matthew. She was channelling a spirit, wasn't she?'

Matthew Byrd, a younger, rather good-looking man, appeared somewhat embarrassed, but he agreed with Jonathon. 'She knew everything about daily life at the Hall, almost as if, well, she had first-hand experience of it.'

'Exactly! Because she did! And not only—'

'Please, gentlemen!' Gary said. 'We really aren't here to discuss, er, spiritual matters, we need some down-to-earth help with our enquiry.'

Both men looked apologetic.

'Sorry, Detective, but it's a bit of a passion of ours, and we tend to get carried away,' said Jonathon. 'So, erm, you want to know about Gino Lombardi, that right?'

'Nice man,' added Matthew. 'Not a believer, per se, but he kept an open mind, and he admitted to a certain susceptibility to atmosphere.'

'He was good friends with another of our members, Arthur Brownlee. You'd do well to talk to him. He often comes on our ghost walks with us.' Jonathon pulled out a diary from a pile of books on his desk. 'I've got his number, if that helps?'

'Thank you,' said Kevin, 'but we've already got it, and we've left a message for him to contact us.'

'We were all gutted when we heard that Gino was dead,' said Jonathon. 'He was a good bloke, and everyone liked him. We honestly believed that he'd got fed up — I mean, members do come and go — and Arthur told us he'd had a barney at work, so we thought he might have moved away to another job.'

'Was there anyone in the group he didn't get on with?' asked Kevin.

Both men shook their heads. 'No one,' said Matthew. 'This is a friendly group. Okay, we have our moments — as Jonathon says, it's a bit of a passion, but we don't take ourselves too seriously.'

'That's right,' said Jonathon. 'People come for a variety of reasons, and no one is critical or deprecating of others. We have a laugh, and occasionally we do come across something none of us understands, and that sparks some great debates.'

Kevin took from his bag the five images generated with facial recognition software. 'Okay, gentlemen, we'd like you to take a look at these and tell us if any of them look familiar.'

Both men frowned when they came to the picture of Gino.

'That's definitely Gino, but something about it is not quite right,' said Jonathon. He looked up at Kevin. 'Oh I get it! It's one of those computerised things they reproduce from dead people's faces, isn't it?'

The picture fell from his fingers and fluttered to the floor. Gary picked it up without comment.

'Recognise any of the others?' Kevin asked.

'Shelley?' Matthew said. 'Yes, that one. It's Shelley Kershaw, who used to work at the pub in Bartoft.' His face took on a look of horror. 'Oh Lord. Does that mean she's one of those dead people in that bunker?'

'Did you know her?' Kevin asked.

'Er, well, yes, in a sense. She was one of the barmaids at the Full Moon. I used to have a drink there sometimes.'

It wasn't lost on Kevin that Matthew probably knew Shelley rather better than he was letting on. No wonder he was shocked.

Neither of the men knew any of the others, so Kevin and Gary prepared to leave.

'One final thing,' said Gary. 'When is the next meeting? And do you generally meet here, or at the venue for the ghost walk?'

'It's not for a couple of weeks,' Jonathon said, 'and we'll be driving ourselves there, as it's out at one of the old World War Two airbases over towards the coast. However, I can always call an extraordinary meeting here, if that would help? Most of our members are pretty flexible, even though they won't all be able to attend.'

'That would be an enormous help, sir,' said Kevin. It would have been a long job getting round thirty-odd people spread out across the area.

'Okay, I'll get on the phone. Seven tomorrow evening, is that all right?'

Kevin and Gary stood up to leave. 'Perfect, sir. We'll see you then, and thank you both for your time.'

Matthew stopped them at the door. 'I wonder if I could take another look at those photographs? I was rather distracted when I realised they were pictures of dead people. I'm not sure, but I think I might have seen another of them before.'

Kevin took out the images and passed them to Matthew.

'This woman . . .' He stared long and hard at the photo of the older woman that Rory had named Juno. 'I live in the middle of the village, close to the post office, and I swear I've seen someone just like her . . . Yes, that's it. She was walking across the village green, and she had binoculars around her neck! She was very well dressed, but sort of old-fashioned, you know, like tweeds? Clothes posh people used to wear for the country.'

That figured. Juno's clothes had practically decomposed as they were made of natural fibres, and quality woollen tweeds would certainly come into that category. 'That's very helpful, sir,' Kevin said. 'But it was quite some time ago, wasn't it? Are you sure that's the woman you saw?'

'Oh yes,' Matthew said. 'It stuck in my memory because we don't get many strangers in the village. Certainly not tourists, that's for sure. And she reminded me very much of my grandmother. I can see her now, with her expensive binoculars, a brownish jacket with a suede collar, and a matching pleated skirt.'

It gave them something else to follow up, and the full forensics report would give them the colour and origin of the fibres clinging to Juno's bones. Plus, she could very well have been a birdwatcher, it was a big thing in the Fens.

They were making progress, and it felt good.

* * *

On their way to Dudley Nailer's house, Jackman received a call from Vic Blackwell.

'I've just heard from Corbin's lawyer. He's very eager to talk and would like us to meet at the prison tomorrow morning at eleven. Can I accept?'

'Absolutely. Go ahead. Did he mention what this meeting is to be about?'

'Not really, sir, he just emphasised his client's eagerness to help.'

'Given the incontrovertible evidence of a recording of his voice from inside Hartwood House, he couldn't do much else, could he?' Jackman said.

Vic laughed. 'No, indeed, sir. Still, if he can give us any kind of lead that helps us catch Chaos, I'll be first to hand him the keys of his cell and wish him bon voyage!'

Call ended, Jackman said, 'I can't help thinking this'll turn out to be a waste of time. I'm certain Chaos is too clever to be caught out by some art thief.'

'You never know,' said Marie thoughtfully. 'There's always the chance he underestimated Lucas Corbin, thinking like you did that he was just some art thief. I had a read-through of the Met's list of unsolved crimes involving the theft of valuable antiques and artwork, and I could be wrong, but as the MO was identical for a whole bunch of them, I'd put money on the fact that Corbin is a master thief, and that he's got away with a fortune in stolen artefacts. You have to admit that the Hartwood House job was carried out meticulously, and Corbin was only caught because Chaos turned traitor on him.'

'In which case I shall pay very careful attention to that gentleman at tomorrow's interview.' They were now approaching an old-style gabled house. 'Is this it? Reed Lodge?'

Marie nodded. 'Home to Mr Dudley Nailer. This should be interesting.'

As Kevin had foretold, they were welcomed like old friends and ushered into the famous kitchen that Kevin had raved about. On being offered a choice of different teas, Marie said she'd go with Russian Caravan, something she'd never heard of, let alone tasted.

'Then you are in for a rare treat, Detective Sergeant Evans!' chortled Dudley. 'Just a splash of milk and enjoy! Now, do tell me, did you get more than two words out of our Mad Sally? Your delightful colleague told me that you were the brave soul who drew the short straw.'

Marie had no intention of sharing anything with this man, despite his cheerful disposition and his tea. 'Could have been worse, I suppose. I was wondering why you told my colleague that she was far from mad, given her nickname.'

Dudley perched on the edge of a chair as he waited for the kettle to boil. 'She simply isn't what she makes herself out to be. She watches everything that goes on while pretending to understand none of it. I think Sally actually understands more than most. She's like a hunting dog, or that fox she walks with, scenting out anything that occurs within a ten-mile radius of this village.'

'Are you suggesting she engineers things, causes them to happen?' asked Marie.

'Oh no, nothing like that. They're often perfectly random things that are no one's fault, like when the bus shelter collapsed and narrowly missed a young mum with a toddler in a pushchair. Well, Mad Sally was there before the dust had even settled. How do you officers put it now? First on scene?'

'Yes, sir, first on scene,' Jackman said.

'And then there was the time when old Jimmy Haynes collapsed in the village store. Sally was there long before the first responder. She never helps, or interferes, just watches.' He shivered dramatically. 'I told your young constable, Kevin, she's like a dark wraith, a harbinger of doom.'

Kevin had told them that Dudley reminded him of an elderly actor, retired from the stage, who couldn't help being overdramatic. They could see what he meant.

'We wanted to thank you for your suggestion of calling on old Jeannie Roberts at Laburnum House,' said Jackman, changing the subject. 'It has helped us identify one of the dead victims as Shelley Kershaw, and if it's okay with you, we have some images that we'd like you to take a look at — composite photographs of two of the other bodies found in the pillbox.'

'Oh dear. Let me make the tea first, Officers. I might need a restorative if I'm to gaze upon the dead.'

'Don't worry, sir, they are wholly lifelike,' Jackman said. 'I assure you we wouldn't show you anything unsuitable.'

A short while later, Marie was breathing in the delicious aroma of the Russian Caravan served in a bone china cup. It was fragrant, but with a slight smokiness that made it more full-bodied. Jackman was smiling appreciatively, so it clearly came up to standard.

Dudley was carefully studying the two photographs, those representing Juno and Eamonn. 'The woman seems vaguely familiar, Officers, but I have no idea where I might have seen her, and indeed, I might be imagining it. The man strikes no chord. I have a good memory for faces, so I'm pretty sure I've never seen him, but the woman . . . no, I'm sorry, I can't help you.'

'No worries,' said Marie. 'I don't suppose you have had any more thoughts since our Kevin's visit about anyone else in the neighbourhood who might be able to assist us?'

Dudley sighed. 'I've thought of little else, Sergeant. This terrible thing has cast a blight on our lovely village, and I'd readily give any help I can offer, but the only person who comes to mind is a man called Seymour. I don't know his first name as I've never heard him called anything else. He comes to the village every Thursday morning with the fish van. He parks in the layby by the village green and sells fresh fish that his son brings direct from Grimsby. He's never in a hurry, and chats like there's no tomorrow. The old girls love him, but the reason I mention him is because he travels around the local villages and carries the news from one to the other, like his father and his grandfather before him. He's a real old local and he hears a lot, and believe me, he doesn't miss a trick, that one. If I were you, I'd show him those pictures. If anyone can help you, it's Seymour.'

They finished their tea and made ready to leave. Marie was glad to have tried the Russian Caravan, but decided good old builders' was still her preferred daily brew.

'Your thoughts?' asked Jackman when they were back in the car.

'I honestly have no idea,' she said. 'Part of me wants to take him at face value, and another wonders if I just spent half an hour in fantasy land.'

'Same here,' Jackman said. 'I'd like to think that someone who has such excellent taste in teas cannot possibly be capable of murder, and then I decide I've just played a small part in the Dudley Nailer Show.'

Marie laughed. 'Not like us to be totally bemused about someone, is it? But one thing that does make me think he's for real is his stature. I mean, he's so short and, well, rotund. I can't see him hefting a bloody great spade and caving someone's head in. I think our killer has to be taller than Dudley, don't you?'

'Rory will be able to clarify that from the angle and trajectory from which the weapon was swung. Maybe we should consider that before we start grilling suspects.' Jackman quickly rang Rory, who confirmed that the murderer had to be at least five foot nine and most likely taller. It was impossible to be exact, as their footwear had to be taken into account, and the terrain at the scene of the crime. It was possible that the killer was standing on a slope, or slightly raised above the victims in some other way.

'So we can't really rule anyone out,' sighed Marie, 'but it's more likely that we are looking at a fairly tall subject, which lets Dudley off the hook.' She felt rather pleased about that, as she'd rather taken to him, and she fully understood how Kevin had fallen in love with that wonderful old kitchen.

'So, where to now?' asked Jackman, starting the car.

'Why don't we tie up with Kevin and Gary, if they are still around, and see how they are doing,' suggested Marie.

'Good move. And don't forget, we need to have another talk with that farmer about our Albanian man. I rather wanted to take a walk down to that pillbox now it's been cleared; I'm hoping that seeing it empty will dispel any remaining demons. Plus I'd like another chat with Bryson's mum and dad.'

'Then let's arrange to meet the others there.'

'Ring them now, and we'll head towards the bungalow. Let's go lay a few ghosts.'

CHAPTER TWENTY-EIGHT

Superintendent Ruth Crooke gazed pensively at her phone, thinking over the call that had just ended. Another crime foiled by the timely intervention of Chaos, this time in Fenchester. On this occasion it was a big-time drug dealer who found himself in the back of a police van, and DCI Ivan Barclay who was cracking open the bubbly. Upon learning that the arresting officer had been DS Ralph Enderby, Ruth smiled. Marie would be pleased.

Was this Chaos person really out to help them? So it seemed. But why? For some reason she pictured a paedophile offering sweets to a child. Ruth shook her head to dismiss the image, stood up abruptly and strode from the office.

She rarely had occasion to visit the IT centre, but now she decided it was time to have a personal word with Orac.

The low buzz of chatter stopped as soon as she walked in.

Orac called out to her from the other side of the room. 'Superintendent Crooke! To what do we owe the honour?'

Ruth made her way over to where Orac sat in front of an array of screens, all filled with figures and symbols that made zero sense to Ruth, who shook her head. 'It's beyond me how you can make head or tail of all that.'

Orac gave Ruth a look of what she took to be amusement — it was hard to tell with those disconcerting eyes. 'I guess it takes the mind of a genius, but then . . .'

Ruth sat down. 'Does any of that,' she nodded to the screens, 'give any indication as to who Chaos might be?'

''Fraid not, but it might, given time.'

'Which unfortunately is in rather short supply at the moment.'

'Take heart, Ruth, what you're seeing here has nothing to do with Chaos.' Orac pointed across the room. 'But those do.'

Ruth looked across to the other side of the room, where two data operators were working at a bank of screens similar to Orac's.

'To put it in layman's terms, we've set up a kind of cyber net, and my colleagues are fishing for all they are worth. We are hoping that the big fish, namely Chaos, will swim into our net, and we can follow him back to his lair — if fish can be said to have lairs. Well, whatever you call them, you get what I mean, don't you?'

Ruth did. 'I expect DI Jackman's told you that the man caught inside Hartwood House is saying he wants to help you trace the money transfers?'

'I have, and DS Vic Blackwell is going to report back to me the moment he returns from HMP Marshfield. Although I wouldn't bank on him telling us anything useful. We all know how smart our joker is, and I'm betting he uses a different channel for every single transaction. He probably has accounts on various obscure offshore islands that we can't even spell the names of.'

'Yes, I'm aware of that,' Ruth said. 'But I'm hoping he might at least give you an idea of how they are made — like does he use cryptocurrency — and especially how the villains get in touch with him.'

'That's what we are banking on. At some point, he has to slip up. He'll make a schoolboy error and when he does, we'll be waiting for him. We're watching twenty-four hours a day,

Ruth. And not just us, nor Spooky, either. There are others with their eyes on his every move. All it takes will be a single mistake, and Chaos will be history.'

'Well, I'll leave him in your capable hands, Orac. I'm sure I don't have to tell you to contact me at the slightest hint of a breakthrough.'

'You'll be the first to hear, Ruth.'

Ruth made her way back upstairs. They could do no more. They had the best facilities and the best operatives there were. All they needed now was Lady Luck to smile on them.

* * *

Marie was surprised at the extent of the Telford Farm Estate office. Attached to Telford's residence, it boasted three desk areas, carpeted floors, and lots of healthy houseplants. Two of the desks were occupied by women who were busy typing and making telephone calls. At the farther end of the room, a more imposing desk obviously belonged to the farmer himself.

Donald Telford sat down heavily. 'Fact is, I rarely get to know any of the field workers by name. The only person I have any dealings with is the gangmaster. Sometimes I never even see them. They are ferried in minibuses to wherever they'll be harvesting — usually cutting cauliflowers, cabbages, or gathering broccoli. At the end of the day they are taken straight back to where they're staying, and it goes on like that until the fields are cleared.'

Marie had seen them, out there in all weathers, bent over the crops. It was tough and repetitive work, and was now almost all done by migrant workers.

'I only ever use licensed companies regulated by the Gangmasters Licences Authority, and we are using fewer and fewer of them, since we're going over to other crops like wheat, rapeseed and barley, which are harvested using heavy equipment. All I can say is that to my knowledge I've never personally employed anyone by the name of Dalmat Tabaku.'

Jackman handed him the photograph. 'And you've never seen this man before? I don't mean on the farm, but you might have noticed him elsewhere, like in the village.'

'Never seen him, Inspector. Sorry.'

'That's all right, it was a long shot anyway. But would you mind giving us the names of the companies you use to recruit labour? They should have records of the people they take on.'

Telford asked one of his secretaries to look them out. 'I tend to use a couple of reputable companies, but sometimes we need more manpower, depending on how many fields need harvesting, and the people they supply are mostly migrants. You wouldn't believe it, but even on our basic minimum wage they can send home three times the amount they'd get paid in their own countries. And they earn it, too. They're out there in the fields every single day, come rain or shine, working their socks off.'

'Mind if I show this picture to your ladies here?' asked Marie.

'Go ahead,' said Donald. 'And if you have a spare one, leave it here, and we'll ask anyone who comes in.'

Jackman took two pictures from his briefcase. 'Thank you, sir. And while we're here, I have another face here for you to look at. Is this woman familiar to you from around eighteen months to two years ago?'

Donald shook his head. 'Can't say I recognise her, but my secretaries might. Do either of you two know this woman?'

Marie handed them the picture, but again it was met with shakes of the head. 'She was seen close to the village green, and had some expensive binoculars around her neck.'

'Then if I were you, I'd have a word with Gabby. She's the landlady down at the Full Moon,' said one of the women. 'She runs a birdwatching club, only small, just a few enthusiasts, but they help out with those counts and surveys they do to find out how the birds and wildlife are faring.'

Marie thanked her, and handed the picture back to Donald Telford. 'Let us know immediately if anyone here recognises either of these two people, won't you, sir?'

'One last thing, sir,' Jackman said. 'The pillbox. As from today, it's no longer a crime scene, and our people will all be pulling out. I'm afraid we don't have the resources to leave a car there just to stop nosy parkers trying to take a look. Can I ask if you have any plans for it?'

'I bloody well do,' said Telford. 'The moment we get the go-ahead from you people, the damn thing is coming down! I've got men just waiting for the word, and that horrible monstrosity will be history.'

'I'm afraid you'll need to hold them off for a little longer, sir,' said Jackman. 'I fully understand your wish to get rid of it as soon as possible, but I'm sorry to say that until we make an arrest, or get some satisfactory answers as to what occurred there, it will have to remain.'

'If that's the case, I assume I'm within my rights to fence it off until it can be demolished? I don't even want to see that evil place.'

'Of course,' said Jackman. 'We'll be doing the occasional drive-by to check that it hasn't been disturbed, and if you do get any trouble, ring us and we'll get a couple of our people down to sort it out.' He and Marie stood up to leave. 'And the moment that pillbox ceases to be of interest to us, I'll be sure to let you know. There's nothing I'd like more than to see it eradicated from the landscape.'

When they were outside again, Marie said, 'That's the second time the Full Moon has come up, isn't it, boss? Shelley was the barmaid there, and now it's been mentioned in connection with Juno.'

Jackman looked at his watch. 'After we've met up with Gary and Kevin, I suggest someone gets themselves over there with all five photos. If nothing else, it tells us something, doesn't it?'

It took Marie a moment or two to latch on. 'Yes, almost everyone passes through a public house at one time or another. Rather than a personal connection, those five victims could be linked by a place they've all been, like the Full Moon.'

'Exactly, or another similar sort of location. And if it turns out that anyone from the Full Moon does know Juno, we'll look long and hard at that place and everyone who frequents it.'

As they pulled up at the Smiths' bungalow, Marie received a text from Rory asking her to ring him as soon as she was free. She called him at once.

'Ah, the inimitable detective-extraordinaire, Marie Evans-Enderby! I'm hedging my bets with the name, you understand, not being too sure which one I'm currently addressing.'

Marie laughed. 'How can either of us help you, Rory?'

'Well, once again it is *I* helping you, dear heart. Having been requested to take an in-depth look at the jewellery found on our Juno, as well as the fibres of clothing found clinging to her, I think I've done rather well, even for me.'

'Naturally, we expect nothing less, but do reveal all, Rory. In your own time, of course.'

Marie glanced at Jackman, who was shaking his head. 'He never changes, does he? Milking every last detail for what he can get from it.'

Rory's voice issued from the phone. 'I heard that! Anyway, despite your comment, here's what we know about the jewellery. Expensive, very expensive indeed. I'm surprised the killer didn't remove it, as one of the items was easily traceable to an exclusive shop in London's Burlington Arcade.'

This was a good lead. 'Great!' Marie said.

'I've got all the details here, but if you are hoping for a name, she did not purchase it herself, it must have been a gift. However, you stalwart detectives will no doubt easily find who bought it, and who they gave it to. I'm telling you, that lady — and she was a lady — was deposited in that filthy pillbox with at least three-and-a-half-thousand-pounds-worth of trinkets on her person.'

'Bloody hell!' exclaimed Marie.

'Exactly. Now, pin back those delicate lugholes, because this is the clever bit: the clothes.' He gave a little chuckle. 'I had to almost forcibly prevent my little gumshoe Spike from undertaking the job himself, by the way. I said it was a distinct possibility that you might come to rely on him too heavily if he indulged in much more clever sleuthing, so it will be over to you to follow this one up. Now, this lady had money, she loved her clothes and took care of her appearance. Both Jan Wallace and I deduced this fact from nothing but the few remaining fibres we were able to test. Brilliant, eh?'

The call now on loudspeaker, Marie and Jackman both listened intently.

'Our Juno was indeed wearing tweed, as your observant witness stated, and his memory for colour was very good, as I can confirm that her jacket was Harris Tweed and the colour and design was a kind of Dijon windowpane check. I say "kind of" because both fabric and design were bespoke, and those do not come cheap, believe me!'

'And all from a few threads. I am impressed, Rory.'

'And so you should be! Anyway, dear Spike said to tell you that when you embark on your search for this lovely tweed, you need look no further than the Hebrides. Sayonara! And good hunting.'

Marie stared at her screen. 'I swear he gets worse by the day.'

Jackman grinned. 'You can say that again. But this is fantastic information, isn't it, Marie? Ring Max and ask him to follow that up as a matter of urgency. We could well have another name by the end of the day.'

Marie was just finishing her call to an excited Max, when Kevin and Gary approached their car.

'Time to pool our collective findings,' said Jackman, getting out. 'And time for Betty Smith to close down her emergency café.'

'After we've cadged one final brew, I hope?' Marie was ready for a drink, and in her book, Betty's tea was much more acceptable than Dudley's Russian Caravan.

As soon as Betty saw them approach, she called out, 'Kettle's on! Come on into the kitchen. Teddy's in the garden somewhere, probably glaring at the cause of all this trouble and wishing Donald Telford would pull it down.'

Thanking her for her offer of tea, Jackman said, 'You can tell Mr Smith that the farmer wants it pulled down just as much as he does, he's just waiting for us to give him the go-ahead.'

She sighed. 'Oh, that will be such a relief. Teddy spends far too much time down there staring at the damn thing! Anyway, is it four teas, or is anyone on the coffee today?'

Drinks ordered, Jackman told her that the remaining officers would be gone by the end of the day, but if she had the slightest concern about anything, or if the media became a nuisance, she should ring them immediately.

'Luckily, our Bry isn't returning to London just yet,' said Betty. 'I feel safer with him around, although I know he won't be able to stay for ever. He's been so good to us over the years, and now he's offered to help us find another home if we decide we can't stay here after, well . . .'

'Do you really think you might leave?' asked Marie. 'Oh, I'm sorry to hear that. I know it's been awful for you, but you've made such a lovely home here, it would be a pity if you felt you had to move.'

Betty shrugged. 'We really don't know, Sergeant. Neither of us wants the upheaval of a move, and we do love this place. Anyway, we won't decide immediately. When he's finished doing this job for you, our Bry is going to spend a few more days working with young Colin Reynolds on the garden, and we'll make our decision before he goes back.' She placed four steaming mugs on the table. 'I'll go and leave you good people to enjoy your tea, while I try to prise my Ted away from that damn pillbox.'

After she left, they began to compare their findings. All in all, Marie thought they'd done better than expected, especially regarding Juno. Now, only one of them was a complete mystery — Eamonn. A man of fifty to fifty-five, who died wearing outdoor country-style clothes. Apart from the fact that he had brown hair and was of average height, they knew nothing about him. He was an ordinary man with no distinguishing features, who had met with an extraordinary fate.

'Penny for them, Sarge,' said Gary.

'Sorry. Wool-gathering. I was just thinking that we seem to be racing ahead with identifying the victims, but we're no closer to finding our killer, who could well be one of the people we've been talking to. It's a scary thought, isn't it?'

No one responded. It was indeed scary.

'Then we'd better get our arses in gear and find the bugger, hadn't we?' said Gary. 'What's next, boss?'

With a grateful smile at him, Jackman said, 'I just want a swift walk down to the pillbox, and then Marie and I will go and see how old Jeanie at Laburnum House is doing. Now she knows that her old lodger is dead, she might need a bit of support.'

'Then take a hard hat and don't slam any doors,' said Gary. 'You take your life in your hands just knocking on the door in that place.'

Jackman grimaced. 'Thanks for the warning. Now, would you and Kevin head over to the Full Moon at Bartoft and ask Gabby, the landlady, about birdwatching.'

Both men looked puzzled.

'One of Donald Telford's secretaries suggested it,' added Marie. 'Gabby runs a small birders' club, and as Juno, whom I very much doubt was a Peeping Thomasina, was seen carrying binoculars, there's a chance the members of that club either know or know of her.'

'I see,' said Kevin. 'We'll go as soon we've finished here, then.'

'Has anyone heard how uniform are getting on with the search for the murder weapon?' asked Jackman.

'Nothing as yet,' said Gary. 'We had a word with Stacey Smith earlier. They did find one spade of the same make and design, but it was almost new and the owner still had the receipt, so it definitely wasn't the murder weapon.'

'There's a lot of properties to search, though,' added Kevin, 'and they're being very thorough. It could still turn up.'

Unlikely, Marie thought, but it was always a possibility, especially as the same spade was used on all of the victims over a number of years. Their murderer was clearly attached to it.

Not for the first time, Marie found herself wondering about Mad Sally, and what had happened to her to make her the way she was now. An intelligent, well brought up woman turns into a silent ghostlike figure, choosing to live alone and off grid, repelling all efforts at contact. Marie resolved to check in with Robbie as soon as she could, to see if he'd made any headway with the mystery woman.

Jackman pushed back his chair and stood up. 'If you've finished your tea, I suggest we press on. And I think we should organise some sort of a thank-you gift for Betty Smith for her support, what say you?'

'Why not have a whip-round, boss?' suggested Gary. 'Everyone who's been out here, especially the crews on obo, will certainly put their hands in their pockets. That lady has been a real diamond. Want me to organise it?'

'If you don't mind, thank you. Then we'll have to decide what to get her — other than a year's supply of tea bags and three gallons of milk!'

Marie was pleased. The likable Gary was very good at that kind of thing, and generally did better than anyone when it came to getting money out of his colleagues.

As they dispersed, Marie said, 'Do you mind making your pilgrimage to the pillbox on your own, Jackman? I want to phone in and get updates from both Robbie and Max, if that's okay?'

'Of course. See you back at the car. I won't be long.'

Marie pulled out her phone. Why was she so certain that Mad Sally had witnessed something that would help them? She would have dearly loved Jackman to meet her, but bringing him in would destroy the tenuous link she'd managed to build up between them. No, she needed to deal with Sally alone, and before she made another attempt, she wanted some solid information to take with her. There was a serious problem somewhere in Sally's past, if only Robbie could dig it out.

* * *

Bob Ruston was amazed at how well his house guest, Craig's gran, was getting on with Troy. With her calm, easy-going manner, she was one of the few people his son seemed able to relax with. Since Emily Sharpe had been staying with them, Troy hadn't had a single outburst of fury. Come to think of it, perhaps this wasn't so surprising. Troy had adored Bob's own mother, and taken her passing badly. Maybe Emily was a surrogate granny?

Whatever, it was lovely to see, and it was giving Bob some respite from the pain of seeing his son suffer. He often watched them together, Emily happily crocheting away, Troy beside her in his wheelchair, both chatting like old friends.

'He's a lovely lad,' said Emily, gathering up her balls of wool. 'You must be very proud of him.'

Troy was in his room with his mother, sorting out his medication. Bob smiled at her. 'Oh yes. The lad's a fighter, all right. But it breaks my heart to see him like this. He was such a fit young man and he had a brilliant future ahead of him.'

'Well, what's to stop him!' Emily said with feeling. 'He's got a very good brain, he just needs to channel it into something he *can* do, rather than dwelling on what he can't.'

'But—'

'Come on, Mr Ruston! It's up to you to get him out of the doldrums. Encourage him to find a new interest, something that might lead to a job at some point. So many people nowadays work from home, don't they? What your Troy needs is stimulus. I could see that at once. Stop pitying him, and no matter how much it hurts you to do so, put a squib up his backside.'

Bob burst out laughing. 'Ever considered a career as a life-coach, Emily? You'd make a fortune!'

Emily chuckled. 'I spent years as an occupational therapist in a rehabilitation centre, and I was famous for cracking the whip when it was called for.' She sighed reminiscently. 'And though I say so myself, I had one or two heartwarming success stories, so it was all worth it, even if I never made any fortune.'

'I can imagine you had quite a few successes,' Bob said.

'And if your boy fancied working with computers, I could always get my Craig to have a chat with him. He helped a friend of his get a job not long ago. He might not have been too keen on making a career of it, but he's very good at it. He designs things using this new-fangled AI whatchamacallit, did some lovely New Home cards for his mate's girlfriend. It's a shame he never took it up professionally. I hate to see talent wasted.'

Bob didn't say so but he knew Craig had to be good. Good enough to get himself kidnapped and nearly killed.

'And not long ago, he helped that same girl set up this brand-new hi-tech computer system in her home. Well, I say home, but really it was more like this luxury annexe attached to her dad's mansion. Craig wondered what on earth he did for a living, it was so posh! He said Cindy was lovely, though, really down to earth, even though her parents were obviously rolling in it.'

Bob was about to answer when he was struck by what Emily had just said. He'd spoken to Craig in some detail about the jobs he'd done for different people, but he hadn't mentioned this girl. Who was she? More to the point, who was her father? In his head, the clamour of alarm bells sounded, urgently. He looked at his watch. He hadn't been planning to visit Craig today. Now he was eager to get there as soon as he could. He had a few very important questions for that lad.

* * *

As Jackman approached the field edge, he paused for a moment and looked across to where Bryson and Colin had been working when they made their gruesome discovery. Standing alone, just a few yards inside the gate, was Edward Smith. He seemed to be in a world of his own, and had clearly not heard Jackman, who was about to go over and talk to him. But something in Smith's expression made him change his mind. Instead, he quietly opened the field gate and went through.

Two officers were outside the pillbox, clearing away the last of the debris before they too left.

'Halogens are all down and packed away, sir,' said one of them. 'So not somewhere you'd want to come to after dark from now on.'

'I don't think it ever was, was it?' said Jackman. 'But I guarantee we'll get the odd idiot wandering about here in the pitch black.'

'Well, they're welcome to it. I'll be glad not to have to come here again. Place gives me the creeps, even in daylight. Sod it at night, and with no lights!'

This prompted his crewmate to take the rise out of him, but the banter soon fell flat. This place seemed to leach the life out of everything in its vicinity.

'Mind if we get away, sir? Or is there anything we can help you with?' asked the first officer.

'You get off. I don't intend staying here long myself. I'm just checking that all is in order before we pull out.'

After the two constables had left, Jackman gathered himself for a final look into the pillbox. The door and it's rotting frame had gone, and some of the decaying concrete structure itself had been dismantled to aid the removal of the bodies. It was empty now, yet a sinister air still clung to it. Even in broad daylight, the place had an unhealthy darkness about it. He stepped back a few paces and stared at it. It was just a hunk of old concrete, built in another lifetime to do a job it had never been called upon to fulfil — protect Britain's coastline from invasion. He'd seen more than a dozen of these things dotted around the countryside, utterly unremarkable until this one had been put to its sinister use. Jackman felt that something of the killer's black heart still haunted it.

For goodness' sake, Jackman, he told himself. He had come here to lay the ghosts to rest, but it seemed they refused to lie down.

There was a snap, as of a twig breaking somewhere in the bushes that surrounded the pillbox, and Jackman jumped. He squinted at the place he thought the sound had come from but saw nothing. An animal? A bird? Was someone else out here, watching?

Normally, he would have called out and challenged whoever it was, but for some reason he remained standing, rooted to the spot, listening. Then he recalled the uniformed officer who had been struck with a heavy branch in this very pace, and he did shout. 'Okay, whoever's in there, come out! Now!'

No response. A silence hung over the wooded area and its solitary edifice, and Jackman began to relax. Imagination, that's all it was, just imagination.

With one last look back at the brooding old pillbox, Jackman turned tail and hurried back out to the field path. Maybe his idea of paying a last visit to this place hadn't been such a good one after all, it had only made him unsettled and jumpy. His heart only stopped pounding when he caught sight of Marie leaning against the car, waiting for him.

* * *

By the end of the day there had been further developments, but Marie was still mystified when she went home. Max had given it his all regarding Juno, and had been ecstatic when he discovered her real name. Their rich woman in bespoke clothing and beautiful jewellery was called Marion Sandon-Hayes, but then he ran into a dead end. The deeper he looked into her past, the more puzzled he became. This older woman, who had lived for most of her privileged life in Chelsea, had gone missing more than three years previously. It wasn't until he started to unravel her life that he began to understand. At seven that evening, Jackman had been forced to order him out of the station, fearing that if he didn't do so, Max would still be there when they arrived for work the next day. Jackman even refused to listen to Max's story of what he had uncovered, telling him to go and get some food and sleep. Max could give them the whole story at the morning meeting, when, hopefully, they would all be fresh and fit enough to take on board yet another mystery.

By the time Marie drew up outside Peelers End, their lovely old police house in the village of Corley Eaudyke, she was practically out on her feet. It was mental exhaustion. Every person they spoke to was a potential murder suspect. It was draining work, summing up the information they gave, and deciding how much of it was true and what was fabrication. You trained yourself to pick up anomalies and statements that conflicted from person to person. You logged things that cropped up more than once from different sources, such as the Full Moon pub in Bartoft. You never ignored or made assumptions about anything you were told, even if it seemed likely to lead nowhere.

'Are you planning on sitting here all night, madam? Because if so, I could bring your dinner to you on a tray?' Marie looked up to see Ralph smiling at her through her half-open window.

Marie laughed. How she loved this man! He *got* her, plain and simple. Relationships between serving officers were notorious for coming to a bad end because of the job. Theirs flourished, for the same reason. She and Ralph were wired the same way, dedicated to the work they did, and in love enough to understand that what was good for one was good for the other. Plus, they made the most of their time together.

'I don't think I'll dine al fresco tonight, waiter,' she said. 'There's not room for a tray behind the steering column. I'll opt for silver service in the grand dining hall, thank you all the same.'

'Then, if madam would like to follow me, I'll see if we have a table free. The chef's special is going down rather well tonight.'

Arm in arm, they walked up the drive, giggling like a couple of children.

CHAPTER TWENTY-NINE

The morning meeting got underway earlier than usual, as everyone seemed to be in long before their normal time. Jackman gave a brief status report on what was happening with the pillbox, and uniform's unsuccessful search for the murder weapon, then he handed over to Max.

'Okay, so here's where I am at present.' Max added a new photograph of the woman they had called Juno to the whiteboard. 'Marion Sandon-Hayes, widowed at thirty-five and never remarried. Lived in an exclusive apartment, in what they call a "reimagined" Grade II-listed building in the Chelsea area of London — and man, that is one cool, upmarket pad! Thing is, it's empty. She hasn't been seen there for almost two years. She was one seriously rich lady, and although I've barely scratched the surface of her finances, it appears she owns the entire building. Upkeep and maintenance is handled by a team of accountants and solicitors, and is funded by renting out the other apartments, along with the proceeds from several very successful businesses she owned.'

'Hence the posh clobber and expensive jewellery, I suppose,' said Robbie. 'But why wasn't she reported missing? She's been dead for eighteen months or more.'

'Our Marion was very much a free spirit, mate. She used that classy pad as a base and never spent much time there. She travelled extensively, and was sometimes gone for long periods of time. I've got a Zoom call with her accountants later this morning, which should be interesting, but I did manage to have a chat with the bloke who bought her the wristwatch she was wearing. His name is Andrew Shearing, a retired university lecturer and old friend of her late husband's. He was probably the only one of their friends she remained close to after her husband's death from cancer. He has always believed her disappearance to be suspicious, but no matter how many waves the poor bloke made, her financial advisors blocked or dismissed them. He reckons, and I think he's right, that they didn't want to upset a very tasty and lucrative applecart. They all made a bloody fortune from Marion, and if she was found to be brown bread, all that would change.'

'So, has this friend of hers any idea what she would have been doing in the Fens?' asked Marie.

'Oh yes,' said Max. 'In fact, he came here looking for her around six months ago, but since by then she was in that pillbox and dead as a dodo, he had no luck finding her. According to him, she was not just a birdwatcher but an ornithologist of quite some repute, and at the time she was writing a book on the waterfowl species of the fenlands. He said if we ever found her phone, we'd see it was chock full of photos, as well as notes on the various birds she was studying.'

Gary sighed. 'Well, her jewellery was all there, but no phone. If we only had that, it might tell us where she was just before she died.'

'He gave me her mobile number, but as you'd expect, it just comes back with "unknown number".'

'And he was the only person worried about her?' said Jackman. 'That says something about her, doesn't it?'

Max shrugged. 'He's coming here to have a chat with me about her today, should be on his way right now, in fact. He said it was a bit of a long and complicated story, and better

332

told in person. He's retired, so he didn't mind driving up from London. He's really gutted, boss, but he's angry, too, because no one would listen to him. He said something like he always thought it would end this way.'

'Get all you can from him, Max, even what seems irrelevant. And, Kevin? Gary? What luck did you have at the Full Moon? Now we know she was an ornithologist, she might well have met the local birders.'

'Gabby wasn't there when we called, and neither were there any club members, so we're going back first thing this morning, boss,' said Gary.

'Make that a priority, okay? I get the feeling this lady could be the very person who leads us to her killer.'

After his fit of the heebie-jeebies the day before, Jackman now felt a growing sense of urgency about the need to solve this case. In the back of his mind was the thought that the closer they got to the killer, the more likely it was that he would strike again. He was certain that whoever it was had not moved on, but was right there in Fendyke Village. It could be a dangerous time for all of them.

'Robbie? Where are you at present?' Jackman asked.

'Marie asked me to get some background on Mad Sally, sir,' he said. 'Not an easy task, I'm afraid.'

'That's right,' confirmed Marie. 'But I'm convinced that whatever caused her to retreat into herself and refuse to speak is vital to the case. I swear she saw or heard something that is connected to the killings. I need a timeline of some sort, and a lot more knowledge about her than I already have. Fortunately, I've had some success in getting her to talk to me, but even then, she gave nothing away. I want to go back, but I need to have the right questions ready, or it will be a waste of time.'

'Fair enough,' said Jackman. 'So, Robbie, have you made any progress at all?'

'Not much, but I do know that she's lived in that house for fifteen years, and she bought it in cash — no mortgage or any other kind of loan. Her full name is Sarah Nugent, and her name is on the deeds, but I can find no birth certificate on record, neither can I find a marriage certificate, so we must assume she is unmarried.'

'She said she's a Fenlander. She detests incomers, along with anyone else who wants to bring change to the village and its way of life,' added Marie. 'She was quite vehement about that. What I'd like to know is where exactly she came from originally.'

'I thought the conveyancer might help,' said Robbie, 'but I couldn't get hold of them. The person who handled the sale wasn't with any of the local firms, and has since moved on. The house itself had been empty for a few years before she bought it. The original owner was this really old boy who was moved to a home up-county after he became ill with dementia, and eventually died there. I don't know, I keep chasing down all these leads and hitting brick walls.'

'I'm not sure if it's worth spending any more time on that particular avenue,' Jackman said, 'especially as she might turn out to know nothing at all. She could well be exactly as she appears — an eccentric. I'm sorry, Marie, I do understand where you're coming from. Perhaps you could try taking a less direct route, and get Robbie to go out to the village and try to pick up on the gossip about Mad Sally. These village rumours often have a seed of truth in them.'

'That's fine by me,' said Marie. 'Just be really diplomatic, Robbo. Don't let anyone know why you are asking about her — you know what the village grapevine is like. They could get the wrong end of the stick, and we find them on the village green building a bonfire so they can burn her at the stake!'

Robbie grinned. 'I'll be discretion itself, Sarge. I'll get onto it as soon as we get back from our "Interview with the Vampire" at HMP Marshlands. After prison, and Gareth Rock, I'll be glad to get outside into the fresh air.'

The meeting ended, and just as everyone was moving off, PC Simon Laker walked in.

'Sorry to interrupt, sir, but my sergeant asked me to pass on a piece of information I've just received from Bob Ruston, the retired copper who has been keeping an eye on young Craig — you know, Handcuff Boy?'

Jackman immediately brightened. 'Aha! Does this mean Bob has made some headway?'

'I think so, sir. It's a possible lead, for sure.' Simon proceeded to tell him of what Bob had discovered. 'As you know, people often asked Craig to sort out the odd IT problem for them, but he couldn't think of anything that might have led to his abduction. Well, yesterday his gran mentioned to Bob that he'd set up a computer system for a girl called Cindy, whose dad was apparently extremely rich. Bob went to see Craig last night, and asked him to tell him more about it. According to Craig, Cindy had always given the impression that she was a just an ordinary working girl, but when he got to her house it turned out to be massive. The computer system Cindy wanted his help with was in an annexe her father had had built for her. Craig spent several days there setting everything up and then helping her get to grips with the new system until her father suddenly decided he'd outstayed his welcome, and paid him over the odds to finish up and clear out. Craig assumed her dad thought he had the hots for her and didn't like his little princess hob knobbing with riff-raff, so he didn't think any more about it.' Simon looked at his notebook. 'The father's name is Sean Fairweather.'

'I know that name!' Jackman said. 'Greenborough have had him under surveillance for months, but they've never managed to catch him stepping out of line. Rumour has it he's into all sorts of illegal deals, but no one has been able to pin anything on him.'

'After Bob asked him about it, Craig started to think he might have seen or overheard something. He reckons there were a lot of comings and goings in the main house while he was there, which made him wonder what kind of business Cindy's father was in. Craig also said that from what he saw, the security in the main house was top notch. Cindy also said her dad had an extremely sophisticated computer system, and he didn't think it was for playing *Call of Duty*.'

His thoughts racing, Jackman said, 'Thank you, Simon. Can you give Tim, my office manager, all the details please, and then we'll get this straight down to IT in case it's connected to Chaos.'

Even if there was no connection, this was the first hint as to why Craig had been abducted. Although it was only a hint, the fact was that Sean Fairweather was a person of interest to the police. DI Jenny Deane would certainly be interested to hear of it when she got back from whatever emergency had dragged her away.

At that very moment, the CID room door opened. Speak of angels!

'Oh, I'm *so* sorry! I really left you in the lurch, didn't I! Anyway, I'm back now,' Jenny said, pulling off her jacket. 'I'll tell you all about it later. What's been going on in my absence? Where's Vic? Any updates on—'

'Whoa!' Jackman held up his hands. 'Just sit down and relax while Gary gets you a coffee, and I'll fill you in. And I'm very pleased to see you.'

Jenny did as she was told. 'It sounds awful of me to say it, but I'm so glad to be back. I've had a seriously shitty few days.'

'I know just what you mean,' Jackman said.

Jenny lowered her voice. 'Dad disappeared from the home again. As you know, it's way down on the South Coast, so I'm in a bit of a cleft stick. I either bring him to live closer to me and confuse him even more, or leave him where he is in familiar surroundings, where I run the risk of him staging another Great Escape, and having a four-hour drive to get there and help find him.'

Jackman's heart went out to her. There was no easy compromise between dementia and a demanding job, and having almost two hundred miles between her and her father made it all that much worse.

'Anyway,' she said, 'never mind all that, what's the state of play with Chaos? And our art thief? And with your Pillbox Killer?'

Jackman brought her up to date, leaving her with Tim's printout of everything Bob had extracted from Craig Sharpe.

'Hmm, tasty,' said Jenny, looking more like her normal self with every line that she read. 'Well, well, well. Sean Fairweather! What have you been up to, I wonder?' Her face then darkened. 'I really do need to get straight onto that because — and I could be wrong there — but there was a rumour doing the rounds that Fairweather could be connected to the Westerham brothers.'

'Really? That would certainly answer a lot of the questions about young Craig's abduction. Keep me in the loop on that, won't you?' said Jackman.

'Oh I will, never fear. As soon as I've caught up with Vic Blackwell, I'll be paying a call on Craig Sharpe. I'm very interested in that place where his friend Cindy Fairweather lives, and the "comings and goings" he spoke about. Very interested indeed.'

Jenny went out, leaving Jackman feeling considerably relieved. With the exception of Charlie Button, they were back to a full complement, which meant that after their prison visit, they could pitch back into taking the village of Fendyke apart, until they found something that Jenny would call 'tasty'.

* * *

Although he had never admitted it to any of his workmates, Robbie Melton had a phobia about prisons. He was more than happy to chase down villains and have them consigned to one, but where he was concerned, they filled him with dread. Whenever he was obliged to enter one, heard those metal doors clang shut and lock behind him with a click, he went cold all over. It was no different this morning, although having the boss beside him helped to a certain extent. The trouble was that he feared having to talk to Gareth Rock even more than the doors slamming at his back.

Rock was a tall imposing figure, and with his rugged good looks could easily have passed for a celebrity sports star. The man certainly had presence.

Introductions over, they quicky got down to business, and as the negotiations proceeded, Robbie was surprised to find himself feeling very much in control. He reiterated that there was no question of any deal being made, but that Mr Corbin's compliance would most certainly be taken into consideration.

'Then my client wishes to confess to arranging the robbery at Hartwood House, and would like the fact that this is his first offence to be taken into account.' Rock's smile could have frozen hell. 'Until this one misstep, Mr Corbin has been a model citizen. He is a well-respected buyer and seller of mainly Art Nouveau antiquaries, and has always paid the relevant taxes in full, as your own investigations into his finances have undoubtedly shown. Unfortunately, when he heard of the extent of the Greenes' collection, he succumbed to temptation, which he now bitterly regrets.'

Every single question that either Robbie or Jackman posed met with a smooth, well-rehearsed response or expression of contrition. When asked about his fellow thieves, especially the woman Lucas had called Nina, he told them she only ever went by that name, which was in all probability an alias. He said that if Mr Corbin had known the real names of any of his associates, he would have said so, but all of them used nicknames to hide their identities. He had already given the police the address of his rented cottage on the fen, but admitted that he had told Nina to dispose of any of the contents that might incriminate him. At the time of his unfortunate entrapment, Mr Corbin had assumed that Chaos had accidentally set the alarm system to the wrong time, and would let him out as soon as he became aware of his mistake. His client also admitted to asking Nina to take care of their stolen goods, and use an emergency procedure set up beforehand. The stolen items were to be taken to a warehouse rented prior to the robbery, whose address he would give to the police, although it would almost certainly be empty by the time they got there.

At this point, Lucas spoke up on his own behalf. 'I've never done anything like this before, but I'm meticulous in everything I do. It took over a year to plan, and although I knew I was taking a terrible risk, I truly believed we'd pull it off without a hitch.'

And you would have, too, if it hadn't been for Chaos, Robbie thought. 'But you were double crossed, weren't you?' he said. 'So whatever help you can give us to find the person who did that to you would go a long way to having him locked up, and for a considerably longer period than you.'

Glancing briefly at his solicitor, Lucas said, 'As you already know, he goes by the name of Chaos. He's something of a legend in the underworld, or so I was informed, and it took me over six months to finally make contact with him. The thing is, I needed him, because when I finally got to see the place where those vile brothers kept their precious collection, I knew there was no way I could bypass or disable their security system. I simply didn't have the knowledge. So I did some research, which eventually led me to the dark web, and that's where I found Chaos.'

Robbie pricked his ears up. The dark web. If this guy had found Chaos that way, then Orac easily could.

Lucas requested a short break so he could consult with his solicitor. Upon resuming the interview, Rock said, 'My client would like to state that the information he is about to divulge may result in the identification and arrest of the person known as Chaos. Should this be the case, he would like to be assured that his assistance be recorded and brought to the attention of both judge and jury at his trial.'

Here Robbie deferred to Jackman.

'*If* this information leads to an arrest, I can assure your client that his assistance will be made known to the court, including the source,' Jackman said.

'He advertises,' Lucas said.

Both Robbie and Jackman frowned.

'And before you tell me that he uses a different means of contact with every transaction, of course he does,' Lucas said. 'But the wording of these adverts always follows the same lines, they have a common thread. It took me a while to work it out, and once I did, I was still anxious about making contact.'

'But you did?' questioned Robbie.

Lucas shrugged. 'Well, obviously. Once you've made contact, explained what you want and paid up front for his services, he contacts you. He provides you with a couple of devices that you use to gain access to your target location. Via these small devices, he is able to scan the security system and override it. You are given a set timeframe within which the security system is inoperative before he reactivates it.' Lucas smiled bitterly. 'Or that's what's supposed to happen, anyway.'

'So where are these devices?' asked Robbie. 'You didn't have them on you when you were arrested.'

'Oh, so you never found them then?' Lucas looked surprised, then mildly amused. 'Well, the laptop used to initiate the procedure was in the back of my car. I can only think that Nina must have removed it and taken it with her.'

'And the other device?'

'It was a small hand-held device with a tiny display window on the front. You use it to get through the locked door, and the display on the screen lets you know exactly how long you've got before the alarms are due to be reactivated. When I realised I would be arrested, I left it in plain sight, next to the remotes for the TV and Sky box in the lounge at Hartwood House.'

Robbie glanced at Jackman. If Lucas was telling the truth, the forensic sweep had missed it.

No one spoke for a while, until Lucas said, 'Here's the thing, officers, what I'm about to tell you has to be already known to anyone wanting to use Chaos's services. It's no good thinking that one of your clever computer engineers can work it out for you, it would take them years.'

'Go on,' Jackman said. Lucas remained silent. 'Look. I've already told you that we will inform the relevant authorities of the extent of your cooperation, and that if what you say results in a conviction, we will do all we can to have your sentence reduced, if not dropped.'

Lucas glanced at Gareth Rock, who nodded. 'As I am sure you are aware, the dark web is used for selling things that cannot be got legally — from drugs, or guns, to stolen data. It also serves as a marketplace for hot goods, which is where he hides. What he advertises isn't important, it's just a cover. What you have to look out for is the name of the contact.'

Robbie braced himself. This was it.

'It's always a different one,' said Lucas slowly, 'but it's always a moon. Chaos took his name from a dwarf planet in the Kuiper belt beyond the orbit of Neptune. The last time he posted, he signed off as Ganymede, one of the moons of Jupiter. Find an ad selling bogus stolen goods that uses a moon's name for the contact, and you'll find him.'

'I think my client has said enough for now, Officers,' Rock said. 'He is prepared to provide you with the details of how he originally came upon the method of contacting your nemesis, as well as how the money changed hands, but that's for a later date. My client needs a break, and we'll see you again soon. Thank you, gentlemen.'

'Just two very quick questions, Mr Corbin, if you don't mind,' Jackman said. 'What made you risk what you tell us was an honest and respected business and decide to perpetrate this theft?'

Corbin spread his hands. 'Simple. A love of beautiful things that I couldn't afford.'

'And you mentioned a technician — a *legitimate* friend, you said — who helped you access the dark web. Can you tell us his name? You won't be putting him in trouble.'

Lucas glanced at Rock, who said, 'In the interest of transparency, I can see no problem with my client answering that question if it serves to verify the truth of his statements.'

'His name is Johnny Millard.'

CHAPTER THIRTY

By midday, it had become patently obvious to both Bryson Smith and Vic Blackwell that they were no longer welcome at Hartwood House. In the face of an increasingly hostile atmosphere, they had worked hard, and arrived at a total of fifty-four stolen items, ranging from huge heavy-framed paintings to tiny items of jewellery, but the theft that most distressed the two brothers was that of the stained-glass window.

'Where do you think it is now?' whispered Vic, when they were alone for a few minutes.

'Hidden somewhere safe, and it'll probably stay there until the hue and cry dies down. It'll then be shipped out at the dead of night, never to be seen again. It will grace the private home of some big collector who isn't too fussy about where his precious acquisitions come from, or how they were obtained,' said Bryson.

'Jackman thinks the thieves probably had a shopping list, and were working on behalf of a client, a sort of steal-to-order job,' Vic said.

'I think he's right, but when the man in charge got caught, you can bet your bottom dollar the rest of the gang would have decided to dispose of it all themselves and pocket the takings,' Bryson said, keeping his eye on the door in case the Greene brothers returned. 'One thing is for sure, those items won't ever be found. Until that final calamity, it was a very professional heist. I worked with an insurance company for a while, who brought me in following a series of art thefts in the city. It was quite an eye opener. I had no idea until then that there is such a massive market for art treasures, especially abroad.'

'You never know, one or two items might turn up after a while,' said Vic. 'We'll be circulating descriptions of all the items among the major auction houses and other outlets. Sometimes people get twitchy about handling something that's as hot as this lot, and they try to move it on sharpish. We had a stolen diamond ring turn up in a pawnbroker's in Greenborough once — worth a small fortune, it was, and the guy who pawned it accepted peanuts for it, he didn't even haggle. Luckily, the manager of the place had CCTV, and rang us immediately. We got the ring back to the owner, and caught the fence!'

Before Bryson could answer, the door opened and Norman Greene came in.

'My brother and I have finished compiling the inventory, and we are certain that there are no more missing items. You have all the relevant paperwork, I believe, so your work here is complete.' He shifted uncomfortably from one foot to the other. 'This has all been a terrible strain on us both, and as you probably realise, we are very private people, and so . . .'

Beside him Vic had bristled at the words 'leave us in peace'. It was as if they were a couple of intruders! Curtly, he reminded Greene that they were merely being thorough. 'If we miss something now, sir, then we'll only have to come back, won't we, and I'm sure you wouldn't want that.'

Bryson watched Greene's face, across which a number of emotions seemed to pass. They were hiding something, but what the hell was it? Greene turned on his heel and left.

'Are we done?' asked Vic.

343

'Pretty well, just a few loose ends to tie up,' said Bryson. He looked thoughtfully at Vic. 'Would you have any objection to asking the Brothers Grimm if we could do a final walk-through before we go?'

'If you like, but why?' Vic said.

'I don't know, Vic, but something is bugging me. Those two are growing more twitchy by the hour, and they want us out badly. Something is really wrong, and I'm damn sure we won't find it in the paperwork. I just want another look around in case I missed something obvious.' He shrugged. 'Though I don't even know what I'll be looking for.'

'Right, then,' Vic said. 'I'll go and tell them I need to check the whole place as a crime scene one last time before we sign Hartwood House off — and leave them in peace!'

He returned five minutes later, with a face like granite. 'I swear I'll deck one, or both of them before long. Condescending arseholes!'

Bryson laughed. 'Couldn't happen to a more deserving pair. So, do we get our walk round?'

'Yes, but only as long as one of them accompanies us. I told him we are investigating a crime, not committing one!'

Twenty minutes later, they were back in the car and ready to leave.

'Well, I didn't see any cause for concern,' said Vic, 'but what do I know? I've never seen a place like that in my life before, it's like a film set, only more over the top.'

Bryson didn't answer immediately. Nothing had leaped out at him either. Even so, he still couldn't shake the feeling that there was something not quite right in that house, something so small it had barely registered. 'I guess it was a waste of time. Sorry.'

'Oh, it wasn't wasted,' said Vic with an evil grin. 'It was worth it just to inconvenience that pair of ungrateful sods.'

Bryson spent the drive back to the station worrying about what he'd missed. It had to be related to the collection somehow — after all, that was his field. Maybe he had seen some item that had once been reported as stolen. It wasn't beyond the bounds of possibility that the brothers, obsessives as they were, had acquired some of their treasured possessions under the table, as it were.

Vic gave him a quick glance as he swung round a bend in the narrow lane. 'They've really got to you, haven't they?'

'Yes, I'm afraid they have.'

'If it helps, I feel that way, too,' Vic said, accelerating forward. 'I know nothing about this art business, but I do recognise a crime when I see it, and those two brothers have sent up warning signals. And I never ignore those. I'm going to have a closer look at our two Mr Greenes, and what their story is.'

'And I bet you find something shady,' said Bryson. 'Can I help at all? Once I've gone through this lot,' he glanced down at the thick folder in his lap, 'I'll have nothing to do but garden for my mum and dad, so I'd be glad to lend a hand.'

'You certainly can,' said Vic. 'As soon as I get to the "arty-farty" — forgive the expression — part of their history, I'll be glad of a bit of help.'

'Well, there you are then. "Arty-farty" happens to be my speciality, so I reckon I'm your man.'

* * *

Marie hurried down the back stairs to the staff car park, unlocked her car and flopped into the driver's seat. Suddenly, and totally out of character, the noise and hubbub in the busy office had got to her, and she needed to go somewhere quiet.

What had sent her in search of peace was what Robbie had told her about their art thief being an associate of Johnny Millard's. Corbin — who, she reminded herself, was probably a consummate liar — had said that he and Johnny had become acquainted when they both attended a function in London. Johnny — a thoroughly likable young man — had offered to help Corbin out if ever he needed any advice on

IT, and they had subsequently kept in touch, albeit infrequently. Corbin had told Jackman and Robbie that he had been deeply shocked on learning that Johnny was in prison, and was convinced that he had been framed for a crime he didn't commit. Corbin told them he had rung Johnny to ask for his help in gaining access to the dark web. Anna had answered, and henceforth had acted as a go-between, since he and Johnny never spoke on the phone, fearing the prison authorities might be listening in.

Marie closed her eyes and considered this story. There might be a grain of truth in it, but to her mind, Lucas had left an awful lot out, and the sequence of events was probably very wrong. She did not believe for a second that Hartwood House had been Lucas Corbin's debut into the world of art theft. Their records showed that there had been far too many similar unsolved jobs over the years, and Marie was certain that the man behind them had been Lucas Corbin.

Marie massaged her temples, telling herself to concentrate. If she was to assume that Lucas had indeed been the mastermind behind all these unsolved heists, he could not have carried then out without Chaos's help. Which meant he had first made contact with Johnny Millard years ago, not recently, as he tried to make out.

She opened her eyes. Okay, what about this for a scenario? What if Lucas rings Johnny's number. Anna tells him her husband is incarcerated. Lucas tells Anna his problem, and Anna asks Johnny if he will help Lucas get onto the dark web. Johnny agrees, but wants to know what Lucas is looking for.

Marie blinked a few times, trying to crystalise the vague idea that was fast becoming a possibility. 'So,' she muttered to herself, 'Lucas tells Johnny that he's heard about a tech wizard with the ability to manipulate security systems, and he wants to make contact with him via the dark web. Johnny, bitter and vengeful at having been made the patsy for a cybercrime he didn't commit, wonders just who this mysterious super-hacker might be. Was this the person who was behind his wrongful incarceration? It was possible, if he was as clever as Lucas said.'

Marie frowned. Had Johnny somehow managed to track down Chaos himself? Or failing that, was that why he had worked so hard to obtain an early release, so he could go after Chaos? And then what?

Marie opened the car door and climbed out. It was only a theory, but Jackman should hear it.

By the time Marie was back inside the station, she was certain that Johnny Millard was not only alive, but hiding somewhere, hell-bent on seeking out his nemesis — and ten to one, Anna was now with him. Marie still believed Anna when she said she'd been afraid for her husband's life. But Anna had misjudged the depth of Johnny's hatred for the man who had stolen a piece of his life. Anna had been convinced that Johnny would contact her if he were able to — after all, he loved her and wouldn't want her to have to undergo months and months of anguish. She, and everyone else who knew him, were certain he'd stick to the terms of his licence, to do otherwise would be foolhardy in the extreme. But that was the old Johnny, and that man no longer existed.

To her relief, Jackman's door was open, and he was alone at his desk. She was talking before she was even properly inside. 'Boss, I need to run something past you, and if you think I'm on the right track, we need to tell Orac, fast. Oh, and it also means I won't be angsting about Anna Millard anymore, and can commit one hundred per cent to the Pillbox Killer.'

Jackman closed the file he'd been working on. 'Suppose you sit down and start from the beginning . . .'

* * *

Orac's department had never before operated at such a pace and with so much concentration. Every member of her team had dedicated all their time to the task of finding Chaos. They scanned internet traffic for unusual activity or attempted security breaches. They found nothing. There were no further reports of crimes having been foiled. Indeed, there weren't many crimes at all, which came as a relief to some, but Orac was suspicious. Had Chaos tired of playing games with small-time crooks and was on the lookout for something more challenging?

The only other person who seemed to share her misgivings was Coral McIvor. She started work earlier each day, and was often at her desk by six. She would have stayed late, too, she said, but her father's health was failing. He hadn't said as much, but Coral suspected he'd had bad news regarding his latest test results, and he was obviously far from well.

As usual before she left work for the day, Coral stopped by Orac's desk to report on her day's work.

'He's planning something, isn't he?' said Coral.

'I think so,' said Orac. 'And the longer he stays quiet, the more anxious I get.'

Coral was about to reply when two familiar figures walked into the room.

'Marie! And DI Jackman, too. This *is* a pleasure!' She grinned at Marie. 'How many proper coffees and Danish pastries did it take to persuade your revered boss to put in an appearance?'

'On this occasion, not even one. This visit was all his idea.' The smile left Marie's face. 'And if we are correct in what we're about to tell you, it will mean a lot more work for you guys, I'm afraid.'

'I'll fetch a couple more chairs,' said Coral. 'Is it okay if I join you?'

'Of course,' Orac said.

When they were seated, Jackman told Orac and Coral about their art thief and his connection to Johnny Millard, whom they suspected to be somewhere in the vicinity, also on the hunt for Chaos.

'So we could well have two dangerous and invisible people to find,' Orac said.

'One with murder on his mind, and the other planning God knows what kind of techno havoc,' muttered Coral. 'Just peachy!'

'Well, this might help lift your mood,' said Marie. 'Our art thief has given us what might be some very helpful information.'

She glanced at Jackman, who went on to describe the way potential clients got in contact with Chaos, in a part of the dark web where people traded in stolen goods.

'According to Corbin, he regularly changes his contact name, but it is always that of a moon. Corbin said the last one he used was Ganymede, and the one before that Dione.'

'Is that so?' said Orac. 'Then I need to update my knowledge of astronomy. I've had operatives wandering in and out of the dark web ever since this whole thing erupted, and finding nothing, but that little nugget could be our key to tracing him. Who'd have guessed it was that simple? However, finding the ad is only the first step, we'll need to know how to proceed after that, or he'll smell a rat. Has your little grass told you any more about what happens next?'

Jackman smiled. 'He has. He's desperate to get a suspended sentence, or at least, to get it reduced, and he's talking pretty freely. Surprisingly, it's all done by phone. You ring the number on the ad and say you need his help. He rings you back, and asks a number of questions about what you need. He gives you a price for the job, which is non-negotiable. If you agree, he gives you the details of how to make the transaction. That done, he sends you one, or sometimes two, electronic devices, depending on the kind of crime. These you use, in conjunction with him, to control the CCTV cameras, alarms, or security doors.'

'And the good news is that we have secured one of these gizmos,' added Marie. 'Uniform are picking it up now, and they'll be bringing it directly to you.'

Coral beamed delightedly at Orac. 'Looking good!'

'Looking very interesting indeed,' Orac said. All of them were silent for a moment or two as they considered the possibilities of what they'd been told.

'Incidentally, have you had any more reports of Chaos turning over any more unlucky villains?' asked Marie.

Orac shook her head. 'We were just discussing that when you arrived. Our Chaos has gone ominously quiet, which doesn't bode well. However, our security has been ramped up to the max, and we have eyes everywhere. One wrong move, and we'll be down on him like the proverbial ton of bricks.'

'And did you manage to salvage anything from Johnny's computer?' Jackman asked.

'We're almost at the point of saying that we've extracted anything that was retrievable. It mostly consists of names, contacts and addresses, but don't get your hopes up. My staff have looked into every single one, and none seem to have any connection to major cybercrime. If you have a quiet day sometime, you could use them to tidy up a few petty crimes, and even feel a few collars for fraud or theft, but nothing more than that. There's no trace, either, of the person who fried his hard drive.'

'There's not even a recognisable pattern or signature way of working to point us to a certain kind of operative,' added Coral, 'but we are still working on it. From what we've seen, Johnny Millard was a very smart guy, so it must have taken a real genius to break through his firewall and mess with his data.'

'I think we'd already worked that out,' said Jackman grimly. 'A genius who is playing with us, and most likely enjoying every minute of it. A genius who goes by the name of Chaos.'

'I can't disagree with that,' Orac said. 'But he can't keep this up for ever. We have the whole country watching for his every move. Even if this new information you've given us fails to bring him to light, he's bound to cock up at some point, and then, by all that's sacred, I'll have him!'

'We can't ask more than that then, can we?' said Marie. 'But damn it, I hate these faceless people who operate from the shadows.'

'And I especially hate it when they try to manipulate *us*,' added Orac. 'But at least we now have a talkative art thief to guide us, so who knows what magic we can work? Huh, Coral? What say you?'

Coral's dark eyes flashed. 'Oh, just hand me my wand and call me Tinkerbell!'

* * *

Max stuck his head out of the interview room door in the hopes of spotting someone who might be free to fetch his guest a cup of coffee. Seeing no one who didn't look rushed off their feet, he went himself.

As he fed money into the vending machine, he thought about the man he'd just been speaking to. He liked Andrew Shearing, and felt terribly sorry for him. It was perfectly obvious that he had been in love with Marion Sandon-Hayes, and although he had suspected that something had happened to her, to find that she had been murdered had come as a terrible blow. He had tentatively asked if he might formally identify her, and when Max had gently explained that the body was too decomposed for a visual identification to be made, Andrew Shearing had broken down and wept. 'Oh, how she would have hated that,' he had said softly, wiping his eyes with a tissue. 'She was one of those women who always look immaculate, whatever the occasion. Her looks were important to her, and to end her days like . . .' He swallowed. Max had expressed his sorrow for his loss, and had tried to steer the conversation to Marion's life, but Andrew was struggling. At that point Max had gone in search of coffee, so as to give Andrew a few moments alone to compose himself.

On his return, Max found that Andrew had pulled himself together enough to be more helpful. Fortunately, he had a very good memory for detail.

'I've been wondering how come no one ever wondered why there had been no activity on Mrs Sandon-Hayes's credit or debit cards, sir,' said Max. 'Surely that would have indicated that something was wrong?'

'Because no one ever checked,' said Andrew bitterly. 'When I expressed my concerns, no one was interested in following them up. Though it is true Marion didn't make things easy. She kept her private finances separate from all her business accounts, and the accountants who dealt with the income from the rent from her property in Chelsea had no access to what she referred to as her little "piggy bank". She told me she dealt with that herself, and believe me, it was a considerable sum. I have a feeling she employed a different accountant to help with her tax returns and that kind of thing, but she never mentioned their name or what firm they belonged to.'

'We'll be able to check that when we get access to her home,' Max said. 'And at least that answers my question. Now, you said you came here looking for her, didn't you? Did you ever go to a village called Fendyke?'

Andrew shook his head. 'No, I only made enquiries in Saltern-le-Fen and the surrounding towns — Greenborough, Fenchester and Fenfleet. There are so many little villages and hamlets around that I hadn't a clue where to start, other than that I knew she was studying the local waterfowl. I spoke to people from the RSPB, but no one remembered seeing her. Then I checked all the better hotels, as she liked her comforts, but again, no luck.' He sighed. 'It was like looking for a needle in a haystack, Max. I'm obviously not cut out to be a detective, and I failed miserably.'

'At least you tried, sir, and you clearly cared, whereas it seems few other people she knew did.'

Andrew gave a hollow laugh. 'Oh, I cared all right. It was hard enough living *with* her, but I had no idea how hard it would be without her. And now I know that I'll never see her again—'

Max waited. It was clear that Andrew wanted to say more, but wasn't sure how much he should give away.

'Basically, I grew up with Marion. Our families were close, and as children we often spent the holidays or weekends together. She was younger than me, but she was definitely the leader. And, oh my, what a headstrong girl! What Marion said went! Or woe betide you. I was convinced she would never marry, she was just too strong-willed, which was partly why I never found the courage to ask her. And then she married my best friend.'

For an instant Andrew's face twisted in pain, and then he resumed. 'I loved them both, so I never let on that I was anything but happy for them. I remained close to both of them, and when Philip died, I became Marion's trusted confidante and dearest friend, but never anything more than that.' His gaze rested on the table in front of him. 'She began to travel, and immersed herself in ornithology. I remember her taking off on the path of some migrating birds, and when she finally returned she'd been studying their breeding grounds in the high Arctic! Not a word, not a message for months, then one day there she was on my doorstep, demanding tea and biscuits and rambling on about purple sandpipers!'

Max was starting to understand why people hadn't been too concerned about her failure to communicate. If she didn't even contact her best friend, she certainly wouldn't be ringing her business associates or accountants for a chat.

Max asked Andrew if he knew who her solicitor was, and whether she'd left a will.

At this, Andrew became more businesslike. 'Oh yes, I have his name. In fact, I brought it with me. Marion was meticulous regarding her affairs, so there is a will. Naturally, there is a copy with the solicitor, and I hold her personal copy. She gave it to me for safe keeping when she began to travel. She trusted no one but me, and was concerned that her apartment would remain empty for long periods of time. She also entrusted me with an attaché case full of documents, and now I know what has happened to her, I will be handing them over to her solicitor.'

353

'Would you mind very much if we took a look at those before they are deposited with her solicitor? As this is a murder enquiry, we really need to see everything that relates to Marion.'

For a moment Andrew looked doubtful, then he nodded. 'Of course, as long as the solicitor gets them as soon as possible.'

'Naturally. A member of CID, possibly me, will be speaking to them anyway. If we need one we can always get a warrant to access her business and personal papers, which I suspect will be the case where her business associates and her accountants are concerned. I spoke to them this morning, and they were less than amenable.'

'Load of leeches and spongers, that lot. They've spent years feathering their own nests at Marion's expense,' muttered Andrew. 'They were downright obstructive when I began making waves about her disappearance. I'd give a lot to be a fly on the wall when they realise that their goose will no longer be providing golden eggs for them.'

Half an hour later, Max escorted Andrew to the door, saying he would arrange for the document case to be collected and brought in. Now armed with far more information about Marion Sandon-Hayes than he had ever hoped for, he returned to his desk. Her home would have to be searched and those documents gone through with a fine-tooth comb, but the bottom line was that they had a confirmed ID.

Max smiled. Not bad. In fact it was bloody good going. Four victims out of five now had identities, just one left. Then his smile faded. All well and good, but there was a sixth person still unaccounted for — the shadowy figure binding them all together. The killer.

* * *

Robbie stared at the door of the CID room, willing Marie to walk in. He should be out there talking to the people of

354

Fendyke as Jackman had asked, but there were still one or two promising avenues of enquiry that he hadn't yet explored. Half an hour and several blind alleys later, he was ready to give up. He would never get anywhere in his search for Mad Sally.

Yet he couldn't let it go. He fully expected that at any moment, that heart-stopping 'Access Denied' warning would explode across his screen. It had happened before, and that time the person he'd been searching for was on a witness protection programme. Unless he'd forgotten everything he'd ever been taught, Mad Sally, or Sarah Nugent, simply didn't exist. He would have liked to ask one of the others what they thought, but they were all out — Kev and Gary at the Full Moon pub, and Max elsewhere in the building, and with no Charlie Button around, he was flying solo.

Robbie shut his computer down and irritably snatched his jacket off the back of his chair. He couldn't sit here staring into space all morning, so he might as well sod off to Fendyke and do as he'd been told, hunt down the village gossips.

As he drove to the village, he continued to mull over why this woman should apparently have no history. He knew that some of the very old fenland families going back to pre-war days, had never troubled to register births or deaths, simply because they lacked the means of getting into town. There were no cars, and some were too poor to even own a bicycle. Some deliberately avoided registering a marriage, aware that they and their spouse were a little too closely related. Some people didn't even know they were supposed to obtain a certificate. But that was then. Now even land workers had cars, and everyone owned a mobile phone, and the public transport system, albeit sporadic, connected most parts of the county. No, there was something else behind Mad Sally's apparent non-existence, and Robbie's thoughts kept returning to the idea of witness protection. Maybe Nugent simply wasn't her name, and she kept her real one hidden. But why should she do that? Was she hiding from an abusive partner?

By the time he pulled into the church car park where he'd agreed to meet Gary and Kevin, he no longer knew what to think.

'Oh, she's got a past all right,' said Gary grimly, when asked. 'If I were you, I'd keep it simple. And you can forget witness protection. If you do come across it, the people involved are high-profile criminals. Someone the likes of Mad Sally is hardly likely to be implicated in a major case of that sort.'

Kevin agreed. 'What did the sarge say about Sally after she had that chat with her?'

'Well, Marie thought she must have come from what she called "good stock", as she was quite well-mannered. She's lived alone in that house for fifteen years, with almost no mod cons,' Robbie said. 'She's obviously no local-yokel, though she insists she's Lincolnshire born and bred.'

'Imagine living for all that time with no neighbours and no friends,' said Gary. 'What must it be like to have absolutely no one in your life?'

'She does have one friend, though,' said Kevin.

Robbie and Gary stared at him.

'The fox.'

Robbie rolled his eyes. 'Yeah, right, Kev! A bloody fox isn't going to give me much of an insight into that woman's past, is it?'

When they stopped laughing, Kev said, 'We can glean one thing from what you've said, though, Rob. If she's been the same way all the time she's been living here, and your supposition that something traumatic happened to her is correct, then it must have occurred over fifteen years ago, and not in this village. It might just be worth checking the county newspapers for some incident that took place before then.'

Rob smiled at him gratefully. 'I might just do that, our Kevin. Nice one!'

CHAPTER THIRTY-ONE

As soon as she got home, Coral McIvor put the kettle on for tea. Because they were so busy at work, she had stocked up on ready meals, and had prepared a few simple home-cooked ones for her father. Every morning before she left for work, she would take two out of the freezer to defrost, ready to take them over to her father as soon as she got home. When she moved to the village, they had agreed that they would eat together every evening, and had continued to do so without fail. Now that he was more or less housebound, routine had become important to William, and any deviation from the norm made him anxious. He insisted that their daily meals should be 'just right', the table perfectly laid with his best chinaware and the cutlery precisely aligned. He polished the wine glasses until they shone, and fretted about the exact time their bottle of red wine should be opened so that it might breathe. It didn't seem to matter that the dinner might consist of nothing more exciting than a Sainsbury's lasagne, it still had to be done just so.

Coral took her tea into the lounge and sank into her armchair. This was *her* time. Fifteen glorious minutes of peace and quiet — no computer, no television, her phone on mute. Her lounge was her refuge, uncluttered and tastefully furnished. Two comfortable chairs, a large coffee table, a fireplace, two bookcases, a number of flourishing house plants, a bowl of crystals and two contrasting paintings on opposite walls. Both abstracts, one was all exuberant colour, dramatic and powerful, while the other had been made in delicate pastel shades reminiscent of fen mist.

She often used these two paintings as an aid to meditation, and now, needing to clear her mind, she rested her gaze on the paler one. She was extremely anxious about Chaos, and was concerned that her father might pick up on it. Early in her career she had made the decision never to burden her dad with issues he could do nothing about. Work was work, and family was family, however much she would have liked to confide in him.

They had always been close, even when her mother was alive. Her poor mother had often been bewildered by some private joke the two of them shared. It made his latest action all the more painful for Coral, as if he had been trying to elude her. She had always driven him to the hospital for his appointments, but this time he had booked a taxi and gone alone. She hadn't even known that he had an appointment. Not even when she still lived in London had he done such a thing. So, why now, all of a sudden? The only answer she could come up with was that he had expected bad news and didn't want her to know about it. When she asked him, he had said that it wouldn't look good for her to take time off when she'd just started a new job. But from that point on, there was something different about him, and it wasn't just that the wine glasses didn't sparkle so brightly. There was something he wasn't telling her, and it had to do with that solo visit to Greenborough General. It seemed that a reluctance to burden your dearest relative with your issues cut both ways.

Coral sat, quietly sipping her tea, wondering if she dared broach the subject again. He'd been almost curt the first time she'd asked, and after that, he simply became upset. It hadn't helped that he'd recently lost an old friend to cancer. Maybe that was why he was finding it so hard to give her his own bad news. All she could hope for was that he'd tell her when he was ready.

What a curse old age was! Her dad had been a truly remarkable person. Well, he still was. He always would be, no matter what.

She finished her tea and went back to the kitchen to gather up their evening meal, such as it was. It was certainly unworthy of the carefully laid dining table. She sighed. Tomorrow, Chaos allowing, she would cook him something special.

As she packed the food into a bag, she realised that for once, her fifteen minutes had been no help, and she was still worrying about Chaos. Worse still, a new hypothesis had entered her mind. What if Chaos didn't have a guardian? What if this other person who had appeared on the periphery of Chaos's affairs wasn't protecting him, but doing the exact opposite? What if it was Johnny Millard?

* * *

By four o'clock, Bryson Smith had done all he could for the day. Hopefully, a few hours on the phone the following morning would see all the missing items from Hartwood House listed and certified as genuine purchases made by the Greene brothers. Their record-keeping had certainly been impeccable, but this alone worried him. He would swear it was a cover, but for what? He'd spoken to as many of his contacts as he could get hold of, and although they were unanimous in their dislike of the brothers, all their transactions had been without fault.

Bryson had been given a spare desk in the CID room to lay the photographs out on, so they could be tallied against the items that had been reported as stolen. From here, he could see across the whole room, from the end occupied by DI Jenny Deane and Vic Blackwell's team to where Jackman's detectives

359

were working. As the working day drew to a close, he began to see faces he recognised. He guessed there would be reports to complete and their individual findings pooled. He'd been in police stations before, called in as a consultant or an advisor, but never while a high-profile murder case was in progress, and he was glad not to have to work in such an environment. His work was conducted mostly in silence, often alone, especially if he was dealing with one of his own canvases and not that of some long dead artist. It was a world of creativity and beauty, whereas this one was ugly and harsh. Well, someone had to maintain order, and without them, the world would be a grim and terrifying place.

Bryson slipped his completed work into the clear plastic sleeves that Vic had given him and stacked them into neat piles, keen to get away before the mayhem of the shift change. Although he would hate to have to work here, he had rather liked seeing an investigation unfold, and was secretly rather pleased at having been part of it.

'All finished?'

It was Vic Blackwell, looking over his shoulder. 'For today. Just a few minor things and a couple of calls to make tomorrow morning, and then it's all yours.'

'Lucky old me,' grunted Vic. 'I'm still wondering what the f—, sorry, what the devil those two jokers are up to, though.'

'Trouble is, if they aren't actually dealing in stolen goods, and nothing I've found indicates that they are, what are they trying to cover up?' Bryson said.

'What indeed?' Vic said. 'It's the million-dollar question, ain't it? Anyway, I'll let you get away. And thanks for all your help. I might still give you a call if I come across anything fishy about those brothers, so if your phone rings in the dead of night, it'll be me burning the midnight oil.'

'Please do,' Bryson said, 'even if it is in the dead of night. And if I ever remember what it was that was bothering me at Hartwood House, I'll be sure to return the favour.'

'Any time, mate. It keeps bugging me, and I must say it would give me a great deal of satisfaction to find something to pin on that creepy pair. Come on, I'll walk you out of the building.'

As they passed Jackman's end of the room, Bryson heard someone call his name. He looked up to see DI Jackman himself approaching them, waving a handful of papers.

'I know they will soon be plastered all over your village, Bryson, but would you take these home with you?' Jackman handed him copies of five photographs. 'These are likenesses of the pillbox victims. You'll see there are names on four of them, one is still unidentified. We are desperately trying to place them in the village at some point. We're looking to see if they have anything, or any person, in common.'

Bryson looked at the portraits and swallowed. He was looking at what that horrible tangle of bones in the pillbox represented. For the first time it was brought home to him that they had been real people, with real lives. For a moment he was speechless.

'I felt the same when I saw them,' said Jackman softly. 'It brings it all home, doesn't it? And it makes it all the more urgent to find who committed that heinous crime.'

It took Bryson a moment to get a grip on his emotions. He folded the printouts in half and pushed them into his pocket. 'I'll show them to Mum and Dad when I get home.'

Jackman thanked him for his support and said they were grateful for his expertise. 'Look, I know this might sound melodramatic, but be careful, won't you? Keep your eyes and ears open. We all believe the killer is still around, and the discovery of the bodies may have made them very unstable indeed. You and your family are at the heart of it, whether you like it or not. I saw your father down by the pillbox earlier today. He was alone, and it's been worrying me ever since. Please, tell your parents to stay well away from that end of the garden.'

'You mean because the killer always returns to the scene of the crime?' Bryson said. It was a chilling thought.

'They weren't killed there, but that's where he left them, so that place must mean something to the murderer. Just make sure no one goes down there. Oh, and you can tell your parents that as soon as we give him the go ahead, Donald Telford is going to demolish that pillbox and clear the ground.' Jackman gave him a half-hearted smile. 'I told him you most probably wouldn't object.'

'Like hell! The sooner it's gone, the sooner we can all get a good night's sleep. I have nightmares about that monstrosity.'

'You're not the only one,' said Jackman. 'I'll do all I can to speed things up, but we dare not authorise its destruction before the investigation is complete.'

'Of course,' Bryson said, adding that if his parents decided to remain there, he would probably have a high solid timber fence constructed to block it from view. 'It would be worth losing a quarter of an acre of ground if it meant that they wouldn't have to look at it again.'

'Hold fire on that for the time being,' said Jackman. 'I've an idea that Mr Telford may have something in mind for that area that might provide a better solution for you, so before you start spending all your money, sit tight for a bit and I'll keep you posted.'

Bryson thanked him, and he and Vic continued on their way. He wondered what Telford could possibly be wanting to do with that obscure corner of his field, but he supposed there was no rush to start putting up fences. At least the damn place couldn't be seen from the bungalow, or the main part of the garden, and who knows, maybe Donald Telford's idea might turn out to be viable. He and his dad often had quite a long chat in the pub, though they weren't great mates, so it was probably worth waiting.

Vic opened the door for him. 'See you tomorrow, and don't forget, ring if you have a eureka moment.'

Bryson grinned. 'You too. And good luck digging the dirt on the Gruesome Greenes.'

* * *

As Jackman watched Vic and Bryson leave the room, he thought of Bryson's father standing with his gaze fixed on the pillbox. According to Betty, he had been there the day before, too, supposedly seeing off rubberneckers and sneaky journalists. The man Jackman had seen earlier hadn't been watching out for trespassers. Jackman had been a mere few yards from Ted, but he hadn't even noticed him. There was something about that still figure that he found very disturbing.

'Boss?'

Jackman turned to see Marie giving him a quizzical look. 'You okay?'

'Sorry, I was miles away.'

'I gathered that,' said Marie. 'Anything I can help with?'

'No, Marie, it was something I saw earlier, and it's kind of haunting me. Anyway, if everyone's back in now, we might as well have a swift review of the day.'

As he turned to walk away, she said, 'Don't be haunted, share it with me. It might be important.'

'Don't worry, I'm probably just being paranoid. Let's get this meeting over, shall we?'

All thoughts of Ted Smith soon vanished amid the animated discussion. The pace was ramping up, although in which direction they were heading wasn't all that clear. Everyone agreed there was an atmosphere in that village, a gathering tension, almost as if a storm were about to break.

'Gary and I are off to meet up with our ghost-hunters this evening,' said Kevin. 'The bloke that runs it, Jonathon Bush, rang me earlier and he said it looks like it'll be well attended despite the short notice. We are hopeful that those Identikit images of the victims might stir up some memories.'

'It'll be interesting to see if the ghost-hunters are as twitchy as some of the villagers seem to be,' added Gary.

As the meeting progressed, Jackman noticed that Robbie appeared increasingly restless. At first he thought he just wanted to get off home, then he realised that Robbie was anxious to get back to his desk, so as soon as the meeting had ended and everyone was moving off, he asked Robbie what the problem was.

'It's Mad Sally, boss,' said Robbie. 'Kev mentioned something about her earlier. I set up a search just before the meeting, and I'm itching to see what it's thrown up.'

'Search on what?'

Robbie explained Kevin's theory that Sarah Nugent may have had a traumatic experience, probably not long before she moved to Fendyke. 'It would explain a lot, wouldn't it, sir? Even why she always gravitates toward any strange or bad event that happens in the village. It's like she *has* to know exactly what's going on, either out of fear, or maybe because she's expecting to see someone she recognises from her past.'

'I see,' Jackman said thoughtfully. 'Well, it's possible, I suppose.' He smiled at Robbie. 'So your lovely girlfriend will be spending the evening alone, while you sit here with your eyes glued to your screen?'

'Not quite, sir. Ella's been called out, so she's coming here after, hopefully with a pizza, since I could be here for a while.'

'Well, in that case, what with Kevin and Gary out hobnobbing with ghost-hunters, Max still negotiating with the Met about getting entry into Marion's swanky Chelsea apartment, and now you slaving away at your desk, I think I'd better hang on here too.' Jackman winked. 'As long as you ring Ella and tell her to up the pizza order — my treat.'

Robbie grinned. 'That's a deal, boss! And I'll check with the Sarge as well — we'll all have a party, on you!'

Jackman went to his office and sat at his desk, thinking about the information that had been amassed in the past few days. He needed to get all those interviews into some sort of order. Bottom line, had it resulted in anyone who set up warning bells? Had any one figure emerged who his detective's instinct flagged up as being a likely cause for concern?

'Need another perspective on those deep, deep thoughts?' Marie smiled at him from the doorway. 'I think Robbie mentioned pizza, in which case I'm happy to stay on for another couple of hours. My Ralph is helping a mate puzzle out some flat-pack furniture this evening, so I'm in no rush to get home.'

'Then you're most welcome. Let's see if we can pinpoint some names that might call for a closer look. Grab a chair.'

They whittled down the dozens of names to a handful. None of them leaped out as being likely suspects, but were people who had something about them that made the good old copper's nose twitch a little.

Marie pulled a face. 'Well, I can't see anyone here who makes me want to grab my handcuffs and call for back-up.'

'Ah well, I guess we can hardly expect a multiple murderer to jump up and down waving at us. Whoever it is, they must have a pretty calculating brain to be able to conceal five murders for over eighteen months without arousing a whisper of suspicion. So, let's go through them again and see what we've got.' Jackman read out the names: 'Dudley Nailer, because he seemed a bit too helpful. Then we've got Gary's suggestion of the guy who organises the ghost-hunters, Jonathon Bush. He was also very helpful. Now, what was it Gary said? Oh yes. Just as they were leaving, one of the others, a chap called Matthew Byrd, asked to see the photos again. He'd just remembered seeing the woman with the expensive binoculars, meaning Marion Sandon-Hayes. Apparently, this seemed to make Jonathan annoyed. Gary said he gave Matthew a look of absolute fury. Gary dismissed it at first, because nothing had been said, but later it started to bother him. He's going to be keeping a close eye on that man tonight.'

'Then we have the farmer, Donald Telford, yet another very helpful man,' Marie said. 'Normally, I'd have passed him over, but for the fact that he could well have known Dalmat Tabaku, even though he denied it, and that pillbox *is* on his land. He's the one person whose presence at that copse would not have seemed odd. Bryson said he put owl boxes up there at one point, and often went to check on the birds. I liked the man personally, but the more I think about it, the more I wonder about him.'

Jackman said he'd also liked Telford, who had been a great help to Rory and his forensic team. 'But he is in a hurry to demolish that pillbox, and — keep this to yourself for now — he's going to offer to purchase the strip of land along the bottom of the Smiths' garden where the pillbox now stands. It would be a handy bit of cash for them, and could be a blessing, since the garden is getting to be too much for them.'

'Hmm,' Marie said thoughtfully. 'Meaning he could be trying to get hold of it for another reason.'

'I hadn't seen it that way, but we need to keep an open mind. Looks like he's moving to the top of the list, am I right?'

'And that's it?' Marie said. 'That's not so bad.'

'Not quite.' Jackman wondered how she would receive his next suggestion. 'Edward Smith.'

'What! Bryson's dad? You're kidding.' Marie stared at him. 'Why?'

He told her about seeing Ted gazing at the pillbox, and that Betty was worried about the amount of time he spent down there.

'No, Jackman. I really can't see that. He's probably just drawn to it, like people who can't help gawping at traffic accidents.'

'You didn't see him, Marie. There was something very sinister about the way he was staring at that horrible place. He seemed totally mesmerised by it.'

'Okay, well, put him on the list if you must, but for heaven's sake, don't let on to Bryson — or Betty for that matter.'

'As if I would. But the person we're looking for is a murderer. We can't afford to look back later and say, Oh, if only we'd looked deeper at him, but he was such a nice, helpful person.'

'True,' Marie said. 'After all, we've come up against some very surprising killers in our time, haven't we? And as you rightly say, you saw him, not me, and I trust your judgement, so Mr Teddy Smith is added to the list.'

'And I can't see anyone else who qualifies, so we'll start digging into their backgrounds and see if anything nasty pops up.'

'Agreed, and just like you being haunted by that image of Ted Smith at the pillbox, I keep seeing Mad Sally out there in that creepy house. Something must have scared her very badly to have caused her to behave the way she does.' She pushed her hair back from her face. 'I wish you could see that place, Jackman. Trouble is, I'm afraid that if I took you there with me, it might cause her to retreat into her shell again.'

'I understand,' Jackman said. 'You've painted a damn good picture of her and her home, so I'm happy to stick with that. Unless anything serious occurs, of course. Then I'll be the first one there.'

'That's good to know. And if it's all right with you, I'll get back out there tomorrow, especially if our Rob can uncover something that might confirm his theory about a past trauma.'

'Absolutely. Talking of Robbie, why don't we go and see what he's come up with?'

Out in the CID room, they found DI Jenny Deane at Robbie's desk.

'Hi, Jackman. I hope you don't mind, but Vic and I have added our names to the guest list for tonight's Pizza Party.' She grinned at them. 'And you won't have to foot the entire bill, I promise. It's just that we're the only two left standing out of my team, so I thought we might join you.'

Jackman liked Jenny. She was a great person to have as an opposite number. He'd worked with some dreadful senior officers in his time, some were competitive to the point of being obstructive, while others had just been plain lazy. Jenny was a breath of fresh air — supportive, generous with offers of help and never unwilling to ask his opinion.

'Don't worry, Jen. I think my wallet can stand two more pizzas. Even if all this money I'm supposed to be earning in overtime never seems to find its way there.'

'Tell me about it,' Jenny said grimly. 'It's a good thing we love what we do, isn't it? So. Got a lead?'

'Nah, we're all just trying to follow up hunches. How about you?' Jackman said.

'Same with us,' Jenny said. 'Vic's got a real bee in his bonnet about those Greene brothers, and now Bryson Smith has the screaming abdabs for the same reason. Apparently, he's had one of those *what the hell did I miss* moments.'

Marie grinned. 'Ah, *those* moments! Bane of my life. Poor Bryson.'

'Vic's praying for a call from him, but I'm not hanging by my eyelashes,' Jenny said. 'Well, I suppose I'd better get back and help him. When's pizza time?'

'Ella says it'll be half an hour,' said Robbie. 'She's heading for the takeaway right now.'

'Perfect. See you all shortly.' Jenny turned and hurried away.

'I hope Bryson doesn't end up getting the screaming abdabs over anything to do with his dad,' Marie said quietly.

'Me too,' said Jackman. 'Now, Robbie, anything interesting shown up?'

Robbie shook his head. 'Rather a lot, boss, I'm afraid. Several horrific domestic disturbances, a couple of violent crimes including one robbery in which a whole family were held at gunpoint. What else? Ah yes, various muggings, and that's just the ones that made the headlines. This being the second largest county in England, and I'm not looking at anything specific, there's a helluva lot of crimes to trawl through.'

'Then share the load, brother,' said Marie. 'Throw some my way, and I'll pitch in.'

'Me too,' said Jackman. 'Our stuff can wait till tomorrow.'

The look of relief on Robbie's face was almost comical. 'Welcome aboard! I've printed out all those that occurred before Sarah Nugent moved to Fendyke, but more keep appearing. It's a bigger undertaking than I expected.'

'Nevertheless, it was a very good idea, and worth following up. We'll do as many as we can tonight, and tomorrow I'll try to drag in some extra help. It's something that can easily be tackled by civilian officers. So, let's get cracking, shall we?'

* * *

Despite the appetising smell of warm pizza drifting across from the other end of the room, Vic was loath to tear himself away from his screen. He couldn't make sense of what he was reading there. Was he overtired and had made a total cock-up of his search strategy? For the third or fourth time, he read through the statement that Lucas had made regarding what he had found from his research into the Greene brothers. Lucas had been adamant that everything in that statement was the truth. So why did his own research not bear out the facts in it? Surely, it was in Corbin's best interests to stick to the truth if he wanted to get his sentence reduced? According to him, the brothers had been born to wealthy parents in Saltern-le-Fen. So where were the birth certificates? Corbin had also said that they had made their money legitimately in the clothing trade. Well, if that was the case, he hadn't found any record of it, not even a company name.

'Vic! The best bits are all getting eaten! Get yourself down here if you don't want to starve!'

He looked up to see Marie waving to him from Jackman's end of the room. Resisting a strong urge to kick his computer, he got to his feet. Perhaps if he got some food in him his brain would start functioning again.

'Blimey, mate! You look like you've lost a pound and found a sixpence.' Grinning broadly, Max offered him one of the boxes of pizza. 'Not going too well up your end?'

'You can say that again,' muttered Vic. 'I think I must be having an attack of brain fog, or else I've lost my touch. Nothing's making any sense.'

'Welcome to the club,' said Robbie. 'I'm sat here hunting for a woman that the records all tell me doesn't exist.'

Vic stared at him. 'Really? That's my exact problem. The Greene brothers aren't showing up anywhere.'

369

'Bloody hell,' said Max. 'It had better not be catching. Chasing real people is hard enough, but phantoms, well, that's a whole other kettle of fish.'

With way more pizza than was good for him weighing him down, Vic returned to his desk, armed with a cup of strong coffee.

A couple of minutes later, Robbie arrived at his desk. 'A problem shared, and all that. Only you mentioned Lucas's statement, and I just wanted to say that at this stage of the game, he can't possibly be lying. It's just not in his interest.'

'That's what I reckoned,' said Vic. 'So why can't I find anything to corroborate it?' He ran through what Lucas had said in his affidavit. 'So, now I'm wondering where Lucas got his information from. All my searches have brought up zero results, even when I spell the name Green without the "e". All I do know is that they *are* wealthy, and a large sum is paid regularly into their joint account, but I'm struggling to find where it comes from. Unfortunately, I can't go any further with that until tomorrow when the banks open.'

'Well, in the meantime, can I give you a theory I've got about our Lucas? I've talked to him, see, and he spins a great yarn. He's very convincing about this being his first heist, which has got to be bullshit. The man's a pro. He's good, and I'm sure he's responsible for any number of the thefts of artworks that have been reported over the years. That being the case, where would he get his information from? Where else than the criminal grapevine?'

Vic took a moment or two to catch on. 'Ah, right. So you think that the story he got his research from was leaked by the Greene brothers themselves! It's what they want people to believe.'

'And it's all a load of bollocks.'

'You're dead right, Rob. Even a clever sod like Lucas couldn't see through their carefully constructed wall of lies.'

'What I don't know is why,' Robbie said thoughtfully. 'Although I reckon it could be one of two things: either they

370

are true zealots, obsessives driven by a need to possess more and more objects, or they are criminals too.'

'Thanks for that, mate. It makes a great deal of sense, plus it confirms my belief that Lucas was telling the truth as he knew it. I appreciate your input.'

'No problem, and if you manage to sort these guys out, you can give me a hand with my mystery woman. Talk about brain fog! Anyway, better go and get on with my search, I suppose. Since I've roped in Marie and the boss, I can't be seen skiving off. Good luck.'

Vic smiled at him. 'Right. Back to the drawing board.'

* * *

Rory raised his wine glass. 'Here's to the next time!' He winced. 'Oh dear, I could have put that better, couldn't I? Nevertheless, you have been an absolute star, and it has been a joy working with you again. You've steered this ship through some very stormy waters in the last few days, and you have my eternal gratitude for having brought us safely to port.'

'Oh, do shut up, Rory,' Professor Jan Wallace said. 'This particular case could only have been handled by a forensic anthropologist — which is my field, not yours. I'm just sorry that we haven't been able to give Eamonn his real name yet, although if the tests do come up with anything interesting, I'll be back here like a shot. Our Eamonn could take his time to divulge his secrets, but I won't give up on him. I don't do failure! I shall be in the lab tomorrow morning, tying up loose ends, then I plan to spend a few days at a small hotel in North Yorkshire that overlooks the sea. Three peaceful days, and then I'll head back to my students, who I'm sure are all missing me.' She laughed. 'Not.'

They were dining in a small local restaurant that Rory had happened upon by chance and fallen in love with; a thank you for all the help she had provided. Four victims from the pillbox had been identified at almost lightning speed, thanks

371

to Jan's skilful manipulation of the reconstruction images. As far as Rory was concerned, it was just a pity that there was no way he could justify keeping her here simply to wait for the test results.

Their food arrived and they chatted amicably. It was probably a good thing, Rory thought, that the tables were well spaced out, as their conversation might have put their fellow customers off their food.

'I must say you have a remarkable team of detectives at Saltern,' said Jan, expertly skewering a pan-fried scallop. 'I remember the first time I met them, way back during the Children's Ward case. I was impressed by their dedication then, and they haven't lost any of their enthusiasm, despite all the subsequent changes in the way the force is run. You, my friend, are one lucky pathologist.'

He chuckled. 'Well, don't tell them I said so, but I'm very aware of that. Mind you, dear heart, they are also lucky to have such an incredible genius as yours truly at their disposal, are they not?'

Jan rolled her eyes. 'Oh, that goes without saying. It's just fortunate that you have such brilliant contacts to call upon when you flounder!'

'Flounder! Nonsense. I've never floundered in my life!'

By the time dessert arrived, they were deep in conversation about their remaining unidentified victim.

'It's odd,' said Jan, digging into her sticky toffee pudding. 'Even though his image is probably the most lifelike of the five, yet he is the only one not to have been recognised.'

'I can't say I'm surprised that he hasn't appeared in the national databases,' said Rory. 'He just seems so *proper*, if you know what I mean. His clothes, his general state of health — not quite the country gentleman, but not far off. He wasn't a criminal, dear heart, I'd swear to that.'

'Oh, I agree,' said Jan. 'Though even I know that not all criminals are rough and ready. Why shouldn't they be well dressed and well groomed, given all the money they make? I'm wondering if at some point, the press might like to publish that picture. Someone will recognise him, I'm sure, and I'd dearly love to know what his story is.'

'We'll find out one day,' Rory said. 'I hate to leave that man with a black notice. Rest assured, I'm not giving up on him, or he'll haunt me! But now, dead people aside, what would you say to a cognac and a coffee, since neither of us has to drive? The coffee here is excellent, by the way.'

'That would be very nice indeed,' said Jan. 'You know, I'm going to miss you, Rory Wilkinson.'

'Not nearly as much as I will miss you, dear lady. Just remember that the door to my mortuary is always open, to you and your doppelganger, the Elephant Man.'

Jan snorted. 'You do say the sweetest things, Professor. I don't think I've told you, but I plan to step back a little from my duties at the uni, and reduce the number of lectures I give, so I'll have more free time to help you out if you find yourself flound— if you find yourself in need of my assistance.' She gave a cherubic smile. 'However, one more mention of the Elephant Man, and you may well end up on your own dissecting table!'

CHAPTER THIRTY-TWO

As the evening drew on, no one seemed inclined to go home, so at ten o'clock, Jackman decided he'd better call time. 'We'll all be fit for nothing tomorrow if we don't get some sleep. So get home, the lot of you.'

Robbie screwed up his face. 'Sir, can I please just give it another half hour? Something came up a while back and I dismissed it, but I'm thinking maybe I should give it a swift check. I won't stay too long, honestly.'

'Oh, I suppose so, but only half an hour, and not a minute longer,' Jackman said.

Fifteen minutes later, Robbie was alone in their end of the CID room, while in Jenny Deane's section, a single light glowed — Vic Blackwell, still sitting in front of his screen.

As Robbie's deadline of thirty minutes was about to expire, he heard a gasp.

'Rob! Come here!'

Rob hurried across. 'Got something, Vic?'

'Look at this! Who do you think these people are? And take a look at their surroundings.'

On Vic's screen was a photograph of three men and a woman lined up in a row, all wearing smart clothes dating from another era. From their artificial smiles, it looked like they were attending some function that they'd rather not have been present at. For a moment he wondered why Vic was showing him this. And then it came to him. He recalled the sight of two men being escorted to an interview room. One was tall and thin, the other shorter and rather plump.

The Greene brothers? He squinted at the image. They were fifteen or twenty years younger, but it was almost certainly them.

'Got it?' said Vic softly.

'Yeah,' Robbie said. 'Norman and Derek. But who are the others? And where are they? It looks like some art gallery or something, it's very upmarket wherever it is.'

'Oh, it's upmarket all right. It was a high-end London gallery that specialised in Art Deco and Art Nouveau paintings and glassware. It closed years back, but in its time it was as famous as the Saatchi Gallery is now.'

'Okay . . . I'm clearly missing something here, so what are you showing me, exactly? And where did you find this old picture?'

'I was playing with some software that I've used in the past, but now it uses AI, so it's vastly improved. It's like the one the force uses for identifying a face in a crowd. If you have an image, it will search through the internet to find pictures containing that specific face. While Bryson Smith and I were working in Hartwood House, we photographed certain parts of the rooms items had been stolen from, in particular, that stained-glass window. While we were at it, I took a couple of shots of the brothers, without them knowing. I uploaded the one of Norman, as he's got the most distinctive features, and this is what it came up with.'

Rob peered closer. 'It's from a newspaper, isn't it?'

'You got it, Rob, and there's an article beneath it. I've also uploaded the editorial from that issue from the paper's archive. Have a read.'

Robbie took the printout and read it through. Now he understood Vic's excited reaction.

This is the last known photograph of the Verde family, taken before the brutal murder of the oldest brother, Peter Verde, in their home in the Lincolnshire Fens. The atrocity was witnessed by his sister, Sasha.

'I get it!' Rob said. '"Verde" means green in Italian. Hence Greene.'

'That's why they are so secretive and don't want anyone inside their house.' Vic ran a hand through his hair. 'I haven't had time to follow it up yet, but we need to look at this murder case very carefully. I'm ringing my DI right away. She needs to know about this. And I'll ring Bryson Smith too. He's going crazy about something he thinks he saw in Hartwood House. This might jog his memory.'

'And I'll go and find everything we have on file regarding the Peter Verde killing. I seem to recall the name, but it was way before my time.'

'If you would, mate.' Vic pulled his phone from his pocket. 'I'll just get hold of Jenny now.'

Back at his computer, Robbie wondered if he should ring Jackman. If only they hadn't all gone home. This was big, he knew it, it was going to affect them all, not just Jenny and her team.

'Evenin' all!' Gary appeared in the doorway, closely followed by Kevin. 'Didn't expect to find you here, Robbo. What's occurring?'

'I'm not sure, Gazza, but hell, am I glad to see you two. Come and have a look at this.' Robbie showed his two colleagues the newspaper article with the photograph.

'Well, I never! The Gruesome Twosome,' muttered Gary. 'And Peter Verde! I remember some of the older officers talking about that case. So the Greenes are the Verde brothers, are they? That's bizarre.'

Having already retrieved the case file, Robbie skimmed through an overview of the investigation. 'Hey, listen to this! The sister, Sasha, saw the whole thing, and apparently it was a vicious attack. She was found soaked in her brother's blood, screaming like a banshee!'

'Am I right in thinking that they never caught the man who did it?' asked Gary.

Robbie read on. 'Ah, here we are. No, they never got him, even though when Sasha had recovered enough to talk, she was able to give a fair description of the bloke.'

'How was Verde killed? And where?' asked Gary.

'Bludgeoned to death, apparently,' said Robbie. 'In the garage of the family home. Extensive injuries, mainly to the head.'

'With a spade?'

Robbie looked up at Kevin, who had turned pale. 'Spade? 'Just check that out, Rob, please?' Kevin said.

Rob skimmed though until he found it. 'How did you know that, Kev?'

Kevin pointed to the photograph, his finger trembling. 'Because the sister . . . you called her Sasha, didn't you? That's the woman with the fox. That's Mad Sally!'

* * *

Jackman and Marie arrived at almost the same moment, and soon the two teams were working to piece together the story that a chance hit on an old newspaper photograph had brought to light.

Seeing that they all looked rather shell-shocked, Jackman asked a constable to go out and buy them all some real coffee from the late-night takeaway close to the station.

'Well, it looks like you've certainly found the trauma that sent her off the rails,' said Marie. 'And I may be wrong, but I think the reason she keeps turning up at every incident is that she knows the killer and is looking for him.'

'Or trying to make sure she knows exactly where he is, in case he comes looking for *her*,' said Gary. 'My God, what that poor woman must have gone through!'

'But why didn't she stay with the two surviving brothers?' asked Jenny Deane. 'Why go and live on her own in the middle of rural nowhere? It's the last thing I'd do!'

'It's something we'll have to ask both her and her brothers,' said Jackman. 'And that's not going to be easy, especially in Mad Sally's case.'

'Suggestion, boss,' said Marie. 'Why don't we get hold of Julia Tennant, and first thing tomorrow, she and I can go and talk to her? A man would give her the heebie-jeebies, but two women, one of whom she already knows, and the other being as understanding as our lovely force psychologist is, might stand a chance. I reckon it's our best bet, don't you?'

'Normally I'd just have her brought in, but in this case it would be a disaster. Yes, Marie, I think you are possibly our only chance.'

Just then, Vic's phone rang.

'Bry! You got my message then. Sorry it's late, but there's been a development, and I thought you should know about it.'

They heard a tinny, excited voice and then Vic put his phone on loudspeaker. 'Sorry I missed your call,' Bryson said. 'I dozed off, and when I woke up, I realised what had been bothering me.'

Vic glanced at the others. 'Okay, Bry, go ahead. We're all listening.'

'I had been looking at an exquisite glass vase on a writing desk, and next to it was a framed photograph of four people. Four, Vic! Three men and a younger woman. Then I remembered where I'd seen it before. There had been an article not long ago in one of the papers, about unsolved murders. My dad showed it to me on one of my visits down here. The photograph I saw was the very one that appeared in the paper just above that article. What on earth would those two brothers have been doing with the original in a frame?'

'We're pretty sure we know the answer to that one, Bry, but it's after eleven now. I'll see you tomorrow and explain.' Vic let out a sigh. 'And thank you, Bry, that confirms a lot. Speak in the morning.'

'Vic! Hold on! There was a second framed picture, only it had been laid face down. When Norman wasn't looking I sneaked a glance, and it was of the same four, but when they were much younger. I'd get hold of that, if I were you. I only caught a glimpse of it, but I remember thinking there was something slightly odd about it.'

'We'll do that, Bry, and thanks again. Try and get some sleep now.'

Jackman shook his head. 'Well, looks like we've got a lot of investigating to do. Between us, we need to go over that whole murder investigation, and pull out everything we can find about the Verde family. Then maybe we'll see where the Greene brothers, as they call themselves, get their money from, and why their sister is living alone off the grid on a desolate corner of fenland — possibly with the man who murdered her brother in close proximity.'

'I think the best thing we can do tonight is draw up a plan of action, don't you, Jackman?' said Jenny. 'Then we can come out of the blocks at full speed in the morning.'

'Agreed,' said Jackman. 'While Jenny and I do that, the rest of you get away. As Jenny said, we need to hit the ground running tomorrow.'

This time no one demurred. Kevin paused on his way out. 'Boss, I've just had a thought. Do you think Sarah, or Sally, or Sasha, is in imminent danger?'

'Let's call her Sally to simplify things, shall we?' Jackman said. 'And you're right, she is, but it sounds like she's been in danger from the moment she witnessed her brother's murder.'

'Then shouldn't we be going out there now, and getting her out of danger?' Kevin said anxiously.

Jackman smiled at him affectionately. 'Think about it, lad. Having experienced the trauma of seeing her brother killed, she would then have found herself in the midst of all the mayhem that follows a serious incident. She'd have been surrounded by police officers, police cars, vans, forensic people in masks and protective suits, photographers and ambulance crews. The sight of a police car could trigger a panic attack, so how do you think she'd react if we steamed out there now, in the dark? We could do more than frighten her, Kevin. We could push her over the edge.'

Kevin nodded. 'I get you. Then it's all down to the sarge, isn't it?'

'*And* Julia Tennant. If anyone can help Sally, it will be them.'

When everyone had left, Jackman and Jenny got down to drawing up an action plan for the following day.

'First thing tomorrow, we bring those brothers in. And we shan't be treating them gently. There'll be no more tiptoe-ing around their delicate sensibilities. They'll have to be made to realise the seriousness of the situation. I want them in an interview room, away from their familiar surroundings,' said Jackman. 'Agreed?'

'Absolutely,' she said. 'And I suggest we get Vic to fetch them, along with a couple of uniforms. He's not one to take crap from anyone.'

'Good choice,' said Jackman. 'Meanwhile, Marie and Julia will go to Fendyke and do their best to get Sally to talk to them. I've just had a text back from Julia, and she says she'll be here early tomorrow morning.'

'Excellent,' Jenny said, scribbling in a notepad. 'Meanwhile, we've got a whole shedload of enquiries to get underway. Why don't we list them and put them in order of priority, and then decide who does what.'

Jackman cleared his throat. 'First off, we go over the Verde investigation with a fine-tooth comb. Our killer is somewhere in that case file, and we need to find him. And if the Greene brothers aren't forthcoming, we can get the details of their real family history and the source of their money from that.'

Busily writing all this down, Jenny said, 'It could also explain how although Sally doesn't work, her home was paid for and she has enough money to cover her basic needs. I'm assuming the parents are long gone by now, so it could be part of an arrangement in their will.'

'It's something to check up on for sure,' said Jackman. 'And it's the kind of thing Sally might not want to reveal initially.' He gave a little groan. 'Oh, Jenny, I think Marie and Julia are going to have one heck of a difficult time with that poor woman. I just wish I could be there, but I daren't risk upsetting her and ruining their efforts. I gather it's simply unheard of for her to allow anyone to even get inside her door, so she must have seen something in Marie that she felt she could trust, or maybe even — I don't know — identify with on some level?'

'I'm glad Julia is going with her. She has years of experience behind her, whereas Marie is flying by the seat of her pants.'

Jenny was right, but Jackman still worried. He'd dealt with unstable people before, as had Marie, and there was no predicting their reaction. Sally had been badly damaged, and the last thing he wanted was to compound her suffering.

Jenny glanced at him. 'I know what you're thinking, Jackman, but bottom line is the need to keep Sally safe. There's a killer out there, and if he recognises her, or decides that she's a danger to him — well . . .'

'I get what you're saying,' Jackman said. 'And thinking about that killer, it's imperative we get the forensic report on the murder weapon used on Peter Verde. If the spade is the same as the one used on the pillbox victims, we have our connection — Sally. We need to establish if any of our five victims were known to her and her brothers.' He winced. 'And I think we should ask the brothers first. Showing pictures of dead people to Sally might not be a good move.'

After another hour, Jenny threw down her pen. 'I'm bushed! And I think we've got enough here to get working on. Do you want to take the lead, Jackman?'

He raised his hands. 'I'm happy for you to be OIC. It'll keep me free to get out into the field if I'm needed, and act as liaison between the different lines of enquiry.'

'If that suits you best, I'll man the fort here, and make sure you get regular updates.' She stood up. 'I'm going to type this up and then get off home for a large drink and bed. Depending on what Marie and Julia come back with, we could well have a manhunt on our hands tomorrow.'

* * *

As Jackman was about to let himself into Mill Corner, he stood still for a moment, bathed in an unexpected feeling of peace. The night was still, not even a leaf rustled. When he went inside, the house was warm, with its own familiar smell. Everything was as it should be, even the note from Hetty Maynard, who had apparently become clairvoyant in her old age.

Cold supper in fridge, Mr J. Thought you might be working late and too much pizza does you no good whatsoever. Mrs M.

Jackman laughed softly. Good old Hetty. In actual fact, he'd had very little of the pizza, and the cold supper looked inviting. He took a beer from the fridge and sat down at the kitchen table. He'd seen Julia's vehicle parked outside the mill again, but he decided not to disturb her at this late hour. There'd be plenty of time in the morning to brief her about what to expect from their visit to Mad Sally.

As he ate, he remembered all the meals he and Laura had enjoyed, sitting at this very table. For once, he felt none of the anguish that usually accompanied his memories of their time together. That didn't mean he no longer felt her presence. If possible, she was more present than ever, and he almost believed that if he looked up, he would see her sitting opposite him, sipping her glass of wine and smiling at him.

'This is a tough case, Laura,' he said softly. 'If I'm honest, there's something about it that scares me. I know what you'd say — that I shouldn't doubt myself, or the team, but . . .' He looked across at the empty seat on the other side of the table. 'Yes, this one scares me.' No answer came, but the feeling of peace remained.

Jackman put his dinner things away and walked around the house, checking that the doors were locked. He took one last glance across at the mill, and pulled the curtains. Time for bed, although that didn't necessarily mean sleep. He rarely slept these days.

Still feeling strangely content, Jackman washed, cleaned his teeth, pulled on his pyjamas and climbed into bed. He closed his eyes, and for once, thoughts of the day's events didn't immediately flock into his mind. For once, he didn't toss and turn. For once, Jackman slept.

CHAPTER THIRTY-THREE

'So, what's the plan of action?' Marie said.

Julia held up her hand, the fingers crossed. 'Suck it and see, I reckon, and perhaps throw in the odd prayer for good measure.' She laughed. 'Doesn't sound very professional, does it, but it's a rule of thumb to observe and respond accordingly. It's tricky, because we'd normally avoid any reference to something that could trigger an episode or a panic attack. Unfortunately, in this case that's the very thing we want her to speak about.'

'So, we need a really cautious and mindful approach?'

'Oh yes, the gentle touch, my dear, by the bucketful,' said Julia. She gave Marie a sympathetic smile. 'I know how important this is to you, and you know better than me that we probably only have one chance to get it right, but just be yourself. Most people are capable of picking up on whether someone is being sincere, and I don't expect Sally to be any different. Now, I'm afraid that to start with, it'll be down to you to introduce me, but as soon as I've made a swift evaluation of her state of mind, I'll be right there with you, and then . . . Don't worry. We'll do this.'

It was reassuring to have Julia by her side. And at the very least, it would provide someone else with an opportunity to get a look at Sally's unbelievable house. Marie looked at her watch. 'I reckon we ought to go early, what do you think?'

'Absolutely. I have a good idea Sally's always up with the lark.' Julia got to her feet. 'Ready when you are.'

As she drove, Marie felt oddly ill at ease. She was almost never apprehensive about talking to anyone, whoever they were, but she supposed she was feeling the weight of responsibility. It was down to her to persuade the one person who had actually seen the murderer to speak about it. This interview was going to be crucial.

'How did she react at your last meeting?' asked Julia, gazing out across the endless blue-green fields of cabbages.

'She was mostly angry,' Marie said. 'Not with me, but she obviously resents change in any shape or form. She loathes the villagers, but the worst of her ire was directed at the incomers.' Marie dropped a gear to navigate a bend in the lane. 'She's educated, though, even though her language is a bit outdated, or maybe literary. I remember her saying something about "lies falling from lips in torrents". It sounded almost Shakespearian. The villagers all call her Mad Sally, but she was far from that.'

'Anything else strike you as odd?' Julia asked.

'There was one thing, I suppose,' said Marie thoughtfully. 'When I asked her why she wouldn't answer my questions and said she wasn't helping me, she said that she couldn't help. "And it's *can't*, not won't," she said. It sounded like she wanted me to believe she really couldn't, even if she wanted to.'

As they drove further, Marie's mood became as bleak as the landscape. She began to wonder where her old feisty self had gone to. If she didn't get it back soon, she'd never get anywhere, and then she'd be letting everyone down, including Sally herself. 'It's a strange house, Julia. I found it a bit of a culture shock.'

'Does it have a name?' asked Julia.

'Rivendell.'

'Really?' Julia sounded surprised.

'*Lord of the Rings*, isn't it?'

'It is, but it's more than that, Marie. The book says, "*It represents both a homely place of sanctuary and a magical Elvish otherworld.*" More curious still, it is the place where the quest to destroy the One Ring began. Now, doesn't that suggest that our Sally thinks of her house, this Rivendell, as her own sanctuary, the place from which she can set out on her own quest?'

'Hmm. Quest. As in hunt for the man who killed her brother?' Marie said.

'Most certainly. Oh, and it also confirms your assumption that she is an intelligent woman. As we know, she's not exactly the type to take herself off to the movies, and if she did deliberately name her home Rivendell, as I suspect she did, it takes some doing to read JRR Tolkien from cover to cover and comprehend all its complexities.'

'You are right, she did name it,' said Marie. 'When Robbie was researching her background, he found that the two old cottages, which were originally part of a farm estate, had no names, and the man Sally purchased them from didn't name them either.'

Marie recalled that she'd noticed a lot of books in the kitchen. She hadn't taken too much notice at the time, but they all seemed to be hardbacks, and pretty hefty tomes at that. She tried to recall if she'd seen any of the titles. The only one she did remember was *Titus Andronicus*.

'Pardon?'

'Oh, I didn't realise I'd spoken out loud. It was one of the books in Sally's place. She had lots, but the only one I really noticed had a beautiful cover. It was *Titus Andronicus*.'

'Oh dear,' Julia said. 'Do you know it? Ever seen it performed?'

'No, I'm more of an Agatha Christie kind of person myself.'

Julia didn't laugh. 'What would you say if I were to tell you that it is referred to as a historical revenge tragedy, and of all his works, including *Hamlet*, it is the bloodiest? And that it deals not only with revenge, but brutality, and the cycle of violence.'

'I'd say, "Oh shit."'

They drove the next half mile or so in silence, until Marie said, 'She's lived there for fifteen years, and according to the reports on Peter Verde's murder, it took place a good few years before that. We need to ascertain if she lived with her brothers following the murder, or whether she moved out soon afterwards.'

'And why did she even leave?' Julia said. 'Well, we won't know the answer to that unless she tells us. If she continues to refuse to speak, I'll just have to try and figure it out from the extent of the damage caused by having witnessed such a terrible event.'

'We may have the brothers' statements to help us,' added Marie. 'Although I'm not sure that they'd recognise the truth if they fell over it. Seems to me they've lied their way through their entire adult lives. Still, you never know, when they realise that we are aware of their real identities, they might cough. No telling how people will react when they're threatened with being charged with withholding evidence or perverting the course of justice.'

'Only time will tell,' said Julia softly, gazing out at the farmland. 'So, how far are we from the famous Rivendell?'

'Two minutes, if that. We'd better gird our loins!'

To their dismay, no one answered their knock. Swearing loudly in frustration, Marie banged the old doorknocker. She hadn't for a minute considered that Sally might not be at home. The curtains were pulled back and washing hung on the line to the side of the house. She was definitely up, but must have gone out.

'What now?' asked Julia.

'I guess we either wait, or try again later, or go into the village and see if anyone has seen her this morning.'

Julia put a hand on her arm. 'No need. Look.'

387

Striding purposefully towards them was a tall woman, with — Marie blinked. Trotting happily at her side, a fox.

'Oh, so Kevin wasn't hallucinating,' murmured Marie. 'That is *so* weird.'

While they watched, the woman took a treat from her pocket and offered it to the animal, who accepted it politely. It was clearly their customary morning ritual.

On seeing the two women, Sally drew to a halt and glared at them. The fox sank to its haunches, staring at them, ears back. Sally gave it some more treats, tickled its ears affectionately, and pointed back the way she had come. The fox slunk off into the reeds lining the ditch at the side of the road and disappeared into the dense shrubbery along the edge of a field.

Sally stood at the gate, eyeing them suspiciously. Marie took a deep breath. Now it was all down to her.

'Good morning, Sally!' she said brightly. 'You're an early riser.' She hadn't expected an answer, and didn't get one, so she went on. 'I'm sorry to bother you again, although you probably guessed I would after our last conversation.' She smiled, looking Sally straight in the eye. 'There's been a serious development, Sally, and it's very important we talk to you. I respect your wish for privacy, so it's just me and my colleague, Julia, rather than a whole crew of uniformed officers. May we come in, Sally? Please? It really is most important.'

As before, Sally walked past them and unlocked the door, leaving it open. They followed her through the dingy hallway, into the kitchen.

Once they were inside, Sally pointed to Julia. 'Who is *she*? She's too old to be a detective.'

'She's my friend. This is Julia, she's a counsellor, and I've brought her along to help. You see, what we need to talk to you about might be rather upsetting for you. Do you mind if we sit down?'

Sally's expression remained stony, but she pointed to a couple of chairs. 'Just don't expect any tea.'

'It'd be best if you sit down, too, Sally,' said Marie firmly. 'This isn't going to be easy for any of us.'

Sally's eyes narrowed. 'Say what you have to say and get out — and take your *psychologist* with you, because I will not be needing her help.'

* * *

'They are in interview room one, boss. Vic's just called from downstairs.' Max grinned. 'I think he rather enjoyed bringing them in.'

'Okay, I'll inform Jenny and get down there. Let him know I'm on my way, Max.' Having let Jenny know, Jackman hurried down the stairs, glad to be finally getting his teeth into something concrete, instead of organising others and worrying about Marie.

Vic met him outside the interview room. 'I've told them you will be interviewing them, sir, and that the conversation will be taped. They asked if they needed a solicitor, and I assured them this was just a preliminary interview to ascertain certain facts, but if they wished to have a brief present, it was their prerogative, but they would be paying, and it would hold up proceedings somewhat. They asked if they were under arrest, and I assured them that that was not the case. Yet.'

'So, are we waiting for a solicitor?'

'No, sir. We are good to go.'

They went inside, sat down, and after introductions for the benefit of the tape, Jackman explained why they had been called for interview. He told the brothers that the police were now aware of the terrible tragedy that had befallen the Verde family. As he spoke, their expressions changed from polite anxiety to what appeared to be sheer terror. It was not the reaction he had expected. He saw one of the brothers grasp the other's hand and grip it tightly. At his side, he felt Vic stiffen.

'We are very sorry to have distressed you,' he said kindly, 'but we are concerned about your sister and her safety, and you are the only people who can help us.' He paused for a moment. 'Can we get you a drink? Or . . .' He really didn't want to ask, but under the circumstances felt he had no choice. 'Or perhaps you feel you *do* want a solicitor after all? We can get the duty brief in for you, if you like.'

The brothers were silent. Jackman began to feel very uneasy indeed. For once, he didn't quite know how to proceed. Nevertheless, they had not accepted his offer of a solicitor, so he decided he might as well plough on.

'Would you please confirm that you are Derek and Norman Verde. That you are the brothers of murder victim Peter Verde, and also that Sasha Verde is your sister.'

Norman's lips moved. Jackman waited. It seemed to take Norman a great deal of effort, but eventually he uttered a whispered, 'Yes.'

Jesus, thought Jackman. How long is this going to take? He decided that if they were to get anywhere at all, a short, sharp shock was required.

'Then, gentlemen, I suggest you both take a deep breath. My colleague here will fetch you a hot drink, and then you need to talk to us, *properly*, because your sister's life is in danger.'

Neither he nor Vic had expected the roar that erupted from Derek's throat.

'No! No! This can't be happening!'

Derek leaped to his feet, and if the table hadn't been bolted to the floor it would have gone over.

Before either Vic or Jackman could even move, Norman jumped up, grabbed hold of his brother and shook him violently. 'Sit down, you fool! We've always known this would happen one day. It's over! Get it? All over. I've had enough, Derek! This has to stop!'

He forced his brother back onto his seat. Derek leaned forward, put his head in his hands and began to weep.

Jackman started to say that he was terminating the interview, but Norman cried, 'No! No, Detective Inspector. This *has* to be said, and now.' He took a long shaky breath. 'My name is Norman Verde. I understand my rights, and it is my wish that what I am about to say should go on record, even in the absence of legal representation. We will deal with the aftermath later.'

Gritting his teeth, Jackman reminded Norman that he and his brother were neither under arrest nor under caution, but that their assistance would be greatly appreciated. He then asked Derek whether he would like the FMO to have a look at him, cursing the fact that Julia was miles away, and out of reach. He reiterated that a duty brief could be called at any time.

They all sat back down, and after a short silence, broken only by Derek's intermittent sobs, Jackman asked Norman if he would begin by giving them some background on what had happened to the family following his brother's murder. He especially wanted to know about Sasha, who at her own request, they were referring to as Sally.

Norman, who seemed to have aged ten years in a matter of minutes, straightened his back and looked directly at Jackman. 'I had better give you the whole story, because it is not as it might seem.'

* * *

Max, Gary, Robbie and Kevin all had their heads down, working furiously, when Tim, the office manager, called out from across the room, 'Can someone take a call from forensics? Prof Wilkinson asked for the boss, but he's tied up.'

'Put him through to me,' called back Robbie.

'Robbie, dear boy, I've got the cross-reference here that your revered master required — the comparison between the weapon used in the Verde murder and our trusty but as yet undiscovered ground-breaker spade from the Pillbox Killings.'

'Yes, Prof?' Robbie tensed up.

'A match, dear boy.'

'Shit,' Robbie whispered to himself.

'Language, young man,' said Rory, 'although I must say I concur with the sentiment.'

'Thanks for that, Prof, I'll pass it on to the boss.' Robbie hung up and called out to the others, 'Same weapon used, guys! Peter Verde and our own victims, all topped with the same spade. I'm going to tell DI Deane, but if Jackman comes back, let him know, will you?'

A few minutes later, he was heading back to his desk when he saw Bryson Smith walk in.

'I've just called in to finalise the inventory of the items stolen from Hartwood House,' explained Bryson. 'And Vic said he'd fill me in about last night's finding. Is he around?'

'Sorry, he's interviewing, mate,' said Max. 'He's got the pleasure of talking to your two happy householders whose house traps robbers, saving us the bovver of looking for 'em.'

'Pity,' Bryson said. 'Not only am I itching to know what went down last night, I asked him to collect a photograph from Hartwood House, and I hoped he'd have it here for me to look at. It bothered me when I first saw it, but I didn't know why.'

'Then your luck's in, Bry,' said Robbie. 'I've just been down to the other end, and there's a framed photo sitting on Vic's desk in an evidence bag. Want to take a look?'

The two stood at Vic's desk, staring at the image. It was exactly the same as the famous 'last photo' from the newspaper, but the four people were very much younger, possibly only in their late teens.

'So, what's your beef with this?' asked Robbie, seeing nothing much amiss, apart from their appalling fashion sense.

'That,' said Bryson, pointing to Sasha.

Robbie looked closer, and saw what Bryson meant. The three young men were smiling broadly, but Sasha's face was set in an expression of absolute fury.

'Blimey! Some bugger really upset her, didn't they?'

Behind them, Max said, 'Yeah, not a happy bunny in that pic, is she?'

'Who's she looking at?' asked Bryson.

'Impossible to tell exactly, as her head's turned in the direction of all three brothers, but if I were a betting man,' said Robbie, 'I'd take a punt on Peter.'

'Could that be significant?' asked Bryson.

'We are ignoring nothing in this case, Bry,' said Max. 'I'll tell the boss as soon as he's back from downstairs. I wonder how they're getting on. Those brothers aren't exactly dutiful citizens when it comes to helping the police.'

They headed back to their desks, leaving Bryson to finish up his inventory. Halfway across the room, Robbie stopped and called back, 'By the way, Bryson, have you ever heard of a place called the Verde Gallery in London?'

Bryson laughed. 'Who hasn't! I thought everyone must have heard of the Verde. It was one of those iconic sixties places where people went to be seen. You know, like Biba, although the Verdes weren't into fashion. They started out with Art Deco and Art Nouveau paintings and glassware, then added other collectibles, and more merchandise. They had a restaurant with an amazing roof garden. Why?'

'Because I was just about to get into the background history of the Verde family, and you, my friend, are going to help us all over again,' said Robbie.

'But what on earth have the Verdes got to do with anything?' asked Bryson.

'Quite a lot, mate. You are at present cataloguing goods stolen from the home of Derek and Norman Verde, grandsons of Ricardo and Rene Verde, whose names you will no doubt recognise.'

Bryson's jaw dropped. 'Bloody hell! So that's where their love of that period of art started. They were brought up with it!'

'And that's where their money came from,' said Robbie. 'So, when you are finished with what you're doing, perhaps you'd like to come and give me a hand.'

'Why not?' said Bryson, shaking his head in disbelief. 'In which case, I'd better pull my finger out and tie this up fast.

Oh my, this all gets stranger and stranger. Remind me not to book another week of gardening for my mum and dad, it's far too stressful!'

* * *

'Okay, Norman, the whole story,' said Jackman. 'But if it's going to take a while, I need to remind you that we are very concerned about Sally's safety, so time might be of the essence.'

At this, Derek began to laugh hysterically. 'Fools!' he spluttered. 'You haven't the slightest idea what it's about. You really don't get it at all, do you?'

'I have to stop this interview,' said Jackman, reaching to switch off the recording. 'Your brother is in no state to continue. He needs help. I'm going to call the FMO. Interview terminated at—'

'Wait! Just listen to me, will you?' Norman said. 'Derek's right, you don't understand. Let me just tell you the most important part, and I'll explain the rest later.'

Wearing a puzzled frown, Vic glanced at Jackman.

'Okay, Norman, what have we got so wrong?' A horrible thought was beginning to take shape in Jackman's brain.

'Sally herself is not in danger, DI Jackman, but others might be. Anyone who upsets her. Our sister suffers from a condition called IED, or Intermittent Explosive Disorder. It takes the form of uncontrollable fits of rage, she's suffered from it since her teens. As long as she's on her own, and not too badly disturbed, she's fine. Well, on an even keel, let's say. Living in isolation, at least the only person she can hurt is herself.'

Jackman felt an icy claw of fear clutch at his heart. Marie! And Julia! 'Oh, my God,' he breathed. 'Norman! We have people with her now. Are they in danger?'

Norman turned pale. 'Where?'

'At her home.'

'At Rivendell? Oh no! You need to get them out of there. That place is utterly sacrosanct to Sasha. One wrong word and . . .'

Gripped by a rising sense of panic, Jackman said, 'Will it help that my sergeant is a woman? She has spoken with Sally before, and there was no problem then.'

'It might, but she'll be walking on eggshells and not know it. It's still dangerous. And the other officer?'

'She's not a police officer, she's an older woman, a psychologist.'

'Sweet Jesus! Then get them out as fast as you can. Most of her life, our parents kept telling our sister she would be sent to a psychiatric hospital, and she's terrified of anything to do with the mental health profession. After Peter's death she was forced into therapy, as everyone believed that witnessing a murder had traumatised her! DI Jackman! Get those women out of there!' Norman was visibly shaking.

Jackman looked at Vic.

'I'm coming with you, sir! These guys are going nowhere. I'll inform the custody sergeant and catch you up. We have to get to Marie!'

His hand on the door, Jackman stopped and turned back. 'Two things, Norman. Straight answers. What's my best approach? Blues and twos, or will that only make her worse? Or should I try a silent approach? What is best for my sergeant and our friend?' Jackman knew his voice had risen and he didn't care.

'Sorry, but I can't advise you. To my mind, neither will make a blind bit of difference. You'd need to be specially trained to manage her anger, and if it's a full-blown rage, then no one . . .' He shook his head. 'Just get out there and see for yourself. Do whatever you can to save your colleagues, and if anything happens to our sister as a consequence, it can only come as a blessed relief.'

'She killed your brother, didn't she? And you covered it up?'

He didn't expect an answer, but as he hurried out of the room, he heard Norman say, 'Yes, she killed him.'

* * *

Marie was beginning to think it had been a mistake to bring Julia. Not for a moment had she expected Sally to be so antagonistic towards this softly spoken and likable woman. Gradually, she began to realise that it wasn't Julia herself that was the problem, it was the fact that she was a psychologist. If only she had known this beforehand she would have come alone, but as it was, it was making getting through to Sally all the more difficult.

Sally was staring off into the middle distance, silent and rigid.

Marie tried again. 'Look, I realise this is difficult for you, Sally. I'm aware that you're a very private person and this must feel like a bit of an intrusion, but what I have to tell you is important. It concerns your safety.'

Still no response, but at least Sally hadn't told her to get out of her house.

'We believe that there's someone, either in the village, or somewhere close by, who means you harm. I also think you know who this person is.' Marie waited.

'A dangerous person, you say?' Sally made no move to turn towards them, as if she were addressing some unseen person on the other side of the room.

'Very dangerous. The thing is, Sally, we know about your past. I really didn't want to put you through even more suffering, which is why I brought Julia with me. She understands about the kind of traumatic experience you've undergone and can offer you help and guidance. She's here for you, Sally, as am I. Both of us only want to help, nothing more.' Marie was trying to sound reassuring without being patronising. 'And I need your help too. We have to catch this person, and if your assistance helps put him away, the fact that he's no longer around might give you a measure of peace.'

'Peace?' Sally said bitterly. 'Peace? Me? Ha. There's no peace in my life.'

'Oh, but there is,' said Marie. 'I saw you with that little fox this morning. You care for it, it accompanies you when you're out walking. That's a form of peace.'

Finally, Sally turned and looked at her, but her expression was unreadable.

'Please, Sally, I'm begging you. I need to catch this killer, mainly before he gets to you, but also before he hurts someone else. We know he's killed before, and we don't know why or how he chooses his victims. Come on, Sally, you are all I have! Help me, please.'

From the corner of her eye, Marie saw Julia give her a reassuring little nod, but Julia was wise enough not to interject. By now, they had both realised that Sally must have received a great deal of therapy following her brother's murder, and that it hadn't worked, which was why she had reacted so negatively towards Julia. Marie was beginning to run out of things to say. She couldn't be as forthright as she had on her previous visit, yet she couldn't keep pleading with her either. In the end, she decided to take a leaf out of Sally's book. She sat and stared at her, waiting for her to say something.

After what felt like hours, Sally finally said, 'I've told you I can't help, so I don't know why you're wasting your time and mine. If I were you, I'd give up and go. Now.'

'But you aren't me, are you, Sally — or should I say Sasha? And I'm not leaving you here unprotected. For heaven's sake, you know who the killer is, so tell me. That's the only way you're getting me out of your house.'

'Oh, I know who the killer is all right,' growled Sally, 'but telling you won't make any difference.'

In Sally's lap, her hands were clenching and unclenching, as if she were trying to restrain herself.

Fighting to keep her voice steady, Marie said, 'It's okay, Sally, and I'm sorry if I shouted at you. It's just that I want to help you, that's all.'

'Oh really? And I suppose this quack you've brought along with you wants to help me as well? How exactly? Is she going to pump me full of drugs so I can't think straight? Is she going to make me so ill and half dead that I can't even function?' She turned on Julia, and spat, 'Your kind make me sick!'

'You don't know me any more than I know you,' Julia said evenly, 'and I can only guess at what you've suffered. But I'm telling you right now that I've never used drugs on *anyone* in that way. In fact I don't use drugs at all if I can help it. All I do is help you to help yourself, so that you can lead a happier life. What happened was no fault of yours, my dear, and you don't have to imprison yourself here out of fear. You see, I'm not like the people you've spoken to before. I will listen, really listen, and I will do my utmost to guide you through what you experienced, and so help you to help yourself.'

The seconds ticked by. The tension in the room was palpable. The air seemed to vibrate, like a string stretched almost to breaking point. This situation was one of the most stressful Marie had ever been involved in. She knew it could go either way, and she had absolutely no idea how it would end.

Sally got slowly to her feet, her hands clenched tightly into fists.

'Listen to yourself. "Help you to help yourself." Do you not think that if I could have done that, I would have done so years ago?' Now pacing to and fro like a caged animal, she spat, 'I'm damaged! Damaged! Get it? You think I can have a, what was it you said, "happier" life again, all violins and roses? What a joke.'

Sally lowered her head, staring at Julia, eyes hooded like a caged beast about to attack. Marie really didn't want to have to use force to restrain her, knowing it would only inflict more trauma, but she had a feeling it would come to that.

Julia remained calm, making no move that might antagonise a normal person. The trouble was, they now realised, Sally was not normal. Dudley Nailer had been wrong when he opined that Mad Sally was not, in fact, mad. Sally was an extremely disturbed woman.

'How dare you,' Sally hissed. 'You come into my home, preaching at me like some sanctimonious old parson. Changing my responses indeed. Well, here's my response!'

The next few minutes seemed to pass in a blur.

As she uttered those last words, Sally came to a halt at a high-backed chair covered in a woollen throw. Before Marie realised what was happening, Sally had reached down and snatched something from beneath it. A spade. An old, heavy, ground-breaker spade.

With a yell, Marie was up on her feet and charging towards her. But she had underestimated the older woman's strength. Winded by a blow to her solar plexus, Marie staggered back. She could do nothing but watch in horror as Sally raised the spade in the air about to bring it down on Julia's head.

Marie's cry of 'No!' ended in a gasp of surprise.

Sally was fast, but not as fast as Jackman. She still had the spade raised above her head when he burst through the door and grabbed her arm. The spade clattered to the floor at Julia's feet. By the time Marie had recovered her breath, Sally was in handcuffs, kicking and spitting like a crazed animal caught in a trap.

'Please, don't hurt her!' Julia was on her feet and running towards the two constables. 'She's ill, terribly ill!'

'And she's strong, terribly strong, lady!' grunted one of the constables, wrestling to retain his grip on her. 'And why should you care anyway? From what I could see she was trying to kill you. Ouch!'

Getting shakily to her feet, Marie felt Jackman's arms around her, holding her tight.

'Oh, thank God! All the way here I was thinking we'd lost you,' he breathed. 'And Julia too.'

'It's her, isn't it?' Marie said into his shoulder. 'She's the Pillbox Killer.'

'And she killed her own brother. And I have an awful feeling that when we finally get the whole story from Norman Verde, their statement will be a catalogue of other violent incidents, all the result of her uncontrollable rage.'

'Intermittent Explosive Disorder,' said Julia, and sighed. 'Poor woman. I recognised it almost immediately, an impulse

399

control disorder characterised by a failure to resist aggressive impulses. Often, after an outburst, the sufferer is stricken by remorse, they have feelings of guilt, or shame. Sally, however, is at the far end of the spectrum. Frankly, it's the worst case I've ever seen.'

Marie extricated herself from Jackman's hug, and brushed herself down. 'I thought you were a goner, Julia, I really did. When I saw that spade I thought it was all over, and we were both going to die. Brilliant timing, Jackman! Once again, you've saved the day. First Charlie, now Julia — and probably me too! That punch in the gut was a real doozy.' She winced. 'And you, Julia, how come you're so calm? Anyone would think you've just come back from a trip to the shops or something.'

'Oh my dear! You've no idea how many disturbed people — men and women — have decided I'm the devil incarnate and must be done away with on the spot. I've been threatened with knives, hammers, and heaven knows what kind of tool, but I have to say that's the first time anyone's tried to use a spade.'

Not knowing whether to laugh or cry, Marie suddenly felt very, very tired. 'Can we get out of here? I've seen enough of bloody Rivendell to last me a lifetime. All I want now is a cup of dreadful coffee in our dreary down-to-earth CID room.'

CHAPTER THIRTY-FOUR

'Blimey, boss. Don't you ever go doing anything like that again. You had us all shit scared wondering what was happening.' Max was beside himself.

Jackman squeezed his shoulder. 'I'm so sorry, Max, and the rest of you, too. As soon as I heard what Norman Greene said about his sister, I had to make a judgement call, so I took off with a couple of uniforms and drove like a maniac to Rivendell. Even then I didn't think I'd make it in time.' He shivered at the thought of just how close a call it had been. 'I even left Vic in the car park, and I didn't dare ring Marie to warn her in case my call alarmed Sally. I acted on instinct, and thank heavens the fates were with me.'

'Then I guess we'll have to forgive you,' said Max, 'even if you have taken ten years off my life. And you, Sarge. The whole bunch of us wanted to be there. We'd have been willing to take on twenty Sallys to save you and Julia.'

Marie smiled at him affectionately. 'I know that, you muppet. In this team it's all for one, and one for all.'

The sound of her ringtone interrupted the conversation. Anna, calling from her burner phone.

'Marie here. Anna? Is that you?' Gesturing urgently to Jackman, Marie put the phone on loudspeaker.

'Marie, I'm so sorry. Someday soon I'll get to explain properly, but right now I have something very important to tell you.'

'Okay, I'm listening. I've been so worried about you, you know.'

Anna took a moment to respond. 'When I first came to see you, I honestly didn't know my husband was alive. I really didn't. But now — listen to me. Chaos — you know who I mean — Chaos did not set Johnny up. There was more than one master hacker out there then, and it wasn't Chaos. The man who sent Johnny to prison has fled the country. Yes, we all know that distance means nothing to a hacker, but in his case we're pretty certain he won't ever be heard of again. He got into a . . . different kind of cybercrime, tried to be too clever and crossed the wrong people.'

'And Johnny discovered this? And he's safe?' Marie asked.

'He's fine, Marie, but . . . he knows what violating the terms of his parole means, and he's not going back to prison. It would kill him. We're going away. He asked me to send you a leaving present.'

'A present?'

'Something I think will help you resolve an ongoing thorn in your side.' Anna gave a little laugh. 'He says you should go down to your IT department in about ten minutes, and your IT boss, Orac, will receive a message that, well, let's say will be to your advantage.'

'Okay, I've got that.'

'He also said to tell Robbie to say hello to his friend Harry for him. Tell him he thanks him for being such a loyal friend, and that one day they'll get together again. Now, I've got to go, but thank you, Marie, for everything.'

The line went dead.

Down in the IT department, Orac's mouth dropped open when she saw the whole team file in, one after the other. Marie gave her Anna's message, and they waited.

After what seemed like forever, Orac's phone rang, making everyone jump.

It was a recorded message, and the speaker had clearly used a voice changer:

'A gift for Marie, because she never believed I was guilty. In my search for the man who stole seven years of my life, I took a wrong path. I believed it was the hacker they call Chaos. I was wrong. Nevertheless, I found him. I had the assistance of nameless people who would never help the police, nor any other official body. Don't worry, I'm not going to send you off on a treasure hunt, I've done all the work for you. Chaos was hard to find, his use of VPNs, encryption, proxies, steganography and all the rest, was the work of a genius, but how I found him isn't important. All I'm giving you is an address. Not an IP address, a physical one — a house name, a road and a village. All I ask is that you don't go out there mob-handed. He won't put up any resistance. Chaos is dead, and I'm sad about that, but not as sad as someone else will be.'

The distorted voice then reeled off the address.

For a moment, no one spoke. Then, from behind them, came a horrified gasp. Coral McIvor stood there, her face ashen.

'Dad?'

* * *

As requested, they didn't go in with blue lights and sirens. A single police vehicle drew up quietly outside the cottage in Kirkby Fenside, closely followed by Jackman's car. In it were Marie, Orac and Coral. They tramped up to the front door in silence.

Coral took her father's front door key from her jacket pocket, and they all went inside. The two constables went ahead, checking the rooms one after another. The house was, as usual, neat and tidy, with nothing out of order.

They found William McIvor in the main bedroom. He had probably been dead since the night before. In his hand was an envelope, addressed to his 'darling daughter'.

Somehow managing to keep her emotions in check, Coral asked Jackman if she might open the letter and read it. He agreed that she could, as long as she wore gloves.

Marie handed her a pair of gloves from her pocket, and they averted their eyes as she read her father's last words to her.

When she had finished, Coral said, her voice shaking, 'It's mainly personal. I was right in thinking he'd had bad news from the hospital. He was terminally ill, and decided not to prolong the suffering for either of us.' She swallowed, and cleared her throat. 'This last part is what concerns you:

'After I lost my mobility and could no longer do the things I enjoyed, I looked for a project to keep me occupied. Sudoku had never interested me, and in the firm belief that daytime television is the fastest route to brain rot, I turned my attention to the noble art of hacking, and I must say, I think I became quite good at it. Must run in the family, mustn't it, darling? I apologise for giving you all so much trouble, but I have to say, being Chaos was enormous fun!'

Coral was shaking her head in disbelief. 'He says we are to go out to the garden and look in the old storeroom next to the garage.' She looked helplessly at Jackman. 'He told me he'd rented that out to a neighbour to keep his gardening equipment and mowers in. He says the key is on his personal keyring.' She indicated a bunch of keys on the bedside cabinet.

She took a shaky breath. 'The rest of it is a farewell message to me.'

'I'm sorry, Coral, but we'll need to bag the letter,' said Jackman gently, 'but you'll get it back as soon as we've confirmed that no one else was involved in your dad's death.'

Five minutes later, they were all standing in the doorway to Chaos's headquarters. The inside of the store had been partitioned into two halves. The front part was open, and contained all the gardening paraphernalia normally kept in the shed. The second half was closed off with a solid metal door. Jackman went through the keys on the keyring and found a small key that fitted the lock. The door swung back.

'Chaos's command centre,' whispered Orac. 'I can hardly believe this is it. How could he have achieved so much with so little?'

Marie agreed. She had expected to find a setup resembling mission control for the space programme. Instead, all it consisted of was a long table that served as an office bench, bearing a couple of desktop computers, two monitors, a tower server, a laptop, a printer, and a load of little electronic devices that meant nothing to either her or Jackman. Incongruous amid the electronic equipment was a large photograph in a leather frame — Coral as a beautiful young woman, smiling out at the world.

After a swift appraisal of the setup, Orac nodded approvingly. 'He lined the walls with soundproofing, and up there,' she pointed to a panel set in the roof, 'I think you'll find he had someone mount a nice little Starlink antenna, so he would have got a great signal, even out here in this rural location.'

Besides the shock of her sudden bereavement, Coral was utterly dumbfounded by her father's 'project'. 'I can't get my head around this,' she kept saying. 'I've been tracking Chaos for years, and he's always been one jump ahead. And no wonder. My own dad!'

'Well, you did say he had a wicked sense of humour,' said Orac, linking her arm through Coral's. 'I think you gave your father a purpose in life as his health started to fail. I mean to say, aiding criminals only to turn the tables on them. That's what I call inspired!'

'I think it's time to go, folks,' said Jackman. 'Arrangements will have to be made for William, and I'm afraid this house is going to be a possible crime scene for a time. I'm sorry for your loss, Coral, we'll get all that done as soon as we can. Given the letter he left, which he obviously wrote himself, there is little doubt that there was no foul play involved. If you wouldn't mind giving me the keyring, we'll lock up, and then it'll be in your hands, Orac. I'm guessing you'll have quite a lot to sift through.'

'I'm looking forward to it. But all that can wait.' Orac turned to Coral. 'Right now, I think you need some support. The unit can run itself for a while. I'm here for you, Coral, you don't have to go through this alone.'

Jackman watched the two women walk away, arm in arm. In appearance, they couldn't have been more different, yet at heart, they were two of a kind.

Jackman shook his head and told himself to stop blathering. They still had countless questions to resolve, and the sooner he found answers to them the better. Last out, he locked the door, and made a brief call to DI Jenny Deane. He caught up with Marie and put his arm around her shoulders. 'Shall we arm ourselves with caffeine and chocolate and shut ourselves in my office? It's going to take a while to absorb what has happened today. Or, perhaps after what you've been through, you'd rather go home to Peelers End and Ralph?'

Marie raised her eyebrows. 'Do you really need to ask?'

'Then caffeine and chocolate it is! Let's go.'

CHAPTER THIRTY-FIVE

Two Weeks Later

Jackman had just finished going through the transcripts of the interviews with Norman Greene. It made harrowing reading, and Jackman found himself becoming increasingly sorry for what Sasha must have endured as she grew up. Her entire life from childhood onwards, had been plagued by a series of uncontrollable rages, which often resulted in quite serious damage. It seemed that Norman mostly took the brunt of these fits of fury, and it was he who was most concerned about her. Life became increasingly difficult as they grew older. They were a prominent family, and the four siblings were often required to put in an appearance at various social gatherings. Whenever they attended a function, the four siblings kept close together, the brothers never letting their little sister out of their sight. By now they were familiar with the warning signs — Sasha would lower her head and stare up at whoever had provoked her from beneath her eyebrows. Marie had seen this look of Sasha's for herself, at Rivendell, and it had been truly frightening. Norman swore that no one had witnessed their brother Peter's death, but it was obvious who was responsible. Sasha had come up with an implausible tale about a stranger attacking him, and rather than have the family brought into disrepute, their parents had insisted they go along with it. The only part of her story that rang true was the fact that the murder weapon had never been found, Sasha insisting that the killer had taken it with him.

For some reason, maybe because the family had a lot of clout, Sasha's IED diagnosis was never brought to light, nor was she ever under suspicion. Nevertheless, the strain of maintaining the fiction eventually became too great, and Sasha's father insisted that she should leave the family and go to live elsewhere. Much to their surprise, she agreed, even going so far as to say that it would be best for all of them if she were to sever all contact with her family. As she was now in her thirties, and no longer needed parental care, arrangements were made for her to move to a lonely farmhouse in Fendyke, with an allowance for her upkeep and day-to-day needs. By this time, Norman and Derek were themselves mentally unstable and unfit for both employment or for sustaining any sort of relationship, including ordinary friendship. Norman was consumed with guilt at having let their sister down in sending her away, while Derek believed his life would have been in danger had she stayed. Isolated by what they knew about their brother's death, they gravitated towards each other and began to shun social contact. United, too, in their passion for art, they began collecting Art Deco and Art Nouveau in a serious way. After their parents died, their love of this period became an all-consuming need. They sold the family home, along with some of the artworks that were of a different style, and purchased Hartwood House. Norman insisted that he and his brother had no idea that Sasha had murdered anyone else. Until, that is, they read about the Pillbox Killings and put two and two together. Then came the robbery, and the consequent invasive presence of a policeman in their home, which almost sent Derek over the edge.

Jackman rubbed his eyes. He and Jenny, and sometimes Vic, had spent hours with Norman, but they were still not entirely sure if he'd been telling the truth or not. Possibly only Sasha could give them the real story.

Jackman was still pondering the question of the Verde family when Superintendent Ruth Crooke came into his office. 'Ruth! This is a surprise. We don't often see you down here. Is everything all right?'

Ruth sat down at his desk. 'It's just a brief visit. I'm meeting the members of the special unit dealing with the Westerham case in about twenty minutes, and before I go I thought I'd update you on a few things.'

'I'm all ears.'

'The main thing is that Craig Sharpe, your Handcuff Boy, as you called him, may now return home. Poor lad got caught in a nest of vipers through no fault of his own, and I'm sorry he had to suffer so badly. However, the knock-on effect is that we've managed to link the father of the friend Craig was helping to Lars and Giles Westerham, and he's finally where he belongs — locked up in a cell.'

Jackman smiled broadly. 'I can think of a lot of police officers who'll be very happy to hear that.'

'And none more so than the special unit, who've been watching Sean Fairweather for months. Craig was shown a series of mug shots of various felons and picked out both Giles and Lars, whom he'd seen drawing up at Fairweather's house in a chauffeur-driven car. Unfortunately for Craig, his friend, in all innocence, took him to see her father's computer system, which led Sean Fairweather to have him abducted for fear he might have seen something he shouldn't.' Ruth shook her head. 'Poor kid hadn't seen a thing, and had no idea why he'd been kidnapped.'

'I suppose they found him through Fairweather's daughter,' Jackman said.

Ruth nodded. 'Again, through no fault of her own, she dropped Craig right in it. She says she thought her dad liked

409

Craig and was just asking her questions like any father would about one of her mates.'

'We have a lot to thank Bob Ruston for, don't we?' Jackman said.

'Fear not, he'll get official recognition. He's been a trooper.'

Jackman leaned back in his chair, 'And as for us, I'm pleased to report that Charlie Button will be back on light duties in two weeks' time, and Max is also back on track, having got over the shock of seeing his best mate go down. Things are looking up.'

'I'm relieved to hear that,' said Ruth. 'I've been told that Max Cohen is a bit of a reluctant hero. Nevertheless, I think he'll enjoy showing his two children the commendation their daddy got for bravery.'

'I'm not so sure about that. He still insists it's no more than anyone would have done in his position, but that's definitely not the way it looked to me. He deliberately placed himself in the line of fire to protect Charlie. Westerham was definitely pointing the gun at him.'

'Until you floored him,' said Ruth. 'An action you later repeated when Sasha Verde was about to bring a spade down on the head of our force psychologist. You're not suddenly becoming a caped crusader by any chance, are you, Rowan?'

Jackman looked embarrassed. 'No way! On both occasions I simply had no choice. I was hardly going to stand by and let two officers get shot, or our psychologist get her head caved in. I mean, really!'

'And we are all very grateful that you acted as you did, but you have to admit you did show a certain disregard for your own safety.' Ruth raised her eyebrows.

'I acted instinctively, that's all. Like Max said, it's what anyone would have done in the circumstances.'

'All right,' said Ruth, and gave him a rare smile. 'I'll say no more about it, although you might leave the heroics to someone else next time. Now, tell me, what have forensics found at Rivendell — apart from the murder weapon, of course.'

'Three mobile phones belonging to Gino, Shelley and Marion. We have no idea why she kept them, and there is no sign of Dalmat's, or of Eamonn's, which is odd as I'm sure they would have had mobiles on them. They are down in IT now, and Orac's team is extracting what information they can from them. We are hoping they'll tell us why the victims were in Fendyke, and whether they had had anything to do with Sasha.'

'And Sasha herself?' asked Ruth. 'Has she offered any explanation for why she perpetrated these horrific acts against those particular individuals?'

'As you know, she's being held at the secure psychiatric hospital, and we haven't been able to see her yet. However, Marie is being allowed a short visit this afternoon. Apparently, Sasha is considerably calmer, and is asking for her. I must say I'm far from happy about it, but Marie insists she wants to go. She thinks she might be able to help, since she's the only person who seemed able to get through to Sasha.'

'You'll go with her, won't you, Rowan?' Ruth said.

'Oh, don't worry about that. I'll be on hand if I'm needed,' Jackman said. 'Although Julia seems to think that Sasha could be entering a new phase of the illness, and is beginning to feel some remorse. Apparently, that's new for Sasha.'

'Is she aware of her situation?' Ruth asked. 'I mean, that she is being charged with six counts of murder and one attempted murder?'

'Oh yes, she knows that. She's quite lucid, but she insists that she won't speak to anyone but Marie.'

'Lucky old Marie,' muttered Ruth. 'Well, I suppose I'd better go and meet with my spooks, or whatever they are. Do let me know how Marie gets on, Rowan, won't you?'

As soon as Ruth left, Vic Blackwell poked his head in the doorway. 'Have you got a moment, sir?'

'Sure, come on in, Vic.'

'I heard from Bryson Smith just now, sir. He's planning on going back to London next week, and he wondered if he could come in and see us before he leaves.'

'Certainly,' Jackman said. 'I'd like to thank him for all his assistance.'

'Good, I'll get him to call in tomorrow if that suits you. Maybe after lunch? I must say, I don't know what I'd have done without his help with the inventory of stolen goods.'

'Tomorrow is fine, Vic. He has been a real diamond, especially considering the shock of finding that pillbox.'

'That reminds me,' Vic said. 'He asked me to tell you you were right about holding fire on putting up that fence. He says Donald Telford has offered to buy that part of their garden. He's going dismantle the pillbox, clear all the overgrowth, plant it with trees and put up new owl boxes. Bryson said the offer has persuaded his parents to stay on after all.'

'That is good news,' said Jackman, recalling Teddy Smith gazing at the ill-fated stretch of ground. Now he could turn his attention to pottering around in his garden, knowing that those poor souls had finally departed.

About to leave, Vic said, 'Oh, and Bryson has been in touch with some of his contacts in the art world. Apparently, not one single item from the Hartwood House robbery has turned up on the market. The gang are either sitting on them, or they've delivered them to the collector for whom Corbin made the heist.'

'And if it's the latter, they won't be seen again.'

'Yep. My thoughts exactly,' said Vic, and closed the door.

* * *

Reluctant as she was to admit it, Marie was feeling distinctly nervous about the coming interview with Sasha Verde. Julia had told her that despite having only been administered a mild sedative, she had had no further episodes of rage. Indeed, one of the doctors said she seemed almost relieved at no longer

412

having to pretend to be someone she was not. This, apparently, was why she had asked to speak to Marie.

While she was ruminating on Sasha and what she might have to say, Marie received a call from Anna.

'Are you alone?'

'Hang on a minute.' Marie made a dash for Jackman's office, which she knew to be empty. 'Okay, Anna, go ahead.'

'Your loudspeaker's not on, is it?'

'There's no one here but me.'

'Well, you know I said we were going away — well, we're leaving tomorrow, meaning you won't be able to use this number from now on. It's just that I think I owe you an explanation before I disappear.'

Marie thanked her, hoping she didn't sound sarcastic.

'The thing is, I had no idea that Johnny was so eaten up by revenge. If I'd known, I would never have involved you, but I'm afraid I mistook his desire for vengeance for fear. He finally contacted me while I was still at my friend's house.'

'I thought you seemed changed, especially when you suddenly agreed to move out,' said Marie.

'I was shell-shocked, Marie. I was ecstatic knowing he was alive, but furious with him, too, for leaving me believing that he was dead. That man's put me through a lot, I'm telling you, but despite all that, I still love him. And at least I'm able to understand why he acted as he did. He was always a free spirit, and being locked away nearly destroyed him.'

'And the hacker who put him there? I seem to remember you saying he'd fled the country. What was his reason for taking Johnny out of the equation like that?'

'Greed. Like I told you, Johnny was a fixer for a fairly small criminal organisation. Well, as it turned out the boss-man wasn't as small fry as he first thought. He'd been trying Johnny out to see how good he was, with the intention of using him in something very big indeed, a major and very daring cybercrime. Anyway, another organisation got to hear about it and decided they weren't going to let it happen. And my Johnny, being the linchpin, was removed.'

Marie frowned. 'Let me get this clear. They had their own fixer, and it was this person who destroyed Johnny's computer system and set him up for a fall?'

'Exactly, but before he wiped it, the hacker found the plans for the cybercrime, liked them a lot and thought he might do a little private work for himself, and reap the profit.'

'Bad move?'

Anna laughed. 'Very bad move, Marie. Yes, he did flee the country, but the people he cheated were hot on his tail. We have a pretty good idea that one extremely talented hacker will never be heard of again.'

'And Chaos?'

'Johnny chased him for weeks, before realising that he'd made a terrible mistake, and had wasted his time. Ultimately, Chaos was a joker. Oh, sure, he swam in shark-infested waters, but the last laugh was always on him. Johnny admired him tremendously for the way he would set up a crime, take the money and then make sure the villains went down. My husband was not exactly an angel himself, but he thought Chaos was the ultimate trickster.'

'Tell me, did Johnny ever shadow Chaos?' asked Marie. 'We began to notice that someone was watching him and sometimes kind of tidying up loose ends. We thought he had what they call a guardian.'

'Sorry, I know nothing about that, but I very much doubt it.'

Marie felt a little disappointed, but supposed it didn't really matter anyway, now that Chaos was dead. Though she had an idea that not knowing who had been lurking in the shadows watching Chaos would probably bug her for a long time to come.

'And that is that,' said Anna, 'other than to say I appreciate your help, and that you cared about a miscarriage of justice, even though the victim was a criminal himself. Thank you, Marie, from both of us.'

'One last thing,' said Marie with a smile. 'We were very grateful for the information Johnny gave us, even though discovering Chaos's real identity and what subsequently happened to him was both shocking and sad. Anyway, I've arranged with our IT expert, Orac, to reciprocate with a gift of our own.'

Anna was silent for a moment or two. 'What kind of gift?'

'If you give me an email address — I promise it'll be perfectly secure — I'll send it to you.'

'Present? Come on, Marie, don't be cryptic.'

Marie decided she'd better put her out of her misery. 'Orac has retrieved Johnny's photo gallery from his corrupted hard drive. The videos were a step too far — Orac said she didn't have six months to spare — but all his precious photos are safe.'

Anna was silent again, and Marie wondered if she might be crying.

'Orac will send them as soon as you text one of us that email address.'

'You are a star, Detective Sergeant Marie Evans. I won't drag this out, but I'd just like to say I'm sincerely sorry we won't meet again.'

The call ended. In one way, Marie was sorry too, but mainly she hoped never to meet Anna again, because if she did, it would probably be to arrest her, and she'd really hate that.

CHAPTER THIRTY-SIX

Before Marie left for the secure psychiatric hospital, she went to see Orac and tell her that she'd passed on the message about Johnny's photo gallery.

'How's Coral?' she asked.

'Devastated. Shocked to the core, as you can imagine. She was very close to her father. She's a bit like me in that she doesn't have any close friends.'

'It's good of you to help her, Orac,' said Marie. 'She hasn't been here very long, and you've been a real rock.' She grinned at her. 'I mean, I have never, ever, known you to take time off work before.'

Orac waved it aside. 'Ah, it's no big deal.' Orac glanced around to make sure no one was within hearing range. 'I went with her to see the solicitor, and, oh, what a dryshite that man was.'

'A what?'

'Sorry. Irish expression. Means as boring as f—'

Marie grinned. 'I get it. Go on.'

'The long and the short of it is that there's an awful lot of money coming Coral's way, and she's terrified it's from all the illegal deals he was doing as Chaos.' Orac pulled a face. 'I spent a whole day looking into it, and I couldn't find a thing that hadn't come from perfectly legitimate investments. I'm guessing his finances will be taken apart by the lawyers and accountants, which could be a long, drawn-out process, but I'm willing to bet that William was always a step ahead of the legal beagles, and in the end they'll throw their hands up.'

'And Coral will be one rich lady.'

'I'm not so sure. Her plan at the moment, as soon as she gets the go-ahead from the solicitors, is to sell his property, which was definitely acquired legitimately, and keep the proceeds from that, but that's all. She says she earns enough to keep herself comfortably, so should that money flow her way, she'll give it all to charity.'

'Phew! She really is worried about it, isn't she?' said Marie. 'Mind you, I totally understand. She works for law enforcement, so she probably feels she can't accept the proceeds of crime, even if no one can prove that that's what it is.'

'But what crime did he really commit?' asked Orac. 'Yes, he helped thieves steal things, but then he trapped them and told the police. Who exactly is going to bring a case against a dead man who was little more than a cyber Robin Hood?' Her loud laugh caused several heads to go up in surprise. 'Oh, I know it'll be a right legal circus with all the fun of the fair, but I'm betting that at the end of the day, the whole thing will be written off, brushed under the carpet, and the money will finish up in Coral's bank account, or worst-case scenario, HMRC's coffers. Who knows?'

Put like that it did seem a real possibility. 'Mind you, didn't Coral say they'd been tracking him for years, and for some pretty serious offences?'

'Ah, but don't forget there were two hackers out there,' Orac reminded her. 'One was Chaos, and the other was the hacker who had Johnny banged up, and I'd like to know who would take on the job of trying to sort out who did what, because it won't be me! Let's go with our hearts on this. Coral's dad was doing what he said, having fun and dumping thieves in the shit.'

'So, we watch this space. Talking of that, my conversation with Anna got me thinking, and I'll bet you a pound to a penny that one day there will be another Chaos. I don't know what he'll call himself, but he'll do all the same things — make a shed load of wonga, stick villains in the doo-doo and generally have fun. And d'you know what his real name will be? Johnny Millard.'

* * *

From her apartment in London's upper-class district of Belgravia, Nina Hagen looked out across Eaton Square Gardens. They could hardly be said to possess the majesty of her beloved fjords, but they were a peaceful oasis of serenity in the heart of the bustling city. The only thing that spoiled her pleasure in the view, was the fact that Lucas would probably be looking out at a wall of concrete. If his cell even had windows. She hated Chaos for what he had done to Lucas, but she hated even more the fact that he had managed to record Lucas shouting out her name from inside that locked house. She had only discovered this after a surreptitious phone call from Jean-Paul, Lucas's cousin. Sure, Nina was a pseudonym and she was perfectly safe from detection, but nevertheless, it made her angry. Despite the popular belief that there is no honour among thieves, Nina respected those criminals who exhibited cleverness and skill. She viewed a perfectly planned robbery in much the same way as a work of art, and admired a skilful production. Lucas had been a master craftsman, and the fact that he was now languishing in prison was not the result of any flaw on his part, it was down to treachery. So, with that in mind, Nina had taken up the reins. Using the laptop she had taken from Lucas's rented cottage, she completed the transaction with the client. It went off without incident, and within the following twenty-four hours, Crispin Payne had received his consignment and paid what was due, just as Lucas had arranged. It was a pity Lucas couldn't be made aware of this — there was no way she could possibly visit him, neither could she contact Jean-Paul, as he was certain to be under surveillance.

Nina went to the kitchen and poured herself a glass of wine. It had been an exciting few weeks, full of rapid decision-making and swift action. Luckily, like her incarcerated friend, she had a mind like a razor, and her plan came together with all the smoothness of velvet.

Back in her comfortable reclining chair on the balcony, she sipped the wine, and hoped that Lucas would appreciate the measures she'd taken. On the whole, she thought he would approve. The most difficult problem had been what to do with the van-load of Art Nouveau treasures Lucas had appropriated for himself. She had no wish to store them and risk some cunning detective tracking them down, so in the end, she had selected a few particularly special pieces and kept them in her apartment, where they would await Lucas's release. The bulk of the items had been sold off to those clients who had no objection to receiving stolen goods. This meant that when Lucas was back in circulation, he would find a nice little hoard of cash waiting for him.

And maybe that wouldn't be too far in the future. From Jean-Paul's single phone call, she had learned that Lucas had acquired the services of Gareth Rock as his brief. That told her a lot. If Rock lived up to his reputation, Lucas could well end up either out on bail, or serving a considerably shorter sentence. Lucas would not come out of prison an old man, as he and Nina had both feared. And when he did, he would find that his business partner, the woman he knew as Nina Hagen, would have kept his brainchild afloat in his absence. She and their trusted team would keep working and the money would continue flowing in. She already had another interesting little heist lined up and ready to go.

Nina looked at her watch, put down her wineglass and picked up her phone.

'It's Nina,' she said in her finest English accent. 'I need your help.'

A brief conversation ensued, in which arrangements were made, and money began its circuitous route into a distant bank account. Times and dates were agreed and the programme confirmed. She then repeated the details back to the person on the end of the line, and, satisfied, said, 'Perfect. I will contact you at the agreed time. I appreciate your assistance.'

He assured her he was always available should she need his services in matters relating to security or access; she need merely use the channel of communication he had provided.

'I have to say, you come highly recommended, so if you succeed in facilitating safe access to this particular place, I will certainly be using you again. Thank you, Johnny, it's good to have you in our team.'

* * *

'I'm not quite sure what I should call you,' said Marie. 'What name do you prefer?'

'Sasha. After all, that is my name, and there's no longer any need for me to be Sarah Nugent or Sally.' Her voice held none of its former aggressiveness, yet she didn't sound drugged or confused, either.

Marie stared through the reinforced glass panel separating her from Sasha, and had a strange feeling that she was being played for a fool. The woman seemed so perfectly composed. Was she putting on a clever act? Or had she completely disassociated herself from the woman who had killed six innocent people in a fit of rage?

Despite the presence of the two psychiatric nurses standing behind her, Sasha sat quietly, her hands loose in her lap as opposed to clenching and unclenching as they had before her attack on Julia. Yet something about her made Marie profoundly uncomfortable.

Marie shook herself. This was the first time anyone had interviewed Sasha in any formal way, so she had to do it right. Hitherto, Sasha had been too disturbed for anyone to even make the attempt. Marie informed her that the session would be recorded, and that it was her right to have a solicitor present. Initially, Sasha had flatly rejected the offer, but Marie explained that having a lawyer was in Sasha's interest, if only to ensure that Marie's questions were acceptable and relevant, so Sasha finally relented, and a solicitor was called.

Now it was crunch time. As before, Marie decided to treat Sasha just like any other person, while hoping not to let slip anything that would bring on another fit of rage.

'So, Sasha, let me begin by saying that we have been granted access to your medical records, and are aware that prior to the onset of puberty, you began to suffer from Intermittent Explosive Disorder, a condition which has persisted into adulthood. We have also spoken to your brother, Norman, who has given an account of the form these episodes took. That said, I wish to ask you whether, in the course of one of these fits of violent rage, you killed your brother, Peter.'

Through the glass, Sasha's gaze met hers without flinching. 'That is correct.'

'And is it also true that while you were residing in the village of Fendyke, you bludgeoned to death Gino Lombardi, Shelley Kershaw, Marion Sandon-Hayes, Dalmat Tabaku and one other man who is as yet unidentified?'

Sasha continued to regard her steadily. 'If you say so. I never knew their names. On each occasion it was done during an episode — that is, a fit of blind rage.'

Marie hesitated. This was chilling. According to the psychologists treating her, Sasha was relieved at having finally been caught, and could drop the pretence of being someone else — Sarah Nugent. Even Julia had suggested that she could be entering a phase wherein she became aware of the consequences of her rages and was beginning to feel some remorse. But Marie couldn't sense any of that in the woman on the other side of the glass partition. All she felt was that something in her manner was terribly wrong. She wished that Jackman were with her, and not waiting outside, unable to see what was going on.

Abruptly, Sasha began to speak. 'I should never have been allowed to live. Then all these . . . things would never have happened. People are dead because of the way I'm wired up. I should have been stopped when I was young, not allowed to grow into a woman with the strength to do real damage.' Her lips parted in a rictus. 'What's so stupid about it is that most of the things that sparked my anger were misunderstandings. I got things wrong, misinterpreted something someone said . . . so what was the point of it all?'

'Was that the case with Shelley Kershaw, Sasha? What did you think she'd done that made you so angry?' Marie asked.

'Oh, Shelley.' Sasha tossed her head contemptuously. 'No, there was no misunderstanding with her. It was her sheer stupidity that got me so angry. I overheard her telling someone about this wonderful man she'd met, who was going to take her away from Fendyke and treat her like a princess. Ha! I knew who she meant. I'd watched him over the years, and he was a predator. He would have treated her just like all the other women he'd had — used and abused her, and then tossed her aside. I don't know why, but I actually felt sorry for the silly little girl. So, I got in my Land Rover and followed her to the bus stop intending to warn her off. I even spoke to her — me, who never said a word to anyone. I told her just what her Prince Charming was really like. And do you know what she said? She said I was jealous of her.' Sasha lowered her voice, and said flatly, 'I don't remember what happened next. I never do. Which is all for the best, I suppose.'

Marie tried to follow a possible order of events, and came to the conclusion that Sasha must have had the spade with her in the Land Rover. She hit Shelley, dragged her into the vehicle and drove off. But where? To the pillbox?

'What *do* you remember, Sasha?' she asked evenly.

'I don't. They say I block it out in order to distance myself from what I've done.' Sasha shrugged. 'Makes sense, I suppose.'

'So, even though you block it out, you still believe you've killed these people? After all, you've confessed to murdering them.' Marie frowned. 'I'm not sure that makes too much sense.'

Sasha gave her a cold smile. 'What else am I supposed to believe? I was with those people. They all angered me. I know what I'm capable of, and they are all dead. Ergo, I killed them.'

'Tell me about the pillbox,' Marie said abruptly.

Sasha stiffened. For the first time, she appeared unsure of herself. 'You found the bodies there, didn't you? So I must have taken them there.'

'How?' Marie countered. 'We are the same height, and I carry more weight than you, so I'm probably stronger, but I couldn't even *lift* a dead body, let alone carry it as far as that pillbox. So, how did you do it?'

Sasha hung her head, and for a moment, Marie expected to see that terrible, baleful glare. Instead she looked up, and sighed. 'It seems I have a lot to tell you. Could we take a break?'

The lawyer agreed, so Marie suspended the interview and got to her feet. 'I'll be back in a quarter of an hour or so.'

Outside she found Jackman and Julia, both looking grim.

'Sorry, but don't think this is going as I hoped,' said Marie, sinking into a chair. 'I'm picking up all sorts of mixed messages from her.'

'You're doing fine,' Jackman said. 'None of us thought it would be straightforward. And from out here, it sounds like she's going to actually tell you something concrete.'

'I'm not so sure about that,' said Julia. 'Obviously, I can't treat her, having been the subject of one of her episodes of rage, but from what I've heard today, as well as my discussions with the people who are working with her, I can't agree that she's making all that much progress. She projects a very different persona when she's talking to Marie to the one her mental health team sees. I think she's manipulating the latter into believing that she's responding positively, whereas she's more honest with Marie. It's like she thinks Marie can see through her, so there's no point putting up a front.'

'Maybe she can, Julia,' said Jackman. 'You've always been able to read people, Marie, and I get the feeling that Sasha can see that in you.'

Marie told them about her feeling that something just wasn't right. 'And now I'm wondering what I'm going to hear next.'

'Aren't we all,' said Jackman. 'Are you okay to do this, Marie?'

She drew in a breath. 'Oh yes. We need answers, and if I'm the only person she'll talk to, then so be it.'

Ten minutes later, she was back facing Sasha through the glass partition.

'Talk to me, Sasha,' she said softly. 'Let's start with the pillbox. How did you discover it?'

'Because of the fox.'

Boy, thought Marie, *this woman does like to throw curve balls.* 'The fox? Okay, tell me about him — or is it a her?'

'She's my friend. I found her with her tail trapped in some broken fencing. I freed her, and she ran away, but the next day when I went for my walk, I passed the place where I'd found her, and I saw her watching me from the trees. She was there the next day too, and gradually over the next few months she came to trust me, until she was walking quite happily at my side.'

This tale of the fox revealed a very different Sasha, and Marie was certain that whatever else this woman might have told her, this time she spoke the truth.

'One day we walked along the field edge on the Telford estate, and I sensed that the fox wanted me to follow her. She led me to her den. It was in a copse on the boundary between the farmland and the gardens of some of the Fendyke residents, people called Smith.'

'And you saw the pillbox?'

Sasha nodded. 'I . . . I was drawn to it. It was like some horrible magnet. It squatted there, an ugly, malignant presence among the owls roosting in the trees, where my little

424

russet red friend had her den. It shouldn't have been there, it spoiled the place, and I hated it.'

God, thought Marie, that evil place even affected Sasha.

'You asked how I got them — the dead bodies — to the pillbox. I don't know for sure, because I really have no clear memory of it, but I believe I must have driven them as far as the edge of the copse, and then tipped them out of my Land Rover into a wheelbarrow. I always carried a wheelbarrow, a spade and some tools in the back.'

'And no one ever asked you what you were doing there on Telford's land?' asked Marie, trying to keep the disbelief from her voice.

'Telford's son has an old Land Rover, too, so no one would have given me a second glance. I suppose I must have gone in the evening or early morning. That would make sense, wouldn't it?'

'Probably,' said Marie doubtfully. 'Though I'm still wondering how you managed to get those heavy bodies into that pillbox.'

Sasha shrugged. 'Well, you know what they say about the mad having superhuman strength. We are complex beings, Marie. Don't underestimate what a sudden burst of adrenalin — or rage — can enable a person to do.' Sasha ran her hand through her hair. 'I'm tired, Marie, so I'm making a couple of stipulations. First. I will not talk about my family, nor do I wish to see them — any of them. I will not talk about my brother's death. I've accepted culpability, and that will have to suffice.' She continued in a monotone as if she were reading from a list of points. 'Now, for the facts. I know none of the names of the other people I murdered, but they all provoked a catastrophic episode of IED. One patronised me, one kicked a stray cat I had been feeding. One expressed a bigoted opinion about something I held dear, and the last one would have killed the fox. That one prompted the greatest explosion of anger I have ever experienced.'

Marie believed her. 'Thank you, Sasha. If you wish to terminate this interview, I respect that. Just one last thing. Did you go out to the copse one night and attack a policeman who was on duty there?'

Sasha gave a tired laugh. 'It was hardly an attack, more like an act of self-defence. Yes, I hit him, but not that hard. I went there most nights, even when the police were around. I was worried for the fox and didn't want her den disturbed.' She smiled reminiscently. 'She once brought her kits for me to see. That's what they call baby foxes — kits.'

'I get it,' Marie said. 'You didn't seriously injure that policeman because you weren't actually angry.'

'Exactly. I was just trying to get away unnoticed.'

Marie suddenly felt as tired as Sasha. 'You get some rest now. I am grateful to you for talking to me.'

Sasha nodded. Her face took on an expression of deep sadness. 'If it hadn't been for my fits of murderous rage, I could have had a wonderful life. I had everything money could buy, but I had no compassion for others, nor did I receive the help I so desperately needed. For the sake of keeping up appearances and protecting the family's good name, my parents turned me into a pariah, and a callous killer. I hope they thought it worthwhile.'

Marie terminated the interview.

* * *

Back at the station, Marie and Jackman sat in his office going over everything Sasha had said. By the time they had pulled apart every single word and examined it for subtle nuances, they were no closer to an understanding.

'I still think she couldn't have moved those bodies alone,' said Marie.

'I agree,' Jackman said. 'When we got back, I spoke to her brother Norman about how they got on as siblings. If anyone helped her, I reckoned it would have been either Norman or Derek, or both.'

'So what did he say?'

426

'That he loved his sister, and felt the parents never got her the treatment she needed as a child. He said he always tried to quell her anger when he saw a fit of rage coming on, once receiving a broken arm for his trouble. Peter dismissed her as being attention seeking, nothing but a spoiled brat. Derek, on the other hand, was terrified of her, and she teased him for it, making him her little slave. Apparently, he never got over his fear of her, even when they were adults and she had been sent away.'

'So, if Sasha told him to get over to Fendyke and help her with something, he'd do it?' asked Marie. 'Even down to moving the odd dead body?'

'Fear can make people do terrible things. Love, too, so maybe Norman would have helped as well. Who can say? I guess we just have to accept that we may never know.'

They fell silent. After a while, Marie said, 'So that is that, I suppose. We have our killer, and she's confessed to all the deaths. We have four identified victims, with only one on the black notice. Maybe we shouldn't expect a perfect result. What we have is actually pretty good.'

'Don't forget that our Handcuff Boy and his gran are safe too, and that your friend Anna is also safe and well in the arms of her beloved — even though that beloved is a rather naughty boy.' Jackman smiled. 'Yes, I'd say that is a very good result indeed!'

* * *

After they had called it a day, Marie drove out to Fendyke, but not to the village itself, her destination was Rivendell. There was cordoning tape still flapping from the gateposts and the place seemed even more desolate than it had when 'Sally' had lived there. Now it felt like there was no life there at all.

Before leaving the station, she had gone down to see the dog handler and cadged a handful of training treats. Now, she sat on the grass verge with her back against the gate and waited.

It was over half an hour before she saw a movement on the other side of the lane. The fox emerged cautiously from the bushes, stopped and regarded her suspiciously.

'Hello,' she said softly. 'I hoped I'd see you.'

The fox didn't approach her, but neither did it run away.

'I thought someone should come and tell you that your friend won't be coming home. She's sad not to be seeing you again, because she really loved you.'

For a moment, Marie felt like laughing at herself. What on earth was she doing, sitting on the grass and holding a one-sided conversation with a wild animal? Nevertheless, she felt it was somehow important.

She pulled some treats from her pocket and scattered them across the lane. 'The dog handler tells me they're chicken-flavoured.'

The fox remained stock still, its eyes never leaving hers.

'Well, Foxy, your friend is going to miss you, and I guess you'll miss her too. You knew the best side of her, didn't you?' Marie suddenly felt as if she wanted to cry. 'I'm really glad someone did, because I think that was the real Sasha. The other one was just another victim.'

Slowly, she raised herself to her feet and went back to the car. 'Stay safe, Fox! And it might be a good idea to find yourself a new den, because I've heard that your copse is going to be cleared.'

As she opened the car door, she saw the little animal sneak across the road and grab the treats. Then it stood looking after her with its head to one side, and for a fleeting moment Marie felt a connection. Then it was gone, a flash of russet disappearing into the reeds at the side of the lane.

THE END

THE JOFFE BOOKS STORY

We began in 2014 when Jasper agreed to publish his mum's much-rejected romance novel and it became a bestseller.

Since then we've grown into the largest independent publisher in the UK. We're extremely proud to publish some of the very best writers in the world, including Joy Ellis, Faith Martin, Caro Ramsay, Helen Forrester, Simon Brett and Robert Goddard. Everyone at Joffe Books loves reading and we never forget that it all begins with the magic of an author telling a story.

We are proud to publish talented first-time authors, as well as established writers whose books we love introducing to a new generation of readers.

We won Trade Publisher of the Year at the Independent Publishing Awards in 2023 and Best Publisher Award in 2024 at the People's Book Prize. We have been shortlisted for Independent Publisher of the Year at the British Book Awards for the last five years, and were shortlisted for the Diversity and Inclusivity Award at the 2022 Independent Publishing Awards. In 2023 we were shortlisted for Publisher of the Year at the RNA Industry Awards, and in 2024 we were shortlisted at the CWA Daggers for the Best Crime and Mystery Publisher.

We built this company with your help, and we love to hear from you, so please email us about absolutely anything bookish at feedback@joffebooks.com.

If you want to receive free books every Friday and hear about all our new releases, join our mailing list here: www.joffebooks.com/freebooks.

And when you tell your friends about us, just remember: it's pronounced Joffe as in coffee or toffee!

9 781805 731740